Hollywood
Buzz

Books by Margit Liesche

Lipstick and Lies
Hollywood Buzz

Hollywood Buzz

Margit Liesche

Poisoned Pen Press

Poisoned
Pen
Press

Copyright © 2009 by Margit Liesche

First Edition 2009

10 9 8 7 6 5 4 3 2 1

Library of Congress Catalog Card Number: 2008931502

ISBN: 978-1-59058-579-5 Hardcover

Poisoned Pen Press
6962 E. First Ave., Ste. 103
Scottsdale, AZ 85251
www.poisonedpenpress.com
info@poisonedpenpress.com

Printed in the United States of America

For the WASP
who gave so much and continue to inspire

Author's Thanks

My thanks to Julie Dickson, dear friend, who first introduced me to the WASP and whose love of a good book is an inspiration to me and to so many.

I am grateful to my circles of first readers: Amy Beauchamp, Claudia Bluhm, Caiti Collins, Mary Cone, and Terri Tate; Susan Bono, Christine Falcone, Chuck Kensler, Elizabeth Kern, Mark Sloan, and Pat Tyler. Wonderful writers and friends who sift through my untamed fields of words, gently weeding and pruning, while tipping their caps to the well-turned blooms.

I owe a great debt to several author/teachers for their generosity, encouragement, insights, inspiration, and advice: Katherine Forest, Lynn Freed, Judy Greber, and Susan Trott (also my advisor at the Squaw Valley Community of Writers). Sagely foreseeing a good match, Susan, pointed me to Poisoned Pen Press. My heartfelt appreciation goes to the hardworking professionals at Poisoned Pen, especially Jessica Tribble, Annette Rogers, Barbara Peters, Rob Rosenwald—I am more grateful than I can ever say.

I also thank my band of WWII experts, former OSS agent Betty McIntosh, former WASP Peggy Slaymaker, and Hollywood screenwriter assigned to the First Motion Picture Unit, Mal Wald, for sharing their personal experiences and historical perspectives. For their invaluable assistance in helping me uncover a trove of historical treasures at the National Archives, a very special thanks to Senior Archivist, John Taylor, and researcher, Mia Waller. Also, thanks to Horst Meyer, who took Pucci's creator up for a test run early in the game and who generously made available his flying expertise.

My appreciation goes to Barbara Hall, Research Archivist, as well as Janet Lorenz and the rest of the dedicated staff at the Margaret Herrick Library-Fairbanks Center for Motion Picture Study in Beverly Hills, CA, for graciously leading me through the riches in their collection, in particular the WWII First Motion Picture Unit holdings. These materials were significantly enriched as a result of interchanges with a number of knowledge-able individuals, including Doug Cunningham, doctoral student in Film Studies (FMPU emphasis) at UC Berkeley; and Ned Comstock at the USC Cinema-Television Library.

My deepest gratitude goes to Peter Lillevand, longtime part-ner in the delicate dance of wordsmithing and so much more, and to Liz, Rose, Tunde, Jason, Evan, Theresa, Kate, Sean, and Chris for their unwavering love and belief in me.

Chapter One

It's nice when someone is there to greet you; disconcerting when it's the general's aide.

The assignment had started normally enough. Yesterday, I'd ferried a factory-fresh pursuit fighter from Long Beach to New Jersey. I was all set for a direct flight home to repeat my standard routine, but juggled orders put me on a hopscotch course, ultimately delivering a P-47 Thunderbolt to Long Beach shortly after dawn.

I jumped off the fighter's wing.

"Pucci Lewis." Lieutenant Hatch, a true ramrod in a natty, sharply creased uniform, addressed me.

"Yes, sir."

"Forget the paperwork, Lewis, and leave the gear. Cochran wants you in the general's office, on the double."

My fingers fumbled as I unstrapped my parachute for the ground crewman waiting nearby. "Yes, sir."

Jackie Cochran, my boss and head of the Women Air Force Service Pilots—WASP—operated out of her ranch in nearby Indio or from Washington, D.C. Why was she here? And what was so urgent that standard procedures, including the postflight paperwork at BaseOps, were being set aside?

A month ago, we'd met under similar high-priority conditions at the Willow Run aircraft factory near Detroit. I had been "loaned" to the Detroit FBI field office to assist with an industrial espionage case. My pulse quickened. Was I needed on another home front security mission?

Hatch pointed with his chin to the leather bag I'd parked on the asphalt next to me while shedding my chute. "Bring the grip. You're gonna need it."

No kidding. My B-4 bag went everywhere with me, as much a part of my day-to-day existence as the purse I'd carried in more traditional times. And, like a purse, the standard issue tote had too many essentials crammed into too small a space.

I lifted the bag and hustled to catch up to Hatch.

◇◇◇

Miss C sat behind the general's highly polished desk, absorbed in an important telephone conversation. Her posture was rigid; her expression was tight. Holding up a finger to signal she needed another minute, she spun around leaving us to stare at the tall back of the general's swivel chair.

General Griffith and Miss C went way back, but she was chummy with a number of Army Air Force generals, having competed against them in air races before the war. I knew about her in admiring detail. In 1932 she received her pilot's license after only three weeks of lessons and immediately pursued advanced instruction. By 1937, she'd set three major flying records against all comers. In 1938, she won the prestigious cross-country Bendix Race, much to the chagrin of her male competitors, some of whom became those AAF generals.

Scuttlebutt about her association with the brass-hats frequently made the rounds in airport ready rooms, where we whiled away the hours waiting for our orders or for the weather to clear. It was assumed that we'd fill the time wisely, reading flying regs or the Pilots' Information File, a.k.a. The Pilots' Bible, but usually we just plain needed a break. We'd tell jokes, play cards, devour movie magazines, gossip. And there was plenty to dish when it came to Miss C. Her mysterious origins, her eccentricities, her millionaire husband and their unconventional marriage, her numerous professional accomplishments, the climb to her current executive position, and the cargo hold of enemies she'd assembled along the way.

A good ready room yarn would've been welcome as Hatch and I stood by. Looking sideways, I studied his chiseled profile. Muscles twitched at the edge of his tightly drawn mouth; otherwise, shoulders back, eyes ahead, he remained a statue. My gaze drifted to the wall above Miss C where a life-size portrait hung of President Roosevelt, complete with pince-nez, cigarette holder, and jaunty smile. Reflexively, I returned the smile. Shifting my weight from foot to foot, hoping to work off some nervous energy, one calf brushed against the other. Adrenaline suddenly coursed through me, turning my face lobster red. I'd left my ankle holster on! I was authorized and trained to use a gun, but the pistol strapped to my leg was a non-regulation Smith & Wesson .38, a gift from my Gran Skjold who knew things could get rough for a single woman on the road. She'd been a dancer in a traveling vaudeville troupe when she first arrived in the States fresh from Sweden. At WASP graduation, Gran had passed along the holster and the S&W break-top, along with a few lessons on its use. Turned out to be the ideal gift. Whenever I was assigned a plane with specialized equipment, a .45 got handed over along with my orders. A .45 was large and cumbersome; the break-top, on the other hand, was compact and lightweight. Wearing nonregulation items required discretion, so normally I took the holster off before exiting my plane. Hatch had distracted me.

I felt the heat of a second burst of adrenaline. The .45! Check-in procedures required turning it in. Because they'd been waived, I still had that gun, too, inside the B-4 bag positioned on the floor next to me.

Packing a hidden arsenal at my feet could account for the rise in my body temperature, but my flight gear wasn't helping either. I peeled off my leather helmet and unzipped my jacket, quickly patting the WASP insignia over my heart. Filling the insignia's center was Fifinella, a cross-eyed winged gremlin and official mascot of the WASP, designed by Disney Studio.

We considered Fifinella a good luck charm, protection against storms, mechanical failure, and any other danger that may cross our paths. *Don't let me get caught with two hidden guns*, I silently pleaded to her.

Miss C's voice crescendoed behind the chair. "Don't bully me. I'm working on it."

She swiveled and the receiver hit its cradle with a clunk. "Hatch, that's all."

Hatch jerked to life. Miss C and I exchanged greetings while he about-faced and exited the room.

"What? Hasn't grown out yet?" Miss C was gaping at my hair as the door clicked shut.

A couple of months ago, on the road and bored, I'd decided to do something about its standard-issue color. From a corner drugstore I purchased a kit that promised to transform dishwater blonde to Tahitian Gold. What I got was tabby orange, the shade resembling the pelt of Sarah Bernhardt, my childhood cat. A self-trim to lop off the damaged ends and frizz had left me with a short, shaggy Amelia Earhart do.

"Ah c'mon, Miss C. We've been over this. You know how hectic ferrying coast to coast gets. Plus, hours under a leather helmet, my scalp gets sweaty." I finger-combed my hair. "This style fluffs right back into shape."

Miss C did not look convinced. "And the color?"

I grinned. "It's fun?"

Her dark eyes bore into me. My grin wobbled.

Miss C was a fanatic about appearance. *It's a woman's duty to always be as presentable as time and purse permit*, she liked to say. Polished steel in a jeweled case, she had a purse with deep pockets, affording the fine designer clothes she loved. Today, decked out in a navy designer suit and cream blouse, every shimmering golden hair smoothed into gently permed waves, she looked as though she'd just stepped out of Central Casting.

"It won't matter," she said at last. "You'll be in flight gear most of the time you're on camera."

"*On camera?*"

"Sit." She motioned to the chair opposite her.

I dropped to the edge of the seat. She shot her square jaw toward the telephone. "That was Roland Novara in Hollywood, director for a Victory short on you gals. We're *lucky* to have him." The lift of her brow reinforced the false ring of enthusiasm in her tone.

Victory shorts were documentary-style films about home front participation in the war effort. Usually twenty minutes in length, they showed citizens how to conserve, assist, and sacrifice, while painting rosy pictures of military branches for recruiting purposes.

"So the film's on again," I said. "That's terrific. Someone pull some strings?"

Directors, like all goods, were scarce these days, and the WASP Victory short had been in the works for some time. Several months ago, Miss C sent me to Hollywood for a look-see. But I never set foot in the studio. The film was quashed after the director was recruited to work on an urgent hush-hush AAF training film.

Miss C's lips curled into a small smile. "General Griffith got involved. Thinks we can use the film to help build support. It's shameful we're being forced to lobby for a service that's so clearly needed…" She sighed. "But it's got to be done. Opposition keeps coming out of the woodwork. Mainly returning vets, claiming my program is taking stateside jobs from them.

"But by God—" She smacked her fist into the palm of her hand. "You gals have worked hard. We're not about to let them waltz in, pull you off the flying jobs just because some men out there happen to want them. That tired argument that women aren't as qualified, don't have the same physical and mental stamina as the men—ha! A plane doesn't give a damn whether a pilot's male or female; what matters is whether you know its capabilities and can fly it. You gals are proof of that."

I nodded, acknowledging the vote of confidence. "Did you say, er, something about me and a camera?"

Miss C ignored the question. "The War Department's breathing down Novara's neck to finish up our film. He's feeling pushed. We're only one of several he's got in the works, including a training film with Clark Gable. AAF wants the Gable movie yesterday, too."

Clark Gable? Who'd care about unreasonable deadlines if Clark Gable was involved?

"Novara's also vying for a feature," she added. "Something with Cary Grant and John Garfield."

The stars' names tripped off her tongue as though they were all old friends. But then, why was I surprised? The guest book at Miss C's ranch read like a *Who's Who* of notables from film stars to baronesses to top ranking corporate executives, military officers, and politicians. Even the President. More intrigued by the moment, I leaned forward in my seat.

"Something else." She cleared her throat. "Frankie Beall. Several weeks ago, when Novara started on our film, I reassigned her to Hollywood to assist him. Do you know her?"

I nodded. Frankie had been in the class ahead of me at Avenger Field in Sweetwater, Texas, where we'd done our training. Although in different classes, we'd been assigned to the same dormitory or bay. The gals in our bay had come from a cross-section of backgrounds: an actress, a radio commentator, a flight instructor, a journalist. Frankie had been a schoolteacher. What was particularly memorable about her was how she always carried two cushions in her parachute bag for scooting herself forward in the cockpit to reach the rudder pedals with her feet. In spite of her five foot two height, Frankie could outmaneuver anyone in a PT trainer, and she'd earned a reputation as our unit's aerobatics ace. Though the bases we'd been assigned to weren't all that far apart, we hadn't seen one another since graduation. Too bad, I thought, suddenly reminded of our promise to keep in touch.

Miss C leaned across the desk toward me. The brown eyes that moments before had bored a hole through me, were suddenly so soft that I sensed she was holding back tears.

"Something's happened to Frankie?"

She nodded. "Yesterday, at March Field she took an A-24 up. They were rehearsing a target-towing segment for the film. She made a pass over the filming crew a-a-and—" She swallowed. "—engine quit."

My stomach roiled. "Oh no…"

"Tower said she knew right away the trouble was big. Told 'em to get the crash truck out. Film crew saw it all. Said the plane lurched, then hung mid-air for what seemed an eternity… Nose dropped all of a sudden, and the plane plummeted down. Incredibly, Frankie managed to level out. But when she hit the runway…fuselage just snapped."

I blinked several times. "Sh-she alive?"

Miss C's nod was barely perceptible. "A miracle. Tail section was completely demolished, but the wings and everything forward stayed intact, more or less. Cuts, broken bones, head injury's the worst of it. She's in critical condition. She struck something, maybe the control stick. There's a deep gash. Too soon to know if there's brain damage."

She looked away for a moment. "I…was in Hollywood on business, so I stopped at the hospital last night. She's been unconscious since the accident. They've got a close watch on her."

I took a deep breath, then let it out slow. "Stray bullet?"

Target-towing involved letting anti-aircraft gunnery crews practice their marksmanship by firing live ammunition at a muslin target shaped like a long wind sock, which you trailed behind your plane. Oftentimes the plane got riddled with bullets, along with the target.

Miss C shrugged. "Hard to say right now. A crash investigator is sifting the debris. It was an A-24 salvaged from the South Pacific. In bad shape before Frankie took it up." Her lips pulled into a sardonic smile. "Novara had insisted that the tow plane be authentic."

The premium on planes for the front had forced training units to make do with the leftovers. I massaged the muscles at the back of my neck, recalling the "war-weary" I'd been in yesterday. Also a Dauntless A-24 dive bomber, it'd been abused and so poorly maintained that the tail wheel had blown during landing at Camp Davis, Oklahoma. The pull to the right had been so strong, the plane and I waltzed right off the runway. Fortunately, the nose had pointed into a grassy area and not into the row of planes parked on the flight line.

Miss C splayed her fingers on the desk, frowning before folding them, absently tapping the conjoined fists against the desk's surface. She delighted in playing up her great features—the perpetual tan on her flawless skin; the gentle curls and highlights in her blond hair; the couture clothing sheathing the curves of her frame. But she avoided calling attention to her hands. They were very masculine. For this reason, she never used nail polish. But something beyond a manicure was on her mind.

"What is it?" My thoughts tumbled unchecked from my lips. "The crash…You suspect it's not an accident?"

Her focus whisked back to me, unmistakable fire in her eyes. "There's something fishy going on at March. Someone's sitting on the preliminary investigation results. I want to know why."

"Preliminary results? You just said the crash investigator was still—"

"I know what I said, Lewis. But I have my sources. A source. Frankie's crash was no accident."

"*Sabotage?*"

Miss C's sigh was audible. "It's a delicate situation. I can't just rush in, make demands. But I'm not going to let this go. Frankie's one of mine. I need someone from my camp to get up there and dig around."

That's reason I was here. My stomach knotted.

"You're sending me to Hollywood to take over for Frankie? *I'm* the designated camper?"

"It's the perfect cover. You'll ride herd on Novara to see that our documentary projects the proper image. Behind the scenes, you'll be looking into the whys of Frankie's incident."

"Ride herd?"

"Precisely. I'm here for a strategy session with General Griffith. In a few hours, we're off to Washington. Some behind-the-scenes meetings with certain members of Congress. Need to drum up support for a bill to militarize the WASP. It's the ticket to get you gals the recognition and benefits you're entitled to, same as other non-combat military personnel."

Starting the WASP program had been such a sensitive and complex ordeal that to get the service up and running quickly we'd been hired by, and were still paid by, Civil Service. So we were civilians serving under military regulations, a status Miss C despised.

"While we're at it, we're going to try and get a better measure of the tide swelling against us." She grimaced. "And, we hope, find a way to turn it back."

"Can we get back to finding out the whys of Frankie's incident? To riding herd on Novara? What do you mean, exactly?"

She lifted a perfectly groomed, disapproving eyebrow. "You're the one with intelligence training. Behind the scenes sleuthing ought to be second nature."

Three months ago, in early August 1943, I'd been summoned to Office of Strategic Services (OSS) headquarters in Washington to participate in a specially designed, condensed training course. Miss C had not warmed up to sharing one of her assets.

"Sleuthing might be second nature, but riding herd is new. Before I can do the job, I need to know what's involved."

"On my way here from Indio, I stopped off in Hollywood to attend the preview of a feature film. It's about women who fly for the military and it's due to be released soon."

"Great! What's it called?"

"*Ladies Courageous*. But hold your horses. We're not going to be recommending the picture to anyone. *Ladies Outrageous* is more like it! It's sentimental, fictional trash. The women I saw on that screen couldn't be trusted with kiddy cars, let alone airplanes. It'll set my—*our*—progress back years. Think about it."

Her voice rose, she all but stepped on a soapbox. "The primary aim of the WASP may be to support male pilots, but here's a chance to officially document our physical and mental capabilities. Once we show that you gals measure up to the men, the possibilities will be enormous. Opportunities for women pilots will open up across the board. In the military, maybe in the private sector, too. Ideally, we'll get a good foothold and the doors will remain open, even after the war."

She was singing to the choir. Our flying stint with the military, we all knew, was temporary. It was assumed that when the war ended we would return to more traditional roles. Some women couldn't wait. Not me. I wanted the unconventional. A postwar career. As a commercial pilot. Or, dare I dream, *a pilot doubling as secret agent?*

Miss C fluttered a hand through the air. "Now this froth— this *Ladies Courageous*—comes along with the hackneyed message that women are motivated by their interest in men, not by their work. The movie's no tribute, it's a slander to our gender. An insult to my program!"

"Who sanctioned it?"

Miss C rolled her eyes dismissively, but I waited, eyeing her patiently. She might know all there was to know about wheeling and dealing with the brass-hats, but my education in the area was elementary, at best.

"Look, Lewis. The movie's bound to attract a big audience. The studio is billing it as a prestige feature. There'll be a lot of hoopla over the big name stars involved. Loretta Young, Geraldine Fitzgerald, Diana Barrymore…they're all in it." She leaned back in the executive chair and rubbed her trademark lapel pin, a silver propeller set with a large rosette center diamond.

Risking another roll of her eyes, I prodded, "How, specifically, did they manage to muck up *Ladies Courageous*? And who mucked it up?"

"Some boys at Universal Pictures. A big-name, Walter Wanger, produced it. Can't say they didn't get some things right. Loyalty and bravery come across to a relative degree. The women even perform some intricate flying maneuvers. But then the boys wrote in a bunch of petty squabbles, some pouting, beau stealing, a few breaches of discipline and a crash or two. And, *voilà!* They watered down our accomplishments."

Miss C pounded the desk. "They're not going to get away with it! Done right, the WASP Victory short will be the perfect countermeasure to that degrading portrayal. We're going to stick to Novara like glue until we have a true depiction of what the WASP is doing for the war effort." She was loaded for bear. "I've teed things up for you with Novara—let him know that you have the appropriate experience to assist him. And that you're to act as my official liaison on the set."

The shock must have shown on my face.

"It's a lot of responsibility, I know," she rushed on. "I would've stayed on in Hollywood myself, but General Griffith wants me in Washington. He knows the Army needs all the good pilots it can get and he's willing to do battle in Congress to keep us. Thinks my presence might make a difference."

I blinked. Responsibility wasn't what had me worried. "What experience?"

Miss C's eyes widened in surprise. "You mean what qualifies you to act as a consultant to Novara?"

I nodded.

"Your experience at Midland Aircraft, of course."

My mouth fell open. She was referring to what I'd done before joining the WASP. Out of college, I'd wanted to be a commercial pilot. Getting there, I knew, would not be easy. A job—any job—with an aircraft company seemed a good start. Midland Aircraft Manufacturing in Cleveland claimed "no openings," so I went for broke, ad-libbed about the grand things that a public relations writer could do for them, talked them into it. No such position had existed at Midland before. And, luckily, I'd managed to hold on to the job until the Pentagon's high demand for aircraft made my position redundant.

"I made up instruction manuals and informational blurbs to sell airplanes," I protested. "That's not writing screenplays! I'm a pilot. I know zip about filmmaking."

She fortified herself with a deep breath. "Lewis, I need someone capable and trustworthy on this assignment. My source at Midland gave you good marks." Now a smile flickered. "Your record as a cadet and pilot are impeccable as well." Now barely a whisper. "FBI says you're an ace operative, too. Resourceful."

I should have been beaming. Miss C gave out compliments like a Scotsman gave away gold coins. But if I was so resourceful, how come one of the bad guys in Detroit slipped away?

My gaze dropped to the saddle shoes that had bonded Miss C to me. At our first meeting during WASP orientation, she'd immediately recognized the shoes. They'd once belonged to Amelia Earhart. Not one to stand on niceties, she'd asked directly where I'd gotten them. My Uncle Chance, owner of Trinkets and Treasures, a curio shop in my hometown of Chilton, Ohio, found them at a charity auction and later gave them to me. Miss C and Earhart had been close friends before Earhart's disappearance. A common interest, beyond flying, had been extrasensory perception. Miss C later confided that she'd even been tested for it. On July 2, 1937, when Earhart was hopelessly lost on her round-the- world attempt, Earhart's husband, George Putnam, phoned Miss C, requesting that she use her ESP to find his wife's downed Electra in the South Pacific. Miss C passed along the hunches that came to her, but after three days she knew that the opportunity to rescue Earhart had passed. She went to a chapel, lit a candle and said a prayer for her friend, knowing she would never use her extrasensory power again.

At that first encounter, after I confirmed whose saddle shoes they were, I could see the longing for them in her eyes. While I would never dream of giving them up and she couldn't begrudge my connection to them, this mutual link to Amelia created our special solidarity.

Miss C's search for Earhart, mine for Cardillac.

Miss C had said she'd sworn off ESP, but here she was, reading my thoughts. "Anything new on Cardillac?"

Miss C preferred using the escaped agent's code name. A few weeks ago, in my debriefing after the industrial espionage assignment had ended, I'd referred to Cardillac by real name. *We don't dignify traitors with the use of their given names*, she'd chided.

Cardillac. The name sent me back so fast. *Detroit, six weeks ago, a stiletto racing toward me, its needle tip slicing a line of flesh along my forearm, a searing sensation. Blackness, then light, my nemesis gone.*

Exasperated, I shook my head. "Nothing." .

She placed a folded fist on the desk and leaned into me, her dark eyes a piercing slit. "Trust me, Lewis. You have the can-do attitude I need in Hollywood. But understand this. The WASP unit is highly vulnerable just now. We could lose the program if Hollywood isn't straightened out. And Frankie needs our help. You're the woman for the job."

She was right. You lose an airplane, you don't quit flying. You crawl back across the tarmac, heave yourself into the next cockpit. I lost Cardillac. Other sharks swam in the sea.

"When do I leave?"

Miss C quickly filled me in on the background of the Culver City studio near Hollywood where I would be working with Roland Novara. Formerly the Hal Roach Movie Studio, once home of the Laurel and Hardy films and the Our Gang comedies, it was now an official Army Air Force base, known as Fort Roach. The base studio housed the First Motion Picture Unit, or FMPU, organized nearly two years ago in early 1942, when AAF had begun its tremendous expansion. Composed of Hollywood directors, editors, writers, cameramen, and other talents who'd traded tailored suits and studio overalls for AAF khakis, the unit produced training films, propaganda shorts, even full-length features to cover every phase and problem of instructing all branches of the AAF. "You'll be in good company."

It got better.

"Ronnie Reagan's the Personnel Officer. Alan Ladd, Edmond O'Brien, Kent Smith, Van Heflin, Bill Holden, George Montgomery…" She ticked off the names on her fingers. "They're all attached to the unit, too. Don't look so starry-eyed. Actors of their caliber would never be assigned to work with the likes of Novara."

Before I could say *but what about the picture with Gable,* Miss C rolled her chair backwards and lifted a key ring from the middle drawer. "I pulled in a chit with the general. He's agreed to let you drive his automobile to Hollywood. It's yours for the duration of the assignment, in fact. It'll come in handy getting back and forth to the base studio. Fort Roach is a few miles from where you'll be staying."

My eyebrows shot up inquiringly.

"I've notified my dear friends, the Dunns. They're a lovely couple, live in Beverly Hills. They'll be tickled pink to let you bunk with them. I'll tell you all about them while we walk out to the general's car."

She handed over the keys. "I left my Staggerwing at Clover Field in Santa Monica. You'll be working at the studio for the most part, but you'll need to make a few trips to March Field near Riverside. All the flying sequences for our film are being shot there. The trip is a pain, seventy miles of desert. The Staggerwing will come in handy."

She slapped the desktop. "Well, that covers everything. Let's go."

I figured she was oversimplifying things. I had no idea to what extent.

Chapter Two

General Griffith's car was a sight to behold. British racing green with chrome trim, it was Packard's sporty roadster model, the Darrin Victoria.

I folded down the creamy soft-top, climbed over the cut-down door, and eased into the soft leather driver's seat. Firing up the engine made me smile. Like the general, his car had the kind of power that could make mere mortals tremble.

Across base at my barracks, I replenished my B-4 bag: fresh khakis, clean underthings, and a dressy outfit "just in case." Pressed for time, unsure what to do about my inadvertent arsenal, I packed my guns as well.

A call to the hospital was last on my departure list. Miss C had said I needed to check with Frankie's doctor before I visited. A nurse in the recovery ward, where my call was funneled, informed me that Dr. Farr would be at the hospital around noon. I could reach him then. After a little coaxing, she revealed that Frankie's condition had stabilized and she was being moved out of the special care unit.

Back in the Packard, I headed north up the highway, through a brown and olive blur of terrain. Less than an hour later: Culver City. I eased up on the gas pedal, momentarily transported from the commercial-industrial neighborhood around me.

Set back from Washington Boulevard on a grassy expanse of lawn, the studio headquarters was the replica of an elongated

Colonial-style mansion, complete with shutters and columns. Huge, free-standing letters stood atop its two-story portico. U.S. ARMY AIR FORCES.

Miss C had arranged for me to meet with Roland Novara at 0900 and my base orientation was scheduled afterwards, but I was early. I punched the gas and rolled past the studio-base in search of distraction. A block further down Washington, I spied a newspaper kiosk and nosed the Packard over to the curb.

The kiosk was nothing more than a weathered wooden hut painted a dull, chipped green, but it held an impressive array of papers and magazines. In front, a vendor dressed in baggy magenta pants and a cerise sweater vest over a turquoise shirt bustled about straightening and refilling his displays. Stoop-shouldered with flyaway white hair beneath a tweed cap, he was quick and precise, moving like a much younger person.

I drew near and the man pivoted around fast, as if he had eyes in the back of his head. Turned out, he had only one good eye. It pitched up and down, taking me in, while the other, obviously false, stared straight ahead. I stared back, fascinated that the moving eyeball was brown, while the rigid one was icy blue.

"It is what was available," the vendor said.

"Oh." Unable to think of what else to say, I shifted my attention to the array of offerings. The November 8, 1943, editions of Los Angeles' three dailies, the *Times*, *Examiner*, and *Daily News*, were displayed in racks below a waist-high counter. Stacks of *Variety* and *The Hollywood Reporter* sat on the counter above. Inside the hut, along the back wall, slatted trays held trade magazines. Photos of screen stars peeked out between the slats; mastheads stuck out above. *Movie Story*, *Screen Romances*, *Film Pictorial*, *Silver Screen*, *Photoplay*, *Movie Mirror*. An impressive inventory. But then, I'd heard MGM was just a few blocks up the street. Two studios and all the surrounding commercial buildings added up to lots of employees and potential customers.

The vendor moved to a nearby bundle, cutting the cord with a snap. Enticed by the bright red script *Hollywood* superimposed at an angle across its masthead, I reached for *The Hollywood*

Reporter. The word "propaganda" in the opening lines of W.R. Wilkerson's TradeViews column, caught my eye. I scanned the first paragraph, then the remainder of the article.

William Randolph Hearst, Wilkerson said, had allegedly sent an order to a film critic at one of his newspapers demanding that he write another review of Samuel Goldwyn's latest feature, *The North Star*, even though the critic had already endorsed the film. The picture, Hearst argued, presented a romanticized view of the Soviet Union. He wanted the picture labeled as "propaganda," and he expected the critic to go along.

Many Americans, I knew, were sensitive about our wartime alliance with Russia. But had Hearst truly ordered a staff critic to change his review? What did that say about his brand of journalism? Could subscribers ever trust what they read in his papers?

"Young lady—"

I jumped at the vendor's interruption. "You look to need something more than the latest in news or gossip." He held a sprig of freesia out to me. Behind him, a coffee can near the cigarette display held a vivid multi-colored bouquet of the fragrant flower.

Smiling, I reached for the sprig. The vendor pulled it back. "No. The yellow it is not so good. Your uniform is the color of toast. The bloom it will appear like a blob of butter." His gaze veered to my hair. "Topped off by orange marmalade."

His interesting accent and the way his one eye danced at the little joke he'd made got me laughing.

He laughed with me. "The color not so good, but the smell, it will make you feel good the whole day through." He fished out a deep blue blossom from the can.

"Thank you." I sniffed the bud. The sweet smell was like an elixir. My head felt clear again and the butterflies in my stomach had settled.

I slipped the flower into my shirt pocket, letting it protrude at a carefree angle from under the flap. Would the bit of dash, I wondered, be a negative or positive in how Novara perceived me?

Well, this was Hollywood. Why not go with the freewheeling spirit?

I kept the copy of *The Hollywood Reporter* and handed over a quarter. "Keep the change."

The paper's price was a dime, making the gratuity generous, even with the flower thrown in. Especially since he probably hadn't purchased the stash in the coffee can at all. I'd seen several beds of freesias along the roadway, driving in.

If the vendor felt uncomfortable with my generosity, he didn't show it. With a polite nod, he slipped the change into the pocket of the canvas apron tied around his waist.

"Could it be you are in the same unit as the young lady who had the flying mishap the other day?" The vendor eyed the wings over my breast pocket.

The reminder of Frankie pricked my lighthearted mood. "Uh-huh. Was Frankie a customer?"

The vendor nodded. "I miss her. For such a petite young lady, she had much good cheer. What is the saying?" He tapped a finger on his lips. "Ah. Good things, they come in little packages, yes?"

I smiled, nodding automatically.

"How is she doing?"

"Her condition's serious, I'm afraid. Hospital's limiting visitors, but I plan to stop by this afternoon. I'll keep you posted, if you'd like."

"Thank you. That would be good. I am Gus, by the way."

"Pucci." I glanced at my watch. "Gotta run, Gus."

"Don't forget to smell the flower," I heard him call as I dashed across the street.

◇◇◇

At the guard house outside the studio's entrance, a burly MP asked for my orders. He studied them briefly, handed them back. After he gave me directions and a guest pass good for the entire week, the barrier lifted. I drove the Packard onto the studio lot.

The Colonial-style front of the headquarters building was a façade. In back, absent the shutters and columns, the two-story stucco building looked blandly institutional. My base induction was scheduled here, and I would be returning later. Meantime, keeping the Packard to a crawl, my head lurching right and left, I ventured on, following the guard's instructions.

I passed buildings 1 through 4. The structures all looked like aircraft hangars to me, but I gathered they housed the various indoor stages where I'd been told the interior film shoots took place. At last, I saw a heavy metal door with a bold numeral 5 painted over it. I pulled into a parking slot.

An MP who'd been roving nearby sauntered over as I switched off the ignition.

"I'm looking for Roland Novara." I climbed out. "The guard at the gate directed me to Stage 5. This is it, isn't it?"

The MP, without answering, looked me up and down, very slowly, making me glad I was wearing slacks. I took the opportunity to check him out, too. Late twenties, athletically built, Roman nose, oily, bumpy skin, and beady eyes. I read his badge. Sgt. J. Winwar. The name wouldn't hurt his advancement.

Anxious to get his mind back from wherever it had wandered off to, I tried again. "I'm scheduled to meet with Novara at 0830. Know where I can find him?"

"Little early for a test, isn't it?" He winked a weasely eye.

I shuddered. I'd been warned that studio security was tight, but everything about my temporary presence was in order. Where did he get off gawking so rudely? What exactly was he implying about my being here for "a test?"

I huffed up my shoulders and cleared my throat. His rodent eyes met mine and I held them with the frozen steel expression Miss C had mastered.

He looked away. "Novara's not here. He and the boys hustled over to Stage 2 'bout a half hour ago. Off to view yesterday's rushes, part of the morning routine." He tugged up his pistol belt while giving me another roving look. "How 'bout I escort you over?"

I rejected the offer, accepting directions instead.

◇◇◇

A team of soldiers scurried pell-mell out of a nearby building. Some propped large cameras and collapsed tripods on their shoulders, others toted cumbersome black metal cases or pushed trolleys of electrical equipment or large wheeled trunks. I dove into the confusion, narrowly escaping the trajectory of a seemingly rocket-propelled cart carrying a metal milk can labeled WATER, before I emerged in one piece on the other side. Behind me, one of the men cursed as I hopped over clumps of thick cables crisscrossing the pavement and hotfooted it past several clapboard office buildings.

I tugged the door of Stage 2. It only gave an inch.

"Here, let me help."

The offer was from a lanky corporal who had arrived at the door a second behind me. The corporal's face was not what I would call handsome. Exotic, was more like it. Prominent cheekbones, a golden tan, and skin so smooth it seemed almost without texture—the kind that only needs shaving two or three times a week. His black hair had auburn highlights, falling in fine wispy spikes across his forehead. He gave a yank and we entered a small lobby. I looked up into dark, oval eyes behind metal rimmed glasses. We went through the introductions, including why I was there. Serendipitously, Sam Lorenz was the writer assigned to the WASP picture.

Sam combed his fingers through locks that had fallen on his furrowed brow, attempting to brush them back. They flopped forward again immediately. "So, you'll be replacing Frankie. How is she?"

I told him what I knew. Sam nodded, absently. He seemed sad, far away.

"Are you a friend?"

"She's a peach. Lots of spunk. I was at March Field, on a shoot. Saw her just before she went up." Sam's voice dropped. "Uh, just before the accident."

A scene of the horrifying crash began forming in my mind. "Accident? So the final report's come down?'

Sam scratched his arm. "Final report? You saying it might be something different? Someone deliberately wanted to hurt Frankie?" Behind the thick lenses, the look in his chocolate brown eyes was as hard as the frame of his glasses. "It's true…"

I hadn't meant to plunge in so deep, so fast. I pulled in my line a little, then played it out again. "An investigation is standard procedure following a crash. I hadn't heard the results. Thought maybe you had."

For an instant, I thought he might reveal something. But the sad look he'd worn earlier returned and he seemed distant, again scratching his arm.

I shifted gears to break the mood. "What's going on in there?" I nodded sideways toward the theater door.

"Novara and some technicians are looking over the scenes filmed yesterday. Identifying the best takes. I'm about to join 'em. Say, why don't you come inside? The clips are from the film you're here to work on. The WASP short."

"Swell. Let's go." I mustered a confident smile.

Sam smiled in return. "After you." He cracked the door and swept his arm toward the black chasm beyond.

Heads turned as we entered the darkened projection room.

In the light flickering from the screen up front, I could see that we'd entered a movie house in miniature. Four rows of seats—five across—were tucked against the wall to our left. The audience, mere silhouettes, consisted of a man in a beret in the front row and three men in each of the two rows behind him. Sam acknowledged their murmured greetings before the sliver of light vanished with the closing of the door. Only one of the men had seemed interested in my presence. His face was illuminated but an instant, yet I noted that he had strong, handsome features, neatly cut sandy-colored hair, and when our eyes met briefly he reacted with an easy smile.

Sam gestured to the vacant back row. I settled into a plush roomy seat, my attention riveted on the silent images on the screen up front.

A cluster of WASP cadets in flight gear, parachutes slung low over their backsides, strode purposefully across a tarmac, heading for the PT-19s parked near the flight line. The camera lens dropped and focused in on the backside of an inductee whose strut emphasized the rhythmic bouncing of her parachute bustle. She paused, looked back over her shoulder, hands on hips, feet apart, and froze, poster-style, à la Betty Grable. The cameraman pulled back a little, and got the full-body shot. When she began walking again, her sway was more exaggerated than ever.

I crossed then recrossed my legs. What was that all about? Was it a joke? The clip wouldn't actually be used, would it?

Before I could comment to Sam, the camera panned to another student pilot. She sat in the rear cockpit of a PT-19 behind her instructor. I squinted, trying to see if I it was someone I knew, but her goggles made it impossible. The pilot's expression and the way she fumbled with the strap of her helmet, however, told me she was nervous. No surprise. A check-ride, which I presumed the scene was about to demonstrate, was a nerve-wracking ordeal. We all feared washing out and having to say good-bye to the chance to fly full-time. The pilot hit the throttle and the PT lurched forward, then leaped into the air.

All of us in the small theater gave a concerted gasp as the plane zoomed straight up, hesitated a moment, then rolled downward in multiple loops, descending rapidly to the field below. I held my breath. What was wrong? The pilot wasn't pulling up. Had she lost control?

At the last possible moment, the PT broke from the loop pattern, ascending once more in a rapid climb. The plane leveled off and the pilot rocked the wings back and forth.

I grinned. From the chuckles around me, I realized we'd all been genuinely fooled. And thrilled. The exercise was not a check-ride and the pilot was no trainee.

There was more. Rolls, half-rolls, snap-rolls, lazy eights, Cuban eights, cloverleafs. Whoever was at the controls—both cockpits had them—was a real hot pilot. A show-off perhaps, but clearly capable.

My eyes stuck with the action as the plane turned its base leg and made a perfect three-point landing. The WASP gave the camera a thumbs-up and I knew my wish had come true. *She'd* been the hot pilot. The instructor followed, bowing with a flourish this way and that. The dramatics led me to think he was an actor—the kind who, pre-war, would have been cast in B-movies, at best.

Just then the pilot pushed back her goggles. FRANKIE! I should have known.

The scene skipped abruptly to snippets of cadets engaged in various leisure activities. It showed the women in their blue training shorts doing calisthenics, playing volleyball and Ping-Pong. A curvaceous blonde, shown exiting the pool, got me squirming uncomfortably again, especially when a low whistle rose from one of the men in front.

The exploitation of the trainees' physical features, however, wasn't entirely the cameraman's doing, I realized. Whether on the court, in the gym, or poolside, clip after clip showed cadets happily posing enticingly for the camera.

I nearly groaned out loud. I was doomed. Miss C would have conniptions if our film ended up including this cheeky nonsense. These gals and their antics could seriously damage our professional image. What had made them do it? The promise of stardom?

While the cadets-at-play sequence played out, a few more low whistles and murmurs escaped. My cheeks blazed. I wanted to rush up to the projection room and rip the film from the reel. Next to me, Sam cleared his throat. In the line of light from the projector, I could see he was not comfortable either.

The screen went blank. Behind us a strip of film clacked loudly against the metal of a reel.

A voice from the projection booth made itself heard. "We need a couple of minutes back here. Special preview for Colonel Brody and Lieutenant Rask is up next."

The lights came on, giving me a chance to observe the others in the room.

The man wearing the beret in the front row was turned around in his seat, speaking with a colonel in the row behind him. My fella with the easy smile was in the second row as well, seated next to the colonel and involved in the conversation. The light caught the gold bar on his shoulder, pegging him as a lieutenant.

"Who's who in the group down front?" I whispered to Sam.

I must have given away my interest in the lieutenant, because Sam began with him.

"Lieutenant Rask is a film editor. Works for Brody, the colonel next to him." Sam had already been speaking in a low voice. He lowered it another notch. "Rask is fairly new around here, but a good addition. Has a feel for what the men need, training-wise. Used to be a photographer in the Combat Camera Unit. Till it nearly got him killed."

"Huh?"

"A heavy bomber mission drew enemy fire. A twenty-milli-meter shell passed through the cabin at close range. Damaged his hearing. Had to be reassigned stateside. Which got him here, to Fort Roach."

"Is Rask the editor of our film?"

"No, he'd never work for Novara." Sam panned the room. "Don't see Mitch. He should be here. He's editing this picture." Sam adjusted his glasses slightly. "Then again, guess I can under-stand why Mitch *isn't* here. Novara keeps such a tight grip on things, he may as well stay put in the cutting room. It's the very reason Rask refuses to team up with Novara."

My heart sank at learning what working with Novara might be like, but I pushed the insight aside, saving it to muse on later.

"And what about Brody? What's his role?"

"He's a big name director the brass tapped for the duration. Deal is, he oversees work at Fort Roach, but he's free to direct features at MGM, too. Maintains an office there. Special arrangement. He's not involved with the WASP picture, though. It's too minor."

"Have you worked with him?"

Sam nodded. "Uh-huh. We just wrapped a flight character-istics training film—" He lowered his voice, "—hush-hush. I'm also working on an MGM feature with him," he continued, his tone conversational again. "Project's in the development stage, quite the ordeal. Last writer was fired...or quit." Sam's forehead creased as though reflecting the strain. "*Heavy* revisions."

My experience at Midland had ingrained in me a genuine respect and empathy for the rewrite process. "Hmm," I offered, sympathetically.

All at once, the man in the beret in front hollered up to the projection room. "We're waiting. You guys ready up there, or what?"

In the brief lull that followed, I sensed Sam's foot tapping the floor next to me. I looked over. His profile was expressionless, but his jaw muscles were knotting and unknotting.

An ominous feeling crept through me. "If Rask and Brody aren't involved in our film, why are they here?"

"They've been invited to look at a clip. 'There are no rules in filmmaking, only sins,' Brody likes to say. 'And the cardinal sin is dullness.' Novara thinks they might want to splice the piece into a training film he's heard they're working on. For dramatic impact." Sam' s voice had developed an edge. He narrowed his eyes. "Brody wields a lot of power in the industry, particularly in directing circles. Novara's trying to butter him up."

"The man in the beret. Novara?"

"Yup."

Dark, intense-looking, Novara appeared to be about forty, with strong features, full lips, a prominent nose, and thick eyebrows. The only one in the room not in uniform, he had a cravat tucked inside his open-necked white shirt. Beneath the beret he wore at a jaunty angle, his head looked completely bald.

Clearly, Novara didn't give a hoot about the impression he made on me. Our meeting had been scheduled to start a half hour ago, yet he was ignoring me, acting as though I hadn't arrived.

A major in the row behind Novara flanked Colonel Brody's other side. He had drawn back from the discussion with the others and now, pivoting in his seat, sent a nod our way.

"Major Beacock," Sam said. "From March Field where we're shooting the in-flight scenes. He's here to make sure nothing classified ends up on film and everything AAF is accurately represented."

Had he seen what I had? Nearly everything about the WASP I'd seen so far had been misrepresented!

The lights went down and the projector started up with a clackety-whir.

I squinted, baffled by the shadowy images up on the screen. A technical glitch had damaged the picture's quality, making it nearly impossible to follow what was going on. But I tried.

First, an unidentifiable person backed away from another individual standing near a plane inside a hangar. Next, as though in slow motion, the figure, the fuzzy image of a woman pilot, walked toward the camera. Shoulders sagging, she appeared to be blotting her eyes with a handkerchief. The picture quality sharpened at the moment her head snapped up as though in reflex to something being said or, maybe, at realizing she was being filmed.

The hair on the back of my neck stood on end. Frankie again!

The cameraman continued filming her, though she was shaking her head and begging him to stop. Suddenly, her hand shot out toward the lens as if to grab it.

The screen went blank. I turned to Sam. It was too dark to read his expression, but I would have had trouble even in the light. He'd put his hands to his head and was massaging his temples.

"What the hell was that all about?" a voice echoed in the dark.

"Who the hell cares," Novara retorted angrily. Turning, he shouted to the back of the room. "You guys asleep up there, or what? Cut that or I'm cutting your throats! Where the hell's the clip we're waiting for?"

The projector started up again. There was some flickering, then blue sky filled the screen. An A-24 approached from the right. As it flew across the screen, a sleeve-shaped target being towed behind came into view. My fingers tightened on the arm-rests of my chair as the camera's powerful lens closed in on the plane's dull gray fuselage, catching its beat-up condition, before zooming back to the target to pick up a tattered area riddled with bullet holes. Was it the angle of the shot or was the sleeve closer to the plane than normal? While I made a mental note to ask someone later, the plane bumped a bit as though it'd been bracketed by flak.

I leaned forward in my seat, but the A-24 had begun flying smoothly once more. An instant later, it faltered again. Horrified, I saw the plane's nose drop. I stopped breathing, watching while it plummeted to earth. At the last second possible, the pilot leveled out. The plane's touch down was a blur of metal careening across the desert floor, skidding, tearing apart until, at last, a cloud of dust and smoke mercifully blotted out what followed next.

My mind went numb as an emergency crew arrived on the scene. Moments later, after the cloud had settled some, the crew's frantic efforts to contain the damage and rescue the pilot were lost on me, too. I was in a sort of shock.

Slowly, I turned to face Sam. "Frankie?"

He nodded stiffly.

"Hair-raising stuff, no? Lights, Farella."

Novara's voice and the sudden brightness snapped me out of my trance. I blinked several times. How could he sound so flip? Frankie had been in that plane. Couldn't he show some compassion?

I fought to keep my composure. An emotional outburst now would almost certainly obliterate any future chance I had for steering the film in the way we wanted. Part of me hated Miss C for placing me in this den of goons, part of me was stirring with the challenge of outsmarting them.

"What do you think, Derrick?" Novara asked Colonel Brody. He gave a *heh-heh*, then added, "That clip could put a little samba in your flick, don't you think?"

I cringed.

Brody turned to his sidekick. "What do you think, Lieutenant? Can we use it?"

Lieutenant Rask, elbows on the armrests of his seat, his chin resting on the peak of his hands, folded steeple style, thought a moment. "Uh-huh," he replied at last, straightening up in his chair. "And don't toss the piece with the gal sobbing. I want that, too."

I clenched my fists. They wanted the clip of Frankie coming out of the hangar, crying? Why? And how exactly were they planning to use the scene with her crashing?

It was the kind of thing Miss C feared most.

Major Beacock was first to leave; the technical crew followed. Brody and Rask lingered in front, talking with Novara, while Sam and I hovered near the door. Sam had offered to do the honors in finessing the overdue introduction between Novara and myself.

After a while, a tall and well-built Lieutenant Rask wandered our way. My gaze veered to his face and I was struck once more by his strong and handsome features.

I straightened my shoulders. Stop it, Pucci. Good-looking or not, Rask was out to hurt Frankie, destroy the WASP program.

Rask, smiling his easy smile, put out his hand to Sam. "Hey, Sam."

They shook hands, then Rask turned to me. My sensibility gave way.

"What are you going to do with the crash scene?" I demanded. "Attack our safety record? Ridicule our flying ability? And, what's with wanting that clip of Frankie coming out of the hangar blotting her eyes? *Sobbing*, you called it. You want to show how emotional women pilots are? Make a statement about how cry babies shouldn't be trusted with our military's valued planes?"

Rask lost the smile. "Easy, lady. Shhh." His tone was soothing, the kind one used when trying to calm an animal or a small child. "You're a little quick on the draw. Maybe you'll find a beef with how Novara plans on using those shots, but my intent is honorable."

I didn't like his placating tone, I didn't like the amusement in his eyes, and I didn't believe for moment he could distinguish an honorable intent from a hole in the ground.

"Oh sure," I spouted, before I could get my lips clamped shut again.

Sam cleared his throat. "Pucci, say hello to Gunnar Rask. Gunnar, Pucci Lewis."

Gunnar, how appropriate. Aerial combat photographers recorded the enemy forces in action—showing their tactics and type of equipment used—as well as Allied raids on enemy installations. But they didn't just shoot film. They were also required to man a waist gun on missions.

I nodded, coolly ignoring the hand Gunnar offered. There was an awkward silence as his hand hung mid-air.

Sam gave me a pleading look. "Gunnar's okay, Pucci."

Reluctantly, I reached out and gave the hand a limp shake.

Gunnar, an amused smile on his face, acted as though everything were hunky dory. "You're one spunky gal, aren't you?" He glanced over at Sam. "Did you tell her about my injury?" Sam nodded. Gunnar turned back to me. "Just the right ear's bad; other one's fine."

I was still fuming but I had to appreciate the way he was handling things. I was also mesmerized by his eyes. They were a gorgeous shade of gray-blue, like a sky at dusk.

I blinked, dismissing the distraction.

"Funny thing is," Gunnar was saying, "the eardrum was already damaged. Result of some high fevers and infections when I was a kid."

"And you passed your induction physical?" Sam asked. "How'd you do it?"

Gunnar gave a sly wink. "There are ways. Actually, a punctured eardrum is not that big of a deal. Did you know that Stuka pilots intentionally perforate their eardrums?"

What a sad sack. Was he trying to impress me? First he'd called attention to his hearing to be sure I knew the heroics behind how it'd been damaged, now he wanted us to think he had something in common with Stuka pilots, the terror of the Eastern front. Stukas were highly maneuverable dive bombers. For psychological effect, they were fitted with a wind-driven siren to enhance the natural scream of their high speed maniacal attacks. Some thought the pilots fearless, I thought them crazed.

"Why deliberately poke a hole in your ear?" Sam asked.

My eyes swung to Sam's face. What a disappointment. He seemed genuinely interested.

The corners of Gunnar's mouth turned up a little. "Some brainy someone figured out that equalization of air pressure occurs through the perforation. Without the pain and distraction of pressure on the eardrum—or, worse, a mid-air rupture— they're able to concentrate more intently on what they're doing during a dive."

Part of the swagger associated with Stuka pilots was their ability to withstand the inevitable blackouts caused by the intense centrifugal pressure of their steep pullouts. I hadn't heard about the deliberate eardrum piercings, but I wasn't surprised.

"But now the ear is bad enough to keep me stateside," he added. "On the bright side, I discovered I could transfer what I knew behind the camera to film editing and still do my part."

"Gunnar's developed a knack for splicing actual footage into studio-made training sequences, Pucci," Sam said. "He's absolutely the best when it comes to cutting deadly realism into what otherwise might be a mind-numbing piece. What he does grabs a soldier's attention. Helps get him to do his job right, first time."

"No room for second-guessing when it comes to air warfare," Gunnar added, solemnly.

I nodded in agreement. But we'd veered off track. "Your intentions regarding Frankie's crash clip? Can we get back to that?"

"We're doing a short training piece to demonstrate a new foam that's come out for extinguishing fires. We need to show what the foam can do and how to use the new equipment necessary to apply it. Preparing ground crews saves lives, too, you know."

"Uh-huh." I was being deliberately vague. The cause might be worthy, but I wasn't convinced our WASP reputation, or Frankie's, wouldn't somehow suffer as a result of his creative efforts. Who could blame me after what I'd just witnessed on the screen?

The door swooshed open and the projectionist entered the theater to speak with Novara. He waited while Novara wrapped things up with Colonel Brody.

An awkward silence hung over our threesome.

"How 'bout I give you a tour of the cutting room?" Gunnar suggested finally. "You really should see for yourself how we'll use the crash clip. I could show you a couple of other instructional pieces that could use its boost, too."

Just what I was afraid of. Monitoring the additional ad hoc uses they'd find for the segment would be impossible. Still, why pass up a chance, no matter how slim, to influence how it would be used?

"That'd be swell. When?"

His reply had to wait.

"Watch your flank," Sam whispered out of the corner of his mouth.

I turned as Novara, adjusting his cravat, swaggered up to me.

"May I?" he asked, stopping nearly toe-to-toe with me.

Not bothering to wait for my reply, he lifted my chin with his fingers, angling my face this way and that. "Porcelain skin, good cheekbones, nose…hmm, bump on the bridge." I cringed under the spray of a surprise raspberry. "And, what pray tell, happened to the hair?"

I gave Novara's hand a firm shove.

Sam, who must have been a diplomat in another life, jumped in with introductions. "Roland, say hello to Pucci Lewis. She's here to fill in for Frankie Beall."

Novara looked at my pilot's wings. "Who?"

He knew, the phony. I fought to keep my voice and tone level, matter-of-fact. "Frankie Beall. The pilot who was flying the A-24 up there on the screen." I clenched my teeth against tagging on: The *human being* in critical condition, you insensitive louse.

"Right. Well, the timing's piss-poor. Clark Gable's gonna be here in just two days to do the voice-over for an OCS recruiting film. I've got to have a rough cut ready. We haven't even started shooting yet. Cochran be damned. That's my priority. You'll have to get in line."

I thought fast. "There must be something I can be doing in the interim. You only got a few seconds of target towing in the can, right? What about reshooting the sequence?"

I swallowed hard. It was a desperate offer. I'd only towed target once. Afterwards, I'd vowed to dodge the duty if ever asked again. But if Novara had a new segment on target towing, he wouldn't need to use the one he had—the one with Frankie's accident—right?

Novara's bushy eyebrows shot up. "Hmm…maybe. Film could use a few more flying scenes."

No kidding.

Novara's follow-on thoughts snowballed. "Cochran said you're a ferry pilot, that right?"

I gave a wary nod. He turned to Sam. "We haven't shot the ferrying sequence yet, eh, Sam?"

Sam nodded. Novara glanced back to me. "Okey dokey then, Lewis. Talk to the boys out at March. Set up another target towing shoot. And while you're at it, try to finagle one of their fancy fighters or bombers, would you?"

Before I could respond, he pulled a pocket watch from a trouser pocket. "Gotta dash. We'll get a film crew out there once you've got everything locked up. Keep in touch."

A small sigh of relief escaped my lips as he headed for the door. We hadn't locked horns, he'd been receptive to refilming the target towing segment, and I'd been given some responsibility. Not a bad start for a rube!

Quick as my optimism blossomed, it withered.

At the door, Novara turned. Eyes narrowed, he shot me an even look. "The crash segment stays."

Sam and I stood in silence for a moment, watching the heavy door inch shut.

During the time Sam and I were engaged with Novara, Gunnar had been locked in a private confab with Colonel Brody standing a few paces away.

"Might be useful for you to meet Brody," Sam said softly. "Want to stay an extra minute or two?"

I nodded. The wait gave me a chance to observe the colonel more closely.

Lieutenant Colonel Derrick Brody had a wiry build, and thin, dark hair that was graying and receding. His disposition seemed to work off of Gunnar's. While he talked, the colonel, as though animated by a force of nervous energy, sliced the air with his hands and his body shifted constantly. Gunnar on the other hand remained silent, hands crossed over his midriff, his head angled toward Brody, as though using the stoic exterior and the occasional nod to deflect the tension Brody threw off.

When we were at last being formally introduced and shaking hands, I noticed that Colonel Brody had self-manicured fingernails, chewed to the quick. Brody clasped his hands behind him almost before I'd let go.

"Your boss' husband, Floyd Odlum, is a friend of mine. Invested in one of my pictures a while back." He rose up and down on the balls of his feet a few times. "Got another one coming up I'd like him to consider."

Before I could formulate a reply he'd unclasped his hands and begun edging toward the door. "Well, men," he said, his eyes darting back and forth between Gunnar and Sam, "there's work to be done. Sam, don't forget we're meeting with the OWI rep this afternoon, after lunch. Wilma Wallace. She's got ideas for improving the script." He stuck his index finger inside his shirt collar and whisked the back of his neck. "'Fraid you'll be doing some tinkering afterwards."

Sam's top lip curled in a surly manner, but if he had a notion of objecting, he dropped it. He adjusted his glasses. "'Course I'll be there. No problem."

"Good." Brody placed his hand on the door.

"I have some free time this afternoon," I interjected hastily. "Miss Cochran, uhm, Mrs. *Odlum*, would be grateful, I think, if you'd let me attend your conference. I've got lots to learn and the experience, I'm sure, would be ideal." I gave him an imploring look but expected the Odlum name had already worked its magic.

The colonel's eyes met mine for the first time since we were introduced. "Sure. Why not?"

With a shove to the door, he made his exit. Gunnar, following in his wake, assured me he'd be in touch soon regarding my editing room tour. "The flower's a nice touch," he said smiling at me before the door could close.

Chapter Three

Sam left the theater with me.

"You were smooth in there with Brody," he burbled.

Sam's buoyancy surprised me. I looked up into his face. He was staring back at me with truly flattering appreciation. My face got warm under his gaze, and I couldn't help smiling.

"Figured it was too good an opportunity to miss. And, if I didn't invite myself, who would?"

Sam returned the smile. "Me. *If* I'd thought of it. But good for you. I like the way you asserted yourself. Just like Frankie—" He started to smile, but this time the effort seemed too great. His expression turned suddenly glum. So glum, I nearly reached over to pat his arm.

"Where you heading now?" Sam asked.

"Base orientation." I grimaced.

"Ugh." Sam chuckled. "Say, how 'bout I walk over with you?"

"I have a car, but it's parked near Stage 5. Think it'd be quicker to hoof it?" The lot, I'd noticed, was more active than when we'd entered the rushes theater earlier.

"Definitely. Things tend to heat up this time of day."

Sam wasn't referring to the weather, though even by Los Angeles standards it was balmy for early November. Balmy enough for the oversized doors of a nearby Quonset building to be left wide open. An invisible buzz saw screamed, seasoning the air with pine. I looked around, orienting myself and trying to determine in which direction to head.

Sam noted my momentary confusion. "Seriously, I'd like to escort you. My office is near headquarters anyway."

At that, hand at my elbow, he began steering me along a broad street dividing the sound stages. We strolled past the Shop Building, a sprawling garage-like structure with tall doors and walls of paned glass windows. A soldier carrying a faux section of brick wall rounded the corner. We ducked sideways to avoid becoming part of the set.

Sam's eyes filled with concern. "You all right?"

I laughed and assured him I was. "Can't help it, but I'm half-expecting that the next corridor we take we'll see Laurel chasing Hardy with a cream pie."

Sam laughed and began steering me again.

"I hear Ronald Reagan is base personnel officer."

Sam nodded. "Uh-huh, but I don't think you'll meet the lieutenant. At least not today. Bumped into him leaving his office earlier this morning. Off to the recording studio."

Sam chatted it up with Reagan? I tried to sound casual. "Another Recognition picture?"

I'd seen *Recognition of the Japanese Zero Fighter,* starring Reagan, a year ago. The film had been rushed into production because the Zero and the P-40 look so much alike—practically indistinguishable at 1,000 yards—that some of our boys in the air and on the ground were shooting down their own buddies. Up until then, I'd only been exposed to uninspiring nuts and bolts training shorts. But this had been like watching a big screen feature with Reagan playing a U.S. flier who nearly downs a colleague's plane after misidentifying it.

"Nah, Reagan's not being cast in instructional films any more. Base commander decided he's too famous a face."

"Too famous? But the movie was effective. No more reports of confusion after its release."

Sam shrugged. "I'm just a lowly scribe. And for the duration, Reagan is Fort Roach Personnel. No cushy job. Post roster's up to nearly a thousand men. He's still called up to do the occasional voice-over though. Like this morning."

An Army transport truck barreled toward us. Sam, gripping my elbow, herded me to one side. Ordinarily, I wouldn't have put up with a man nudging me this way and that. While some women considered the gesture gentlemanly, I thought it patronizing. But I let it go. Other matters were pressing in on me, like my initial meeting with Novara and the growing awareness that I was operating in an industry completely foreign to me.

The truck, an Army six-by-six, roared past, its warm slipstream washing over my face. I stared. The tarp closure was open in back and two soldiers sat opposite one another on side benches. Their uniforms were that nasty field-grey color we'd all come to despise—not khaki; on their heads, the distinctive coal-scuttle helmets. What was this? Two Nazi prisoners of war being transported to some desert prison camp?

Something fired them up. They stood—displaying more of their offensive German-issue outfits, complete with belts, daggers, and tall black boots. They shook knotted fists. Angry guttural curses spewed from their ugly twisted mouths.

Shocked, I turned to Sam. He was laughing. My gaze whipped back to the truck. It was nearly out of sight, but I could see the Nazis laughing too.

"Couple of writer pals," Sam said. "Real cut-ups. Must have been recruited as extras over at MGM. A top-secret project's being shot on a special set over there."

"Oh." Feeling more than ever like Dorothy in the Land of Oz, I sighed. Did I really have what it took to turn around Novara and his perverted ideas of what we did?

Sam picked up our pace as we vectored between clapboard buildings, many with running balconies. Sam explained that the buildings had once been dressing rooms or offices in the studio's previous life as Hal Roach Studios. Since conversion to the First Motion Picture Unit, they mostly functioned as barracks.

Sam pointed to the Writers' Building, a tin-roof, plywood and tar-paper GI structure where he had his office. Seconds later, we paused before a two-story brick building.

"Film Editing," he said. "Gunnar's territory."

A dark green Buick Roadmaster rolled to a stop across the street in front of the Music Building. The convertible top was down. The driver wore a red scarf over her dark hair. I knew immediately by the dark eyebrows and red lips who she was.

I blurted, "Judy Garland?"

"Yup. That's her husband David Rose, the composer. Miss Garland always drops him off around this time on her way to MGM. They live off post, near George Montgomery and his wife Dinah Shore. Keep alert. Miss Shore also does the chauffeur thing now and then."

He apologized with a wink. "I could bend your ear until it was blue, talking about the stars' comings and goings around here. Maybe you'd like to know something unusual about the military side of FMPU?"

I would have preferred the star talk, but his boyish grin was infectious. "What?"

"Regulations require that an air base be under the command of a flying officer. Our CO is Paul Mantz, the former stunt pilot. He's the only flying officer on the entire base."

I chuckled. Miss C hadn't been exaggerating when she'd called this a loose military operation. *Miss C. My dilemma with Novara.* How was I going to convince him to change our film? I decided to hit up Sam for advice.

"Those rushes with the WASP cadets…they looked like posy prima donnas on leave from their college sororities. Any tips on getting Novara to present our program in a more professional light?"

"Not really," Sam said. "It's his film. But don't sweat it too much. You've seen the worst. We've got some footage of cadets marching in review on the parade grounds, and there are more classroom scenes, I think."

Pretty dull stuff. I was getting more discouraged by the moment. "How about the segment of Frankie crashing? Any ideas on getting him to drop it?"

"Waste of time, even trying. I've worked with him, trust me. When he says something stays, it stays; he says it goes, it goes.

Your boss Cochran's request is a good example. She wanted a scene of cadets learning instrument flying in those tiny box-like compartments with wings that simulate flying conditions…" Sam paused, reaching for the right word.

"Link trainers," I filled in absently.

"Yeah, link trainers. Novara rejected the request, flat out."

The nerve! Novara wouldn't listen to Miss C's advice, yet she expected me to get him to take mine. The sudden burst of anger, brought on by my boss' brazen expectations, lit a fire in my belly. Scattered vague thoughts on how I might get Novara to follow my lead began chasing through my mind. Sam's voice drew me back before they could gel.

"Novara has a casting couch reputation," Sam warned next, as if it weren't obvious. "And he treats women like merchandise. But you handled him just right. Put up the hands-off sign, made sure he read it, straightaway."

Sam stopped in his tracks and faced me, his mouth fixed in a half-smile. "What he said about your looks, don't take it personally. Directors and studios don't seem to get it. To them, 'different' means inferior. In my opinion, in pictures, *anytime*, it's more original—and more appealing—not to be perfect."

I accepted the observation as the compliment I thought it was meant to be. "Why, thank you, Sam."

We'd reached the administration building with its weathered colonial façade. Before he left to go back to his office, Sam gave me directions to MGM where the meeting with Brody and the OWI representative was scheduled for that afternoon. He also said it might facilitate security matters if he accompanied me. Delighted with his willingness to help, I agreed to pick him up outside the MGM entrance.

◇◇◇

On a short break during orientation, I tried the hospital and was put through to Dr. Farr.

The doctor cleared his throat. "I wish I had more positive news. Miss Beall's condition is grave, ah, very grave indeed. She has a broken wrist, cuts and contusions—ah, those injuries are healing as expected. The coma is our main concern. That, and the internal injuries which may be numerous—and potentially serious. A visit from you will be good…" He cleared his throat again. "Ah, good for Miss Beall. It's beneficial for comatose patients to have someone whose voice they recognize talking to them. In some cases, it's enough to bring them out." Dr. Farr hesitated. "We continue to hope for the best, but there's been no response since she was transported here."

"I have an appointment coming up that's carved in stone. But I'll be there this afternoon." It was my turn to hesitate. "Ah… what's her prognosis, long-term?"

"The next couple of days are critical. While it's not unusual for a patient to be comatose for as long as a week after a severe head injury"—there was a pause—"the chances of emerging diminish significantly after that."

My stomach tightened. "My gosh," I whispered. "Frankie might not emerge…" I couldn't seem to bring myself to try pinning him down further. I swallowed. "Shouldn't someone, er, related be with her?"

"Miss Lewis," Dr. Farr said firmly. "I'm telling you this because you're needed. It seems she has no immediate family."

"No family?"

"There is an uncle, her father's younger brother. Efforts are underway to locate him. I'm afraid, however, getting him here will be impossible. He's overseas, serving in the Pacific."

Poor Frankie. All alone. In a coma. No family. "I'll be there this afternoon."

◇◇◇

True to his word, Sam was waiting for me. He climbed in the car and a trail of tangy aftershave—Old Spice?—followed.

"Sorry I'm late," I said. "*Reams* of paperwork to cut through before they'd let me escape. And no assistance from Reagan. You were right."

Sam looked over. Errant locks of fine dark hair, though damp and lined with the marks of a fresh combing, flopped forward onto his brow. His eyes, mellow pools of brown, took me in. "Worth the wait," he said, softly.

Blood rushed to my cheeks and I swallowed hard, at a loss for a comeback. Then, as if my drippy schoolgirl blush and sudden muteness weren't embarrassing enough, my foot hit the accelerator with a firmer press than was necessary. Sam's head snapped back with a jerk.

"We've actually got plenty of time," he said, once he'd recovered from the abrupt start. "Meeting's been delayed an hour. OWI rep's running late." He turned to me. "Bumped into my buddies doing the extra work. They introduced me to the set supervisor. We're cleared to take a quick look. Wanna do it?"

"A top-secret filming? Sure. What's it called?"

"Project 1699. I'll brief you in more detail on the set."

I braked at the guardhouse in front of the arched stucco entrance. There was no gate. The guard, acknowledging Sam with a nod, motioned us through. We passed under the METRO-GOLDWYN-MAYER sign with its signature roaring lion. I felt tiny prickles of excitement dance across my shoulders as the reality of where we were took hold.

Fort Roach and MGM might be only a few blocks apart, but there was a world of difference in their appearances. Fort Roach was a bare-bones operation with tired-looking, low-lying, clapboard buildings. Personnel roaming the grounds were predominantly male, mostly in uniform. Driving into the MGM lot was like entering a bustling Technicolor metropolis. Modern stucco buildings, many newly coated in yellow paint, lined both sides of the street. Civilian men and women from all stations of studio life, clad in everything from coveralls to shimmering gowns, meandered freely along the length of the route.

I gawked openly as we inched along. Near Stage 8, I spotted a small cluster of men in AAF uniforms. "Ah-ha," I said. "I'm no longer in Oz."

"Ah-ha, but you are. Those 'soldiers' are actors."

I slowed the Packard to a crawl, squinting to get a better look.

"They're working on a picture about a bomber pilot who gets killed on a failed reconnaissance mission," Sam continued. "He dies heroically, but then comes back to earth as a guardian angel to watch over a rookie pilot."

"Th-Th-That's Spencer Tracy in the leather jacket…" I sputtered. "Van Johnson's next to him!"

"Uh-huh. Film's called *A Guy Named Joe*. Tracy is the guy who gets killed, Johnson is the pilot in training. Irene Dunne plays Tracy's bereaved girlfriend. She falls for Johnson, eventually. It's a—a nice love story." Sam gave me a sidelong glance, smiling when my eyes met his. "OWI likes the flick 'cause it leaves the audience with a consoling note they can carry into real life—the dead hero lives on, in memory, in heaven."

At Stage 2, I parked the Packard. The truck that had been carrying the ersatz German soldiers sat unoccupied nearby. Cleared by the sergeant at the door, we entered a dim cavernous space. In the near distance, tall portable lights, scattered around the set, illuminated a castle and a crew of khaki-clad soldiers operating cameras and sound equipment. One man on a low stepladder held a long boom-mike pointed in the general direction of a path leading to the castle entrance. Of course, the castle was only a façade, but from a distance it looked real.

"Intelligence gathered the images from postcards and pictures taken by tourists on their summer vacations. Set department did the rest. Look—" Sam pointed slyly as we crept closer to the action. "There's my buddies."

The two German soldier cut-ups weren't laughing now. Armed with prop rifles and standing at attention, they flanked the castle's main gate, seventy feet or so from the assemblage of cameras and men.

"But a castle? German soldiers standing guard? What's going on?"

A tall, clean-cut captain seated in a chair marked "Director" looked our way and frowned. Sam waved. The soldier-director nodded, got up to peer through the camera finder.

"It's about the process of interrogation. Show air crews what to expect by depicting what happens to a B-17 crew shot down over Germany. Put the airmen through a program of subtle German interrogation. Let the viewers see how the Nazis separate even the most well-meaning, tight-lipped American flier from his military knowledge."

Sam had been whispering. I whispered too. "How do we know what the Germans do?"

"That's a replica of the place in southern Germany where they take our men. A couple of fliers who escaped are acting as advisors…"

The director stepped back from the camera. With an imperious wave of his hand, he shouted, "Ac-tion!"

A soldier snapped the arm of a clap board. Men in German uniforms and captured GIs in leather flight jackets approached the gate.

"Edmond O'Brien? Barry Nelson? Arthur Kennedy?"

Sam nodded. I gave in to a smug smile. I got it right. Things were looking up.

Sam bent in close. "Kennedy's also in the Flight Characteristic picture I just wrapped with Brody and Rask."

He'd mentioned the hush-hush training film in the rushes theater this morning. He started to say more, but a rifle belonging to one of the writer-stand-ins clattered to the ground. The group by the gate burst out laughing.

"Cut!" yelled the director, his face beet red. "And cut the funny business. I've had it with the pranks. It's a simple shot. Let's get it done. NOW. There's a war going on, dammit!"

Silence followed.

I sensed something plunging toward us before I saw it. Barely saw a blur. Heard a dim noise that increased to an ear-splitting sound. I turned. A torpedo-like object screamed as it dove toward Sam's head. He started to look up as I shoved him hard. We tumbled forward, stumbling, rolling in a tangle on the ground. Slamming into the floor inches from us with a vicious thunk, the missile bounced sideways, landing and ricocheting against the floor several times until finally it settled, rocking nervously. Was it a mailing cylinder? One of the grips rushed over to pick it up.

"Wait!" I jumped up, holding out my hand. "Don't touch it. Could be a bomb!"

The entire crew burst out laughing. I was aghast. One of the men, noticing my horrified expression, hushed the yokels.

Above us, footsteps bounded down one of the catwalks, heading away toward the far end of the vast sound stage. I looked up at the maze of planks crisscrossing the ceiling, following the sprinting footfalls and, at intervals, glimpsing a khaki-clad figure. The running stopped. He'd reached the stairway along the exterior wall. My gaze whipped to the crew clustered nearby. A grip held the tube in his hand; the others looked amused. The entire event had played out at such an accelerated speed that I could only think they hadn't yet caught up with what was going on. What else would explain their complacency?

The grip turned the tube so I could see an amateurish whistle device attached it its side. "It's another prank…"

"If that cylinder had hit home, you'd be calling the medical examiner instead of making like it was Stan Laurel up there having a little fun."

I glanced down. Sam's glasses had flown off and he was crawling toward them. "Sam, you okay?"

He looked up. "Yup. Fine." His voice was a little shaky, but he was mobile. I believed him.

I squinted toward the staircase. The airman's legs appeared, starting down from the top of the stairs. I took off after the prankster, the soles of my saddle shoes clapping against the wooden floor. I could see a silhouette of his frame as he descended the final stairs. He'd removed his tent cap, using it to shield his face, but I noted he had black, slicked down hair. I was closing in on the stairway, my arms pumping, my breath coming hard. Pushing off the final step he bolted for the door, shoved it open, and ducked outdoors. I followed, seconds behind.

Outside, I panted, fighting to catch my breath while I surveyed a deserted alleyway.

Back inside, the crew members had returned to their duties. The director, looking exasperated, huddled with the principal actors to one side waving his hands to emphasize his words. A few airmen glanced over as I returned to Sam, his face drained of color, holding a poster and staring at the image.

I came up beside him. "The contents of the tube?"

Sam's voice was so quiet I had to strain to hear it. "No bomb, but it may as well be."

He turned the poster so I could see the illustration. The confident, commanding figure of Hitler, brandishing a swastika-emblazoned red flag, dominated the forefront. Behind him, a sea of uniformed troops with swastika armbands gave the stiff-armed Nazi salute, many of them also waving flags like their imposing leader. The winding river in the background had to be the Rhine. In the sky, glorying over all, an illuminated cloud formation cast far-reaching beams of white light. In the border beneath the bold German phrase along the bottom, the poster's message had been translated: GERMANY LIVES!

"Outrageous!" I was furious. "And they think this sort of thing is all a big joke? Your head nearly got split open."

Sam forced a smile. "It's war. We like to keep things light. Other incidents have been funny…"

"Like?"

"The other day, just as the actors reached the gate, a banner flipped down over the castle entrance. Someone had drawn a good caricature of Bela Lugosi. His mouth was open and a dialogue bubble said, 'Velcome to de castle of my ancestors.' Everyone cracked up."

I rolled my eyes. No wonder the director was at his wits' end.

Sam tossed the poster on a nearby folding chair that also held the mailing tube. "They'll have to set up another take. We should go. Commissary's near Brody's office. How about we leave all this fun behind, grab some lunch?"

His invitation reminded me I hadn't eaten a thing since breakfast. I accepted.

◇◇◇

A pedestrian path led us through a warren of institutional buildings and into an open courtyard surrounded by Spanish-style structures of white plaster and red tile. Outside the Dutch door entrance to the casting department, a line of people stood waiting. I panned for famous faces. A little further on, at the studio schoolhouse, I honed in and thought, eureka!

Sam chuckled. "Sorry, that's not Mickey Rooney. Only a stand-in. Don't feel bad," he patted my arm, "a double is supposed to fool you!"

We laughed and continued walking. I asked Sam to prepare me, best he could, for what would be going on in the upcoming story conference.

"Like Brody said at the rushes theater, an OWI rep has found some problems with the script. He's called the meeting to iron them out."

The Office of War Information, or OWI, served as the non-military propaganda arm of the State Department. Dedicated to making the war pervade everyday lives, the agency also helped interpret the war for the public. I knew OWI representatives were in Hollywood "coaching" movie makers on how best to advance the war effort and keep the public informed on war issues; I didn't know the full extent of their control. "Can't a studio produce a picture without OWI's blessing?"

"Sure. But OWI holds a trump card. The Office of Censorship relies on its input and they control the almighty, highly lucrative foreign distribution rights."

"Ah, gotcha," I said.

We walked a bit further. "Who else, besides Brody and the OWI rep, is expected at the meeting? Will Rask be there? And what's the film about?"

"It's a wartime story set off the coast of Long Island," Sam said. "No, no Rask. This is a major studio feature, he's strictly AAF.

Producer's supposed to attend, but I doubt that he'll show. Someone from production should be there, though. Russell Chalmers, too, I heard. He wrote the novel the movie is based on."

Sam's expression turned suddenly dour.

"What?"

"Studio's already paid Chalmers a hefty fee for the novel's rights. Still, he's fighting Brody's every change tooth and nail. As the script writer, I'm caught in the middle."

"So why did Brody invite him today?"

"He didn't. Chalmers insisted. Why Brody agreed"—Sam looked heavenward, then he frowned—"Hmm…OWI demands could be a blessing for this particular picture."

"What do you mean?"

"If the OWI rep wants major adjustments, there'll be another rewrite. Script rewrites mean delays. The studio will have to cough up more money."

I wasn't following Sam. "But you said OWI demands might be good for the picture. Won't Brody's reputation suffer if he goes over budget?"

"You're partly right. In Hollywood, you're only as good as your last picture. Brody's last was a box office flop. Meaning this time around the studio coffers weren't opened as wide for him." A sly smile played on Sam's face.

"But?"

"If the OWI rep makes a fuss, Brody will be able to go to the studio for more bucks. He's no rube—he'll spread the funds around. Pump up the areas he thinks got shortchanged. Like casting, or location, or set design, costumes, special effects –"

My tongue snapped a 'tsk'. "Sounds more like the plan of a desperate man than that of a highly regarded director." I shook my head. "And how pathetic that someone at Brody's level needs to scheme and manipulate to get the picture he wants made."

Sam shrugged. "That's war."

Chapter Four

The studio dining room, a high-ceiling open space with linoleum flooring, Formica tables, brass chandeliers, lacquered columns and heavy drapery, was a strange mix of elegance and function. Clinking cutlery, glass and china, and the din of a hundred voices speaking at once, reverberated through the room. I trailed Sam through the crowd, evading waitresses in pink uniforms and caps darting among the diners.

We found a table along a bank of windows with a view of the studio lot. After ordering, Sam peppered me with questions about my background.

The pattern continued after our salads were served. We were up to my college years when Sam stopped his fork midway to his mouth. "A journalism major. That's swell. We're fellow writers."

I shifted under the sudden intensity of his stare. His eyes glazed over and for the briefest moment I wondered, *What is he thinking?*

"What got you interested in writing?"

"Money." I laughed, eager to lighten things up. "I was a PK, Preacher's Kid. When I was ten, some of my Sunday school pals, probably thinking I had an inside track, asked for my help composing prayers the teacher made us write. I agreed, for a fee. Something got passed down in the genes, all right. I churned 'em out like a machine. Penny-a-Prayer Lewis, they called me." I gave a demure Judy Garland smile. Sam chuckled. "Later on,

I took up flying. But the writing bug stuck. It got me my job at Midland."

With all the questions, I wasn't getting much to eat. Jabbing my fork into my salad, I tried to grab a bite but Sam was faster. "When did you learn to fly?"

"Took CPT in college."

He whistled. "Way to go! I heard only one woman for every ten men was accepted."

When I'd applied, I hadn't known about the odds. Or cared. The Civilian Pilot Training course, a government program to build a stable of pilots, was offered on college campuses before the war. "It was exactly what I'd been waiting for, the something that would catapult me out of the ordinary for good."

"Tell me more about the promotional writing you did at Midland."

"Hold on. I'm doing all the talking, and I'm starving here. What about your family? Where did you grow up? When did you know you wanted to be a writer? Where did you go to college?"

Sam held his hands up, traffic cop style. "Your journalist training is showing in spades. Enough." He laughed and checked his watch. "We better get over to Brody's office. How about we discuss me over dinner? Tomorrow night?"

My heartbeat quickened as his eyes met and held mine. Was "dinner" what the odd staring had been about earlier?

◇◇◇

There was a minimum of small talk as we assembled in Lieutenant Colonel Derrick Brody's office, a masculine space, its dark-paneled walls studded with glossy autographed movie star photos. Behind a polished mahogany desk, a credenza held a gold-framed photograph of Brody's wife and their two daughters. His wife appeared rather plain, but the girls had sweet expressions and big bows tied in their hair. Nearby, several leather-bound books were sandwiched between brass roaring-lion bookends.

Sam had been right. The producer would not be joining us, but someone from production would be arriving shortly to take his place. After making the announcement, Brody introduced us to Wilma Wallace, OWI's Hollywood representative and the reason behind the gathering.

Miss C, I thought, would have had mixed feelings about Wallace's no-frills appearance. No hint of lipstick had touched her primly pursed lips. A tall stick figure of a woman, she apparently saw no reason to gloss over her other God-given features either. She wore no make-up at all and her dull ash-blonde hair—the shade hauntingly like mine pre-peroxide—had been yanked into a severe bun. Her sharp blue eyes were piercing, even behind the thick, horn rimmed glasses.

On the other hand, Miss C would have commended Wallace's no-nonsense attire: a gray hopsack suit and a white blouse cinched at the neck with a brooch. The serious bearing followed through in the perfunctory handshake she gave me.

I was also introduced to the novelist Russell Chalmers. Looking scholarly in a tweed jacket, chino slacks, and a white shirt open at the neck, he had a casual appearance. Many men on the home front not in uniform felt they had to explain immediately, and Chalmers was 4-F due to an irregular heartbeat, he told me, shaking hands.

The session began once we were all squared away in leather chairs that circled a round conference table. Brody took charge with an ease suggesting he did so always, whether in uniform, as he was now, or not.

"Miss Lewis could use a quick recap of *Adrift With The Enemy* before we start. Let's do it while we're waiting for Wexler, agreed?"

Fine by me. Sam hadn't given me much background on the story. In fact, I hadn't heard the film's title before this. The heads around the table bobbed in agreement. Brody took center stage. That there were problems with the script became apparent straight out of the chute.

"Story starts out in a small but swank Long Island community. A young naval officer, hailing from a family not so well-heeled as the rest, has recently come home on leave. An average Joe, with a uniform on, he's able to impress the town rich girl. A relationship of sorts develops, and one night, intent on consummating their lust..."

Brody, as though remembering there were women in the room, paused, then cleared his throat. But not before he stole a glance at OWI's Wallace. *Was that a wink?*

"Eh-hem. The young officer and gal take the family cruiser out on the ocean for a joy ride. They know better—not just because they're sneaking the boat—but with the war going on, it's damn stupid: U-boats have been picking off ships on the coast with regularity. Suddenly, with the two of 'em in the throes of passion, a violent storm comes up out of nowhere. The boat gets knocked about; the young officer, topside now, gets knocked out. His leg breaks. Compound fracture. Bone protruding through his pant leg."

I grimaced and looked around. The others appeared at ease, but then they'd read the script.

Brody had been speaking in the rapid-fire style I'd observed this morning when we'd met. This afternoon, however, his energy level seemed to be percolating at an even higher rate. He stood and began pacing.

"The girl, bounced around pretty good, too, takes over, best she can. Time passes. Now and then, the young man rallies from his semiconscious state to give the gal various instructions. But the engine has been damaged; compass and radio destroyed. They're completely helpless.

"Suddenly, from over the side, a hand grabs the railing. Gal's not sure whether to scream or shout for joy. She rushes to the boat's edge. A bedraggled man is laboring to climb aboard from a partly deflated rubber raft. Adrenaline rushing, she struggles to help him."

Up to this point, I had been willing to suspend my belief. What happened next was overboard.

"The gal tries to get the man to tell her what happened, but he says nothing. His clothes are tattered and he's weak. Renewed by his presence, she fixes broth for him in the damaged galley. Still, he doesn't speak—it's all been meaningful eye contact to this point. A little later, he's mumbling in his sleep; she realizes the speech impairment has nothing to do with being injured at sea. He's German!

"Now she's frightened, but still desperate. Next day, wary, she stands by while he fixes the engine, then sets her boyfriend's leg. When he gets them puttering toward shore—thanks to a small compass he has with him—she lets her guard down a little. She's grateful. They become friendly, discussing this and that. He speaks broken English—" Brody tossed his voice my way.

Still pacing nonstop, but at an accelerated rate now, he went on. "The boyfriend thinks they're flirting. He starts smoldering. Later, when he spots the Nazi consulting a secret map, he figures out they're being navigated in a direction where the Nazi intends meeting up with an enemy ship."

Brody paused, derailed by something on his desk. An oversized white envelope. He studied the writing on the outside then, using a letter opener, unsealed the flap. A 5x7 photograph wrapped in a pink satin ribbon slipped out, pinched between his fingertips. A quick concerned glance our way—directed more at Miss Wallace than anyone—and his focus returned to the photo and an accompanying letter, leaving the rest of us to stare wide-eyed at one another around the table. Sam moved to take up the slack.

"Uh, while the boyfriend is putting two and two together, the Nazi makes a move on the girl. He kisses her and she tries to push him away. But then, the girl begins responding…" Sam's voice caught and he gave in to a sudden coughing jag.

The girl responds to the Nazi's kiss? No wonder Sam was hacking uncontrollably. What a flight of fancy. No red-blooded American woman would do that! Nor, should any American movie portray that. Whose idea had it been? I glanced over at Brody.

Sam began again. "Eh-hem. The boyfriend makes his move. Adrenaline pounding, he separates the two and overpowers the Nazi. He shoves him overboard to the sharks."

With a compound fracture? No wonder they called this place Dreamland!

A smile flickered on Sam's lips, suggesting he saw the absurdity of the situation, too. But he finished up gamely. "The girl embraces her hero while denying she'd felt anything but revulsion for the Nazi. An Allied vessel appears on the horizon. Fade out."

Brody, who'd rejoined us, began tapping the table with the letter opener he'd brought from his desk. He looked worried. He transferred the look to Wallace. Wallace was eying her pearl bracelet. She'd been fingering the lustrous beads and spinning the adornment around her wrist the entire time Sam had been talking. She glanced up. Brody glanced away.

"What's eating you about the script, Miss Wallace?"

The question was admirably succinct, but stripped of any diplomacy. If Brody wanted to provoke her, as Sam had suggested earlier, he was off to a good start. My gaze swung her way.

Wallace patted the dog-eared script sitting on the table before her. "You've got a problem." Her precise voice matched her prudish looks. "Several problems."

Let him have it, Wilma!

"People living along the Atlantic seaboard are deeply concerned about the German subs operating in their coastal waters. And it's not only the men and merchant ships we're losing out there that has them worried. They've heard rumors that U-boats are casting out raft-loads of spies and saboteurs to infiltrate their communities." Wilma gave her glasses a prim push. "The FBI has been disseminating information to eliminate their fears. This movie will stir up panic the government has been working to alleviate."

Brody had been picking at his fingernails with the letter opener. Without looking up, he said, "Story is fact-based. The entire country knows that Nazis are landing incognito along the coast. They also know they're being captured. Reports have been plastered across the front pages of newspapers, for Christ's sake! So far, no *War of the Worlds* mass hysteria has broken out. Give our citizens credit for being reasonable and intelligent, why don't you? It's the Germans who follow blindly."

Brody placed the opener on the table. "Besides, a reminder to Americans that fifth columnists are among us should be considered a service, not a *dis*service."

Wallace adjusted her glasses again, and gave Brody a stern look. "I'm not finished."

All eyes whisked to Wallace, but before she could continue, Russell Chalmers jumped in, his face livid.

"The girl in that…that so-called script is nothing but a floozy. A dimwit floozy! And the way the badly injured boyfriend recuperates enough to throw the German overboard…" Chalmers' outstretched hand hit the table with a thwack. "…that's way too unbelievable!"

Hurrah! My thoughts exactly.

"In the real story," Chalmers said, pausing a moment to calm himself and to cast Sam a sidelong glance, "it's *clear* the female character is only flirting with the German so he'll drop his guard. She's gotten her boyfriend, the naval officer, the man she *adores*, to remember a hidden gun. At the first possible moment, when the Nazi puts the moves on her, she shoots him between the eyes. *She's* the one who dumps the Nazi to the sharks. Then, with instruction from her fella, she captains the boat to safety."

Better yet! I cheered silently from the sidelines.

Brody tapped the arm of his chair for a few beats. "We've fought that battle, Russell. Moviegoers these days are predominantly women. Or, if a woman has a date, she picks the movie, the man pays. And ladies want romance, not some superhuman gal they can't relate to."

He leaned back in his chair and loosened the knot of his olive-drab tie. "She's only a woman, for Christ's sake. She can't overpower a man, pilot a cabin cruiser." The indignation on Wallace's face and on mine, must have registered. "Sam, help me out here," Brody pleaded.

Sam, head down, doodled with his pencil. To my relief, when he spoke, his position was sound.

"Chalmers has the right idea. The script relies too heavily on stereotype. Women are capable of a lot more than they're given credit for. Besides, I think an audience—both men and women— would find it more romantic if she remained loyal to her boy-friend." Sam tapped the pencil on the table. "We're pushing the envelope on the female lead's moral fiber already: stealing the boat, the love scene with the naval officer before the storm…"

Brody was rolling his shoulders trying to calm down, but his face was taut with irritation. "There you go on that nit-pick again. She wasn't serious about the naval officer, couldn't have been. Her family, her background…He's no match for her, plain and simple."

"Mr. Chalmers, Mr. Brody, Mr. Lorenz!" Wallace snapped the script with her finger as she uttered the names. "Calm yourselves."

She waited with pursed lips until she had the men's undivided attention. "Now that you've raised the morality issue, I'd like to discuss another of my problems. There's no obvious justifica-tion for killing the German. Throughout the story, he's helping the couple, appears to be saving them. The script doesn't even make clear his ideologies. He could be fed up with Hitler and the Third Reich and intent on defecting, for all we know. You don't kill a German just because he's German."

I gave Wallace a supportive nod. Well put! Plus, her tone had just the right touch of emotion behind it. Not whiny or judgmental, yet forceful enough to make her point. To let you know she intended standing by it.

"Why is it a Jap is a Jap, but we're so careful to distinguish between good and bad Germans?"

I looked at Sam out of the corner of my eye. The question had come from him, but his voice had been so hushed no one could have heard it but me.

Wallace was on a roll. "Lastly, my biggest criticism is that the German is presented in a glorified way. Once he's on board, he recovers quickly. By his actions, he's shown as strong, capable, cool under pressure, even charming. So much so, the girl falls for him." Wallace adjusted the brooch at her neck. "The U.S. officer, meantime, is shown as weak. It's as though you want to substantiate the Nazi's claim of a superior race."

Hear, hear!

Brody started to object, but Wallace bounced a fist on the table. "You've got to change it. With slight editing, the Germans could turn *Adrift With The Enemy* into a Nazi propaganda piece!"

So much for Miss C's theory that a woman wasn't worth a grain of salt unless she wore make-up. I smiled. With my next breath, I recalled the propaganda piece we'd been exposed to on the castle set and grimaced.

Brody studied Wallace across the table. If I hadn't been forewarned, I wouldn't have noticed him fighting to suppress a smile. But Sam had been right. The imperceptible smile proved it. This was a game to Brody. He had Wallace right where he wanted: demanding changes which would translate into more money for his picture.

The trace of a smile disappeared and Brody pulled his face into a tight grimace, as though controlling his agitation with great physical effort. An actor couldn't have done better. "Are you finished, Miss Wallace?"

At that moment, Brody's secretary Myra entered the room, carrying a pot of tea. A neat youthful-looking woman with prematurely grey hair, she wore a demure dress in a lovely shade of blue. She also had an unfortunate overbite, reminiscent of Eleanor Roosevelt, causing her to lisp slightly when she talked.

"Anyone el-th?" Myra asked politely, tipping pale amber liquid into a cup in front of Brody. "Chamomile. Good for the nerves." Her top lip tightly cupping the prominent upper teeth, she looked pointedly at Brody.

"No thanks," chorused the table.

Myra held the pot's spout aimed at me, staring as if startled by my presence. But Sam had explained my attendance when we arrived. Perhaps if she'd fawned over him less, she might have noticed me then.

Her gaze returned to her boss. "Th-orry to interrupt." Brody nodded for her to continue. "Three things. Mr. Wexler from production can't make it. Th-ays to call him soon as the meeting's over." Brody grunted. Myra added, "And a call came in from March Field. The colonel would like to see you tomorrow morning, 0900. I'm to call his aide back with an an-ther."

Brody moaned. "As if I had time to go to March." A long sigh. "Tell him I'll be there."

I was going to March Field in the morning to make preliminary arrangements for re-shooting the target towing segment. Maybe he'd like to fly over there with me. Who knew? In spending time with Brody, I might pick up a few clues on how to be more effective in my dealings with Novara.

Brody looked at Myra. "The third thing?"

Her protruding upper lip pulsed with the movement of her tongue underneath. She cleared her throat. "There's been a fire on the castle set. Small. It's out. But Sinclair would like a meeting to dith-cuth a delay."

A pencil snapped. I glanced over at Sam. He shifted in his chair, holding broken pencil halves in his fists, seeming perplexed by what had happened.

"Christ!" Brody heaved another sigh. "Tell him to come on over. Slip him in this afternoon."

Brody took a sip of tea as Myra left, but set the cup back in its saucer the instant the door clicked shut. "Let's wrap this up, shall we?"

Wallace, adjusting her brooch, straightened in her chair. "Perhaps you would like to consider an adjustment I've been toying with…"

Brody hunched forward on the table, biting on a fingernail. The room was a comfortable temperature, but there were tiny beads of sweat on his forehead. He pinned Wallace with his eyes, waving for her to continue.

"It's obvious right from the start, the girl is flirting with the German to get an advantage. She knocks him out while seducing him—say, picks up a nearby wrench and slams him on the head. She ties the German up." Wallace's eyes narrowed behind the thick lenses. "He's their POW now."

Brody picked up the story line. "Throughout the picture, she's an attentive nurse, devoted to the boyfriend. The boyfriend, though suffering, remains stoic. The Nazi is overpowered, but not killed, because we don't know if his intent is evil." Brody glanced around the table, a triumphant look on his face. He beamed warmly at Wallace. "An Allied vessel appears on the horizon. Fade out!" He looked at Chalmers. "Like the fix?"

Chalmers shook his head slowly, with force. "Derrick, the ideas don't send me," he said in measured tones.

Brody stared at him. "Let's just accept that. It wastes time to argue, and time is what?"

"Money, Derrick," Chalmers replied softly. The room fell silent.

Painfully earnest, his brow furrowed, Chalmers added, "I liked you better when you could distinguish art from business… and from feminine government influence, Derrick." He beat the table with his knuckles. "It's not the way I wrote it. I want my name removed from the credits."

Brody threw his hands up in resignation. "You know the studio will never agree."

Seconds ticked by in silence as he and Chalmers stared at one another impassively.

"Let's give it a rest for now, Russ. Miss Wallace's views, I think, are firm."

"Absolutely." Wallace panned the circle of silent faces. "Well, then, we've reached agreement." Rising from her chair, she checked her watch. "And, in record time."

Brody stood as well. "That's why I'm here, Wilma. You got a little problem with one of my pictures, you come see me."

Brody walked to his desk and consulted a large calendar. "Shooting was set to start fourteen days from now. I'll have to do some juggling here and there." He turned from the giant scheduler to look at Sam. "Can you get us a rewrite day after tomorrow?"

Sam scratched the pencil eraser against the crook of his arm. "Can do."

Brody slapped his hand on the desktop. "That's it. I'll notify production we've got a delay."

Those at the table got up and moved toward the door. Brody said good-bye to Miss Wallace—she actually had a beautiful smile—then turned to Sam and me.

"I'm flying out to March Field tomorrow morning from Santa Monica in Miss Cochran's private plane. Orchestrating a shoot for our WASP Victory short. Would you like to come along?"

I shook his hand.

Chalmers appeared at Brody's elbow. Ignoring me, he tugged Brody's sleeve. "Derrick. We gotta talk."

Brody, startled at the urgency in his voice and perhaps taken aback at the rude interruption, glanced at Chalmers, then looked back to me. "Sorry, this will just take a moment." Our hands were still locked together. He let go and took Chalmers' arm, guiding him out of our earshot.

True to Brody's word, they huddled only for a moment.

Chalmers shouted, "Tonight then, Derrick!" and stormed out, slamming the door.

Brody swiped a palm over his thinning, slicked-down hair, then turned to me smiling tightly. "Count me in. Driving would cut two hours out of my day...And time, we know, is money."

Chapter Five

Agog over the opulence of stately homes nestled under palm trees and tucked away in lush foliage, and wondering which legendary star lived in which houses, I nearly missed Benedict Canyon Drive, the road that led to the home of the Dunns. I cut the wheel and the green roadster climbed a steep ravine. At last, nearing a dead-end, I spotted their Beverly Hills address marker.

Downshifting, I turned the rumbling Packard up the inclined drive. At a curve near the top, the fading sun bathed the Dunns' California Spanish-style mansion in a burnished golden glow. I slowed to admire the scene. Tall arched windows were set into a hexagonal turret, anchoring the stucco walls of a wing protruding toward me. Above the roofline, a railed observation deck ringed an open-air cupola. The sights from up there would have to be spectacular, and I could hardly wait.

I pressed the gas again, rounding the turret to the front of the house. The home sat on a knoll amidst terrain partly manicured, partly scrub. In the distance, similar patches of lush greenery dotted the rugged natural landscape of the surrounding hillsides. More home sites of the rich and famous, I guessed.

A wrought-iron fence barred the front of the mansion, but the gate had been left open. I nosed the Packard through, making a slow loop around a circular gravel courtyard.

Arches and deep overhangs covered a stone walkway that ran the length of the first floor exterior. Under the archway, the air was thick with the spicy-sweet fragrance of jasmine climbing the walls. At the front door, I smacked the heavy iron knocker against the doorplate with a solid clank.

My first day in Hollywood had been exhausting. Following the story conference in Brody's office, I'd headed back to Fort Roach. On my way through the steno pool to get to the desk I'd been assigned for my Movieland tour of duty, the reception-ist handed me a message from Major Beacock at March Field. Assuming he was calling to finalize arrangements for my visit the next morning, I grabbed a notebook then headed out to the pay phone in the hallway. I hadn't been issued a personal telephone, but given the open space and the nine other women working at desks around mine, the phone-booth-in-the-corridor arrangement was a blessing.

After Beacock and I finished fine-tuning the particulars of my visit, I'd returned to my desk to review the copy of the script I'd been given for the WASP picture. Then I drove to the hospital for my scheduled visit with Frankie.

On my way down the corridor to her room, a hospital volun-teer, dressed in crisp salmon pink and pushing a cart of toiletries and printed materials, smiled as she passed. I entered the room I'd been told was Frankie's, but retreated. Wrong room—nobody in there looked like Frankie.

A nurse, tray in hand, was approaching.

"Can I help?" she asked.

"I'm looking for Frankie Beall."

The nurse pressed her lips into a line and stared a moment. The prissy look suited her austere appearance but, a half second later, her face softened sympathetically.

"You just left her room."

"She wasn't in th…" My voice trailed off.

The nurse gave a sad, encouraging nod before brushing past me. I followed, hesitating near the doorway, watching as she set the tray upon the bedside table. She adjusted an inverted bottle on the stand beside the bed, then checked the connection point on the hand of the patient. As she worked, the nurse blocked the patient's face from my view. I saw only a small, still form under tight white covers with an arm in a plaster cast, propped on a pillow.

The nurse turned to the tray of medications she'd brought in. My stomach lurched as I took in the disfigured features. Definitely a woman. Her skin, swollen and yellowish to black-and-blue in hue, was spattered with dozens of tiny scabbed-over nicks. A prominent gash ran from the inside corner of one eyebrow, across the forehead, and into a section of hairline which had been shaved. Black sutures and darkened bleeding points straggled from the raised red line. Her black hair was matted, particularly around the hairline, and tufts of it had been clipped or shaved. Her lips were crusty and nearly colorless; her eyelids were closed and puffy.

It was Frankie. I looked away. A wave of shame swept through me at my revulsion, but I didn't want to look back.

The nurse stepped into my line of vision again, bending to give Frankie an injection. She must have seen me from the corner of her eye. She paused, quickly returning the needle to the tray.

"Here. Have a seat," she offered, pulling a chair close to the bed.

I sat. I fought to compose myself, but I still couldn't look at Frankie. Instead, I focused on the nurse. "How's she doing?" I whispered. "Any change? Any sign of improvement?"

"You're the young lady who spoke with Dr. Farr earlier, aren't you?"

I nodded.

The nurse smoothed the skirt of her uniform. She folded her hands, resting them against the crisp fabric, thumbs twirling. "There's been no change. She's very weak, I'm afraid."

The thumb-twirling halted abruptly and her tone lightened. "I'm sure a visit from a friend is just what we need." She adjusted the pillows and bedding.

"No one else has stopped by?"

The nurse walked over and picked the tray up from the table. "No." She knitted her eyebrows. "But there have been a few calls."

"Oh?"

"Nice woman…uhm, a Miss Cochran?"

I nodded encouragingly.

"She called twice." The nurse thought a moment longer. "Then there was the hurried call from another woman, no name…Oh, and a fella phoned a couple of times. Didn't leave a name either. Said he was hard to reach, but would keep in touch."

"Her uncle?"

"Oh, no, dear." The nurse clucked her tongue a few times. "Miss Beall's uncle is overseas. They're doing their best to get word to him, though." She cast a sidelong glance toward the bed.

Her gaze remained on Frankie, but I continued to avert mine. She had just smoothed the bed covering and I placed my hand on the coverlet, mindlessly brushing it, comforted by the rough texture.

A few moments later I felt the nurse's stare boring into the back of my neck.

"Don't worry," she said in a hushed tone, "concentrate instead on helping her get better. Your presence, your voice, your touch, may help draw her out of the coma. Talk to her."

"About *what*?" I whispered, stretching out the words. I recoiled from the look she shot back. "Sorry," I whispered, my voice cracking.

I blinked back tears and turned, hunching forward on the edge of the bed. Nothing I'd experienced before had prepared me for what I was seeing and feeling as I took in Frankie's helpless, broken state. I gently patted at Frankie's side. "Sorry," I repeated, continuing the rhythmic tapping.

"I'll try to reach the doctor to let him know you're here." The nurse squeezed my shoulder and I listened to the fading sound of her footsteps padding out of the room.

I edged my chair to the head of the bed, fighting my emotions. This time, as I forced myself to look at Frankie, I concentrated on what was recognizable. The exercise worked. Her appearance no longer repulsed me and I began to relax a little.

You have a chance to make a positive difference in her recovery, I told myself, cautiously touching the hair matted against the pillow. I began speaking to her. About the weather, the nice nurse, her clean room. Nervous and talking full speed, I was soon desperate for fresh material. The reason for my being in Hollywood. That was it.

"Would you believe Miss C expects me to fill in for you? *Me* towing target with guys shooting live ammunition. Ha! Should be a blast…" Wrong. I forced a laugh. "Ha, ha. Hope not. But I've only done it once. But you…you can probably do it with your eyes closed…"

I became acutely aware of Frankie's swollen, tightly shut eyelids. Why couldn't I get it right?

Disgusted with my insensitive comments, but determined to carry on, I tried again. "To tell the truth, when Miss C asked me to come here, I wasn't all that excited. I thought she was probably overreacting to the way our program was being projected…"

I smiled at the unintended pun and automatically checked Frankie's reaction. Her expression remained locked in its grim mask. The bright moment faded. I went on.

"So, what happens? I arrive in Hollywood and meet El Roland Novara!" I waved my hand. "Isn't he just the most obnoxious man?"

I stood and tucked an errant lock of hair behind her ear. "I've always been able to sidestep his type before. But, after seeing first-hand what he's doing—well, Miss C was right to be concerned." Frustrated, I sighed. "You know all that, don't you?"

What about trying to provoke a response? Might that work?

"What you *don't* know is that Novara wants to use the clip of you crashing in the A-24. Thinks it's the kind of high drama a dry account of women wearing men's uniforms and flying airplanes needs."

I sat and collapsed against my chair, shoulders deflated, my lips flubbering with a sound that usually came from a horse. I finished up on a bitter note. "If he does incorporate the crash into our film, our opponents could—will—jump all over it.

Use it to discredit our safety record or ridicule our abilities. And we've come so far…"

A snigger escaped at a sudden vision of my first and last ride with Frankie. Near the end of training at Avenger Field in Sweetwater Texas, she'd needed a copilot for a cross country. Coming down to the bay, she hauled me out of a peaceful nap and demanded I be of some use. Off we went in an AT-6 advanced trainer. It was a short trip, about two and a half hours, but it was so hot when we took off, it was summertime, the oil temperature went up and we couldn't get above about 1,000 feet. We were roasting, so off came our shirts. It wasn't long before I caught a flick of silver out of the corner of my eye. I looked over, there was a male pilot, and I can still see his grin and the black mustache to this day. He poured on the power and left us almost before I could nudge Frankie. But the memory of our laughter and the aerobatics she did while we got our shirts back on made the quiet form before me all the more heart wrenching.

With a light touch, I stroked her arm, staring at the tape holding the intravenous needle to the back of her hand. "Don't worry. I have some ideas. One, of course, is to remake the towing sequence, but well…" I lowered my voice. "There's a coverup, Frankie." I waited a heartbeat, watching her abused face, hoping for a sign that she heard me. I leaned close to her ear. "Someone sabotaged your plane and the brass is keeping it hush-hush. Do you know why, Frankie? Please tell me what you know."

My ramblings were getting me nowhere. I went with the other subject weighing heavy on my mind. "Don't worry. Miss C has put me on the case. I'll get to the bottom of this. Say…I met a friend of yours, Sam Lorenz. Derrick Brody the director, too.…"

I glanced at Frankie's face in the nick of time. The flutter of her eyelids was barely perceptible; the movement of her swollen and cracked lips ever so slight. In reflex, I bent in closer.

There was a sticky clicking of her tongue trying to moisten the mouth cavity. Next, a low sound deep in her throat. A tiny droplet of blood formed on her bottom lip as her mouth worked with more and more determination. A soft moaning, then the release of faltering, incomprehensible speech.

"...s-s-...s-s-...ah-ah-aaahh...p-p-p...s-s-mmm...m-e-e..."

"Take your time," I whispered.

I remained frozen that way—ear bent to her lips—until I sensed a presence behind me. It was the nurse. She had not been able to locate Dr. Farr.

"She talked!" The enthusiasm in my voice practically bounced off the walls. More subdued, I added, "She tried anyway."

Though the nurse had been upbeat about Frankie's small breakthrough, she cautioned that she may not have been responding to what I'd been talking about—maybe only hallucinating. Still, any reaction whatsoever was considered a good sign. She encouraged me to come back and try again.

◇◇◇

The knocker hit the doorplate with another solid clank. My third attempt and still no one answered. I sighed, and tried the handle. Locked. Had Miss C even bothered to call her good friends, the Dunns?

I decided to try the side wing, following the covered walkway along the face of the house, then turning onto the stone pathway at the side. The kitchen door was ajar. An exotic sweet smell spilled from the doorway, carrying conversation between a man and woman.

"Naturally vee vill go along," said the rich melodious male voice. "It is for home. Our people." The man had a heavy accent and trouble with his 'w's.

"And this?" The woman's voice was grave. "It make you strange. It can kill even."

"But my dear—" The velvety words were steeped in irony. "Dying, it is my living."

I hesitated just outside the doorway to the spacious kitchen. The sweet-spicy scent I'd picked up on my approach was new to my senses, but what I saw before me recalled the castle scene at MGM. At least in that I was staring at a legendary castle occupant.

Clean-shaven, his dark hair slicked with pomade, he was dressed in formal white-tie wear, complete with raised-collar cape. He sat at a wooden table strewn with an assortment of colored bottles and dried herbs. Beside him, a knockout blonde maybe twenty years old. Her simple black dress with a high collar was accented by large buttons sweeping away from the neckline to dash in perfect formation down the side to the skirt's hem.

The twosome eyed a small open case on the table as I walked in. They both noticed me at the same moment. From their startled looks, it was obvious I had surprised them

"I am DRAH-cool-ahhh," the count said, recovering first. "I bid you velcome."

The young woman giggled. I laughed, too, but I didn't miss the graceful swoop of the count's hand as he flipped the lid of the plush-lined case closed.

I got a quick glance. *A vial and hypodermic needle?* A strange vision. But then it had been a strange day.

"Mr. Lugosi," I said, feeling both a thrill and a chill in saying the name out loud. I was a horror picture fan. They scared me to the bone, but I loved them. And Lugosi *was* horror, the embodiment of evil in film.

"Loo-go-she," he corrected me, standing. "Bay-lah."

Lugosi's career had suffered a dip in recent years. An article I'd read in a gossip rag claimed that the star, now in his sixties, had a serious drinking problem, which caused his extra weight, his bloated face, and the fact that he'd begun to look his age. I regarded the Lugosi before me, a tall figure dressed to the nines in his elegant cape. True, his face was no longer lean and so handsome as in his early movies, but he was still good-looking. And his dashing aristocratic bearing was unmistakable–in his posture, in the slight tilt of his head.

Bowing, he took my hand as I introduced myself and kissed it. "Lovely," he said, straightening up.

A pleasant sensation lingered on the back of my hand. I did my best to meet his gaze evenly. "Pleasure to meet you."

The eyes that on screen were luminous and inhuman, menacing and hypnotic, in person looked kind. Human. Especially when he smiled and the expression lines at the corners of his eyes deepened as he repeated my name—"Pooo-chi"—emphasizing the first syllable, drawing it out as though delighting in the sound.

The woman flashed perfect white teeth in a broad smile. "Huh-lo, welcome," she said in a pleasant lilting voice. "I am Ilka Maki, the house caretaker. We did not know when precisely to expect you. The Mr. and Mrs. they have barely just arrived themselves. From Florida. And, well, now with Uncle Bela's surprise arrival, I am afraid I did neglect the front door. So sorry."

She wiped her hands on her skirt, which drew my attention back to the cut of the dress. It fit her shapely Jane Russell figure like a glove. Her shoulder-length hair was movie star gorgeous as well. Waved over one eye peek-a-boo style, ala Veronica Lake, it was dyed Jean Harlow platinum. The silvery blonde shade—definitely not from a drug store kit—looked striking against her olive skin. There was a resemblance to Lake in the full lips, wide-set cheekbones and "good nose" also, except that Ilka's features were flatter. More interesting than the conventional Hollywood beauty, I thought, and she had exceptional tawny eyes.

What was such a dazzling being doing working as a maid?

While I'd been assessing Ilka, she'd been regarding me. "But what has happened *édesem*, my dear? You look as though the day it tossed you this way and that. Maybe you would like to freshen up before dinner?"

"That'd be great."

"Lia, she is making the meal for you and for the others." She gestured to the cook.

A recent Hungarian immigrant, Lia did not speak any English but made up for her silence with a nonstop grin displaying gold-rimmed teeth. When I'd entered the kitchen she'd been at a large, industrial-looking stove, stirring a giant pot. She glanced over as we were introduced then turned back to the countertop near the sink where she rhythmically chopped one of the green apples from a cluster of them nearby. Around her, the walls and counters were lined with built-in cabinets and appliances. Pots and pans dangled from a wrought iron rack attached to the ceiling. Some kitchen. Lia looked content, but I'd take the gadgetry inside a cockpit any day.

"Uncle Bela," Ilka rested her hand on Lugosi's arm, "is going out tonight to a fundraiser—"

Lugosi laughed deeply. "I vill give blood for de vor effort. Imagine. Count Drah-cool-ahhh *donating* blood instead of drinking it."

I laughed, enjoying his sense of humor and theatrics.

"For *the causes*—" Ilka paused, her tawny eyes twinkling. "The cause of publicity for your new A-picture, too!" She shot Lugosi an affectionate smile.

An A-picture was good news for Lugosi. A few years ago, Hollywood had stopped making horror pictures altogether. *The Raven*, in which Lugosi played a mad neurological surgeon with Boris Karloff as his monstrous-looking assistant, with its themes of torture, disfigurement, and grisly revenge was so terrifying that British parents launched a protest, prompting a British ban of horror films. Hollywood studios, which derived a large portion of their income from Great Britain, halted production of the films. The hiatus lasted two years, and when horror made a comeback the plum lead roles were no longer Lugosi's. Instead, he was offered only bit parts by the major studios. Frustrated, he'd opted for lead roles in low-budget B-movies at Monogram.

"Congratulations Mr. Lugosi. You're doing publicity…Is the movie out? What's it called?"

"*Return of the Vampire*." He swept his arm to his face, partly hiding it with his cape. The cape fell away, revealing a different facet of Lugosi. Disappointment. "The premiere, it has been delayed."

Ilka patted his shoulder near the stiff stand up collar. "Universal will issue *Son of Dracula* with Lon Chaney, Jr., this month. When Columbia hear this, they decide not to compete—in spite of having name of Lugosi to tout. *Return of the Vampire* will debut in January now, they say."

"I'll be first in line," I volunteered.

"But first tonight vee vill draw blood from the lines of people who vill attend the gala. It is rumored Paul Litvik vill be there." He flexed his eyebrows at Ilka.

She traced the curve of the platinum wave partly covering her face. "Besides housekeeper, I am actress. I have audition day after tomorrow. Mr. Litvik is the director. Uncle Bela knows Litvik. He thinks there will be chance to whisper in his ear…"

"Hooray. More wonderful news," I said.

"Is only small part. No speaking lines. My accent…"

Lugosi swatted the air with his hand. "Your accent it is part of your charm. Think of how I speak. It has become one of my greatest assets."

Or a curse. According to the gossip rag, Lugosi's sore point was that his roles were not varied, which wasted his talent. Didn't his signature accent—his famous pauses and intonations—play into the typecasting?

Four bottles of wine stood on the table along with the colored bottles and herbs. The small leather case had been tucked in close to the wine. Lugosi noticed where my eyes had strayed.

He lifted a green bottle labeled *Tokaji*.

"Tow-KAI," he said, "is king of Hungarian wines. A sweet white." He set the bottle down and with a flourish lifted another. "*Egri Bikavér*. A full-bodied red we also call Bull's Blood." Lugosi brought the bottle to his mouth and mocked biting its neck. Ilka and I laughed. "I bring *bor*, wine, to thank Mr. and Mrs. Dunn for what they are doing for—"

"For me. Uncle Bela is so thankful for the way they help me…give me job here. He always is bringing gifts. Uncle Bela is here for another reason besides to deliver wine." She looked pointedly at Lugosi. "We are trying to find a cure."

"Yes, is true. I have big problem with chronic sciatica. You know it?"

I shook my head. I hadn't a clue.

"War injury—"

"Last war, Uncle Bela was Captain of Ski Patrol." Ilka began scavenging the array of dried plants as she spoke. "He was wounded on the Russian Front."

"I suffer much. Stabbing pain—like dentist striking raw nerve—shoots down back of thigh and leg from hip to foot. Doctor after doctor I visit. Aspirin is not possible—" He patted his stomach. "Ulcers. Asparagus juice was the recommended cure before—"

"Before he decide to give me chance to find treatment. Ahhh." Ilka held a small cobalt blue bottle up to the light. "This, I think, may be it."

Lugosi's shoulders lifted and fell in an expansive shrug. "Gypsy voodoo, vhy not?"

"Oh, Uncle—" Ilka chided. "Even as joke, this is not funny. It only fuels the bad reputation of the Gypsy."

I frowned. Ilka read my confusion.

"My roots they are with Gypsies. My mother, she was… Grandmamma she is…Gypsy. Gypsies have faced the prejudice of the *Gajé*, or non-Gypsies, forever. There has always been loathing for how we live, for our ways, for our appearance. At best, we are tolerated. Now, with the war, things they are even worse. We are considered 'undesirables.' A people who must be forced out. Eliminated." Ilka paused to look over at Lugosi. They shared a private moment.

"But that is another story," she said, jutting out her chin. "In creating aura of fearful superstition around our race, by pretending to have mysterious powers, we gain certain respect. Fear may be a better word. Slim defense, but better than nothing." Her attention returned to the blue vessel and she squinted, studying the hand-scrawled label.

On the other side of the kitchen, the lid of a pan clattered to the floor. Ilka's hand jerked and I thought she would drop the bottle. The jarring seemed to bring her back to her duties.

Ilka's hand flew to her cheek. "The Mrs.! I forgot! She wants that I show you around a little then direct you to the master suite." She set the blue vial on the table. "Uncle Bela, wait here with Lia. I will be back shortly."

Carefully arranging his cape around him, Lugosi eased back down into his chair. Over near the sink, Lia chopped away.

Ilka bestowed a perfect parting smile on her "Uncle Bela" then turned to surprise me by linking our arms. "It is European style," she explained, patting my hand reassuringly and guiding me from the kitchen to a hallway to the front foyer and into another short hallway that spilled into the living room on one side and into a library on the other.

As we strolled, I recalled my first impression of Ilka, that she might be Scandinavian, possibly Swedish. Deep in recesses of my memory, the name of one of Gran Skjold's friends fought to escape. It succeeded, taking me down a slightly different path. "Maki. That's Finnish, isn't it?"

"Yes, very good. My papa, he was Finnish but I am *Magyar*, Hungarian, born in Budapest."

"Ah, Finnish-Hungarian Gypsy." The blended genes explained the uniquely attractive combination of her olive complexion, tawny eyes and somewhat flat features. Perhaps the Scandinavian blood explained where her desire to be fair-haired came from as well.

"I grow up there, but leave two years ago to come here, to be Hollywood actress." Ilka beamed. "I come as war refugee. Bela, he is sponsor and also my guardian angel in the movie business.

"After you have visited with the Mrs. and had the chance to change"—she eyeballed my uniform—"the Mr. and Mrs. would like for you to join them in the library." She gestured to a room off to our right. "There is cocktails in there before dinner."

Ilka nodded to a grand iron-railed staircase that split at a landing three steps up, before climbing to the second floor. "Your room, it is up there."

I'd been toting my B-4 bag. Ilka suggested I leave it beside the settee positioned by staircase while we completed the tour. An unusual feature of the settee was a small table built into one end. A telephone rested on the table. Beside the telephone was a pair of second-priority airline tickets (the number two slot behind the President). I recognized the high-priority tickets because it was the status given to those of us ferrying Pursuit fighters, they were so badly needed. Only these did not belong to a WASP; these tickets had an international leg. Los Angeles-Orlando-Cairo.

Ilka noticed where my eyes had strayed. Unlinking our arms and deftly whisking the items from the table, slipping them into a pocket in the seam of her skirt, she confided. "Like I say earlier, the Mr. and Mrs. they just return home. Sometimes with them, they bring along a mess."

Past the staircase, two steps led down into the living room. I followed slightly behind Ilka. She walked stiff-backed and made theatrical gestures as she talked.

"The Mr. and Mrs. they enjoy to travel. And, phew—" Ilka fanned her face with her hand. "They find the things to collect along the way. See—" Her hand swiped the air. "Most items here and there tucked around, they have been hauled in from all corners of the world."

Ilka chattered amiably in precise English peppered with her lilting Hungarian inflection and the occasional inverted syntax as we crossed the room, my head pivoting this way and that, taking in the eclectic array of paintings adorning the walls and the colorful bric-a-brac strewn on nearly every surface.

We paused before the room's floor-to-ceiling windows. Commanding views of city, mountain, and canyon were breathtaking. Turning to face the living room's interior again, I regarded the velvet, brocade, and wrought-iron accents of the room's Spanish-medieval décor. Though not to my taste, it was grander than anything I'd ever seen before.

We started back across the room, arriving at the hallway again. Ilka gestured down a corridor to the side wing of the house. "In that part is my quarters and the kitchen. That you will view another time. I must tend to dinner and to Uncle Bela now. But first, let me show you to the master suite."

◇◇◇

Della welcomed me. "You look positively beat, sugah. Bad day?"

Dressed in flowing white satin trousers and a matching tunic jacket, she had tucked one side of her lustrous brown hair behind an ear. She looked just the opposite of beat.

"First day on the job." I feigned a casual air while sizing up the suite. "You know how that goes."

"Sure 'nough do." She gestured to a pair of overstuffed chairs near the fireplace. "Sit a sec, won't you?"

We sat, and I took in her exquisite clothing and the richly appointed room. The reference to work had been stupid. Of course she didn't know what the first day on a job was like. She'd never earned a paycheck in her life, I'd bet. I turned slightly to look at the monstrous bed mounted on a carpeted dais directly behind us. On its burgundy satin coverlet was the suitcase I'd spied upon entering. Yawned open, both halves mounded high with folded garments, it looked suspiciously like she hadn't even unpacked.

I shifted to face Della again. She'd seen me scrutinizing the bed.

"Jackie's notice was seat of the pants," she said. "Didn't even know we had company till we arrived. With everythin' else goin' on, well, I've just had to let some things go. Sherry?"

Miss C's tendency to bulldoze surfaced once again. I murmured my apologies and replied, "Yes," to the sherry.

A small carafe of the amber wine rested on a round table between us. Della poured, and I observed some of the suite's other fine furnishings, like the white fringed carpet covering nearly the entire floor and the cherry wood highboy and nine-drawer bureau. The turret area was at the far end of the room. An inviting space with window seats at tall angled windows, it also contained a wrought iron spiral staircase which I presumed led to the cupola just above.

Della handed over an etched glass. "Call me Della," she insisted, adding that her husband D.B., who I would be meeting shortly over *real* cocktails, would want me to call him by his first name too. With a clink, we toasted to health, friendship, and a quick end to the war.

The first sip, though delicate, warmed me going down.

"Er, the winding stairs," I said. "Do they go up to the cupola?"

"Sort of. They lead to a small study D.B. and I use as an office. From there, you have to climb a ladder to get outside."

I hoped Della would invite me up to look at the sights. My hostess had other ideas. Some initial polite chitchat about their hailing from Tex-*suhs* segued into my training in Sweetwater. How did I like being a WASP? How did I feel about making the sacrifices that came with the job? What made me stick to a job so challenging? Was I prepared to die for my country? And so forth and so on until we arrived at why I was in Hollywood.

"Say, my brother G.R. is based at Fort Roach," she said, topping off our glasses. "Maybe you'll bump into him filmin' some prototype plane or new equipment. Bomb sights, radar…" She let the sentence drift off, suggestively adding, "It's what they're doing there, right?"

I started to nod, but hesitated. Miss C had briefed me about the work being done at the base, but I still wasn't clear on what I could—or couldn't—say openly.

An uneasy silence followed as Della turned an expectant stare on me.

I deflected her look, concentrating on the sherry remaining in my glass. What was she after? Many of the films produced at Fort Roach dealt with confidential material. Did she think I knew about something secret going on inside the studio and was itching to talk? Maybe her interest wasn't actually in what was going on at Fort Roach. She knew I flew military planes.

Did she want me to divulge what I know about secret flight equipment? Radar?

My lips stayed zipped. How green did she think I was?

Apparently, green enough to go a step further. "What do you think of the XP-59A?" she probed, her tone offhanded, as though she were asking for nothing more than my opinion of the weather.

I sipped the drip from the bottom of my glass. The XP-59A was an experimental jet—one of the first. I'd only gotten wind of it day before yesterday, on my stopover at Wright Field.

"How'd you hear about the XP-59A?"

Della twisted a diamond-encrusted earring. "G.R. talks 'bout planes all the time."

That brother G.R. was quite the blabbermouth. If I ever did bump into him, count on it, he'd be getting a piece of my mind.

"Don't you think G.R. should be more discreet?"

Della's eyes hardened. "Are you sayin' my little brother is tellin' secrets?"

I hesitated. My news about the advanced plane had actually come through scuttlebutt I'd heard in the ready room at Wright. That meant the project was probably beyond the top secret stage. I backpedaled a little.

"No…But why broadcast our new developments? 'Be smart, act dumb,' that's the motto. Axis sympathizers have been found in the most unlikely places." I looked over at the bed. "Ilka says you and your husband travel a great deal. *Cairo?*"

Della hesitated, as though now she had to decide whether to explain. She didn't.

With a laugh, she suggested we forget the war for a minute and have a bit of fun. "Let's have a look in my closet, shall we? That officer's uniform looks better on you than most women who wear one, but somethin' more festive is in order this evenin'."

Picking out something to wear *was* fun. We were like a couple of old pals on a shopping lark, in search of the perfect party dress. There was plenty to choose from in Della's walk-in closet. At one point, she let me know that her closet was my closet. "Feel free to borrow anything, anytime," was the way she put it.

At last I settled on a black outfit: wide-legged crepe trousers and a square-necked top with beaded cap sleeves draped matador-style over shoulder pads extending beyond my shoulder line.

I left the master suite, Della's exclamations about how chic the ensemble would make me look ringing in my ears.

Chapter Six

In my room, simply furnished but with its own private bath, I reveled in a luxurious soak. Soap was a scarce item, impossible to find in most hotels these days, yet alongside the tub was a jug of rose-scented bubble bath. What a treat!

A knock on my door from Ilka, saying my hosts were waiting, cut short my grooming time. Standing before the mirror, I gave Della's blouse another yank. When I'd borrowed the outfit, I hadn't realized the top was cropped at the midriff. The style was too revealing for my taste, but what choice did I have? Too late to change.

◇◇◇

Downstairs, I paused in the doorway to the library. D.B., I noted, had classic good looks: eagle's beak nose, slick brown hair, neat mustache. He was standing in front of a bookcase, directly across the room. Another man stood nearby in shadow.

"Hi, Pucci, darlin'," D.B. called out. "You look smashing."

I took a step into the room. My breath caught.

"C'mon over and meet Della's brother." The surprise must have shown on my face. "Say, do y'all know one another?"

You bet we did. Della's brother G.R. was *Gunnar Rask!*

I hovered near the doorway, composing myself. Well, what do you know? Mr. Blabbermouth himself was the film editor I'd met today at Fort Roach...the editing whiz who intended splicing Frankie's crash scene into a training film and into who could guess what else.

My gaze darted about. Something about the layout of the library was different from when I'd peered into the room earlier with Ilka. I walked toward the men. D.B. sported a tweed jacket, an unlit pipe, and a goofy grin. Gunnar wore cowboy boots and had traded his uniform for jeans, a Western shirt with pearl buttons and a string tie. He was grinning as well.

What was so funny? My distress?

An awful thought rattled me. I glanced down. The cropped top was still in place.

"Don't pay them no never mind, Pucci," Della said, breezing in behind me in flowing white satin trousers and a matching tunic jacket. "Boys, y'all get that bar out here right this minute. C'mon, sugah. You look as though you could use a stiff one."

With a tug and a shove, D.B. and Gunnar spun the bookcase they'd been standing in front of around to reveal the well-stocked bar that had gone missing. I laughed wholeheartedly. I'd been truly duped.

D.B. began mixing up a batch of martinis, explaining that the false front bar had been installed during prohibition. The talk about restrictions imposed back then segued into a discussion of current recreational curtailments brought on by the war.

"The drop in tourism has affected the night-club and restaurant business," D.B. said, emptying the clear contents of a frosty metal container into wide-rimmed glasses. After skimming lemon rind around the lip of one of the glasses, he handed it to me. Whisk, whisk, whisk, three more drinks were ready. "Ciro's closes and opens at intervals. Coconut Grove's open Fridays and Saturdays only."

"And yachtin's out of the question. *Verboten!*" Della said, gutturally. "Might bump into a Jap sub."

We laughed, but we all knew the possibility was real. There'd been a shelling of an oil refinery by an unidentified vessel off the coast near Santa Barbara in February last year. Also in February, in the dark of night, air raid sirens went off, huge searchlights flipped on, and the sky south of Santa Monica lit up in a spectacular fireworks show of tracer bullets and thousands of exploding shells witnessed from streets and rooftops by hundreds of residents below. Rumors abounded, but what the antiaircraft batteries had been firing at that night remained a military secret. Another incident that followed later in the year had the makings of a fantastical movie script akin to Brody's *Adrift with the Enemy*. Except this brush with the enemy occurred off the Pacific coast, and it was real.

A Japanese submarine carrying a small plane with folded wings slipped across the Pacific into the unprotected waters off the Oregon coast. In the predawn darkness, the plane and its pilot were shot by catapult into the air. He flew over the coastline, dropping two 168-pound fire bombs into the forest. The outrageous incident didn't end there. The pilot, after landing in the water on the plane's floats, managed to reconnect with the sub. The crew quickly stowed the plane and the sub submerged, successfully evading our Navy's frantic search. Three weeks later, the mission was repeated. Two more bombs and more fires provoked alarm up and down the coast.

Such penetration of American soil was hard to forget. Concern over what else the Japanese might have up their sleeves lingered.

"Most everyone who owns a yacht 'round here has turned 'em over to the Navy or Coast Guard," D.B. said, nudging me from my private thoughts.

Gunnar shrugged. "No fuel to run them anyway."

"Still, they deserve credit for the patriotic gesture," I said. "Could turn the *tide* of the war!"

Everyone groaned, but I'd started something. A skirmish to top my play on words followed, and "yacht donating" gave us plenty to quip about.

As the bantering continued, I began to think maybe Gunnar wasn't so bad after all. He had a relaxed manner and easy sense of humor that made him comfortable to be with, and the work that went on at Fort Roach had not come up once. I decided to save any reproach about "loose lips" and "crash clips" for another time.

Ilka popped her head in to announce dinner was served. Della led us to an annex off the formal dining room. A snug space, the prominent feature of the room was a low table set into a circular pit and surrounded by plump, richly upholstered pillows. Candlelight and a massive tapestry of South Seas natives welcoming a ship's explorers to their shores lent intimacy to the setting. What a blessing I'd worn pants, I thought as we kicked off our shoes and nestled into the pit, legs crossed pow-wow style.

Lia waltzed in with a tray of dishes. One by one, she passed them to Della who, in turn, placed them on a Lazy Susan at the table's center. D.B., in charge of beverages, displayed bottles of red and white Hungarian wines. "Bela Lugosi's treat," he announced, spinning the crowded platter and creating a space for the wines in the center.

We wasted little time digging into a meal that lived up to the intriguing smells I'd detected in the kitchen earlier. The main dish featured rice tossed with coconut, raisins, apples, and chunks of chicken flavored with an exotic sweet spice I'd never tried before: curry. The revelation that Gunnar had selected the menu was another pleasant surprise. He'd brought the recipe back from a trip to the Far East, he confided.

I discovered something else refreshing about Gunnar during our meal. Midreach for something on the table, he accidentally dipped the cuff of his sleeve into the curried dish. Rather than ignore the yellow dab, or make a fuss of blotting it with water from his goblet, Gunnar, without pretense, brought the sleeve to his mouth, dabbed it with his tongue, then got on with the dinner conversation as though nothing at all had happened. While the gesture may have appeared gauche to some, I read it as a sign of a man completely at ease with himself. Perhaps it was the sherry, martinis, or the Bull's Blood, full-bodied as Lugosi had advertised, but I began to like Gunnar even better.

I would have liked to hear more about Gunnar's travels or about his and Della's childhood on the ranch in Texas, but attempts at getting personal information from my dinner companions went nowhere. Della and D.B. dominated the conversation with talk about the zillion war-related volunteer activities they were involved in. They were inundated with committee work which was fine by them. D.B.'s age exempted him from military service and they relished the reward in having found a way to do their part.

We finished our meal and while we were waiting for dessert, Della talked a bit more about their war contributions. "Truth is we get restless if too much time slips by without a call from someone askin' for our help in arrangin' this or that event. Besides, contacting our friends, askin' 'em to volunteer, helps us stay in touch with what's going on around town, know what I mean, sugah?"

Once more, I wasn't sure I got Della's drift. But before I had the chance to clarify what she meant by "what's goin' on around town," a phrase she'd put special emphasis on, D.B. came up with a more vexing matter.

"Della get a chance to tell you the news yet, darlin'? G.R.'s moved his gear into one of the guest rooms. Gonna be staying with us for awhile."

"Oh…" I said, strangely unsettled by the prospect.

"Yup. There's a glut of government workers assigned to Hollywood right now." Gunnar shifted the cross-legged configuration he'd fashioned for sitting at the low table. He fluffed the pillow at his back. "It's put a crimp on housing and I've been bunking at a barracks on the lot. Sis and D.B. having so much extra space and all…well, they roped me into comin' here."

Ilka entered in a hurried flourish. "Mr. Rask. Urgent telephone call. Your office."

While we were taking our last bites of the meal, Gunnar returned. He had to leave. An emergency at the base.

Della turned to address D.B. "What about that important meetin' we have tomorrow, sugah? It's first thing in the mornin', right?"

The tone of Della's question was unmistakably leading. I looked up from ferrying my fork to my mouth and saw the three of them firing discreet glances at one another.

After we bid good-bye to Gunnar, Della announced we'd be having dessert in the dining room. She had a special surprise planned for me.

◇◇◇

The dining room was long and narrow, with rough-hewn beams across the ceiling. At the room's center, tall wood-tooled chairs surrounded a massive dark wooden table festooned with a pair of ornate candelabra.

My "surprise" began when Ilka joined us, wearing an elaborate jacket embroidered with astrological signs. We arranged ourselves at one end of the table. Before taking her seat, Ilka lit the candles. Next Lia entered the room carrying a tray of parfait glasses. Green tea ice cream with a hint of nutmeg flavor. Delicious. Thick black "Finn" coffee was also served.

In between sips and bites, Della and D.B. spoke effusively about their good fortune of having Ilka in their employ. The Dunns' deep involvement in wartime fundraising left little time to devote to household matters. Della had even managed to get Ilka involved in one of her ongoing projects, an innovative popular event that featured Ilka as fortune-teller-to-the-stars.

"Ilka has incredible intuitive powers…"

"Shh," Ilka admonished with a tinkly laugh. "I will tell. For the most part, fortune-telling—fortune-tellers—it is a sham. But I was born with the gift. I did not choose it."

I recalled what Ilka had said about her Gypsy roots. "You said you came here two years ago, as a refugee. You left your family, all that was familiar…it must have been a difficult decision."

"Decide? There was no choice." Ilka's tone was no longer lilting. "Things had become too dangerous," she added softly.

She didn't say more, she didn't have to. In early '41—the year Ilka emigrated—Hungary technically became part of the Axis. My Swedish grandmother and her diverse circle of immigrant friends frequently engaged in heated political discussions. I'd overheard one particularly fiery debate about the political situation there and knew it to be complex. True, a pact was signed and a fascist legislature was established. But an agreement did not mean that all of Hungary embraced Nazi rule. Recent reports in the press had even hinted there was a growing faction determined to undermine the alliance.

D.B. tactfully turned the focus away from politics. "Actin' is in Ilka's blood," he said. "Both her mother and father worked in Budapest's National Theater."

"Yes, Papa was set designer and *édesanya,* Mother, make costumes."

"This was very unusual," Della injected.

"She is meaning, *for a Gypsy.*" Ilka squeezed Della's arm affectionately. "But my mother was strong-minded. At the age I am now, she decide, 'I will follow my own path—a legitimate *Gajé,* non-Gypsy, path.'" She pushed the silvery curtain of hair off her face. "In summers, while both my parents, they are working in the city, my Grandmamma Roza, she tutor me in psychic powers and herbal methods of healing." lka looked suddenly very sad.

With Ilka's blessing, Della explained that Ilka's parents were both killed by an avalanche while skiing during a family visit to Finland. Ilka was sixteen. She went to live with her grandmother. Later, as the war wore on, Roza decided it was no longer safe for Ilka to stay in Hungary.

"My parents, they had many friends at the National Theater," Ilka said, "among them, Uncle Bela. My grandmamma, she find way to make contact and he make arrangements. I am fortunate to be here, safe, with much to look forward to. This I know."

Lia returned and began clearing the dishes. Della stopped her and gestured for her to take a seat. There was a concerted huzzah when Della announced her surprise. Ilka was going to read my palm.

At first I objected—I wasn't one to talk about personal matters, much less have them paraded before a group of people I didn't know—then finally gave in with a "Why not?"

Ilka sat next to me, holding my hand atop the table. D.B., Della, and the Hungarian cook stood behind us, peering over our shoulders.

"Let us begin with the major lines," Ilka said, turning my hand this way and that.

Several seconds of silence followed, during which I got a sinking feeling. Too much doom and gloom? Turned out, it was poor lighting. D.B. turned a knob that brightened the wagon-wheel chandelier centered above us.

"Yes. Better. Here they are –" Ilka traced the most prominent lines of my palm with her fingertip, "—the life line, the head line and the heart line. The life line, it is first."

I shifted uncomfortably in my chair. I'd never had a palm reading before. A bunch of hooey, I'd always thought.

"Ah. A Neptunian life line. You are destined for a life some-how removed from the mainstream."

So far, so good.

Ilka's finger slid back to a deep horizontal line cutting across my palm. "This is the heart line, the representation of matters of the heart. Love, sex, romance…"

"Ooo la-la," Della cheered. "Now we're gettin' to the good stuff."

Ilka ignored the interruption. "A Jupiter heart line," she pro-claimed. She tapped two tiny but distinct slashes along the line. "Ah, but see. The line it is marred. Signs of ups and downs."

Much hoo-ha followed about what the highs and lows might be. Embarrassed and a little miffed at their insensitivity, I felt the blood rush to my cheeks.

Ilka, her finger still on the line, made things worse. "Your nature it is passionate—you rush into romance." She clicked her tongue. "Too often you are blind to the faults of those you love."

Right again! Chalk up falling for my Detroit FBI boss, my latest disaster.

"The line of Saturn it is the career line." Ilka traced a vertical line from my middle finger down my palm. "Yours is likes of which I have never seen."

"It's also called the fate line," Della said.

"Career Line is the designation I prefer," Ilka retorted briskly. "Fate Line it conjures up the notion that I will predict what she will do or what will happen to her…"

Ilka had clammed up. Her eyes were fixed on my palm. My gaze flew to her fingertip. She pulled it away to reveal a star-shaped marking on my hand.

"What?"

"Not much there," she said unconvincingly. "The reading it has ended."

D.B. mentioned the crucial morning meeting, also remembering the ungodly early hour at which it was to start. We called it a night, the others indicating they would likely be up and out before me in the morning.

◇◇◇

My astounding evening with the Dunns at an end, I was preparing for bed, drawing on the satin lounging pajamas that traveled with me everywhere. Pale jade green, they'd been laundered so many times the color looked as though it would disappear completely with the very next washing.

I shuffled across an oriental carpet to the wardrobe against the wall, the comfort of my favorite satin p.j.s helping me to relax. A burst of cool air suddenly swept the room, bringing on a case of goose bumps. I looked around. The sheer curtains at the open window fluttered gently. The B-4 bag on the floor caught my eye. I sighed, remembering the secret arsenal tucked inside.

The clearance beneath the bed frame proved sufficient, and I shoved the bag deep into the dark recess, wondering if anyone at Long Beach had noted the missing .45.

The sheets smelled fresh and felt crisp as I climbed into the bedclothes. A hand-painted porcelain lamp stood on the bedside table. I reached for the delicate chain under its silk-fringed shade. With a gentle tug, I put out the light. Another treasure from abroad, I guessed, snuggling deep under the covers, savoring the weight and warmth of the plush coverlet.

◇◇◇

I awoke with a start, aware the bedside lamp had been turned on. Heart beating madly, leery of laying eyes on whoever had switched it on, I pushed down the fluff of covers, forcing myself to take in the room. No one was there.

Slowly, I inched into a sitting position. I flipped back the covers and ducked over the bed's edge for a peek. My audible sigh filled the room. My B-4 bag had not moved.

Wide awake and still on guard, I propped my pillows against the headboard. I sniffed deeply. A strong perfume scented the air. Jasmine from outdoors?

I took another whiff. Joy perfume! The scent was familiar because Miss C wore it all the time.

Before turning out the light, I noted the time. Oh-three-hundred.

◇◇◇

I was awakened by Ilka's knock sometime after daybreak.

"There is an urgent telephone call for you, *édesem*," she announced from the other side of the door.

What now? Blurry-eyed, I hopped out of bed and scurried into my robe.

Downstairs, Ilka stood by while I picked up the receiver of the phone resting on the settee's edge. The caller, her voice quavering with emotion, identified herself as Derrick Brody's secretary. Mr. Brody, she stammered, would not be going with me to March Field this morning. He had died in the night.

Chapter Seven

The news refused to sink in. Colonel Brody *dead*? I'd been with him less than twenty-four hours ago. He had such a strong presence, so much energy.

"*Édesem*, what is it?"

I didn't answer. My hand still clutched the receiver. I stared at it, transfixed.

"Sit down a minute, *édesem*."

I released the receiver and dropped onto the settee. Shivering, I drew my robe tighter. Ilka sat next to me. I shared the sad news.

"Brody…this name is familiar. Big name director?" Ilka asked softly. "This is too bad." She patted my hand. "He did not go easy."

"What do you mean, *he did not go easy*?"

Ilka's forehead crinkled then relaxed. "A man of his age, he died too early. That is all. Was it heart attack? Accident? The dark deed of an enemy, perhaps?"

I almost smiled at the choice of words and dramatic hush of her last guess.

"His secretary said 'natural causes.' Heart attack would be a good guess, though. He's…" I cleared my throat. "He *was* very intense, high-strung."

"I am so sorry." Ilka gave my hand another pat. "I must go see how breakfast is coming. Anything special you would like?

We have cinnamon rolls, but you would want eggs, bacon, hot cereal perhaps?"

For the first time, I noticed the scent of yeast and cinnamon in the air. "A cinnamon roll would be great, thanks. And your famous Finn coffee."

Ilka smiled. "Good, then. I will see you in the breakfast room. What, in twenty minutes?"

◇◇◇

The breakfast room was off the dining room, the same place where we'd had our curry dinner last evening. This morning it had an altogether different look and feel. A traditional table and chairs set with pastel yellow dinnerware occupied the area where the sunken table had been. Beneath the table, an Aztec rug repeated the green, gold, and sienna tones of the South Seas tapestry on the wall.

Sunlight streaming in through multipaned windows drew me to the opposite side of the room. Della and the men, like the table-pit, were missing in action this morning. I recalled the secretive glances around the dinner table and the curious crack-of-dawn meeting that had come up out of nowhere. What was that all about?

Beyond the stone patio outside the bank of windows, a sweeping expanse of lawn sloped to a kidney-shaped pool. An elderly dark-skinned man, Mexican, I thought, dressed from hat to shoes in white, was digging a hole in a grassy strip alongside the poolside cabaña. A plant attached to a section of lattice and swathed in white cheese cloth rested in a nearby wheelbarrow. Its root ball contained in burlap protruded slightly over the wheel-barrow's edge.

The gardener's shovel bit dirt again. A headstone appeared in my mind's eye. I shivered. My mother's headstone. Memories flooded my brain. Her funeral. A sorrow that cut to my core, draining my slight ten-year old frame of all feeling. The debilitating numbness that followed. The self-blame.

Outdoors, the gardener pushed the wheel-barrow close to the freshly dug hole. He lifted the bundled plant, removed the burlap, positioned his burden in the dirt. Wiping his brow with his sleeve, he began removing the cheesecloth shroud. It caught and he tugged to clear the snag.

If I hadn't been so stubborn, insisting on wearing the patent Mary Jane's, not the brown Oxfords she insisted were better for my feet, we wouldn't have arrived late at the church for rehearsal. She wouldn't have been frazzled, distracted. She wouldn't have tripped, crashing through the loose railing to fall from the choir loft.

A hot stream trickled down my cheek. I blinked. Another tear rained as I heard Ilka's words—*Did not go easy. Died too soon.* My mother's tragic fate; Brody's unexpected end. The finality of death left a hollowness like no other.

The gardener had freed the cloth and begun filling in the space around the plant. A bougainvillea. A splash of fuchsia petals against white stucco. My breath caught at the glory.

"*Édesem…*"

I dabbed my cheeks and turned from the windows. Ilka was at the table with a laden tray. I asked about the room's transformation. As she relieved the tray of its contents—a plate of cinnamon buns, glasses of orange juice, and a coffee pot—she explained. An electric "gizmo," she called it, was mounted on the wall next to the tapestry. The gizmo controlled a floor panel, opening and closing it over the sunken table and seating pit. The Dunns had come up with the idea a year or so ago, and Ilka had supervised the installation. Unfortunately, she couldn't demonstrate the invention without removing the current table, chair, and rug arrangement first.

"Was a mess to put in, for sure," Ilka said in her lovely lilting voice, after we were seated. "And, as you now understand, a not so easy design to use. But, the Mr. and Mrs. so enjoy entertaining. Devising menus from little-known parts of the world is part of the pleasure. The sunken table it gives them a unique place for serving the foreign fare." Ilka sipped her orange juice.

"I wonder what part of the world—or U.S.—the Mr. and Mrs. took off to this time."

"Huh?"

"Yes. They are gone. Off on one of their trips. A note they left it explains everything."

"*Everything*? But you just said you wondered where in the world they'd headed off to."

"Where they go is not important, *édesem*. It is no business of mine. What I need to know, they wrote: *We will be gone for awhile; unexpected committee work has come up*. By such a message I am to know the house it is in my care."

"Unexpected committee work? Gone for awhile? That's it?"

Ilka shrugged. "*Igen*, yes. The Mr. and Mrs. they travel much, often at the drop of a hat. I grew up among Gypsies, remember? Such restlessness I understand." She lifted a bun and nodded, politely waiting for me to take a bite of mine.

"Scrumptious," I murmured, savoring the yeasty sweet cinnamon flavor.

We ate in silence while I pondered the Dunns' departure. It seemed so sudden. Then I recalled Della's suitcase on the bed and the lead she gave D.B. at dinner concerning the crack-of-dawn meeting. I took a swallow of strong Finn coffee. Had this morning's hasty leave-taking been in place all along? Had she actually been packing, not unpacking?

Ilka wiped her mouth with her napkin. "Usually they telephone when they can," she added. "It is a fine system. I have much freedom for tryouts and classes."

"I forgot. How's Mr. Lugosi's sciatica? Did you cure it? How'd the blood drive go?"

Ilka's face went slack. "The remedy I tried, it did not ease the pain. Today I will brew something else." Her expression transmuted. She glowed. "The blood drive, though, it was monster success." She read my expectant look. She blushed. "Yes, Litvik was there."

"Hooray. You're going to get this part, I know." I swallowed the last bite of my bun. "Uh, something strange happened in my room last night." Ilka stared expectantly. "The lamp next to my bed switched on by itself. Around 0300. It woke me up."

"Yes?" Ilka prodded.

"No one was in the room with me, but there was a smell of perfume in the air. Joy perfume."

Ilka's cup paused mid-air. She lowered it to settle unsteadily into its saucer. "This house, it is full of antiques. The lamp it is old. The wiring it may be frayed. I must remove the lamp, have it checked."

"What about the Joy?"

Ilka shrugged. "A mystery. Perfume maybe was spilled into the socket long ago. Yes, then maybe heat from the light bulb or the wiring it stirred up the odor. The Mrs. buys things, expects them to work…"

"Uh-huh…" I checked my watch. "I gotta go—"

Ilka's expression relaxed. She smoothed her platinum wave. "This evening it is Lia's night off. I am fixing the dinner. Gunnar will be here. Will you?"

"Can't." I acted coy. "I have a date."

◇◇◇

I swung the general's Packard through the S-curves of Benedict Canyon, absorbing the serenity and beauty of the early morning hour and lush surroundings. My curiosity over the Dunns' hasty departure returned, but not for long. The loopy asphalt road cut a path through thick ferns and moist greenery. I took a long draw of earth-spiced air, smiling as a pleasant sensation spread through me.

I was looking forward to spending more time with Sam Lorenz in the evening ahead. He'd been going out of his way, trying to help me feel at home in the moviemaking world. He also seemed sincere about wanting my project—*me*—to succeed. And what about our lunch at MGM? I breathed deeply again, savoring my thoughts and the damp blend of soil and foliage. He seemed genuinely interested in me. But was his interest more than professional? Surprising myself, I hoped that it was.

At the mouth of the ravine, the terrain flattened out and I steered the Packard through a neighborhood of opulent Beverly Hills homes, their neat lawns bordered with colorful flowers. Shortly after, I was on a commercial strip, observing small businesses coming to life. I followed Wilshire, then LaCienega. On Washington Boulevard, I pulled over near Gus' newsstand.

This morning, Gus wore the same magenta pants and cerise sweater vest he'd had on yesterday, but instead of turquoise, today's shirt was chartreuse. He stood at one end of the kiosk, talking and smoking cigarettes with the brash MP I'd run up against at Fort Roach. Somehow, the sight of Gus with MP Winwar was a letdown. But at least Winwar was keeping his creeping peepers in check today. In fact, he was avoiding any eye contact whatsoever. What juicy news had the two so riveted, I couldn't help wondering.

Winwar flicked me a furtive glance. Gus waved and hollered he'd be right over. I checked my watch and when I looked up, Winwar was sauntering in the direction of Fort Roach. Gus, madly adjusting his tweed cap in a futile attempt at getting it to sit properly atop his disheveled white hair, hurried over.

Gus' expression, jubilant at seeing me, caved at my mention of Colonel Brody's untimely death. His brow furrowed and his eyebrows, fuzzy white caterpillars, met in an inverted V at the center. "You knew him well?"

"The colonel was going to fly with me to March Field this morning," I informed him, sadly.

Gus shook his head and we stood in awkward silence for a moment.

"There is small notice on page two of the *Times*," he said, gesturing to the newspaper display below the kiosk's counter. "Story broke late last night. Too late for much of a report. But I'll bet you the dirt it all will be splashed across the front pages tomorrow."

I agreed absently, momentarily distracted by the rapid movement of his brown eye and the vacant stare of the icy blue one.

"So, you talked with the secretary," Gus said, continuing. "What did she say?"

I shrugged. "Not much. She—Myra—was all torn up. Her voice broke several times while we talked."

Gus' good eye scrunched in a way that told me he had something to add, but wasn't certain whether he should.

"What? What is it?"

"Did Myra not say anything about her disagreement with the officials?"

"*Officials?*"

"The police. The coroner."

"Myra told me Colonel Brody died of natural causes. That was pretty much it."

Gus stared at me, both eyes completely still. "That is not what I hear is suspected by the coroner."

I recalled Myra's message: They're calling it death by natural causes. The choice of words, the tone of her voice. Yes. It was possible she'd been implying that there was uncertainty about the manner of his death; perhaps that it wasn't so natural.

"What are you saying?" My mind skipped forward. "He was *murdered*? Who says?"

Gus cleared his throat. "I have a source. But we will learn all there is to know about the circumstances of the colonel's death in a few days when the autopsy report it is finished."

Another customer arrived. Gus left to help him and I grabbed a *Hollywood Reporter*. My gaze drifted to the left-hand column. Today's article highlighted the Masquers Club where, on Saturday nights, top names in the picture business entertained, mingled with, waited on, and supplied autographs to servicemen. Meal costs and entertainer time were donated. I'd heard of the Hollywood Canteen, a similar charitable operation, but wasn't familiar with this night spot. A ping of excitement rattled my thoughts. Where would Sam take me on our date this evening?

I glanced quickly through the rest of the paper, thinking I might see something about the blood drive. But as was the case with Brody's demise, the news was too fresh to make the print.

The customer left and I paid for the *Reporter*, including tip. I glimpsed my watch. "0900," I sighed. "The time I was supposed to meet up with Colonel Brody."

Gus, wagging his head sadly, selected a creamy rosebud from the can of flowers on the stall's ledge. Offering the flower—a ravishing specimen, its petals just beginning to unfold—he spoke with surprising eloquence. "Whatsoe'er hath been, there still must be, room for another rose."

A beautiful sentiment. And a remarkable discovery: Gus recited poetry! I accepted the blossom with a smile.

"Florence Earl Coates," he added, bowing his head.

We spent a few moments discussing Frankie's static condition, but then I had to leave.

"Please let me know when you hear anything new." Gus watched me go.

◇◇◇

The clacking of typewriters came to a halt, all conversation ceased, and nine sets of eyes zeroed in on me as I wove through the typing pool, en route to my personal station.

I placed Gus' rose in a water glass on my desk. Before I could even get to my chair, the gals were gathered round me, clucking about the shock of Colonel Brody's death.

"The papers say he kicked from natural causes," spouted a gal with Betty Boop eyes and a voice breathy with excitement. "But we heard the police think otherwise."

"Oh?" Had they heard something Gus hadn't?

What they had were their fast and loose theories. The speculation volleyed.

"Investigators at the scene must have discovered a telltale mark of lethal mischief," lobbed one. "Gunshot wound," fired another. "Evidence of stabbing," thrust a third. *The killer? Motivation?* "A rejected actor—or actress—did it," spewed a fourth.

All eyes turned expectantly on me. "What have you heard? What do *you* think?"

"I'm clueless." Which was more or less true.

The ladies lingered, wanting more. I turned to some papers on my desk, leaving the crime-solving brigade to shuffle back to their typewriters, their parting glances reflecting disappointment as if I had somehow failed them.

After taking care of a few minor things, I placed a call to Miss C in Washington, who was not in. She and the general would be attending numerous meetings to lobby support for WASP militarization, and she'd warned me that it might be difficult for us to connect. So much so, that before leaving Long Beach, we'd scheduled a call for tomorrow. Still, I'd hoped to catch her. I wanted to share my concerns regarding the rushes, and I'd also hoped to enlist her help in securing a plane for the ferrying shoot Novara had suggested. Something told me that if I procured a plane that matched his pumped-up virility, he'd be more open-minded about the ideas I'd begun formulating for improving his—*our*—film.

Back at my desk, I located the WASP movie script, skimmed through it again, making notes, before heading out to Clover Field in Santa Monica.

◇◇◇

The road that led to Clover Field Airport, where Miss C had left her plane while she was away, appeared sooner along Washington Boulevard than I expected. I took a few turns, steering the Packard through a residential pocket.

Miss C had given me a contact at the field. Aware I'd be making the hop over to March Field in Riverside today, I'd called ahead to make the arrangements. A few blocks deeper into the neighborhood of modest homes, I spied the airport in the near distance.

My next turn took me past another landmark I'd been watching for, the AAF Technical Training Command's school for mechanics. I drove slowly, skirting past the unit's barracks and classroom buildings. Men in uniform and in coveralls strolled among the structures.

At last, a small sign indicated the lane to the hangar where I'd been told to park. I took the turn, nosing the Packard out onto a wide-open stretch of grass-patched dirt, coming to a halt in the shade of a small, corrugated-metal Quonset hut.

Prewar, Clover Field had been home to the small planes of commercial enterprise and private individuals. Once we were in the war, civilian pilots were grounded and private flying was all but eliminated. And Clover Field began anew. The mechanics' training school was established on the side of the airfield where I'd just pulled up; on the other side, a sprawling Douglas Aircraft manufacturing plant had been constructed.

Exiting the Packard, I glimpsed the east-to-west runway that divided the airfield. The airstrip had also been altered in recent years. Formerly alive with the comings and goings of small planes, once the factory was built it had been extended to accommodate the testing of the medium and heavy bombers being built or refurbished at the site.

I stood beside the Packard for a moment, awed by all that had been done to disguise the Douglas plant.

A canopy of netting, strung on cables and supported by hundreds of sky-high wooden telephone poles, covered the entire facility. The netting, I'd heard, was four and a half million square feet in its entirety, and made of fiberglass. It spanned the huge factory building as well as the massive hangar next door. Part of it also stretched across an extensive section of outdoor subassembly and storage areas. Beneath the netting, mechanics swarmed over a line of A-20 attack bombers on the tarmac. The A-20s were all painted olive drab, but some had been mounted with glass noses for bombardier visibility, while others were fitted with solid gun-bearing noses. Though not apparent from where I stood, fake housing and phony landscaping on top of the netting disguised the manufacturing site from enemy planes that might breach the air space above.

Other factories along the coast were using similar camouflage techniques as defense against enemy air attack, and I was familiar with the "passive defense" ploy. I'd just never viewed it from the ground. It was a remarkable sight and I couldn't wait to see it from above.

I left the Packard and walked across the grass and dirt to the hangar. A heavyset man in a khaki coverall and billed cap waited in the shade of the doorway. He tossed away the wrapper of his Hershey bar and welcomed me with a handshake. As I'd already guessed, he was the AAF mechanic-instructor "on loan" to Miss C. We'd spoken on the telephone.

His name was Ralph Balke. "But call me Bulk," he said.

I smiled. The nickname suited his full frame, so constrained by the grease-stained coveralls that it threatened to burst the snapped front at any moment. Another Hershey bar, distinguished by its dark brown and foil wrapping, protruded from his breast pocket alongside a wrench.

Bulk and I ducked into the dank darkness of the hangar's interior to go over the course I'd be taking to March Field. The air base, located near Riverside, was about seventy miles east. Using a wall map, we reviewed the route. Then we wandered back outdoors, Bulk briefing me on wind and weather, though the conditions were not expected to present any problems.

Miss C's canary-yellow Staggerwing perched near the end of the runway, ready for takeoff. The path to get to it took us past another hangar where, outside its open doors, models of sections of an airplane had been set up for training purposes. Cadets from the mechanics' school worked in small groups or in twos at the stations.

The Staggerwing looked like a mosquito, albeit a lively strain of the insect, compared to the giant bombers across the runway. The bright yellow biplane's highly polished spinner and prop glimmered in the sunlight as we approached, testament to detailed maintenance. The prop was also symbolic of Miss C's power and influence. Current war restrictions required removing the prop from any private plane not donated for military use.

Known for its clean lines and sporty appearance, the Staggerwing was coveted the world over by aircraft enthusiasts. Its innovative negative staggered wings—lower wing placed forward of the upper—improved performance by decreasing the biplane drag effect. The nose and cowling on Miss C's Staggerwing had been modified, giving it a racier look and suggesting it would show more powerful performance than others of its class. I'd never flown a Staggerwing before and I hadn't been in the air for two days, so I was itching to go up. Before I could, however, Bulk and I walked around the plane, checking out the landing gear, struts, slide tubes and other inspection points. Out of habit, I pulled the speed prop several times to clear it.

Bulk nodded at the numeral "13" painted on the side. "Don't worry none about that. Cochran claims it's her lucky number. It's her official racing number, too." He smiled and his full cheeks ballooned. "Yup. This little plane flew in the '37 Bendix race. Came in third. Not bad."

I smiled to myself. As if I didn't know! I was also aware that third hadn't been good enough for Miss C. The next year she'd entered the race again, the lone woman in a field of ten entrants. This time she flew the AP-7, a civilian prototype version of the P-35 long-range fighter designed by Republic Aircraft. Republic's owner, Sasha Seversky, a former Russian war ace, had personally extended the invitation. Seversky had been trying, without success, to secure a military contract for the P-35. He figured by winning the race—particularly with a woman in the cockpit—he'd gain the attention needed to convince the Army Air Corps of the P-35s superior capabilities. Miss C won the race, Seversky won the contract. They'd remained friends to this day.

"Cochran and Seversky have tinkered a bit with the plane," Bulk chortled, his eyes dancing. "They've installed a new Pratt & Whitney. Cochran says the increased horsepower makes it somewhat overpowered. I don't think she minds." He winked. "Actually, just about the entire plane's been rebuilt and recovered, section by section. Cochran's constantly testing new equipment: instruments, carburetors, spark plugs. You name it. Latest is a high performance fuel she got from a secret stash. Said she noticed an improvement in range and power on the way out here from her ranch." Bulk shrugged. "What's the hurry?"

"Hmm," was the only response I could manage. Resentment toward Miss C and the privilege she enjoyed was nibbling at my usual good will toward her. With severe rationing going on, WASP were having to fly on what was available. Usually the low-octane stuff, which meant that oftentimes engines wouldn't start. Worse yet, poor fuel could cause an engine to quit midair. I'd heard about several incidents where it had happened.

And why had she been so open with Bulk? It must feel good, I supposed, to wield the sort of power to get wherever you wanted, lickety-split. And nearly everyone knew she loved commanding a hot plane. Yet, when others were at the mercy of shortages, wouldn't it be smarter to be more reserved in talking about your privileges? Word got around.

Still, she was our leader. Bulk wouldn't get a negative reaction about her from me.

I led the way up the wing to the cockpit door. Climbing in, I stowed my gear, then settled into the cushiony leather seat. The interior was all black and there was the usual array of gauges on the panel.

Bulk, huddling in the doorway, nodded toward the back. "Rear bench has been removed to make room for two auxiliary tanks. They're on a separate system but share the same flow mechanism." He pointed to a pair of toggle switches on the panel. "Those are the controls. Main tank's in the fuselage, plus there's fuel in each wing. Reserve tank's under the seat." He grinned. "Not that you'll need it—she's full of the high octane still. Besides, you'll be at March almost before you leave the ground."

I'd already anticipated my flight time would be short even without the superior fuel. I smiled back.

We spent several more minutes going over buttons, levers, and switches before Bulk said, "So long," shoving the door shut with a solid thunk.

I waited until he was in sight on the tarmac. At his thumbs up signal, I opened the small side window, shouted, "Clear," and pushed it shut again.

The engine roared to life with the turn of the key. After running start-up procedures and radioing the tower for clearance, I taxied to the end of the strip and opened the throttle.

I slipped on my sunglasses to mute the glare, then vaulted down the runway, rapidly picking up speed to begin my climb. After months of flying the most advanced aircraft, I'd wondered whether I'd experience a letdown flying a small plane again. Not this craft. Miss C had been downplaying it when she'd remarked that with the installation of the new Pratt & Whitney, her Staggerwing had become *somewhat* overpowered. This ship, though small, was strong and fast.

After going full throttle to reach cruising altitude, I leveled off, listening as the fierce reverberation of the ascent settled into a soothing low drone. Scanning the instruments, I set my eastbound course, then looked out the side window.

The staggered lower wing permitted a clear view of the scene below. Just as I'd thought, covered over by the camouflage netting, the Douglas manufacturing site had completely disappeared. In its place, the false neighborhood was an awesome work of deception. Painted streets and sidewalks blended right into those that criss-crossed the surrounding neighborhood for real. Dummy houses built on top of the netting and supported by the roofs of the buildings over which the netting was hung looked completely authentic as well.

I dipped the wing to get a better look at the gently sloping hillside dotted with "war housing" units. Of course, what I was actually viewing was the curved top of the huge hangar covered over in camouflage netting. The "houses," Bulk had told me, were made of burlap specially treated to be weather- and fire-resistant. The painted burlap siding supported by chicken wire or lightweight wood panel frames and the fake roofs were painted red, white, or slate to follow the pattern of the bona fide neighboring homes. I shook my head, amazed. Fake trees, fake shrubs, fake gardens with red, blue and white flowers…What? Fresh "washing" had even been hung on backyard clotheslines!

The illusion was so good from on top, Bulk had cautioned, sometimes Douglas pilots had difficulty finding the runway. I looked for the white markers that had recently been painted on the hills as identifiers. Spotting them, I carefully noted their location for my return.

◇◇◇

Not long after passing over the Santa Monica residential area, I began viewing the concrete and stucco slabs that defined a more commercial area to the east. A few moments later, the terrain was less populated and more arid.

I sat back. The engine's even hum soothed me. It was always that way. A flight, short or long, always improved my outlook. Today, however, the transformation was slow in coming. Brody's death and Frankie's poor condition weighed heavy. Flying off to make arrangements for the production of a film on the WASP seemed trivial compared to the battle she was engaged in. I needed to find out who was responsible—they weren't going to get away with it.

I twisted my head from side to side to loosen the tightness in my neck. Miss C had referred me to the Operations Officer, Major Beacock, for help in orchestrating any filmmaking particulars with the base. We'd already done a good deal of the spade work on the telephone. And I'd reminded him that, in the small world department, we'd already met. Beacock had been part of the group in the small theater previewing the rushes of our WASP film yesterday.

March Field was in sight. The base was laid out in a triangular shape. Hangars, two runways and the tower formed one leg of the triangle; its other two sides were tree-lined. Housing and other standard base facilities packed the triangle's center.

Camp Hahn was just across the highway from March. It was the artillery encampment where antiaircraft training took place and where Frankie's target towing segment had been filmed. I swept the area, looking for the spot where I thought she'd gone down. The blackened patch. Evidence of the crash?

Witnessing the site, merely being in the vicinity of Frankie's crash, stirred my melancholy thoughts again and I felt more deeply connected to her than ever. I banked the Staggerwing and called the tower, eager to get on the ground and unravel the questions shrouding Frankie's incident.

Chapter Eight

I asked the ground crewman who'd guided me in for directions to the headquarters building where I was scheduled to meet with Major Beacock. It was just down the flight line, near the tower, within walking distance. Moving at a fast clip, I passed men in uniform and observed mechanics in coveralls tinkering with a trio of A-24s parked on the concrete apron outside a vast maintenance hangar.

I had the low-lying stucco headquarters building in sight when a throaty female voice behind me exclaimed, "Pucci Lewis!"

I wheeled around. "Mad Max!"

Max was a WAAC I'd gotten to know on my stopovers at Wright Field in Dayton, Ohio. Certified in airplane mechanics, she was a top specialist in engines.

I reached out and clasped the grease-smudged hand she offered. "Hey, Max."

Although Max's thick khaki coveralls were grease covered, she was blessed with the kind of figure that could make even the grimiest of coveralls look good. Somewhat snug in fit, they caused the neckline to gape. A dirty oil rag hung out of one pocket, while a wrench stuck out from another. A small tattoo of a spark plug was visible below the rolled up sleeve on the forearm of the right hand which I now released.

Max was a blend of the bizarre and beautiful. With delicate features, Titian hair, and pale complexion, she was often mistaken for Irish. But she was Polish through and through, hailing from Hamtramck, an east-side Detroit suburb. Her real name was Maxine Koslowski, but the fellas she worked with at Wright had started calling her Mad Max because of the growling sound she made when stumped by a tough mechanical problem. Today, as always, a billed cap topped her buzzed-off hair.

We compared our short hairdos then talked fast, exchanging stories of what we were doing at March. Max, it turned out, had been transferred in only recently.

"How are they treating you?"

"They're getting used to me." Her green eyes twinkled merrily. "There's a war going on. They have to."

Only twenty-one, Max had earned a reputation as one of the finest mechanics at Wright. Her extraordinary skill was due, in part, to coming from a long line of mechanics in her family. She'd also had formal training through one of the government programs in high school.

At Wright, the need for mechanics was desperate, and Max had been thrust into the thick of things. But because she had entered a male-dominated field, she faced plenty of resistance, and the men flat out assumed she'd quit. Months later, when she hadn't—and after they'd witnessed her talent—she'd gotten more and more assignments, and more and more respect. Including mine.

When I'd begun ferrying, the space limitations of fighter planes had presented a problem. Many night clubs and restaurants do not allow women in slacks, which meant trying to pack a dress or dancing shoes into a too-small flight bag already crammed with shirts, pants, and flight gear. On a stopover at Wright, I'd mentioned my dilemma to Max. Laughing, she'd grabbed a Phillips screwdriver and shown me how to access the ideal nooks and crannies for storing wardrobe "extras." Amazing what you can fit into the ammunition box or under an inspection plate on a P-38's wing.

Max was working on a new plane being tested at the base. My eyes lit up when I realized she was talking about a prototype long-range bomber escort fighter.

I quickly brought Max up to speed on my Hollywood assignment, briefing her on my involvement in the making of the WASP Victory Short and explaining that I was on my way to see Major Beacock to discuss the logistics for the film shoot of the ferrying segment.

"Max, I need a really hot plane for the shoot," I finished up.

She shoved the brim of her cap. "Hmm. Get your drift. You want folks sitting up in their seats thinking: Wow, a gal's flying *that?*"

"Precisely. It'd be the sort of coup that would distinguish the director—and his film—from the pack. Novara doesn't deserve the boost, but if I offer him this he'll more likely hear me out about the ideas I have for revamping his picture to meet Miss C's standards."

Max thought a moment. "Go ahead, run the idea by Beacock. But it's iffy the brass will approve it. The P-51 Mustang's their latest, greatest, and *most expensive* toy." A smile played on her lips. "No matter what, come by after your meeting. She's definitely worth a look-see."

Max asked about Frankie. Her fine features skewed into a worried expression as I described my hospital visit. Max hardly knew Frankie, but as a mechanic assigned to the crash investigation team, she'd inspected the wreckage.

"Pucci, when you see tangled metal close-up like that…never fails, it always hits hard. Like a blow to the gut. I can feel the pilot's terror trapped in a powerless free fall. Sometimes when I crawl inside, I can even hear the sounds of the metal grinding, ripping, twisting—like it was nothing more than pretzel dough." Max shook her head to erase the awful thought.

"When I first saw that A-24, I couldn't believe Frankie survived. Thought about her a lot while I combed the mess. Wondered about her mental state…what she'd be like when— *if*—she recovers physically…"

Neither of us spoke for a moment. Then I said, "Novara plans on including a clip of the crash in our film. For 'dramatic impact.' Can you imagine?" My voice reflected my disdain.

Max sneered with disgust.

"It's another reason I'm seeing Beacock. I want to reshoot the target towing scene. He didn't get any actual footage after all, and it's the kind of *va-voom* we want in the picture. Most of all, I'm hoping that if I serve it up to Novara done right, he'll agree to forego including the accident."

Max had been biting her lip. "Don't do it."

"What?"

She lowered her voice. "Don't tow target for the camera." She read my puzzled expression. "Come see me after your meeting with Beacock."

◇◇◇

Before arriving at Beacock's office, I'd mulled over what it would take to win approval to fly the P-51 for the shoot. The biggest objection, I'd concluded, would be giving our enemies a free look at our newest fighter. To better argue my case, I forced myself to consider the opposite view: why might it be *beneficial* for the enemy to get a peek. At last, sitting across the desk from the skeptical Beacock, his bald head shining as if it were spit-polished, it hit me. Now that we, as a country, had at last reached our goal of "overwhelming air superiority," why not flaunt it?

After lagging behind in aircraft design and production, we'd caught up by retooling our automobile factories and transferring assembly line know-how from making cars to churning out aircraft and aircraft parts. Thanks to our ingenuity and sacrifice, our current inventory was superior to that of our enemies.

"Sure it'll take *chutzpah* to put our most advanced fighter on celluloid for everyone to see, but we're giving a message of our confidence to the enemy. Telling them, we don't care if you see what we have. In fact, we want you to know what you're up against. We have the capacity to keep churning out new and better planes engineered to outfly and outfight the best you have. You don't stand a chance of winning the war."

Talk about *chutzpah*! The rush of words that was my logic for flying the P-51 burst from my lips like hot lava spewing from a volcano. It wasn't until I'd finished that I began worrying whether I'd been too assertive.

Beacock, to my relief, listened with his bald head nodding and didn't seem offended by my style or the bold proposal. He brought up the *Flight Characteristics of the P-51* film that had recently been completed. Sam had mentioned it yesterday. Brody had directed, Sam had been the writer, Arthur Kennedy had a role in it. In a film like this, a camera plane stays with the image as it climbs, the narrator giving the speed, rate of climb and so on. In the air, with the plane going through a stringent set of maneuvers that duplicate air combat tactics, the narrator defines and analyzes every action, emphasizing the plane's capabilities.

Such training films are for training, not for public consumption, but what I proposed to Beacock involved only a fly by—a look see—without the particulars. Beacock gave a final nod. "I'll run it past the brass," he promised.

I left the headquarters building feeling satisfied with what I'd accomplished.

◇◇◇

The cool of Hangar Three's interior felt refreshing until a spark fired in me upon seeing the three fighter planes in for repairs and parked in a scattered row along the hangar's center.

Two of the models were familiar. The twin-engine, twin-boomed plane with a 20-mm cannon and four machine guns on its nose was the plane I regularly flew, a P-38 Lightning. This fighter, though, had a larger-than-life tinted headshot of a woman stenciled on its nose. The photo, about two feet by two feet, was likely the wife or girlfriend of the plane's pilot. It was in good taste; a lot better than the naked women some planes boasted.

The snub-nosed fighter next to the P-38 was a single engine P-47 Thunderbolt like the one I'd ferried into Long Beach two days ago. Difference was that this P-47, like its P-38 neighbor, had been personalized to suit its pilot. Fighter pilots were notorious for their cocky aggressiveness, and this plane's pilot had much to boast about. He'd taken out twenty-eight of the Luftwaffe's fighter plane inventory, memorialized by the four rows, seven across, of red, black and white swastika decals on his plane's fuselage. Each decal included markings of either ME 109, ME 110, or F.W. 190—model numbers for Messerschmitts and the Focke-Wulf.

The third plane was a lean, low-wing monoplane with six wing-mounted machine guns. There was no nose art on this fighter, no marks whatsoever, in fact. Brand spanking new, it was the finest-looking fighter I'd ever seen. The P-51 Mustang.

I stood spellbound until a waving motion from inside the plane's closed bubble top canopy drew my attention. It was Max.

She opened the hatch and climbed down. "Some piece of machinery, huh?"

At my emphatic nod, Max grinned. "Its range is phenomenal. Our first fighter/bomber that'll fly all the way from England to Berlin and back. Best part is, even with all the weight, she can do better than 425 miles per hour, easy. And she's responsive. Still a few bugs to work out; but, no doubt, this is one hell of a plane." She beamed. "It's that high-altitude long-distance fighter we've been waiting for."

"Be great to take her up."

Max's eyebrows shot up. "Beacock's gonna stick his neck out for you, then?"

"We'll see," I shrugged. "He's put my request in the hopper."

Max threw a light punch to my upper arm. "Attagirl! But not all that surprising. He's seen your record. Knows you're an H.P."

I couldn't help smiling at the "hot pilot" allusion. "He also brought up the flight characteristics picture that was filmed here. Did you meet Brody, the director?"

"Yeah. Film crew spent a lot of time with this baby." She smiled affectionately at the P-51. "*I* spent a lot of time with the crew. And Arthur Kennedy, Lee J. Cobb, too. Technical advisor." Max sighed. "Too bad about Brody. Didn't know him, but more grim news."

I nodded.

Sam had dropped Arthur Kennedy's name in connection with the hush-hush training film he'd been working on. He hadn't identified it to be the P-51 film, though. "Do you know Sam Lorenz, then?"

"Sure I've met Sam. Kind of an odd fish…" Max chuckled. "I'm an odd fish myself then. Yeah, he's all right. And Frankie seemed friendly with him."

"They're pals. He said he was out here, spoke with her just before she went up…" I paused. "You said I shouldn't tow target for the camera. What did you mean?"

Max glanced around, then steered me to a tool station on the perimeter of the hangar's interior. There were other mechanics at work nearby, but out of earshot.

Max, a grave expression on her face, slipped her hands deep into the side pockets of her coverall. She looked me in the eye. "Give me your word you'll never reveal where you heard what I'm about to tell you."

My heartbeat picked up its pace. I made the sign of the cross over it.

Max lifted her cap off to rub the coppery bristles. "There was sugar in the gas tank of Frankie's A-24."

"What?"

"There was sugar in her fuel," Max repeated softly.

I blinked. The sabotage Miss C had hinted at. Was Frankie, then, Miss C's source? "How do you know?" I asked, my voice now a whisper.

"I made the discovery."

I was in an awkward spot. Had Miss C also promised never to divulge the information and her source? Had she told Max about her sub rosa plan for sending me to Hollywood? I felt certain she hadn't.

Miss C and I had not covered this scenario. Well, Max had had enough confidence in me to confide the truth about what was going on so I made a snap decision and confessed my behind-the-scenes mission. Luckily, Max seemed relieved at having a coconspirator.

"But how could anyone deliberately do such a thing?" A new sense of rage coursed through me as the monstrous nature of the deed set in. "Who would do it? Why?" My voice rose in pitch and volume with each question.

Max twisted the cap in her hands. "Shhh," she whispered. "I don't know. All I know is that the A-24 was serviced Friday, the day before Frankie's accident. The plane was beat-up physically, but it checked out okay. I saw the paperwork. I know the mechanic who signed off on it."

Her voice dropped another notch. "My guess is someone got to the A-24 after the servicing, but before Frankie took it up. Someone who wanted to teach her a lesson. A fatal lesson."

"Lesson? You mean that women shouldn't be flying *military* planes?"

Max nodded ever so slightly.

I fought for rational thinking. "But what makes you so certain Frankie was the target?"

"Not Frankie, necessarily. But a WASP. What's behind the theory?" Max placed her cap back over her stubbly hair, jiggling the bill until it was comfortably in place again. "For one, that plane was earmarked for training exercises; the saboteur knew a WASP was likely to take it up. For another, the A-24 was low on fuel the day it was serviced. The log shows the fuel was added from the same holding tank that fueled two other planes that day. Those planes had no problems."

"But the saboteur...True, he might be an airman taking crazy revenge because a WASP took his plum stateside job. Or he might be someone out to show that women pilots aren't as capable. But he might also be an enemy agent, right? Some fifth columnist out to put the fear of the *Führer* in us?"

Max's half-hearted shrug suggested she favored the crazed airman theory.

I released a long breath. "Whatever the motive, somebody's got to be investigating this. So why keep a lid on the crash results? Any scuttlebutt?"

Max shook her head. "I'm not even sure what the other guys on the investigating team found. We weren't supposed to confer with one another, only with the officer in charge. When I reported my findings, I got orders not to disclose the information to anyone else." She added, "All good reasons why you can't tow target for those film people."

Max pulled a wrench off the peg board where an assortment of tools had been hung. "There's one thing that might play against Frankie if the investigation widens." She tapped the wrench against the palm of her hand. "Frankie took an A-24 up late on Friday for a practice run. Had a passenger along."

"Really? Who?"

Max shrugged and tapped the wrench again. "Don't know. She didn't log in a name."

"But that's against…"

Max had been watching me. Her attention shifted as she caught sight of a colleague approaching, airplane part in hand. "Let it be for now. You'll only raise a flag you might not want to raise, talking about it. It's likely the passenger was legit, part of the film crew. Frankie simply got distracted, forgot to sign him in. Whatever the case, so far no one's brought it up." She turned away. "Pucci, I gotta get back to work, you need to get back to Hollywood. Remember what I said, will ya? No target towing. Stay on the ground."

◇◇◇

Leaving Clover Field, I'd decided to stop at the Hollywood Hospital.

"How is she doing?" I whispered to the nurse bent over Frankie. She was applying Vaseline to Frankie's lips.

"That's better." She pulled her fingers away and straightened up. "No change, I'm afraid." Her voice sounded sad. She snapped the lid back on the Vaseline jar and wiped her fingers. Then with a practiced skill that made it look effortless, she straightened the bed covers around Frankie's inert form, even managing to fluff the pillow which propped Frankie's left arm without disturbing the angle of the cast.

When the bedding was pulled so tight you could bounce a dime on it, she stood with me near the end of the bed. We discussed the efforts to reach Frankie's uncle, which had not yet panned out.

The nurse checked the needle in Frankie's arm, adjusted the inverted intravenous bottle, then picked up her tray. "I'll leave you two alone." Her thick-soled shoes made a soft padding noise as she left.

I went to Frankie's side. Smoothing the dark matted hair around her hairline, I prayed the swollen eyelids would flutter open or that the freshly lubricated cracked lips would move. It wasn't long before the stony silence got to me. I began rubbing her arm lightly. "Frankie, I just came from March Field. Mad Max…you remember mad Max, don't you? She doesn't want me to do the towing sequence. Remember I told you about a cover up? Max found sugar in the fuel of the A-24 you were flying. She's been ordered to keep quiet…"

I paused, conscious of the stillness of the room.

"Frankie, I saw the P-51. You must have seen it. Some piece of machinery, huh? Remember how sleek it looked?" I waited. The reaction I hoped for, a sign of awareness like I'd witnessed yesterday, did not come. I leaned over and whispered in her ear. "C'mon Frankie. You gotta get out of here. That P-51 would be keen to fly, don't you think? They'll let you have a go at it. Miss Cochran will fix it…"

With my mouth bent to her ear, my face toward the wall, my back to the door, it was impossible for me to hear anyone entering the room.

Suddenly, I sensed a presence behind me. I spun around, counting on seeing Dr. Farr, perhaps a nurse. Not Sam Lorenz, the screenwriter.

My hand flew to my chest. "Sam, my goodness. How long have you been here?"

"Just walked in," Sam said in an undertone. With a nod to Frankie, he asked, "How is she?"

"She talked yesterday. Well, she tried anyway. I was just trying to get her to do it again."

Sam smiled. No, it was more of a grimace. He did not look well. His normally golden skin looked pale, an odd shade of yellow; his eyes seemed glazed, his hair was completely disheveled. A few patches of whiskers—and even a few beads of sweat—were present here and there on his otherwise baby-smooth face.

My heart did a leap. Was he here to check into the hospital?

"Sam, what's wrong? Why are you here?"

"Wha…Oh, sorry for my appearance." He smoothed his hair, straightened slightly askew glasses. "I tried to track you down…" Sam glanced nervously at Frankie. "Should we be talking in here?"

I hated to leave Frankie's side. "It's okay. The nurse says she needs to hear voices."

Sam's eyes hardened. "But I'm not well. Let's go in the hallway."

I glanced at him sideways as we left Frankie's room. What was wrong?

There was little traffic in the corridor. We leaned against the wall outside the doorway, facing one another.

"What happened?"

"I've got some kind of bug. Or, could just be exhaustion, not sure. I was working late last night…doing that rewrite for Brody. It came on suddenly. Wiped me out."

Leery of catching what he had, I inched back a little and gave him a sympathetic look. "You heard about Brody?"

Sam nodded. "Didn't help my punk feeling."

Moved by his downcast expression, I reached out to squeeze his arm and was instantly infused with a current of warmth. At first I thought he might be so sick that his fever was radiating through his clothing. Then I realized, with a shock, that I was genuinely worried about him.

"What brought you here?" I asked.

The muscle under my hand flexed as Sam pulled loose from my hold. "I wanted to let you know that, being sick and all, I need to cancel our dinner plans for tonight."

The round trip to March and all that had gone on during the day had been so consuming, I'd all but forgotten about the date. Still, I was let down. I'd built up a candlelight scenario where we would sip wine, talk, gaze across the table at one another. Romance aside, I'd been looking forward to discussing my new ideas for the WASP film, too. I wanted to get a sense of how a screenwriter would shape them into concepts Novara might go for. I also longed for the easy company of a friend I could trust.

"I understand," I said, trying to keep the disappointment out of my voice.

I started to inquire why he had come all the way to the hospital to tell me—how he even knew I was here—but Frankie's nurse approached us. She eyeballed Sam, perhaps wondering whether she should go for a gurney.

"I'm leaving," Sam said for the nurse's benefit. Then he spoke to me. "I'll see you tomorrow morning, then." He read the surprise on my face. "You don't know about the meeting?" I shook my head. "Novara's scheduled one for 10:00 a.m. Wants to hear what you've come up with. He probably left word at your office. The Clark Gable project's heating up, but he's being pressured to get the WASP piece in the can first." Sam rolled his eyes. "Should be an action-packed session."

"You'll be there won't you?"

"You bet. Even if they have to wheel me in."

Chapter Nine

I returned to Fort Roach shortly after five o'clock to find the lot pretty much deserted.

I had in mind putting in another hour of tinkering with the script, seeing where I might insert a scene with the P-51. In the typing pool area, all typewriters had been put to bed, dust covers in place. At my desk, I spied the mug I'd abandoned this morning. A cup of tea, with several spoons of sugar, would be just the sort of boost to get my gears cranking again.

Cup in hand, I headed for the lunch room. At the sink, I dumped out the mug's contents.

Clink. Something hard had been inside my mug. I stared into the flat-bottomed porcelain sink, watching brown dregs drain away from a small metal object. I picked it up. An earring. *A swastika earring!*

It must have been put there by one of the typists. A joke? Comeuppance because I hadn't joined in their loose speculation this morning about Brody's death? Surely they hadn't expected me to take their amateur crime-solving theories seriously. There hadn't even been an official ruling yet that he'd been murdered. And unlike Gus they had no secret source.

But the earring. In not playing along had I hurt someone's feelings? Was that it? They wanted me to know that I was now the enemy? The kettle whistled at the same moment I decided I needed some exercise to blow off the steam fast-building inside of me. I stuffed the disgusting thing in my pocket and left without my tea.

Outdoors, I took a deep breath and let the mild air soothe me. A slight breeze had kicked up and I lifted my face to greet it. In the west, the sky was deepening to slate-blue, the color reminiscent of Gunnar Rask's eyes. Maybe a stroll to the editing building to see if he was in was the ticket. Maybe he knew the story behind his sister's sudden departure this morning. At least one curiosity consuming my overloaded brain would be put to rest.

A short walk later, I was in front of one of the clapboard buildings Sam had pointed out on our walk through the lot the other day. I paused, trying to remember what he'd said the building was used for. A slightly ajar wooden screen door, caught in a gentle gust, flapped softly. Behind the screen, the solid closure had been left open—my invitation to go inside. Looking around, I saw no one to object.

Sam had said some of the old studio structures now served as barracks, but peering into a few of the rooms near the entry it appeared this building was full of unoccupied dressing rooms. I proceeded along a hall and came to a door with the sign CAROLE LANDIS on it. I knocked. No response. I gingerly cracked the door. A couch with a blue satin covering and pillows was positioned along the wall directly across from me. Beside it, a matching blue satin easy chair.

I ventured inside. Blue-flocked wallpaper lent a pleasant homey feel to the space. I sniffed the air. A trace of perfume. Fresh? The studio had not produced a commercial film in over two years. I took another whiff. The scent was musky, heavier than what a woman would wear. Men's cologne, more likely.

I sat on the bench at the vanity table. As I stared in the makeup mirror, my mind conjured up the image of Miss Landis staring in *Topper Returns*, the Roach comedy-mystery picture I'd seen not long ago. In the movie, the beautiful blonde star played the best friend of a gal who got murdered while the two were staying in a creepy mansion. I shivered thinking of the mysterious hooded assailant intending to murder Miss Landis' character but mistakenly killing her friend. Morbid was not the point of this sort of picture, and seconds later, the girl's ghost arose from her body and from there on it was nonstop slapstick as Mr. and Mrs. Topper tried to rescue Landis' character from a similar fate. Just the sort of frothy entertainment I liked for escape.

And escapism was what I needed. I ruffled my short locks and headed back outdoors, on a beeline for the Packard. Time to go home.

◇◇◇

I rolled the general's automobile into my usual spot in the courtyard in front of the Dunns' mansion. I heard the fountain's delicate trickle echoing softly through the quiet of the night, peaceful accompaniment for my stroll to the back entrance. Along the portico, I paused beside the climbing jasmine vines, drawing in deep whiffs of the heavenly scent. Before long, a wistful yearning for my lost date with Sam returned.

All at once, my insecurities skyrocketed like a widget walloped up a Strength-O-Meter scale by Paul Bunyan. I was taken with Sam, but how did he feel about me? He'd come to the hospital to break our date, but he hadn't asked for a rain check.

I shook my head. What selfish, off-the-wall thoughts. *He didn't feel good.* He wanted to go home, be alone. Be glad he cared enough to tell you in person.

As I reached the side door, my outlook brightened. Maybe it wasn't too late to have supper with Ilka. I'd nixed my intended visit to Gunnar's editing studio, but hadn't she said this morning that he was joining her for dinner?

"Anyone home?" I called, passing through the brightly lit empty kitchen.

I stepped into the corridor of the main part of the house. Lights had been left on everywhere, and the house was so still that, in the distance, I heard the cawing of D.B.'s cockatoo in the atrium.

I returned to the kitchen. A piece of paper was propped against a bowl on the work table in the middle of the room. It had slipped to one side and I'd missed seeing it when I arrived.

Dear Pucci,

Hope your date it was good, though if you are reading this, you are home before me.

Gunnar he could not be here for dinner. I called Bela and he invited me. Some Hungarian friends are gathering at his home. See you in the morning.

Ilka

P.S. Édesem, maybe your date it made you too excited to eat much. Food is in the icebox, in case.

Well, that explained the empty house. But not the lights.

I went in search of the promised food. From a tray of pre-made sandwiches, I selected a cheese and lettuce on white bread, and poured a glass of milk. Plate in one hand, glass in the other, I started down the corridor toward the living room, my heels clicking briskly on the tile floor.

Suddenly the house was plunged into darkness. I froze. Stopped breathing, listening for any telltale noise. Hearing only my pulse beating loudly in my ears, I edged slowly in the direction of the nearest wall. *Get a grip, Pucci,* I whispered into the black void. *You're a pilot, trained to react calmly in a flying emergency. Think. Stay cool.*

My shoulder, at last, met with smooth plaster. Pressed flush to the wall, I slid to the floor, anxious to rid myself of the glass and plate before I dropped them. The dishes rattled loudly as they slipped from my grasp to the tile.

Flashing into mind came Carole Landis, her friend, and the hooded assailant in the creepy mansion, the images setting me further on edge. Every muscle rigid, I waited in the dark silent void, anticipating the worst: the sound of heavy footsteps; the sudden grip of a hand on my arm.

I took a few deep breaths, forcing my muscles to relax.

Was that a shuffling noise on the other side the wall? I put my ear to cool plaster. Then I pulled away, listening in the direction of the darkened corridor instead. The house was completely still, not even a peep from the parrot down the hall.

As quickly as the lights had gone out, they came back on. I blinked, then got up, willing my vision to adjust, uncertain whether the movement I detected near the far end of the hall was real. The flap of a cape? An apparition?

I turned and started back toward the living room.

"Pucci! Wait!" a voice behind me shouted.

It was Gunnar. Where had he come from? I noticed he was carrying a flashlight.

Gunnar guided me into the living room, explaining he'd been pulling up when the lights went out. He kept a flashlight in his automobile. He'd taken it with him to check the fuse box. "A few fuses were loose. I tightened them."

By the time we reached the sofa my shock had turned to embarrassment.

"Mother always said I'd regret my addiction to horror movies," I said, breezily. Regrettably, the laugh I tagged on had an unnatural ring.

Seated next to me on the sofa, Gunnar smiled. "Well, you're no lily-livered lightweight, I know that. Not with what it takes to make the grade as ferry pilot."

The compliment was genuine, yet it made me feel uneasy. Praise generally did. I started to look away.

"You were singled out from a thousand-plus women for special assignment in Hollywood. That says a lot, too," he added. "Besides, I'm the one who should be apologizing. Our first meeting at the rush theater…All that hooey about comparing myself to a Stuka pilot." He smoothed his thick sandy hair and chuckled. "I was trying to make light of my hearing problem, but well…" Gunnar pulled his face into an exaggerated grimace. "You must have pegged me as a real palooka."

He'd gotten that right. I started to make a flip retort, but caught myself. I worked at a job where the accolades were few and far between, and I tended to be hard on myself besides. The pat on the back was a nice treat. And I suspected that in calling attention to his foible he'd wanted to make me feel better about mine. That was special, wasn't it?

Bit by bit, because of Gunnar, my built-in bias against hand-some men was faltering.

"You're no palooka," I said. Our eyes met and I felt momentarily hypnotized by his gaze. I cleared my throat. "And thanks for coming to the rescue. So you didn't see anything—*anyone*—when you entered the house? Hear anything?" Blood rushed to my cheeks. Gunnar had a hearing problem.

He shook his head and I rushed to another topic on my mind. "Where did D.B. and Della go?"

Gunnar cocked his eyebrow. "Didn't they leave a note? I thought Ilka said they had."

I nodded. "But it doesn't explain anything."

"They never leave a detailed explanation. They're used to coming and going as they please."

All at once a sensation came upon me that I was on to something. "But what kind of fundraising work would require them to leave in such a rush?"

He shrugged. "They don't fill me in on everything they're asked to do."

"You seemed part of their scheming last night."

Gunnar lifted an eyebrow. "Scheming?" Then he smiled. "What kind of mysterious work do you think a philanthropic couple and a war-injured film editor could be up to?"

"Intelligence," I replied without missing a beat.

Gunnar stared at me, stone-faced. The telephone rang in the hallway just outside the living room. His gaze remained locked on mine. His eyes began twinkling, but he didn't bother explaining what was so amusing. The phone continued its incessant ringing. He got up to answer it, returning almost instantly.

"I have to go," he said, his voice urgent, "but before I do, I need to fill you in on a few things."

I sat up straight. "Yes? What?"

"We know about your special training, about your work for the FBI on the Detroit case."

The tiny hairs at the back of my neck prickled. There could be only one reason for Rask to have that sort of information. "I'm right then. G-2?" G-2 was military intelligence.

His nod was barely perceptible. "And what I'm about to tell you goes no further than these walls."

"I promise."

He continued. "No doubt you've heard the talk going around about Brody's death."

"That he was murdered?"

The flashlight thwacked softly as he bounced it against the palm of his hand. "It's being treated as a suspicious death. We won't know for sure until we have the autopsy and toxicology report, but yes, murder is a near certainty. He was being blackmailed and I'm willing to bet the blackmailer is also our killer."

"Blackmail. Really? Why? Over what? How do you know?"

"Whoa. It's all I can tell you for now. We're on the case and have already set a trap."

"And you need my help? What's my role?"

Merriment flickered in his blue-gray eyes, then he became serious again. "I've put in a request. I'll brief you further once you're approved. Meanwhile, keep your eyes and ears open. Let me know about anything suspicious."

A tall order given I didn't know what I should be looking out for. But I agreed.

"You said *we* know about your training. Are Della and D.B. in on the investigation?"

Smiling, Gunnar leaned to whisper in my ear, "That's it for now."

I snapped away and stared.

He was still smiling. "I'll let myself in later. Meantime, take care of yourself, okay?" He handed me the flashlight. "And keep this close."

◇◇◇

I went to my room and locked the door. My satin pajamas were missing. I retrieved my B-4 bag from under the bed. No p.j.s, but there was Gran Skjold's .38. I loaded it, placed it under my pillow, and crawled into bed. In the buff.

◇◇◇

Early the next morning, Ilka stood beneath an overhead lamp in the center of the kitchen, twirling a rolling pin back and forth over a flattened piece of dough that was getting wider and rounder and thinner. The work table's surface was coated with flour and there were dollops of white on the counter spaces surrounding her. Her long platinum hair was pulled into an upsweep, exposing her forehead and a powdery blotch marring it. The apron covering the front of her peasant blouse and dark skirt appeared to have suffered the least damage. But then it was white.

Ilka's head swayed from side to side and her arms kept rhythm as she cheerily hummed…*drifting along with the tumbling tumbleweeds*…accompanying the radio on the counter behind her. Beside the radio, the lamp's yellow glow was reflected in the large window above the sink. Outdoors, the sun was not yet up.

The music ended abruptly. A moment of silence preceded the announcements that we'd been listening to the *Sons of the Pioneers* and that we should stay tuned for *Don McNeill's Breakfast Club.* As she sensed my presence Ilka's mouth stretched into a broad dazzling smile.

"Pucci, *édesem*," she said, putting down the rolling pin and brushing herself off. "You are up early." She wiped her forehead with the sleeve of her blouse. "Anything the matter?"

"Couldn't sleep."

"Something to do with the date?"

"Canceled."

Ilka shot me a sympathetic look. "Is too bad." She walked over to turn off the radio. "We will have some breakfast. It will help to make you feel better."

I smiled. "Sure, why not. What are you making?" I inhaled yeasty air.

"Biscuits. Lia, she is off today and I decide, why not try the breakfast selection from the War Time Menu?" Ilka nodded in the direction of the icebox where a newspaper clipping was prominently posted on the door. "The ideas often are good, and it is always a help in how to use the ration stamps."

I ambled over. The clipping contained recipes for each meal of the day plus ideas for stretching some items into the next day's fare. The final paragraph tallied up the ration points used if all suggestions were implemented.

Then I caught sight of a menu of a different sort on the counter.

Actually, only the left half of a typed listing protruding from beneath a tin bread box. I had been trained to covertly speed-read during my OSS stint, but spilt flour obliterated most of the text and all I could make out was:

DATE:
FROM: CAI—
TO: I—
ACTION: MO—

The heavy flour shower did not extend to the remainder of the page. The impulses in my brain fired, capturing the visible portion of text:

#29174 REFERENCE MY LETTER OF—
1. KINDLY PLACE ADVERTISEMENTS IN H—
2. START TO OBTAIN MESSAGES RECORD—
   33, 1/3 REVOLUTIONS PER MINUTE.
3. ASSEMBLE A COLLECTION OF MUSIC D—
SEND THE ABOVE MATERIAL BY AIRP—

Not much to go on. But I knew what MO stood for—Morale Operations, the intelligence unit I'd been assigned to at OSS school. Black psychological warfare. The art of influencing enemy thinking by means of subtle propaganda. Rumor, lies, deception. It was all part of the game. The objective: generate confusion and defeatism among the enemy.

What in the world was an MO document doing in the Dunn's kitchen? Had someone carelessly left it there? *Gunnar?* Did the memo have to do with his case?

Ilka had come up behind me. "The table it is set, *édesem*," she said. "If you will scoop the porridge into these—" She handed me two bowls. "I will bring over the coffee. *Ooopla*, I have forgotten. I must first remove the biscuits."

She reached for a hot pad next to the bread box. I watched, wondering if she would shove the memo deeper under the tin. But she was oblivious. She picked up the hot pad, actually exposing more of the page—blank unfortunately—and headed for the stove, leaving me free to ogle all I wanted.

It was a delicate dance. I didn't want to risk exposing Gunnar's true identity—or the memo, if he was the person who'd left it there—but I wanted to learn what Ilka knew about it. She had to have seen it at some point.

Ilka was opening the oven door. "Did you notice anything strange when you returned home last night?" I asked, wandering to the stove, beginning the dance.

"No, why?"

Ilka put biscuits in a cloth-lined basket while I ladled oatmeal into the bowls and explained about the lights going out and Gunnar's arrival.

Her hand, whisking a biscuit from a cookie sheet to the basket, paused mid-chore. "Hmm. There was a problem much the same with the lights not so long ago. The Mr., he had to fuss with the fuses, too. That antique in your room it too was acting up…"

Ilka passed beneath the ceiling lamp. The beam shone on her silvery blonde hair, like a klieg light, creating a luminous halo effect and sparking my memory.

"Your audition is today. What are you doing cooking? Aren't you nervous? Shouldn't you be rehearsing your lines?" I wanted to bite back the words. It was a nonspeaking role.

Ignoring the blunder, Ilka sat across from me at the table. "Yes, today is big day. I cook, it helps me to relax. Uncle Bela, he is picking me up and will drive me to MGM."

"How was the gathering at his place last night? Any stars?"

"Uncle Bela, he does not entertain the movie crowd at home," she said, pouring coffee for me. "Mainly they are artists, writers, musicians and dancers who come." She seemed unable to resist a modest smile. "Well...I have met there the directors Charles Vidor and Zoltan Korda. Last night Ervin Nyiregyhazi, the concert pianist. Bela loves a happy party and often there is Gypsy music...Hungarian friends. Transplants from the old country..." Ilka frowned. "It is expensive to entertain and Uncle Bela, sometimes he is too easy maybe, in handing money to those friends."

I'd taken a few spoonfuls of porridge while Ilka talked. I reached for my coffee. "What do you mean?"

"Nothing," she said, but then quickly added, "Uncle Bela he has always been generous, even when times are bad. Two years ago, when I arrive, the horror industry it had dried up. He lost his home, his cars, he went on relief. Borrow from the Actor's Fund to pay bills. Imagine." She shook her head. A silvery strand pulled free. "He take me in anyway. 'Tomorrow will take care of itself,' he like to say." She twisted the loose lock with her finger. "Think this, it may one day haunt him..."

"What do you mean?"

"Nothing," she said, this time with finality. "He is doing B pictures now. Anyone they can tell you, there is not much money in this."

I sipped coffee and watched her twirl her hair. "You put your hair up. For the audition?"

Ilka picked up the basket, offering it to me. I took one of the light fluffy biscuits, loading on thick apple butter as she continued.

"The War Womanpower Commission has requested that working women wear off-the-face hairdos." Ilka grinned at the incredulous look I gave her. "It is not so strange as it sounds.

Women have taken over much of the assembly line work in the war plants. Long hair hanging loose around machinery is dangerous. It can get caught."

I had just taken a bite of biscuit. I shuddered at my mental image and forced a swallow.

"So the Commission wants women, especially those of us in the public arena"—she wagged her eyebrows—"this will be me, when I get the part—to wear our hair up for the duration."

"But, with your hair down, the long peek-a-boo bang, you're a ringer for Veronica Lake. That would be a selling point for the director I would think…"

Ilka jutted her chin out. "Wearing my hair up it is required. When the call come to audition, this was the instruction."

"Sounds dictatorial. Good thing I don't have to decide whether or not to comply." I smoothed my marmalade locks. Ilka's eyes were hard above the coffee cup. "Hair style is small thing to sacrifice. In the old country, my Gypsy family have no rights. Hitler has declared them enemies of the Reich. Last night there was talk. Gypsies are being rounded up, forced to work on railroads, in factories, clear minefields—whatever is necessary to fuel Hitler's war machine." She stared at the cup shaking in her hands. "There are reports of death camps…massacres."

I had heard rumors that the Jewish people in Europe were suffering under ruthless persecution. I hadn't known of the Gypsies' nightmares.

A kind of numbness settled over us. My cup was empty. I rocked it back and forth on the table. "I hope I'm not being out of line," I began hesitantly, "but you said the other night that Gypsies are travelers by nature. Aren't there remote places where your friends could hide…cross borders into safe countries?"

"What safe countries?" Ilka snapped. Her gaze flicked to the window over the sink. Dawn was breaking and the sky had lightened. Her tone softened. "It was possible once. Even in 1940, before I leave, Grandmama and our tribe, we move our other supplies and…" Her eyes shifted again, this time focusing on the untouched biscuit before her. "…Things."

My synapses unsnarled. Ilka had not left Hungary willingly, but because *things had become too dangerous.* "It's okay," I said. "I know there's an underground movement in Hungary. Were you and your grandmother involved?"

"When my grandfather died, Grandmamma Roza took over the tribe. It was her idea we take on secret transport of fugitives. No one argue. We are all of one mind, wanting to slow the death machine. And we succeed, help many. Escaped prisoners, downed pilots, resistance leaders. We also move food and clothing. Information, too."

My gaze shifted to the OSS memo beneath the bread box. "Courier work?"

Ilka nodded. "Allied printed materials meant for distribution, surveillance reports, war news, eyewitness accounts of soldiers and prisoners."

"Impressive. How'd you manage it?"

"Beneath our Gypsy covered wagons, there is large storage bin used to hold gear for the horses, and tools. Many necessities—even human cargo—can fit in this bin."

"But the danger. Weren't you frightened? Scared for your grandmother? Obviously she must have been afraid for you."

Ilka's eyes narrowed. "Gypsies fear nothing. A lifetime of hate and abuse it make us hard, you see."

My brow furrowed. I didn't see.

"Gypsies have lived on the fringe of the criminal underworld always," she added. "Fortune-telling, stealing, begging, bartering, they are elements of Gypsy culture—it is how we get by." Ilka, sensing my unease, smiled. "Ahh, but the Gypsy ways are no longer my way. Today I am only interested in stealing bit part in small movie."

We laughed, eager to move beyond a further discussion of Gypsy morality. Besides, she'd made her essential point. Their culture made Gypsies naturals in underground work.

"You're a shoo-in for the part. How about the rest of the day? Anything else going on?"

Ilka noticed my empty coffee cup. Lifting the pot from the hot pad on the table beside her, she began replenishing our cups. "Friday night there is fundraiser auction, sponsored by our Hungarian Federation chapter, at the Grand Hotel." She nodded to the folded foreign language newspaper, resting on the table beside her place setting. "It is beautiful beach club, and the event it will be very special. Oh...and tonight there is the Mrs.' monthly palm reading session. Maybe you would like to come?"

The star-shaped mark on my palm itched, as if reminding me of my vow to steer clear of such nonsense. Of course I'd never tell Ilka how I felt.

I gulped the final bite of my biscuit. "Sorry, can't," I brushed crumbs from my fingers onto my plate and pushed back my chair. "You've got your audition. I've got a director to impress, myself. May take awhile. Today's the day I try to sway Novara to see things my way."

Ilka's eyes rolled skyward. "My sessions are helpful, but not that good."

"The other evening, you said you don't do prediction work." I stood. "What *do* you do, exactly?"

Ilka's lips were pursed at the edge of her cup. She blew on the hot liquid, then took a sip. "Everyone has special talents and hidden abilities. I am guide to help people to look within to see their gifts."

"Uh-huh," I said vaguely as I panned the countertops. "Did you happen to see a note from Gunnar? He was called back to the base last night, promised to leave me one when he returned. I can't seem to find it."

"His car it was not in the drive when I went out for the morning newspaper." She shrugged. "He must still be out."

"Hmm, well, I saw an edge of paper over there, under the bread box. It made me wonder."

Ilka laughed. "Gunnar, he did not write that. The Mrs., she has another project in mind." She nodded in the direction of the counter. "My list of what I must buy."

"Ahhh," I said, feeling foolish. I stood, intent on taking my dishes to the sink. Gunnar Rask. It was his fault. *Keep your eyes and ears open for anything suspicious.* Well, I'd uncovered a household communiqué from Della. Wait until I reported this!

I stacked my plate on top of my bowl. "And MO? What sort of action is MO?"

Ilka frowned looking genuinely puzzled. "MO?"

"Below the Date, the To and From, it says, Action, then MO."

Laughing, Ilka stood, smoothing her apron. "MO is MOBILIZE. Sometimes it is like, if she were here, I would salute, perhaps."

A knock at the door. I jerked, nearly toppling my dishes. Bela Lugosi had arrived.

Chapter Ten

A customer clutching a *Los Angeles Times* was leaving the news-stand as I walked up.

"Hello, young lady," Gus called, dropping change into his canvas apron.

Today's shirt selection was a vibrant lemon yellow. With it he wore the cerise vest and the magenta slacks he'd worn before. The ensemble, as always, had the outrageous quality I enjoyed. But, while I'd come to appreciate the extra charge Gus' clothing and company added to my mornings, today the boost wasn't necessary. I was wound up enough already. A half-hour from now I would be pitching the changes I wanted for the WASP documentary.

I greeted Gus, noting the *Los Angeles Times* rack below the shelf was already empty. A fresh stack, still secured with strapping, lay on the ground nearby. "What happened? Get a late start?"

"Second delivery," Gus replied, adjusting the tweed cap atop his unruly hair. "My usual supply, it was snapped up almost soon as I opened."

"What's going on?" I glanced at the top paper on the bundle and read the headline and shouted. "The Marines won in the Solomons! Hooray! Fabulous news!"

The victory, a final step to securing the South Pacific, was a logical reason for increased sales. But there was something else afoot. Using a penknife to cut the strapping, he offered me the top copy, bottom section up. "Like I tell you yesterday, foul play is behind the death of Derrick Brody."

The Marine victory in the Pacific was the *Times'* lead story, but Brody's demise was front page news as well. The prominent below-the-fold headline read: DEATH OF POPULAR MOVIE DIRECTOR UNDER INVESTIGATION; followed by the subhead: Foul Play Suspected.

I tried to read further, but Gus wanted to talk.

"Why bother with the version cast in print, when the one who sells the print has the latest?"

The twinkle in his good eye was irresistible, as was the promise of an insider's account. A juicy bit for Rask, perchance? I tucked the paper under my arm for later.

"Like I say yesterday," he began, "the authorities they discover something out of the ordinary. It alerted them that Brody's death was not as it would appear at first glance."

"Something out of the ordinary? What?"

Clearly relishing his tale, he began, "That evening—night before last—Brody ask the secretary to stay late to help catch up with the letter writing. At seven p.m., Russell Chalmers, he stop by for a meeting with Brody, and the secretary, she take her leave. After a stop or two along the way, the secretary, she arrive home only to discover she left at the office the coin purse which holds her house key."

I cleared my throat to spur him.

Gus looked put out, but picked up the pace. "So, the secretary, she must return to the studio. She arrives to notice light shining through the crack under Brody's office door. She raps. No answer. She knock again, louder." Gus, raising a fist, rapped the air with his knuckles. "Then she try the door. In she goes. Brody is slumped on his desk."

I shrugged. "Why do you—she...they—believe it was *murder?*"

Gus retorted, "Who discovers the body, how it was found, that the secretary call the doctor because she thought Brody had a heart attack—*that* you can read in the *Times*. But the later discovery of a clue at the scene…That is what suggested an investigation was in order…"

The dangling sentences, the dramatic pause, the look on Gus' face, all promised more. "And?"

Gus lifted an eyebrow. "What precisely made them suspicious is being withheld until the tests of the coroner are completed."

Silently, I started counting to ten. I got to five. "And?"

He had a cat-that-swallowed-the-canary smile. "Word is the tests are merely formality—for legal purposes. The investigators already know how Brody was killed…" He lowered his voice. "But they are not talking. Especially, not to the press. What they know is being used to help flush out the killer."

Running tests on a dead body, withholding evidence so it can be used in questioning suspects—that was all usual procedure, wasn't it?

"So, they have a clue that will lead to the killer, but they haven't rounded up the suspects yet? What? A fingerprint? The weapon? A note?"

"That, even I do not know."

I searched for the correct change to purchase the *Times*.

As if the jingling of the coins had jingled his recall, Gus at last said something significant. "I have heard the name of someone called in for questioning."

"Who?"

"Russell Chalmers."

That opened my eyes. Russell Chalmers had been at the story conference. He hadn't liked the way his work had been translated to the screen, or that Brody had agreed to the changes suggested by an OWI representative. But motive for murder? Hadn't Sam said Chalmers and Brody were friends?

"I don't think Chalmers did it," I said. "He and Brody had a long-time personal and professional relationship. I met Chalmers. He seemed like a stand-up guy."

"This is not testimony to a man's innocence. Besides," he wagged his thick wiry eyebrows, "my source tells me Chalmers is about to be charged with the murder of Brody."

"Who's the source?"

He shook his head.

In the rush to leave for Novara's meeting, I missed getting a flower. What a shame—the dusty pink lilies on the ledge of the newsstand had looked divine.

◇◇◇

I swung the Packard into my usual parking space at Fort Roach. At the administration building, I took the front steps of the portico two at a time. An armed guard sat at a small table directly inside the entrance door reading a comic magazine. I glimpsed *Dick Tracy* in the title before the comic was whisked under the duty register conveniently positioned nearby.

Novara's secretary ushered me into his office directly. From behind his desk, Novara signaled with finger and thumb slightly apart to say he'd be a short while longer. As if he'd given me a choice in the matter, I acquiesced with a nod.

While Novara discussed scheduling with the person on the other end, I grabbed the *Hollywood Reporter* from a nearby coffee table, sweeping its front page for news of Brody's death. Nothing. The *TradeViews* column carried another searing criticism of the movie industry by Wilkerson. This time he was lambasting Hollywood and exhibitors for exploiting the greatest boom in the history of the business while shortchanging theatergoers with substandard movies. No examples were given. Would he think people got their money's worth going to see *Somewhere I'll Find You*, I wondered? It was a film of the times. And even I would admit that Clark Gable and Lana Turner were improbable as correspondents. But the love scenes between battles were certainly enjoyable. Did that mean I should feel cheated?

A quiet knock cut short my musings. The door crept slowly open and Sam slunk in, looking worried that he was late. Grinning, I motioned my head in Novara's direction.

Sam, glimpsing Novara pacing at a wall calendar, receiver stuck to his ear, smiled back and wiped his hand across his brow theatrically. Automatically, stray locks of feathery hair flopped onto his forehead. His coloring, I observed with relief, was back to its normal shade of golden tan.

"Feeling better?" I mouthed.

Sam nodded and gave a thumbs-up.

I continued to regard him, studying his unusual looks. Clark Gable might be appealing by popular standards, but Sam's fine sculpted features intrigued me, too. What had Max said: He was an odd fish? *Possibly my trophy catch?*

Sam, smiling self-consciously at the close scrutiny, averted his eyes. It was a mannerism he'd exhibited before and one I found refreshing compared with the brash behavior of many of the men I encountered.

Novara hung up on his call. Cigarette dangling from the corner of his mouth, beret comically askew, he motioned for us to sit. Taking a deep drag, he blew a string of smoke rings in the air. "I don't know if you're aware of the filmmaking system here at Fort Roach, Miss Lewis, but let me explain, if I may."

Novara's polite request was condescending. "When a film like your WASP documentary is ordered by the AAF Motion Picture Division in Washington, it gets ranked according to need. The assignments get doled out to the production office in keeping with the urgency factor. Once we get the job, we break the concept down into a working format. Then I assign a writer to do the script."

Novara sent a smarmy smile Sam's way, but Sam kept his eyes glued to his doodling.

Ahhh. No wonder Sam was keeping so quiet: Novara was handing down the writing assignments. Was that where he was going with this lecture? He wanted me to understand where I fit into the process?

"We're working with an art form. We're seasoned professionals. Yet, ain't it funny?" Novara waited until I looked at him again. "Here we are having this little session because someone seems to think *you* may have ideas for improving *Sky Belles*."

I bit the flesh on the inside of my cheek. Yeah, like changing the dopey title. I hated the frivolous slant it gave our film. But I had to prioritize my battles.

Novara paused to light a fresh cigarette off the stub of his old one. He snubbed out the old butt in an overflowing smelly ashtray. His next move was equally offensive: leaning back in his chair, he put his feet up on the desk.

I stared openly. Shoe rationing had been in effect for almost a year. His new leather shoes were incongruous with the shabby footwear most of us wore these days. *And the sleek style?* Italian, I was almost certain. But how could that be? They couldn't be producing many luxury items over there these days. Horrific battles were being fought on their soil. Italy had surrendered to the Allied forces, but we were still in a seesaw fight with the Germans, who refused to leave. Where had Novara come across the shoes? And why would he choose to wear goods produced by the Italians, who were still, for the most part, aligned with the Nazis?

"Interference from an inexperienced outsider is the last thing I need right now. I'm under tremendous pressure here. I've got several important projects in the hopper. One of them with Clark Gable."

As if I didn't already know.

"The body of work I'm building here is key to my future after the war." Smoke escaped his mouth as he spoke. "And since I intend being up there with the William Wylers and Frank Capras of the world, each and every one of the projects I turn out has got to be a winner."

William Wyler? Frank Capra? I knew Novara had a big ego, but c'mon. Was he nuts? Look what he'd done to our film so far.

"Where I'm going is this…" Novara took a lazy drag. Head back, his thick lips puckered in an "O," he exhaled one smoke ring, then another before continuing. "I have little interest or time to devote to making *Sky Belles*, but the directive came to me over the transom. There's no choice. I'll make it"—from beneath a wreath of smoke, he shot me a hard look—"and I'll make it the way *I* see fit."

His message came across loud and clear: my role in making the WASP documentary was to stay out of his way.

Roland Novara had just laid down the kind of challenge that always brought the best out in me. Confident and relaxed against the back of my chair, I held his look.

Novara gazed at the ceiling, drew his bushy eyebrows together, and creased the skin above the bridge of his nose. "But since we're here, to hear you out"—he took a long drag on his cigarette—"fire away. Rat-a-tat-tat."

These were high stakes. I could knock Novara and his work all I wanted, but if I didn't have something phantasmagoric up my sleeve—or worse, if he didn't buy into the ideas—the WASP film, and I, were doomed. A sidelong glance at Sam told me I wasn't likely to get much assistance from his camp either. He was completely preoccupied with doodling.

"Miss Cochran sent me here as her representative to be sure this film demonstrates to the general public and to the military what women pilots are capable of doing. It should also highlight the ways in which the WASP have contributed to the war effort. You've been kind enough, Roland, Sam"—I nodded politely in each direction—"to show me some clips that exemplify your efforts thus far. I've also read the entire script to get a sense of the other segments that have either already been shot, or that are sketched out for future shoots."

The script was on the table in front of me. I fingered it delicately. "I like your forthright style, Roland. Let me get right to the point as well." I locked eyes with him. "Frankly, I'm disappointed. I'd heard you were beyond B picture work."

The cigarette in Novara's hand halted midway to his mouth.

"This is no second-string project for me and, like you said, it can't be for you either. It will be listed on your credits, like it or not. You have the filmmaking expertise—" I gave a bright smile, trying not to gag—"I'm a WASP. Why not use my enthusiasm and firsthand knowledge to help you turn *Sky Belles* into the award-winner it has the potential to be?"

Novara's feet slid off the desk, hitting the floor with a thunk. He went back to puffing, but I had his ear now. Out of the corner of my eye I saw that Sam had set down his pencil.

"The shots of girls sunbathing or playing Ping-Pong and volleyball in skimpy clothing are sexy stuff," I said evenly, watching Novara's chest swell visibly. "But it's also the stuff of B pictures.

"Now, while there's nothing wrong with your vision," I lied through my teeth, "the ideas I've come up with will give your audience more to think and talk about. For starters, we put in the same number of ground school and flying hours as the men and we're just as good. Most folks don't realize that. We fly our country's very best, most costly, equipment. We fly nearly everything the military has in its inventory—heavy bombers, fighters. One WASP has even flown an experimental jet. So surprise your audience with blown-up photos of each, with a voiceover describing the range of planes. Use real stats to demonstrate our safety record: our accident and fatality records are lower than the men's."

Novara's eyebrows lifted; the tapping came to a halt.

"The B-17 Flying Fortress is impressive—it's one of our biggest bombers—I'll bet I can arrange—"

Novara purred, "Tell me more about the fighters."

The interruption threw me, but I was able to give him a rundown on the preliminary arrangements I'd made for flying the P-51 Mustang at March Field. Novara's nod of approval and the sly curl of his mouth indicated he understood that getting film of a prototype fighter in action would be a feather in his beret.

"Good work," Sam said out of the corner of his mouth.

I looked over and smiled, then turned back to Novara. "I'll know this afternoon whether we've got the go-ahead."

"When you get word, tell Sam," Novara said. "Sam, you'll call a film crew boss, yes?"

Sam nodded switched gears. "What about reshooting the target towing scene, Pucci?"

Too bad I'd been so gung-ho the other day. "Uh, I'm working on that. Still haven't been able to get the necessary clearance." In truth, a call to Miss C was on my agenda later. Max did not want me to do the sequence while a saboteur was on the loose.

I needed to get Miss C's take on the level of danger, hear what she would advise.

I moved on. "WASPs are assigned to 130 bases around the country. In addition to ferrying and artillery training, we're doing test piloting and instructing. Those areas are neglected in the current script as well."

"Blah, blah, blah." Novara wagged his head from side to side in rhythm with the words. "You don't expect me—or an audience—to get excited about that."

The reaction wasn't a surprise. Covering new material meant more effort, more time.

Sam piped in, "Just a minute, Roland. Test piloting *could* be sexy stuff."

I wouldn't have picked the same descriptive, but at least he'd piqued Roland's interest. The floor was mine again.

"WASP pilots test planes after they've undergone major over-hauls. They run the repaired planes through their paces before the ship can be assigned to a male pilot."

A faint smile played on Novara's lips and I guessed the impli-cation that we are expendable met with his approval.

"These ladies have colorful—and brave—tales to tell," I continued. "One WASP, while checking the spin characteristics of an AT-6 at 11,000 feet, suddenly realized all the controls had been hooked up backwards." I paused for effect. "She pulled out at 500 feet then had to stay up in the air until she could figure out how to bring the plane in."

Novara and Sam continued staring blankly at me as though they didn't get it. Did I have to spell out everything? "It's the makings of a gripping pilot interview!"

Novara flicked a mountainous ash at the ashtray, sending cin-ders spilling onto the table. Sam twisted his pencil in his hands.

"Say," Novara said, suddenly. "Mae West was a hit demonstrat-ing how to accomplish a basic flying maneuver, eh, Sam?" Sam had no chance to reply. "Pucci, sweetheart, try to follow what I'm saying here. Maybe it'll give you an idea of what we're going for."

I took a deep breath and clenched my hands together in my lap.

"Okay now, picture Mae West up on the screen in all her glory." Novara held his hands out, thumbs touching, framing the scene he was about to describe. "She talks—her hands seductively tracing the contour of her figure while slooowly describing how, in order to achieve the 'Lazy 8,' you have to use a 'slow and easy' hand on the controls—" He looked at me pointedly. "*Heh, heh.* Then she sings, 'I Like a Guy Who Takes His Time' as animated sequences demonstrate the correct technique for making the maneuver. At the finish, her gravely voice low and slow, she tells trainees: 'When you've learned how to do your Lazy 8s, come up and see me some time!'" He winked and began a rude cackling.

Novara's crass behavior didn't trouble me. I expected as much from him. Sam's chuckles on the other hand, however restrained, did.

I understood the humor of the Mae West piece and realized that a seductive movie star had value in training films—for grabbing attention and driving home important instruction. Still, the technique would be completely inappropriate for a documentary like ours. I hadn't expected Sam to join the laughter.

Before he could notice my dagger eyes, Novara's secretary popped her head into the room.

"Sorry," she said, pinching her face into a contrite expression. "Lou's on the phone. Says it's urgent."

Novara took the receiver. From the way he furrowed his brow as he listened, I guessed the urgent news was not good. Novara's side of the conversation went something like: "Yes." "Uh-huh." "I don't believe it." "Try again." "Air pouch, then." "Call me the sec the plane lifts off."

Novara hung up, propped his elbows on the desk, then rubbed his temples for a minute. "Damn goldbrick in Orlando forgot to fill my reconnaissance order. Let's wrap this, okay?"

"We fly P-39 and P-63 fighters painted with the red Russian star—the Texaco sign, we call it—from the factory in Buffalo to a base in Great Falls, Montana for delivery to Russian women pilots. Part of the Lend-Lease program to help the Russians rebuild their air force. It was decimated by the Nazis, you know." I cleared my throat, fighting a rising giggle. The condescending remark had slipped out inadvertently but, oh, did it feel good! And, though I risked overwhelming Novara with just how much a woman was equipped to handle, I couldn't stop myself from adding, "The Russian women fly combat, can you imagine! One even flew while five months pregnant."

Novara began biting on a fingernail.

"The final suggestion I have involves the B-29 Super Fortress."

Sam gave a low whistle. "That plane's a monster."

I hadn't decided yet whether to forgive Sam for his earlier transgression of siding with Novara. I gave him the slightest of nods. "Seventy tons of armament and power. Biggest plane in our inventory. There's been some problem with fire that's getting the men nervous, but I just heard a couple of WASPs have been chosen to fly the B-29 as demonstration pilots to flight crews in transition to B-29s. Some footage of that would provide evidence that the plane must be safe. You know the patter: If women can do it, anyone can."

Novara sat chewing his fingernail, saying nothing. "Jesus," he said finally, "I'm at a loss here. What do you think, Sam?"

I turned to look at Sam. His jaw muscles began to work as he considered his thoughts. What happened next was a shocker. Sam reiterated the essence of my ideas, using slightly different language. He reviewed the rationale behind why the suggestions would have appeal, both to a wide movie audience and to Novara's superiors.

After he finished, I expected compliments for my good work. Zip.

"You're right, Sam," Novara said. "The suggestions make good sense. Work with Lewis on writing them up, then call me. But do it fast. I needed to get this wrapped up yesterday."

Huh? My mind was spinning. Novara had acted as though Sam deserved all the credit and Sam had taken it.

I got a handshake and we were excused.

My adrenaline was pumping as we walked out into the hallway. I had won some ground, but I wanted to bury Sam six feet under it.

Sam seemed oblivious.

My pent-up frustration exploded. "You're a snake. No, a blood sucker. You sucked up my ideas…made them yours!" Hands on hips, eyes narrowed, I glared. "Why'd you do it?

"I had to go along with Novara," he said, locking eyes with me. "I did it for you, don't you see? It's not in his nature to let a woman tell him what to do. Without that man-to-man stuff, without giving him the chance to accept direction from another male, I was afraid you wouldn't have made any headway."

My nose was bent out of joint, but I could grasp Sam's reasoning. From the little I'd observed of Novara, I knew the outcome was a major coup, given I was a woman. Besides, Sam had been able to express the concepts in the movie jargon he and Novara understood. That also may have helped in selling him the ideas.

Sam's eyes continued to hold mine. The pleading look in them was irresistible. Though I would have preferred captaining my own battle—or at least to have been in on the strategizing—I was on my way toward getting the kind of picture Miss C was after. And, more important, giving Frankie her just due. I put away my anger.

"I'm grateful for the way things turned out," I acknowledged at last.

Before parting company, Sam and I agreed to have dinner together later to celebrate and to get started on putting the ideas for revising *Sky Belles* into script format.

◇◇◇

In the hallway outside the typing pool, I waited beside the telephone. Ten minutes after the appointed hour, it rang.

"Why did I have to go through so many channels?" Miss C asked, steamrolling over the niceties. "I thought I heard the last operator say she'd have to ring you on a pay phone. Don't you have your own phone?"

"No."

"What! Why not?"

I had a mind to say: *Because I'm a woman pilot trying to advise a Hollywood director on how to do his job. That doesn't merit a personal telephone.*

But, fresh from a victory of sorts, I breezily said, "It's no big deal," then steered the conversation to what was. "I heard you called the hospital a few times to check on Frankie."

"I've been concerned," Miss C replied. "Uhm, and there have also been some financial matters to attend to. There's no military assistance for hospitalization of a WASP, you know." She cleared her throat. "I'm having to do some finagling."

Her financial worries paled next to my sabotage concerns.

"The doctor's troubled too. There's been no improvement."

"Yes. I know."

"I bumped into Max." I waited, giving her a chance to come clean about her source. In the lull, I heard the shuffling of papers. "Maxine Koslowski."

"Hmm." More paper shuffling.

"Miss C, Max told me about what she found. Sugar mixed in the fuel. She's your source. Why didn't you tell me? I'm in an awkward position…"

"You're in an awkward position? What about me? I gave Koslowksi my word—"

I cut in. "Max doesn't want me to do the target tow reshoot. Doesn't think it's safe. But I already volunteered."

Because you told me to. I didn't say it, but I wanted to. My back pressed against the wall, I slid to the hard wooden seat and recapped my meeting with Roland Novara.

"Bravo, Lewis. I said you had the kind of can-do attitude to make this mission a success. Now you and that screenwriter have to come up with a new script Novara won't be able to resist. You'll do it. Keep me posted."

"Uhm, what about the P-51 idea?"

"More good stuff. Wish I weren't stuck here in Washington. Would love to fly that new hybrid myself. Seversky's positively gaga over it. Maybe even a touch jealous. That Mustang's more responsive than anything he's got on the drawing board right now." She was so cheerful, I could picture her grinning. "What an impression it'll make on our movie audience, too," she added. "Yup, brilliant idea, Lewis."

"Max also has reservations about taking the P-51 up."

"Why's that?"

I breathed deep. "Miss C, there's a saboteur on the loose. Max is an ace crash inspector. She's certain whoever did this is out to damage our reputation, scare us. She's advised me to stay on the ground. What do you think?"

"Now that we know about the sugar," she said without hesitation, "Max can test the fuel before you go up."

There were other ways to sabotage a plane. She knew that as well as I did. "You think I should do it then?"

"Look, Lewis, I know what I'd do. Someone tampered with a military plane on a military base. High-risk business. Get away with it once, you've pulled off a miracle. Try it twice? Ha! You'd be a fool, or a culprit with a death wish. And what are the odds of that? Besides, if Koslowski is right, and the villain is AAF, the point's already been made. But I'm not there. It's got to be your call. Trust your judgment."

I gulped. Her faith in me was flattering.

"Whether you do the flying scenes or not," she continued, "we need to get the person behind this. Any suspects?"

"Haven't had much time to dig around. Max is our best source…" I brightened. "Tonight I'm having dinner with Sam… er, Mr. Lorenz, the screenwriter. He's a friend of Frankie's. He's also spent time out at March. Worked on the *P-51 Flight Characteristics* picture with—" I hesitated. I'd been about to say Brody. Had Rask's request for my assistance on his case wormed its way through channels and gotten to her yet? She'd have conniptions if she learned I'd gotten wind of the assignment before she did.

"Lewis, are you there? Worked with *who*? I didn't hear you."

"Ah, the director Derrick Brody? Heard of him?"

"Sure I've heard of him. We've never met, though—"

She'd spoken of Brody in the present. She hadn't seen the request. If the cogs continued to churn at this rate, Rask's case would be solved before I could even get involved.

Paper rustled loudly and I sensed the noise-making might be deliberate. "Listen, Lewis I better get back to—"

"Brody was murdered," I blurted. "It's in all the papers here."

"Well, *we're* in the trenches here," she snapped. "I can't keep up with my phone messages. Where do you think I'd find time to read newspapers?"

Before I could drop other hints, Miss C switched the topic.

"Things haven't been going as smoothly as we'd like," she said. "We're up against several hard-core groups—a grassroots organization supported by the American Legion, a delegation of civil aviators, plus a contingent of displaced civilian male instructors. They're all claiming the government's wasting millions of taxpayer dollars training women in a frivolous program that's taking jobs away from the men. It's the same bogus argument, but they're well organized. A smear campaign's in the works, too, we've heard. Hopefully, they're in the dark about Frankie's crash."

I barely heard her running through the other highlights of days of meetings with Congressional representatives and other influentials. I knew it was important. On another occasion, I would have been glomming onto every word. Now, however, I had my own agenda. How could I let her know about Rask and his case?

I needn't have worried.

"It's not exactly clear when I'll be able to leave," she said, winding up the report from Washington at last. "The general has already left, but he's asked me to stay on to continue trying to build more support." There was another crackling of paper.

"Wait a minute. What's this? Note says to call a Lieutenant Rask in Hollywood. Know anything about this, Lewis?"

I swallowed. My armpits were wet with perspiration. "Ahhh, Rask? He's Mrs. Dunn's brother. Staying at the house. Maybe you ought to ring him back. Oh, and while you're at it…a call to Major Beacock or whoever else is involved in decisions of that level might help me win approval to fly the Mustang."

"Hmm. Got a meeting coming up, but I'll see what I can do later today. I'm calling Rask now."

◇◇◇

Before leaving Fort Roach for the day, I took a call from Major Beacock. He advised me that the P-51 Mustang would be available for filming purposes on Saturday, day after next. If the euphoria I got from ferry piloting could be compared to the pleasure of an extended merry-go-round ride, then flying the P-51 should be the brass ring.

◇◇◇

A stop at the hospital was the last thing on my list before heading home for a well-deserved soak in the tub. Then dinner with Sam.

A lively half hour of soliloquy on my day did not induce so much as a blink from Frankie. Her nurse entered as I was about to go and we chatted about Frankie's condition. The signs of life at my first visit had not reappeared, but she mentioned how nice she thought it was that Miss Cochran and her husband were taking care of Frankie's mounting medical bills.

The nurse's remark brought back my conversation with Miss C. So that's what she'd meant about having to do some "finagling" with regard to Frankie's hospital expenses. I was stunned at her generosity. Who would be covering the cost of Frankie's hospital stay if not for Miss C? And, *why* should she have to be doing it in the first place?

The ugly reminder of the second-class status of the WASP made me appreciate, more than ever, the importance of Miss

C's going to the mat for us—this time by accompanying the general to Washington, D.C., to help get us the benefits and stature militarization would provide.

The nurse, after chewing her lip and wringing her hands, added something else. Frankie had had a visitor yesterday evening after I'd left. He left in such a rush, he almost bowled over the nurse who'd come upon him in Frankie's room.

Chapter Eleven

In the gathering darkness, I wondered about Frankie's mysterious visitor as I snaked the Packard up Benedict Canyon Drive, headed for home. Why had he been there?

The nurse's description—dark, medium height, quick on his feet—was not much to go on. No one else in the nursing crew had noticed him. A "No Visitors" sign was posted on the room's door, and the nurse assumed he feared a reprimand for ignoring the order. Perhaps a boyfriend. But if it was someone who cared about Frankie, why the rush to leave? When I'd paid my first visit to the hospital, the nurse had said both a man and a woman had called to ask about Frankie's condition but hadn't left their names. Might the visitor have been the male caller? Or, it had happened so fast, might the "he" have actually been a "she"?

The Packard's engine made a loud rumbling as I rounded the turn off the main road, downshifting to make the steep charge up the Dunns' drive. My gaze climbed the angled walls from the atrium on the main level, to the Dunns' bedroom on the second floor, past the small, narrow windows of the private study just above, stopping at the railed cupola on top. I hadn't yet had the opportunity to take in the view from up there, but I'd seen the spiral staircase that led to the lookout point the other evening when I'd met with Della. Recalling her invitation to borrow from her closet, I smiled. A raid was definitely in order for tonight's date with Sam.

Oddly, I remained attracted to Sam in spite of his upstaging me during our meeting with Novara. Or was it *because* of what had gone on? His handling of Novara had been smooth. And when it came down to it, my objective—the WASP film's integrity—was dependent on my ability to outmaneuver Novara. In sticking close to Sam, I was gathering useful tips. Then there was our writing assignment. I could do a journeyman's job but Sam had the wherewithal to create—how had Miss C put it?—a script Novara wouldn't be able to resist.

Work aside, I was looking forward to an intimate evening with a thoughtful, sensitive man. A bit of an odd fish, perhaps, but the sort of catch I was beginning to find attractive. Just imagining the two of us at a candlelit table, engaged in quiet conversation, his intelligent, caring eyes gazing into mine, made me tingly with excitement.

Impulsive Jupiter Heart line…a tiny voice sing-songed deep inside my brain.

Circling the Packard round the courtyard, I waved to the Mexican gardener, once again dressed all in white. The light clothing was a striking contrast against the charcoal of the early dusk, typical of November. I parked, then watched while he packed the last of his gear into his dilapidated truck. What would Miss C think if she knew I was having romantic thoughts about a colleague? That I was about to set aside my inhibitions? I wondered if she even remembered what it was like to date.

Though powerful and independent as individuals, she and her husband Floyd Odlum found fulfillment through the talents of each other. Mr. Odlum, almost twenty years Miss C's senior, was an investment genius and a millionaire. He had also been stricken with crippling arthritis, and it was said he lived his adventures through his wife. For Miss C, her husband provided the resources she needed for her pursuits. Some even claimed it was Mr. Odlum's vast pool of money, experience, and contacts that had catapulted his wife to Director of Women Pilots. Not that Miss C didn't have abilities and a will of her own. She'd pulled herself up from poverty-stricken beginnings as a child worker in the cotton mills on Tobacco Road, to learning a trade as a beautician—starting as live-in help for the beauty shop's owner—to establishing her own highly successful cosmetics company. No small feat at twenty-three, my age, and in the Depression era. It was her husband-to-be Odlum who, seated next to her at a dinner party, casually commented that competition for any kind of business was so keen because of the Depression that she would almost need wings to cover territory fast enough to hold her own. In 1932, she earned her pilot's license. The beauty operator ceased to exist and an aviator was born. An aviator and also a savvy business woman.

I'd heard about the climb in a talk Miss C gave on goal achievement. Rather than regret her past, she believed the experiences had taught her independence and how to survive on her own. The lessons learned in weathering the difficulties of her youth had become the backbone of her ability and desire to accomplish great things as an adult, she'd said.

The speech had inspired me in a broader sense than flying only. It reinforced my belief that, with a positive attitude and determination, almost anything was possible. It also gave me a new perspective toward marriage. Miss C had returned, again and again, to how a woman's strength comes from having her own thoughts, opinions, and life. Marriage for her hadn't been an escape. She had worked hard to establish a successful career beforehand. And when she married, it was to someone who would treat her as an equal; who was committed to the give and take of a true partnership. She'd kept her own name. It reminded her of where she'd come from, she said.

After her presentation that day, I began thinking I would prove my worth through my work as well. That getting married after establishing my career was the right path for me. All I need now, I thought, exiting the Packard and crossing the courtyard, was to get hired as a commercial pilot after the war, and to find a man who could recognize that my needs, desires, and identity were as important as his. I sighed. No small order.

I left the arched portico still savoring the sweet smell of jasmine as I started for the side door. *A Neptunian life line… destined for a life somehow removed from the mainstream.* If I were to put faith in Ilka's palm reading projections, maybe my post-war dreams weren't out of reach.

I approached the kitchen door. *Passionate nature…rush into romance…blind to faults of those you love.* Ilka's heart line findings charged my brain until I collided with Gunnar Rask, who was making a hurried exit. Momentarily discombobulated, we stared blankly at one another, then burst into laughter.

Gunnar's hair was damp and he had the clean soapy smell of a recent shower. In the dim beam of an exterior lamp, I also observed his freshly pressed uniform and the worn leather briefcase in his hand. He was heading back to Fort Roach, I gathered.

"Sorry, I was on another planet."

"No, I'm sorry." Gunnar smoothed his damp sandy hair. "I'm needed back at the studio. Ah, and no one's home. But I left the lights on. And there's a note from Ilka. Says she'll be back around seven or so."

I hadn't seen Gunnar since the previous night, just after the power outage. I smiled at his look of concern. "Don't worry about my being alone. I'm going out. Got a date."

"A date? Who with?" Gunnar's tone sounded curiously strained.

"Sam Lorenz. We're having dinner. Novara has agreed to make some changes to our WASP film. He wants us to sketch the ideas out in more detail. On paper."

"Your ideas?"

I nodded. "Yeah. But it took Sam to sell them."

I briefly explained what had happened.

"Too bad he stole your thunder. Watch yourself. Around here, people think nothing of stealing ideas from one another." Under his breath, almost as if he were talking to himself, he added, "Other things, too."

Blackmail. Of course, Rask's mind was on Brody and his case. "The trap. Do you have the blackmailer?"

Gunnar squinted into the fading shadowy light. "There was a foul-up. But we'll get them."

"Foul-up? Them?"

Gunnar cocked an eyebrow, said nothing.

"But you know why Brody was being blackmailed. And what the blackmailer had on him." He looked at me. I'd guessed right. My eyes met his squarely. "You asked me to keep my eyes and ears open. I could more effectively carry out my assignment—trivial as it is so far—if I knew what you know." He canted his head. "Miss Cochran said she was going to call you. There's probably a message at your office…"

"I spoke with her. Minutes ago, in fact. She called here." He nodded toward the main part of the house. "Yes—" He read my expectant look. "She's agreed to lend you out. Though I hear you're on a high priority case already."

"She told you?"

"Not in so many words." A little smile quirked the corners of his mouth. "Said you'd fill me in." He shifted the briefcase to his other hand, thought a moment. "Brody was involved in an obsessive affair. He is…he *was,* married."

I nodded, recalling the family photo in his office. "And the blackmailer had evidence. What was he willing to trade it for?"

Gunnar shook his head. "Sorry. No need to know."

"What? It's key information," I said indignantly. "I need it if I'm going to do my job. Who am I going to tell?"

"Pucci, I need one final brass hat to sign off before you're cleared. I'll tell you this much, but it's all you're going to get, understood?" He waited until I nodded my agreement. "Espionage is involved."

My skin tingled, head to foot.

"Your turn. Given how little you've had to go on, but given who you are—" His eyes danced merrily. "What did you manage to pick up?"

I shared Gus' gossip about Chalmers. But Chalmers, according to Rask, was in the clear. He'd simply been brought in for questioning, that was all. Then I reported my observation of Novara's shoes.

"Might be contraband," I suggested. "Purchased on the black market." My conjecturing ballooned. "He could be selling things on the black market as well."

Gunnar smiled. "More likely wishful thinking on your part. But I'll follow up. If you want, stop by my shop tomorrow. I'm wrapping up the firefighting sequence. You can check what we did with the crash footage."

"Thanks. I'd like that." He glanced at his watch and started to back away. An itch in my brain like a mosquito bite demanded to be scratched. "Wait. There was an incident on a high security shoot the other day." I described the prank with the projectile containing the propaganda poster. "Later, in Brody's office, I heard of more vandalism—a small fire—on the same set. Did you hear about it?"

Gunnar knew about the incidents. He'd been called in by Brody to investigate. I listened transfixed while he confided his suspicions. It was not the work of pranksters, but the subversive attempts by enemy operatives trying to work on Brody's fears.

"They wanted him to know they meant business. Jinxing the set, slowing production of a film meant to teach airmen how to resist Nazi interrogation, was the perfect medium. But security has been tightened. The film is back on track." His eyes met mine squarely. "Pucci, word of this must not get out. The possibility of clandestine enemy agents operating in Hollywood would set nerves on edge, create a nervous buzz about other attacks to come. It's just the sort of reaction they want. We're not going to give them the satisfaction."

"Of course, but—"

Gunnar checked his watch and began a backwards exit. "That's all I can tell you for now." He smiled. "The reports were not exaggerated. Your perceptions are excellent." He paused. "Ilka's been acting a little strange lately, have you noticed?"

I stared blankly for a moment, perplexed. "Nooo. She's auditioning for a part. She's concerned about Bela Lugosi. He's got sciatica. She's trying to cure him. Herbs, potions. Sounds strange, I know, but your sister is a believer. Ilka's supposedly been trained in the stuff. Er, the art. Method…"

Gunnar nodded slowly, as though not quite convinced that I knew what I was talking about.

He looked at me. "Watch your back around her." And left.

◇◇◇

I stood in the master suite doorway, uneasy about entering the room in Della's absence. Privacy was something I valued deeply. Yet here I was, about to invade her personal domain.

I took a breath. Della had *invited* me to raid her closet.

The lush white carpeting felt spongy as I padded past the huge velvet-draped bed atop the dais, en route to the walk-in closet. Out the corner of my eye, I glimpsed the wrought-iron staircase. The chance to experience the view from the cupola proved irresistible.

I detoured over to the stairway and mounted it. At the top, I flicked a switch, revealing a hexagonal study with exactly the quaint ambiance I would have expected. A roll-top desk and an overstuffed club chair with a matching ottoman, soft lighting and book-lined walls—the cozy space even had windows, but they were narrow and set high in the wall. Too high to look out.

A wooden ladder led to a trap door in the ceiling. I scaled the rungs carefully. The door pushed open with ease and I climbed outside.

Being out under the tile-roofed cupola was like standing in an open-air bandstand except for the view. Lights glittered everywhere in the distance. They twinkled from homes all along the surrounding hillsides. They sparkled amidst the city sprawl of Beverly Hills and Hollywood below. On the rise directly opposite where I stood, a pocket of lights was scattered fan-fashion; another spilled like diamonds poured from a dark velvet pouch, invisible in the black of the night.

The abundance of lights was surprising, given that war precautions had probably cut the original numbers in half. *Hold it,*

I told the irksome worrywart side of me. Why fret about how much glitter was right for the Hollywood hills? Tonight was my night on the town. A too-rare time for amusement, perhaps even a little pleasure. I smiled. Besides, how could "Tinsel Town" exist without lights?

A soft, cool breeze tingled my skin and gently ruffled my hair. The sensations were delightful and I was tempted to linger at the railing. But my schedule was tight. I had only enough time to select an outfit and take a quick bath before I had to leave for the restaurant to meet Sam.

One hand clutched a ladder rung and the other balanced the hatch door as I retreated down the ladder, one cautious step at a time. Almost predictably, my foot slipped. Instinctively, the hand steadying the hatch door let go to grip the ladder. The door closed with a loud thunk that rattled my nerves and scattered, like a snowstorm, the papers from the desk below.

If only the roll-top had been pulled shut such a thing wouldn't have happened, I groused, scurrying down to retrieve the documents littering the floor. I rifled the pages, sorting and scanning for content. When I'd met Della, I'd dismissed the notion of her holding down a job. Reordering the piles, I began to realize the enormity of organizing charity functions and my perspective changed.

Task completed, I returned the documents to the desk. An edge of errant paper protruded from the narrow crevice into which the roll top receded. I tugged. I tugged two more times before the roll top complied, closing over the desk. The paper—actually a letter sized envelope—remained lodged in the crack.

"Come here you little rogue," I said, grasping its corner with a pinch.

The paper was cream-colored and felt thick in my hand. My first impression was of penmanship, jerky and scrawled. "Which stack do you belong in?" I began reading to uncover the answer. The subject matter had nothing to do with charity matters. Feeling like a spy, and filled with remorse for invading the Dunns' privacy—yet unable to resist—I quickly read on, the paper shaking in my hand.

My Dear Comrades,

Our fears are confirmed. What I have found here in Neubabelsberg I will lay out in this letter in the hope that you can use the information to come up with a swift and resolute plan of reprisal.

Hitler's ruthless maestro of information and rumor mongering has converted the UFA Studio into an assembly plant for making Nazi propaganda. From what I have seen, I think UFA must be one of the largest and finest studios in the world. Under Goebbels' direction, its fourteen sound stages, twenty-one cutting rooms, and five private theaters are humming with activity, with directors, technicians, and artists working around the clock. Shooting and production schedules have been cut in half, sets are being made to do double duty. The reason? The motion picture is fast becoming Dr. Goebbels chief secret weapon.

First-rate battle films are rolling off the UFA production line. They show relentless Nazis in hard-hitting combat shots and in glorious victory scenes overcoming Allied soldiers. But this is only one genre. Goebbels is loading his arsenal with other films, too—features and documentaries that glorify the Nazi ideals of super-race, devotion to state, hatred for the rest of the world!

You and your people must find a way to turn the weapon against him. Unless something is done, the message will spread out of control like a deadly virus.

What do I suggest? I propose that you hijack the Nazis' own images. Why not draw upon material from UFA newsreels, from captured enemy reports, and from Reichsfilmkammer propaganda films? Take the stolen images and manipulate them in ways that will help obliterate the Nazi mythos by exposing to the American public and its soldiers the real-life horror of Nazi fanaticism. For example, a film clip showing Nazi soldiers smoking American cigarettes with a voice-over explaining that the Camels or Chesterfields being smoked were stolen from dead American soldiers would have tremendous impact. Or, why not incorporate, somewhere, speeded-up goose steppers marching in time to a jaunty dance hall melody? What a boost to morale it would be seeing mighty Nazi storm troopers made to look like imbeciles!

Actual enemy footage incorporated into feature films or training films has terrific potential. But I would caution you as well. Do not allow the images to be distorted in a way that will fail to prepare American soldiers being sent into battle. They must know that the Nazi is vicious, skillful, and dedicated. An opponent as deadly as a cobra.

These observations and thoughts are submitted for your consideration. I am confident you will find a way to build on them and apply them with the effectiveness you are known for. Given the situation as I have found it, I implore you: move swiftly with a counter-strategy, whatever it may be.

As always, I am at your disposal.

The writing sprawled across both sides of the sheet, and the ink on the bottom of the back page was smudged, as though it had been splashed with water. I strained to read what remained. From the looks of it, the obliterated portion had included the date, some additional lines including what appeared to be "Cairo," and a signature.

The paper continued to tremble in my hand as I stared wide-eyed, uncertain what to do next. Hitler! Goebbels! Seeing the enemy names and the details of what they were doing to promote their heinous belief in German superiority and Germany's right to rule the world curdled my stomach. I placed a shaky hand over my middle and took several deep breaths.

So much for being appalled with myself for spying on the Dunns. They were *real* spies.

The revelation about my hosts shocked me only momentarily. I'd suspected them of being involved in intelligence work almost from when we'd first met. Still, the cloak-and-dagger memo maintained its overwhelming hold on me.

The dispatch covered a matter important to the outcome of the war. Its author intended that the intelligence on UFA, as well as his ideas, be used in combating Nazi propaganda. What had the Dunns actually done with the information, I wondered. Had they passed it on up the line, or were they the ones actually responsible for coming up with a motion picture counter-strategy like the missive said should be developed?

A curse on Gunnar. Why hadn't he leveled with me about his sister? If she was his sister.

A cold chill gripped me. There were no names mentioned in the salutation. I'd been assuming, because of where I'd found it, that the memo had been sent to the Dunns, that they were intelligence agents involved on our side. But "Comrades" could be anyone. What if the letter was in the Dunns' possession because they'd intercepted it from the loyal American it was actually intended for? What if they were spies for the enemy?

I shook my head. A grotesque idea.

Cairo. The Dunns had recently been to Cairo. I'd seen the tickets—2nd priority—on the table downstairs when I'd first arrived. Enemy spies, I assured my suspicious side, weren't issued such tickets.

My date with Sam was closing in. I needed to make some decisions. The first one was obvious. There was no ready way to unravel the complexities of what I'd found, particularly since the Dunns were away. I would continue the evening as planned and put my thinking cap on again later.

But what to do with the memo? Keep it? Then where would I put it for safekeeping? Whoever it belonged to would notice it missing sooner or later. What if they traced it to me? My note-nabbing might not be appreciated. I could be in danger. Well, then…what if I took it and handed it off to someone official? Uh-uh. Without understanding who the memo belonged to and what was behind it, best to leave it where I'd found it, for now.

I carefully jimmied the paper into the crack as I'd found it, then gingerly opened the roll-top, leaving only the tiniest tip possible showing. A fair compromise, I concluded. It was where

I could readily come upon it again. It was also where anyone else truly interested could find it as well. Maybe.

I bounded down the spiral stairs. A glance at my watch told me that a long soak in the tub was out—a quick shower was more like it. I considered skipping the visit to Della's closet altogether, but a vision of the Spartan interior of the wardrobe in my room spurred me on.

The long racks on either side and in front of me were chock-full. Without Della's guidance I hardly knew where to begin, but after some frenzied rummaging, I came upon a crepe dress in a heavenly shade of purple. Aubergine. The color I'd been told brought out the green in my eyes. Best of all, it wouldn't conflict with the marmalade hue of my hair.

It took some jiggling to get the hanger's hook off the pole. Then, because the dress was packed in so tightly, I had to pull a few times before it wrenched free of the remaining garments. On the final tug, I heard the barely distinguishable *plink* of a button hitting the hardwood floor.

I held the dress aloft, giving it a quick once over. It was in good shape; no missing buttons. In fact, the dress had no buttons at all. It zippered in the back.

I looked at the rack. In extricating the aubergine dress, I'd dragged out the sleeve of the black and white print dress that had been next to it. The sleeve rested at a peculiar angle against the packed rack of clothing making it impossible to overlook. H-E-DOUBLE TOOTHPICKS! A button was missing from its white piqué cuff.

My PK, pastor's kid, conscience kicked in. A proper button was difficult to come by in normal times, but with the shortages these days, finding a replacement would be impossible.

In search of the button, I got down on my knees. Briskly, I shoved a path through the fabric jungle, sweeping the floor with my hands as I went. How curious. There it was, at rest in an ever so slight sliver of light.

It took some maneuvering, but I wedged my way to the rear of the closet. The light was coming through a fissure in the paneled wall. There was enough space between the wall and clothes to stand. The fissure, I discovered, was actually a discreet doorway that had been left ajar. Curling my fingers along the panel's edge, I slowly pried it open.

Peering in, I saw a roughed-in space about the same size as Della's walk-in closet. The area would have been ideal for storage, yet it appeared completely empty.

A barren bulb had been left on. In its glare, I recognized another concealed doorway in the wall to my left. It was secured with a padlock. From its location, I surmised the locked panel doorway led to an interior passageway. A shiver skittered up my spine as I envisioned a labyrinth of dark cobwebbed tunnels and the creepy figures that might exist beyond.

Moving quickly to stem the germination of additional gruesome thoughts, I began a situation assessment.

Grand older homes frequently had secret passageways. In this house, for instance, the library downstairs had a bar that swung around to the inside of the wall. And then there were the floorboards in the dining room alcove that parted with the turn of a "gizmo" to reveal or conceal a sunken table. So, why get all worked up about a hidden passageway off the master bedroom?

But why the padlock?

I took a step inside. Immediately, my foot caught. Metal crashed against the floor. I'd tumbled a stack of film cans. My pulse pounding wildly in my ears, I picked one up. From its weight, I knew a reel was housed inside.

The label was in German, but I didn't need an interpreter to read *UFA Studio*.

The thin round can felt suddenly like a hot potato. I was holding something that belonged to the enemy. Something that an enemy had held in his hands. In reflex, I nearly let the tin drop.

Rallying, I dropped to my knees. I began righting the cans, thoughts about the Dunns chasing through my mind. They worked for intelligence, no doubt about it now. But what was this about? What were the classified films doing on the Dunns' premises?

There were five cans in all. What was this? The bottom tins had toppled atop a large white envelope. For the second time within a quarter of an hour, I stuck my nose into something private. Except this time there was no correspondence, merely a 5x7 glossy. But what an image. Brody with a woman—not his wife. Holding the picture beneath the bare light bulb, I studied it. The woman was likely connected to the blackmail plot, possibly Brody's murder. But who was she? Why was the photo here?

I returned the photograph to the envelope, the hairs at the back of my neck standing on end. Brody had been distracted by a similar envelope at the meeting I'd attended at MGM, hours before his death. The Cairo note. The UFA films. This photo. Rask simply had to take me into his confidence. He valued my perceptions, but didn't he understand I could help him more than just by keeping alert for suspicious activity? I was scheduled to meet with him in his studio tomorrow. What better opportunity could there be to straighten him out?

With care, I set the final can on top of the stack, and retreated briskly to my room, a charge of adrenaline propelling me.

◇◇◇

My shower was replaced by a quick bird bath. Nonetheless I felt refreshed and smelled of strawberries from the soap. Della's aubergine dress fit perfectly and looked just fine with my standard black patent leather heels. Silk stockings would have been a nice touch, but were a luxury few could afford or find these days. Bare legs with no make up would have to do.

A parting glance in the mirror reflected a complexion aglow with the rush of getting ready and the anticipation of romance in the evening ahead. The high coloring might also have been due to the pressure of getting to the restaurant on time. I really was running late now.

◇◇◇

Ilka and Bela were coming down the covered walkway as I was making my dash out to the Packard. They walked slowly, arm-in-arm with a woman dressed in a fur coat, scarf, and huge dark glasses.

Sunglasses at night! Wouldn't you know. They were bringing home an actress on the night I was going out.

Ilka and Bela were on either side of the actress as we closed in on one another. The lamps along the walkway had been turned on, but were so sparsely arranged it was difficult to see much. From their pace and the protective manner of Ilka and Bela, I'd already surmised the woman was elderly. And, though the dimness and her disguise successfully hid whether she was anyone famous, I saw enough to confirm that indeed her face was deeply lined with age. Ahhh. Ilka had said she was going to a palm-reading fundraiser tonight. They'd brought home a movie queen from the past, perhaps a silent film star. Likely in need of a private intensive palm reading. Maybe an herbal treatment of some sort.

"Ilka, Bela," I called. "Hi!"

The greeting startled the group. They'd been concentrating their attention on chatting and navigating the walkway. Ilka's mouth hung open and Bella's eyes remained locked in the wide surprise I remembered from *Dracula* when Professor Van Helsing, supposedly succumbing to Dracula's hypnotic spell, suddenly shows a crucifix and drives the vampire away. The elder woman, her lips coated in a red lipstick vivid even in the semi-dark, twisted them nervously.

What had they expected? A tabloid photographer?

The actress ducked her head as I approached, getting closer.

Ilka was first to recover. She stepped so that the actress was blocked almost completely from my view. "Pucci, *édesem*. On your way out?" The hopeful tone in her voice suggested she'd be disappointed if I wasn't.

"Uh-huh. I have a date."

"This is wonderful. You look very nice." She paused.

"Yes, verr-ry nice," Bela purred. "Perhaps, Ilka, you must look in your herbs for a branch of volfsbane to give our Pooo-chi. For protection."

I laughed. Wolfsbane was a poisonous herb Professor Van Helsing found could be used to stop wolves. Another critical discovery: it was effective for vampire protection.

Ilka's tinkly laugh was almost an afterthought. "Really, Uncle! What time can we expect your return, Pucci?"

"Not sure exactly." I grinned suggestively. "Late, I hope."

Ilka and Bela chortled politely; their guest remained silent.

It didn't strike me as rude that they didn't rush to introduce her—many stars were fanatics about their privacy after all. Maybe they'd fill me in later.

"I better get a move on," I said, taking a couple of backward steps. "By the way, Gunnar's not home. Had to go back to the studio."

"Too bad."

Coupled with the relief showing in Ilka's face, the regretful reply didn't ring true. I noted that her hair was down tonight. She patted the sweep of platinum and grinned. "Pucci, I got the part."

"Great news!" I exclaimed. "Congratulations."

Ilka was beaming now and so was I.

"I should hear tomorrow where the shooting will take place. I will let you know. Perhaps you can stop by."

I agreed to try.

As I stole off into the dark, I thought I heard Ilka say in an undertone to her companions, "Poisons. Maybe this not something we should joke about…"

Getting into the Packard, I was still trying to interpret what I heard when the sound of tires spinning through scattered loose gravel grabbed my attention. Now what? *Celebrity news hounds?*

Chapter Twelve

Benedict Canyon to Sunset Boulevard to Beverly. Sam's directions had been a breeze up until now. The intersection where Sunset met Beverly was crammed with cars and people. I sat waiting for a break, hoping Sam wasn't the impatient type.

I glanced at the sights. The Garden of Allah. The name conjured up Moroccan architecture, Aladdin and his lamp, belly dancers and someone swooping in on a magic carpet. Yet the style replicated the white stucco and red tile so typical of the Hollywood area. Not that I would term anything else about the place before me "typical." A grand two-story main building and a maze of one- and two-story private bungalows dominated lush grounds that included colored spotlights angled to show off select buildings and a smattering of palm trees. I'd heard about the complex, a former estate of Alla Nazimova, now a mix of apartments and hotel rooms favored by members of the literary and intellectual film communities. F. Scott Fitzgerald, Dorothy Parker, Robert Benchley, and Orson Welles were known to stop by; Greta Garbo and Errol Flynn dashed in for drinks or a meal now and again. I zoomed in on the group milling about near the canopied main entrance, hoping to at least spot a celebrity. Bad luck.

Traffic had begun moving again. Slowly. What I wouldn't give to trade the Packard for Aladdin's magic flying carpet.

Back at the Dunns', when I'd been up in the tower looking down on Hollywood, the lights had seemed bountiful. Street

level was different. There was an overall sense the lighting had
been dimmed. But what I was observing also made hogwash
out of D.B.'s claim the other evening that there'd been a drop
in tourism since the start of the war. The sidewalks were teem-
ing, a stream of revelers filing nonstop through the crosswalk,
completely oblivious to the backup of cars waiting to cross.
What was going on? I scanned the crowd. Lots of uniforms, but
plenty were dressed to the nines in evening attire, too. A motion
picture premiere, perhaps?

I strained to see if there was a theater letting out nearby. I
shrugged. Who knew? Maybe a new club or restaurant.

I crept past the Trocadero Restaurant, LaRue's Bar, and the
El Morocco before the pace finally picked up. At the next intersection, I veered the Packard down a side street, across Santa
Monica Boulevard and, a few blocks and turns later, I was in an
industrial pocket of small office buildings and warehouses. The
area was deserted and a little seedy—quite a comedown from
the buzz and glitz I'd just passed through.

Thinking maybe I'd taken a wrong turn somewhere, I pulled
over to the curb, parked under a street lamp. In the dim light,
I strained to read the directions Sam had written out for me.
There would be no mainstream Hollywood night life for me,
I discovered. I was dead on course and within seconds of the
restaurant Sam had selected.

To my further surprise and dismay, the "street" I was looking
for was really an alley. I hesitated at its entrance. The passage was
pitch black except for a well lit building about three-quarters
of the way down the block. A number of cars were parked in
front and a prominent sign atop—in English but with Chinese
characters stacked to one side—confirmed I'd reached the
designated meeting point. MAY Lee's. I locked the passenger
door and maneuvered the Packard slowly down the alleyway to
a vacant slot in front. Bamboo shades covered the large front
windows, but escaping light and moving shadows assured me
that the restaurant was open. I got out and stepped lively to the
entrance.

A tug on the heavy glass door released a blast of warm, oily, food-laden air. A small reception area inside was deserted. I hovered at the cash register, waiting for the hostess and scanning the tables for a sign of Sam.

I felt ridiculous in Della's lovely aubergine frock and my open-toe patent leather heels. Clearly, May Lee's was a restaurant frequented by workers from the neighborhood businesses who'd come direct from their jobs. It was a male crowd for the most part, but even the two women seated at a small table off to one side were clad in coveralls, their heads wrapped in bandannas.

Compounding my discomfort, rather than the white table-cloths and candle glow I'd been anticipating, the tables were laminated plastic, the room harshly lit. All around me the red-tasseled, pink, green and white Chinese lanterns hanging from the ceiling looked as if they'd seen better days. Stained red carpet covered the floor.

There was a bright side. The food must be excellent. Only one of the booths along the walls was vacant and the tables in the center of the room were all occupied as well.

Noticing four men in a window booth staring at me, I blushed. I fidgeted under their gaze until a sudden spray of noise and smells diverted their attention. A diminutive Chinese woman, carrying a tray laden with dishes of steaming food, had pushed through the swinging doors along the wall down from where I stood. I caught a glimpse of kitchen chaos as the doors bounced to a close behind her.

At first glance, the young woman looked ill-prepared to tote such an enormous load. Not only was she a wisp, but she wore a high-necked turquoise brocade dress that was floor length, form-fitting and, by all appearances, restrictive. A hip-high slit and well-toned arms partly made up for the tightness of her costume and slim frame.

I watched the tray glide across the room as though on a conveyor belt to the window booth. The men clearly delighted in the young woman's presence, and there was a lot of friendly bantering while dish after dish was served. As a sort of finale, the waitress slid a platterful of something into a large bowl of broth. Loud crackling and a burst of steam—like a basket of French fries hitting a vat of hot oil—followed.

"Sizzling rice soup," a voice whispered in my ear, as heavy hands pressed down on my shoulders.

"Sam!" I exclaimed, whisking around, hand at my heart. "You scared the wits out of me."

Standing there, an impish grin on his face, silky spikes of dark umber hair veiling his forehead, Sam looked every inch the altar boy. And devilish prankster. Well, why not? He'd pulled one over on me. Appeared out of thin air, quiet as a mouse. I hadn't even noticed the door opening. How had he done it?

Truth was, I didn't care. I was disappointed with the place, uncomfortable in my dress, and uninterested in playing childish games.

Sam, correctly sensing I'd found nothing amusing about his sneak attack, adjusted his glasses and tried getting his mischievous grin under control. He wasn't completely successful. The corners of his mouth remained curled upwards.

"Sorry," he said.

The apology seemed insincere, his behavior odd, but I gave him the benefit of the doubt. Maybe I was being too peevish. The real point in coming to May Lee's was to discuss remaking parts of the WASP film, right?

I smiled weakly. "It's okay. Rough afternoon. I'm a little jumpy."

Sam started to ask about what happened, but the young Chinese woman was descending upon us in a flurry of short, quick steps. Her head inclined slightly, she greeted us with "I May Lee," reached under the counter that held the cash register, grabbed two menus, then gestured for us to follow. A ponytail so long it nearly reached her buttocks swept her back like a pendulum as she shuffled briskly ahead.

Sam steered me by the elbow, the gesture grating on my self-reliant nature. The behavior seemed inbred in him; he'd directed me in this manner before. Well, not tonight. I wrenched my elbow from his grasp.

May Lee led us toward the vacant booth. A few heads bobbed up as we navigated past.

"I should have told you to dress casually," Sam whispered.

Yes, you should have.

"But you look so lovely in purple, I'm glad I didn't."

Hmmm. "Thank you," I said coolly as we slid into the booth.

"Two beers and pot stickers," Sam said to May Lee, tucking in opposite me.

I caught Sam's eye. "Have you been here before?"

"No. I live nearby but I'm not comfortable…"

His appearance projected discomfort, indeed. Hunched forward on the table, arms crossed, brow furrowed, he sat mute, totally at a loss for the right words to complete the sentence.

Geez. The question hadn't seemed complicated to me.

"What were you saying about being uncomfortable?"

"Uh…It's been a while since I've eaten at a Chinese restaurant. I mean, at any restaurant. Uh, I don't like to eat out alone."

Big deal. Who did? Solo restaurant stints were part of the routine for a ferry pilot constantly on the go, but my preference was otherwise. My sister pilots felt the same. But curiously I'd always associated the quirk with women.

Sam changed the subject. "You had a bad afternoon. What happened?"

I spent a moment considering the possible replies. How about: Roland Novara won't listen to me because I'm a woman. Or: Frankie's plane was sabotaged and I don't know what's being done to find the person who did it, nor can I ask anyone about it. Maybe: I found a hush-hush memo and enemy film stashed in the house where I'm staying.

Finally, I turned to the only subject I felt free to talk about.

"They're saying now that Derrick Brody was murdered." I sighed heavily. "To think we were with him just hours before it happened. He seemed like a decent man. Who would do such a thing? I don't believe for a moment it was Russell Chalmers, do you?"

Sam's elbows slid from the table and he sat up straight. "Chalmers? Where'd you hear that? The papers said foul play, but I didn't read anything about him."

I'd forgotten that the news of Chalmers being brought in for questioning wasn't public knowledge yet. Gus had told me about it. Since he hadn't asked me to keep the information secret, I went ahead and shared the scuttlebutt about investigators on the scene making an incriminating discovery.

Sam listened attentively, keeping his gaze on me, but he seemed to be adjusting his socks while I talked. He was in that position—chin jutted forward over the tabletop, hands fumbling somewhere near the floor—when our appetizer and drinks appeared.

While May Lee arranged the glasses and two bottles of beer on top of the table, I leaned back and took a discreet look underneath. Sam had not been adjusting his socks. He was scratching his legs. Had something bit him? Did he have a rash? He'd been sick.

Sam, having satisfied his itch, sat up and took a long pull of beer, then tugged the bottle from his mouth with a jerk and, holding it out mid-air, waited for a toast.

I decided to ignore the rude behavior, attributing the sudden urge to scratch, as well as the parched mouth, to a case of jitters over our date. I took my sweet time, however, pouring my beer into my glass. Bad manners were bad manners. A grown man ought to have a better grip.

"To Brody," we said simultaneously.

Sam took another long swallow, while I took a sip. Beer wasn't a favorite, but it was either that or tea—an even less festive choice.

Sam obviously was satisfied. At the moment he was eying the bottom of his nearly drained bottle.

May Lee returned. "Take you order?"

Sam did the honors. He requested several dishes. It might have been a while since Sam had eaten at a Chinese restaurant, but he hadn't lost his familiarity with favored dishes.

Sam used chopsticks to dip a pot sticker into the soy sauce, quite a feat given its slippery nature. He held the dumpling in a chopsticks vise midway to his mouth as he brought up his visit to the hospital and my mention that Frankie had murmured a few sounds.

"What'd she say?"

Jabbing one of the appetizers with my fork, I slid it around in the soy sauce pool on my plate. "The sounds were really garbled, more a soft moaning, than anything. She seemed to be trying to form words, but nothing made sense. I wonder... Do you suppose if I could repeat the sounds to her, they might bring her back again?"

The idea excited me. I looked at Sam, but he was staring at the wall behind me. His mind was elsewhere.

"Sam?"

He didn't answer. Instead, he pushed his plate away and buried his face in his hands.

After a decent interval, I cleared my throat.

Sam pulled his hands away. "Wha...Oh, sorry. I was remembering the accident."

I'd forgotten he talked with Frankie shortly before the accident. Could he have seen something? Someone? With a little prompting, might what he saw come back?

I sipped my beer. "I heard maybe it wasn't an accident. Did you notice anything unusual? Was Frankie worried about anything? It's important you try to remember. Someone could have tampered with her plane."

Sam scratched the crook of his arm. "Who-o-o told you?"

"No one told me," I answered quickly. "It's a rumor I heard."

"I didn't know Frankie would be hur—hurr- hurt." Sam's eyes welled up and I reached across the table to pat his arm, stop the nervous scratching. Sam was genuinely broken up about Frankie. Was there more to their relationship than friendship?

He'd stopped scratching. I rubbed his forearm. "It's okay. It was just something I heard. Scuttlebutt."

Our main courses, including Sam's beer, were delivered. I pulled back my hand. Sam swigged from the fresh bottle.

The array of food was unlike anything I'd seen or smelled before. There were paper-thin pancakes, sauces, scallions, peanuts, peas, mushrooms and bamboo shoots. Everything but the kitchen sink, though one could speculate some items had backed up through a drain somewhere, by the look of them.

Sam loaded his plate with a spoonful of this and a spoonful of that, while I approached with caution. The rice looked safe so I scooped a hefty portion from the bowl only to discover it was so sticky I had to knock the clump free with a discreet shove of my finger. To top it, I spooned on a small serving of the chicken, peanut, and pea dish.

Sam clamped a scallop with his chopsticks, but didn't lift it off his plate. "In our meeting with Novara you didn't seem so keen on reshooting the target towing sequence. Is that why? You're afraid what happened to Frankie might happen to you?"

For a millisecond I considered telling him the truth. But, much as I wanted Sam to understand the risk I was up against, I couldn't divulge the dark secret Max had entrusted to me. Still, I didn't want him to think I was a sissy or not capable of performing the maneuver.

"Miss Cochran still hasn't given her blessing."

Sam looked disappointed.

My ego got the best of me. "She's bound to say yes. Meantime, we can shoot the ferrying sequence. I was approved to fly the P-51."

The grand announcement was out, now I was committed. I could hope the saboteur would be caught before the time slot I'd reserved for showing off the P-51. I glanced at my watch: approximately forty hours from now.

Sam snapped to life. "Great! When?"

The food on the table was all but forgotten as I filled him in on the arrangements that had been made for Saturday at March Field. A current of excitement ran between us as we automatically began plotting out the details of how the segment should unfold for the shoot. A screenplay, Sam informed me as we jotted down notes and ideas on a spare paper placemat, was actually a series of directives—a one-of-a-kind manual for the director and actors to follow as they transposed the script to the screen.

A boon to my apprenticeship, there was a format to follow. An added bonus—the structure wasn't as foreign as I would have expected. I'd used a similar process in composing brochures at Midland.

After sketching the whole thing out in more detail on yet another fresh mat—including rough scene description, music and voice-over direction—we relaxed against our respective benches, satisfied we'd covered most of the particulars.

"Congratulations are in order." Sam tipped his bottle in my direction. "We just completed writing our first scene together."

The milestone had an interesting ring. We chinked glass to bottle, then I took a sip of beer as Sam took another serious slug.

Novara had charged us with organizing "the works," so, though not ordinarily his duty, Sam promised that first thing in the morning he'd contact the person responsible for getting a film crew scheduled for the shoot. For my part, I agreed to finalize arrangements with the March Field staff.

Sam had a trace of a smile on his lips and a look of admiration in his eyes. "You're quite a woman, Pucci. I'm impressed."

I felt the blood rush to my cheeks under his gaze. Not sure how to respond to the compliment, but hoping for more, I lowered my eyes, fixing them on the peas and peanuts dotting the plate before me.

"I'm serious," he added softly. "You chased after that soldier who dropped the tubing from the catwalk." He shook his head, smiling. "That was something. Then you finagled an advanced fighter for this film. Not many men could have pulled that off. You're attractive, smart, capable…Much more so than I would have expected."

The attention and intensity of his gaze were getting to me. I squirmed. The moment I'd hoped for earlier this evening was here, but now I was unsure about encouraging his advances. Temporizing, I asked Sam to tell me about his childhood. He signaled May Lee for another beer—I would have declined the offer *if* he'd thought to ask me—then began his story.

Sam, like me, was an only child. His father died when he was a boy, and his mother, a seamstress, also deceased as of a year ago, had to work long hours to support the two of them. Her profession frequently brought her to the movie studios where she created and fitted costumes for the stars. As there was no one to keep an eye on Sam when he wasn't in school, many times she brought him along. To amuse himself while she sewed, he read or made up stories and wrote them down.

In high school, Sam won an academic scholarship to the University of California, Los Angeles campus, where he decided to be a writer. Since he'd made a number of friends at the studios where his mother worked, he was able to get a research job at MGM that eventually led to writing screenplays. It was a way to make a living doing what he loved, until he could afford to write at "a more literary level."

Sam spoke freely about the past—the latest beer may have helped—and I enjoyed listening. We shared some common experiences and interests conceived from our lonely childhoods and a love of reading and writing. I felt some of my ambivalence give way.

"Enough about me," Sam said turning his attention back to the dishes on the table. "Time for you to learn how to put together a serving of *Musée* Pork."

I wasn't hungry anymore and, of the platters of food on the table, that dish was the least appetizing of the lot. A gruesome mound of unidentifiable items, it contained numerous spindly things Sam said were mushrooms, but which I was convinced were really slimy slugs and tiny octopi.

Still, like the good soldier I was trying hard to be, I went along, first laying a pancake on my plate, then smearing it with dark plum sauce, then adding a sprinkling of scallions and, finally, scooping on a small pile of the jumbled dish. The idea was to flip in the two sides, tuck the ends to the center, and make a kind of burrito of the whole mess. Wouldn't you know! My first bite dribbled and a splash of plum sauce landed on the bodice of Della's dress. Not only that, the innards of my "meal pod" tasted cold, oniony and oily.

Sam, contrite over the stain on my bosom and my now downcast spirit, offered to pay for cleaning the dress.

"The color blends," I said graciously. But my mood was definitely down. In a moment of pique, I decided to test Sam again. "Say, do you like to fly? I heard Frankie took someone up with her the day before she crashed. The someone was likely from your film crew. Was it you?"

Behind the steel rims, the puppy dog eyes blinked. "Nooo…"

May Lee chose that moment to plop several cartons for leftovers on the table. I wasn't the least bit interested in lugging even one of them home.

"Dessert?" May Lee queried.

Sam turned to me. "We still need to come up with a plan for incorporating those other ideas, right?"

He was talking about the scenarios I'd proposed to replace the frivolous scenes that made up a good portion of the current version of *Sky Belles*. Testimonials, interviews, charts of facts and figures depicting the contributions we'd made to the war effort. Brody had agreed to the ideas in principle, but it was our responsibility to see that they were carried out. No small task. Each concept needed to be treated individually. That meant—while we'd completed a detailed outline for the ferrying segment—we still needed to hammer out similar summaries for each of the other proposed scenes.

Sam smiled and added, "How about going to my place for dessert and at least getting started?"

I checked my watch. It wasn't that late and I wanted to have a rough shooting script and schedule in front of Novara. Besides, my gut was telling me Sam knew more about what happened to Frankie than he was letting on. Strike while the iron is hot.

"Great, let's do it."

Holding out a wad of cash, Sam said, "May Lee, would you please pack up a box of –"

Not fathoming a word that followed, I watched May Lee.

After she left, Sam said, "Guess I haven't been such a good dinner companion, have I?"

His eyes were doleful, his hair disheveled, and, for some inexplicable reason of the heart, my attitude toward him softened. Maybe it had to do with "the something vital" he might know about Frankie.

I shrugged. "Guess we're both carrying around some heavy baggage at the moment."

Sam looked at me the way people look at you when you say something they didn't think you could possibly know. Then his face brightened. "Let's get going."

◇◇◇

Sam lived only a few minutes from May Lee's in a neighborhood that was neat and quiet. Many of the modest bungalows we passed driving along the tree-lined streets were already dark. In others, pulled shades reflected a coppery glow of silhouettes of family life. At Sam's instruction, I pulled the Packard to the curb.

The carry-out boxes had been propped between us on the drive over. I eyeballed the seat for seepage as we divvied them up for transport inside. It was a relief to find none.

The top was up and the smells of whatever we'd eaten were so pungent they'd permeated the car's interior. I left the driver's side window open a crack. I cringed thinking what the stuff must be doing to our insides.

Sam lived in a tiny Spanish-style bungalow. Painted light yellow with white trim, it had arched lead-paned windows and a tile roof. A porch light glowed softly, illuminating the front of the house lined with shrubs. Chest-high rosebushes bordered the sidewalk leading to the front entrance. We followed the path, the intense perfume of the roses overtaking even the cooked cabbage odor of the leftovers we carried.

The living room was to the left, directly off the entry. Distinctively decorated in sparse, modern furnishings, it was not how I would have envisioned Sam's taste. The room's most prominent piece was an L-shaped red velvet couch in a tubular aluminum frame. It faced away from us, in the direction of a fireplace set in the stucco wall. A glass-topped brushed metal coffee table was positioned in front of the sofa. The pieces sat atop an area rug composed of dark geometric patterns. Two chromium-plated pole lamps with pleated shades were positioned on either end of the sofa.

"*Bauhaus*," Sam said, a sweep of his arm indicating he was referring to the furniture.

One of the pole lamps had been left on. Sam turned a dimmer device, softening its glow, then walked to the fireplace. Perching the cartons temporarily on the nearby built-in bookcase, he began stacking logs and kindling on the grate while explaining that Bauhaus was the school of design behind the clean-lined modernist furniture. He confided that he'd gotten the hand-crafted pieces "for a song" at the house sale of a bachelor actor who'd joined the Marines and was being shipped overseas.

While Sam looked pleased as Punch with the bargain, I couldn't help wondering if anyone else had even shown up for the sale. The pieces really looked uninviting.

"Go ahead. Have a seat. Get comfortable," Sam said, lighting a match.

I dropped onto the couch and was pleasantly surprised. The velvet cushions were indeed comfy. Settling into the crook of the L, I felt the urge to kick off my shoes and put my feet up. I resisted. Sam's last moments with Frankie were foremost on my mind. I was determined to stay alert.

A dark marble statue of a Samurai warrior, sword drawn, rested on the coffee table. Across the room, a flame leaped in the hearth as the kindling caught.

The bookcases on either side of the fireplace were flanked by windows. I observed the books, bric-a-brac, and Philco radio on the shelves while Sam gathered the cartons. To his right was a small dining area that was actually an extension of the living room. At the center of a glass top table sat a typewriter; next to the typewriter, a silvery gooseneck lamp. Portions of the dining table's glass surface not covered by the papers strewn across its surface gleamed in the light from an overhead chandelier. The table's aluminum cylinder design was repeated in the four Bauhaus chairs surrounding it. The seats and backs of the chairs were black leather.

"Sorry for the mess," he said, passing through the dining area, dimming the chandelier. "My home office."

From my cozy corner of the couch, I watched Sam disappear behind a curtain of silvery beads, then took another look around. Velvet floor-to-ceiling drapes mounted across one wall's center were a curious feature. It was an interior wall; there was no window. Had they been hung to cover a piece of artwork? I gauged the width of the wall. Maybe. But it was also possible that—given the thickness of the wall—the drapes covered a recessed nook.

I heard running water and the clink of dishes in the kitchen behind the curtain of beads. My visual survey flipped back to the typewriter on the table. A piece of paper sticking out suggested Sam had been called away, midsentence. What had he been working on?

"People deserve their privacy," the ingrained pesky voice leftover from my rigid PK upbringing chided. *"You've done enough snooping for one day."*

At the table, I saw that Sam had been staring at the proverbial blank page. A nearby folder beckoned. Before the censorious voice could tickle my scruples again, I flipped it open.

This was my evening for black and white glossies. Only these weren't of individuals. They were fuzzy aerial shots of trees and possibly a river. Squinting in the dim light, I tried to understand what I was seeing.

A sudden flourish of rattling beads at my back made me jump. I managed to hang on to the photographs, barely.

Sam was at my side, holding a large tray. He nodded at the images. "Stock footage for an upcoming shoot."

"Ah," I said my cheeks hot.

It was an occasion the PK voice in me would be reveling in for months. It couldn't wait. "*You should have listened,*" it chimed in that grating sing-songy tone I hated. "*How will you get him to tell you about Frankie? There's no way he's going to trust you now.*"

Sam continued with the tray to the coffee table. The platter held a Japanese tea service and a half dozen or so miniature custard tarts. Set in strawberry-pink pleated paper cups, the Chinese dessert looked festive, indeed.

Now if only I could recapture the conviviality we'd built up to in our last moments at May Lee's.

The fire had waned while Sam was in the kitchen. I watched while he completed a vigorous pumping of the bellows to fan the fingers of flame. He'd removed his tweed jacket and his shirt revealed the kind of shoulders I liked. Broad, tapering into a narrow waist above long legs.

Time to prove the pesky voice wrong. I walked toward the fireplace, determined to find a way to get him to open up. But how?

I needn't have worried.

He turned from the hearth and reached for the radio. He twisted the knob. The smoky, world-weary voice of Marlene Dietrich crooning *Falling in Love Again* filled the softly lit room.

Sam came toward me. The flickering fire cast his angular face in a flattering glow of shadows and golden light. "Dance?"

He folded me into his arms, holding me so close I felt his heart thumping against mine. We moved slowly, shuffling in a small circle near the fireplace to Dietrich's gravelly lyrics. "Men cluster to me like moths around a flame…"

Sam's lips brushed that most sensitive nook of my neck. I stiffened, unsure of what was coming next. I would never have guessed.

"You don't have to snoop," he whispered in my ear. "I'll tell you everything."

Whether the goose bumps that rose along my arms and shoulders were from the warmth of his breath or from the bluntness of his words, I would never know.

Sam's body tensed and he froze, his grip tightening on my back, digging in so tight it hurt.

"What?" I looked up. My back was to the fireplace. Sam was gaping at something—or someone—over my shoulder. Flames from the hearth danced in the lenses of his steel frames, but the terror behind them in his eyes was unmistakable.

"What is it?" I repeated, squirming to break free of his grasp.

Abruptly, Sam snapped away from me as if a bucket of ice water had been tossed on us. I whirled. A flash of movement outside the window, then darkness. I spun back to face Sam.

"Was someone out there, Sam? Speak to me!"

His expression was dazed. He stood pop-eyed, tongue-tied.

A frenzied rendition of *It Don't Mean a Thing* blared in the background. I caught *if it ain't got that swing* and wanted to swing my fist, knock a reply from Sam's mouth. It'd been a horrendous day, a horrendous couple of days. Now this.

Well, I wouldn't use my fist, but I had to snap him out of it, get some answers.

"I know Frankie took you on a joy ride," I said, going for broke. "She's paying a terrible price. Her career is on the line, maybe even her life. Who sabotaged her plane? The person at the window? *You?*"

Sam looked stunned, then devastated. "Me? No!" He looked away.

"Sam?"

He faced me again. A tear rained from under the steel rims. "I love Frankie. I'm so sorry…"

He wiped the tear and his demeanor changed again. His hand clutched his mouth as though he were about to throw up or scream. He began pacing in front of the fireplace.

"Sam, what is it?" I pleaded.

He continued to pace in silence.

I shouted, "Sam Lorenz, stop that this minute."

He stopped…and moved toward me like a zombie. "Get away from me. Get away."

Before I could react, he grabbed my forearm. Gripping it with superhuman strength I would never have guessed he had in him, he dragged me around the sofa toward the front door. I pretended to trip. Still he pulled me along. With his free hand, he turned the doorknob and heaved the wooden door inward. I struggled to break free, but he held me close and hard.

Outside, he hurled me off the stoop onto the sidewalk as though I was nothing more than a rag doll.

My foot twisted off the sidewalk's edge, thrusting me into mortal combat with the rose hedge. The encounter nearly cost several marauding bushes their lives. My arms flailed at canes, leaves, and thorns, battering them with a wrath they would never forget. Men! First Gunnar, now Sam.

A cold rage filled me. Without so much as a backward glance, I stomped down the walkway, rummaging my pockets for the keys. Tears blurred the journey into watery light and shadow. I slammed the car door. The lingering smell of Chinese food melded with the sweet perfume of crushed rose petals that clung to my hair and clothing. The combination had a sudden sickening impact. My stomach heaved. I got the door open in the nick of time. Dinner with Sam Lorenz spewed out with a vengeance, hitting the pavement with a grotesque splat.

I drove home knotted with confusion and anger. I hated Sam for whatever was ailing him, and I hated myself more. Why did I have to be so nosey? Go prying into his things? Because I thought I was clever enough to single-handedly solve the mystery of the sabotage attempt, that's why. Ha.

Why had I compromised myself? All evening—maybe since I met him—I'd been making excuses for Sam's behavior toward me. Set aside my personal instincts, held back my opinions. Why?

To prove that with enough stubborn determination I could get my way? That I could use Sam's know-how to create the film Miss C wanted? Because I wanted to have a little fling? Because his looks were out of the ordinary? Because his view of women seemed more objective than most men's?

Well, he was different from other men all right. He was *different*, period!

I brooded the entire way back to the Dunns', vowing to listen to the little voice next time.

◇◇◇

In my room back at the Dunns', things brightened. My jade-green satin pajamas awaited me, neatly folded, atop my pillow. A sprig of white jasmine rested across them.

Chapter Thirteen

The sight of roses on the ledge of Gus' newsstand made my stomach lurch.

Huge blossoms in a gorgeous shade of peach—on another day they would have sent me. This morning, they brought to mind my disastrous evening with Sam Lorenz.

Clasping my arms across my midriff, I continued toward the kiosk. Recalling Sam's dating behavior, a Dr. Jekyll-Mr. Hyde transformation straight out of a Lugosi horror movie, I shuddered, then rubbed my arms, trying to shake off the memory. The friction irritated a scratch near my elbow. While it might be possible to bury a bruised psyche, the reminders on my skin would be harder to hide. I looked down and regarded my badly scraped hands, poorly camouflaged with make-up. Last night, the rosebushes had given me a pretty good thrashing. This morning, I'd had to borrow liquid foundation from Della's vanity to cover up my wounds.

Another scar, a permanent one, courtesy of my arch enemy from Detroit, Cardillac, throbbed on my forearm. Cardillac had also surprised me with her transformation. Not a Dr. Jekyll-Mr. Hyde thing exactly. She'd always been evil, I just hadn't seen it. *Too often you are blind to the faults of those you love.* Ilka's clairvoyant insight penetrated my thoughts once again. No, not Cardillac. What wasn't I seeing about Sam? And what—*who* —had he seen at the window? I'd seen nothing myself. Perhaps he'd come forward and explain. Not that I was anxious to see him again.

Time, and steering clear of Sam, I reassured myself, would help heal both the mental and physical scars. Meantime, I had a busy day ahead. I planned to throw myself into work.

A crammed agenda didn't mean I had to forego my morning dose of gossip, did it? My keyed-up state last night had carried over into the early morning and I'd bounced out of bed, wired for another early start. I had a leg up on the day, anyway.

Gus got underway early too. As I approached the newsstand, I saw him huddled once again with the brazen MP who repulsed me—the one with the wandering beady eyes. The two were off to one side of the kiosk, several yards from where I stopped. Gus saw me and waved. Happily, the MP's back was to me. I wouldn't be at the mercy of his suggestive glances.

Today, to the cerise vest and tweed cap he'd had on the last few mornings, Gus had added violet pants and an orange shirt. I smiled. Where did he come up with such crazy combinations? A charity bin? It was possible. Newspaper vendoring didn't pay much. And an immigrant couldn't have brought many possessions with him, right? From his accent, I assumed he was from somewhere in Europe. Which country? What had brought him here?

Grabbing a *Times* from the shelf below the magazine racks, I scanned the front page, my thoughts segueing to our boys serving overseas in foreign lands.

TOTAL OF U.S. WAR DEAD NOW 25,389.

The headline was sobering. I shook my head sadly, attempting to assimilate the huge loss of lives. Beneath the headline, the article continued its grim accounting. Wounded: 35,805—Missing, many perhaps dead: 32,953—Prisoners of war: 26,820. Total casualties: 120,967.

The figures made me think of Frankie, hovering between life and death in the nearby hospital. They also reminded me of why I was ferrying planes, and why I was here in Hollywood. Above and beyond helping to preserve Frankie's dignity and very being, my duty was to uphold the honor of those of us on the home front doing what we could to help bring an end to the war.

I slapped the paper back together at the fold. The personal woes I'd been harboring were swept aside as Sam Lorenz was relegated to an appropriate category: history!

Returning the *Times* to its stack, I cast another sidelong glance at Gus and the MP, still absorbed in conversation. Fresh issues of *Variety* and *Hollywood Reporter* rested beside the *Times*. Curious about the crowds I'd observed along Sunset the previous night, I examined a copy of one, then the other, scanning the bold headings.

Both tabloids had the scoop I was after, and I gave the *Reporter's* version a hurried skim.

The War Department wanted more entertainers to go overseas to entertain the troops. To help the cause, Bob Hope, Jack Benny, Judith Anderson, and Frances Langford had jointly signed and wired invitations to the most famous names in pictures, asking them to come out and hear those who'd already been "over there" tell about their experiences and explain why others should go. Four hundred and fifty stars and studio executives had shown up for the event at the Beverly Wilshire Hotel. Captain Clark Gable had been on hand lending support.

Gus' voice broke my concentration. "How is Frankie? Any improvement?"

I shook my head and returned to the present. The MP, I noticed, was ambling away down the sidewalk. "No change. But I'm planning on visiting her again later today. Going to try an experiment that might reach her, maybe draw her out of her coma." I held crossed fingers in the air, smiling.

Some good had come out of my dinner date with Sam. In bed afterwards, I'd replayed the night's events over and over. While I lay awake, I remembered Sam asking about what Frankie had said the other day in the hospital. The garbled sounds she'd made came to me in a rush, just before dawn. The sudden epiphany felt significant and filled me with hope. I planned to repeat the sounds to her after work.

"Have they discovered what made the plane to crash?" Gus asked.

The Hollywood Reporter, still in my hand, fluttered. Gus ran a pretty good grapevine. Could he know it was sabotage?

"Nothing official yet," I hedged. "Early bets were on mechanical failure. Why?"

The wiry brow above his steadfast blue eye shot up. His brown eye shifted nervously. "Some have claimed the pilot was at fault…"

My jaw dropped. I wanted to jump to Frankie's defense, but Gus held up a hand to stop me. "No, no. Not to worry. That is not my opinion. And only one or two have said it."

That's one or two too many, I thought. The very reason Novara mustn't be allowed to use the accident clip. Why project the incident on screen over and over? Better to let it—and all the inherent speculation that goes with a plane crash, especially one where the pilot was a woman—fade to black, soon as possible.

Gus continued, "Of course, there is the possibility that someone vandalized the plane—" He paused and adjusted the display of *Silver Screen* on the rack between us.

I held my breath. My pulse raced. Did he know *who*?

"Ah, but no one believes such subversive activity is likely," he rambled. "Security at March Field, it is tight as a drum. Not like at MGM."

My shoulders sagged. I released my breath slowly. So he didn't know anything about the saboteur or the fuel tampering. "What's security at MGM got to do with anything?"

He bowed over the tidy stack of *Hollywood Reporters* and began fussing with it. "Look what happened to the director Brody at MGM. And just before his demise, the unexplained fire…"

I stared at Gus' stooped back. The fire had broken out on a high security sound stage. According to Gunnar, it had been deliberately set, likely by the operatives we were trying to chase down. Gus must have gotten the report from his personal all-seeing "source." But how brash. Or foolhardy. The source was either ignorant of the law, or so confident he would not be fingered for passing along classified information that he'd ignored the possibility of facing a firing squad.

"I didn't know there was a fire. Where'd you hear that?"

Gus looked back over his shoulder and narrowed his good eye as if to say, you think I'm going to tell you that?

I quickly shifted. "Hear anything new on Brody's case? His murder investigation?"

Gus straightened up. "No, nothing. Must be the police they didn't have enough on Chalmers to book him. If they had thrown him in the clink, it would be all over the front pages that is sure."

"Heard anything about what's going on that's *not* in the papers?"

Gus shrugged. "My source has no further information." He was staring at me. "My dear young lady. What happened with your face?"

My hand flew to my cheek. "Ah, I was playing with a kitten. They get rambunctious so easily." I faked a smile.

Gus reached for the coffee can full of roses. "How about a rose?"

"NO." The response exploded from my mouth. Gus looked crushed, but I wasn't about to touch another rose, even to please him. "Sorry." I mustered a weak smile. "Big day ahead. Gotta run." To make up for the brusque rejection, I doubled my usual tip.

With a smile, Gus pocketed the money and wished me a good day.

◇◇◇

Talking with Gus about my plan for repeating Frankie's utterances gave me a fresh wave of hope. I felt a sudden inexplicable compulsion to try it, checked my watch, and decided there was enough time.

◇◇◇

A tall, graying, distinguished-looking doctor carrying a clipboard tucked in one hand exited Frankie's room and walked briskly down the corridor in the opposite direction.

"Dr. Farr?" I called. The doctor, his white coat flapping in the gust created by his fast pace and long stride, kept going. He must not have heard me. Or, it hadn't been Dr. Farr. We'd only talked on the telephone. I didn't actually know what he looked like.

The curtain was drawn around Frankie's bed. On the other side, a sniffling noise.

I parted the seam and pushed through the opening. "Frankie?"

The nurse familiar from my other visits stood at the head of the bed with her back to me looking down at Frankie. She lifted a handkerchief to her face, dabbed a few times, and turned to face me.

"Miss Lew-is…" Her voice was nasal, her eyes watery. "I'm so so-sorry. She's g-gone. Dr. Fa-ar…" She paused and cleared her throat. "Dr. Farr was just here. I'm sorry…"

The nurse stepped aside and revealed Frankie's face. My first reaction was that the nurse had made a mistake. Or that she was playing a bad joke. Frankie looked the same. The expression locked in its grim mask, the lips crusty, eyelids puffy…but then the unmistakable difference. Her skin was tinged pasty blue; her lips, a purplish hue.

"Oh no-ooo, Frankie…" The words, her name, emerged in a keening wail. A pounding in my head made it difficult to hear. The nurse sounded like she was in another room, far away.

"Dr. Farr will be back soon. He went to call the authorities."

I nodded absently. My feet had turned to lead, but I reached Frankie's side. Tentatively, I reached for the dark matted hair, gently smoothing it. My fingers brushed her forehead. Cold to the touch. My hand trembled.

The nurse snuffled. Tucking herself quietly in next to me, she wrapped an arm around my waist. "I'm so sorry."

My eyes pooled and Frankie's features blurred. "I'm the one who's sorry," I whimpered. "She was a WASP, my sister in flying, my friend. I was the only family she had here. I s-s-should have been here…"

Miraculously, the nurse pulled a clean handkerchief from her sleeve. I blotted my face.

The nurse shook her head sympathetically. She sensed that I needed to get it out. And get it out I did. The dam burst. Head bowed, my face buried in the handkerchief, I cried in jerky sobs repeating "Why? Why? Why?" until my stomach ached, my throat felt raw, and my eyes burned. All the while, the nurse, gently rubbing my back, matched my distress with calm, quiet talk about having faith in nature and destiny and order.

"Frankie's life had its own meaning, her death has meaning as well," she assured me. "Maybe it's not clear now, but one day her reason for being on this earth will be obvious to you. And there was a reason your life was intertwined with hers. Already that's clear. In your visits with Frankie, you gave her something of yourself. You shared your presence, your friendship. You gave her comfort and your thoughts. Those are wonderful gifts."

The nurse's words soothed me. The tears helped. Like an overflow valve, they drained out enough sorrow so that my grief for Frankie became a manageable lump I thought I could hold inside.

I stared at the handkerchief in my hands, a pathetic damp wad. "Sorry," I whispered hoarsely, absently twisting it.

"For what? There's nothing you need be sorry over."

"I've ruined it. It's stained..." I looked at the nurse through eyes so swollen I could hardly see.

"Not like your grief is staining your heart." She rubbed the small of my back gently.

I squeezed the nurse's hand. "You're wonderful. Thank you." I looked at Frankie. "And, you've given me an idea. A special way we can honor Frankie's life." The nurse's earlier words came back to me all at once. "What happened? How did she die? You said Dr. Farr was making a call to the authorities..."

The nurse glanced over her shoulder. "The doctor should be back soon. Or, maybe he's waiting for them..."

We were on the side of the bed near Frankie's broken arm. The nurse turned and nodded to the intravenous bottle on the other side of the bed.

The nurse nodded. "Over there." I started to circle the end of the bed. "Careful," she warned. "Don't disturb anything."

A vial had shattered near the foot of the I.V. stand, scattering shards of glass in a wild pattern on the floor around it. Moving in close, I knelt down and visually examined what remained of the container. The bold black letters KCl were evident on the green label.

"Potassium," the nurse whispered. She read my perplexed expression. "A high dose injected into the I.V. would cause instant death." Her eyes welled up. "We've witnessed so much of the suffering with this war. Boys crippled, maimed…" Her voice catching, she paused, swallowed. "So many young lives cut short. A-nnd the poor families." Atop her dark hair, the stiff white cap pitched with the slow rocking motion of her head. "Now this monstrous act. Here, just down the hall from the nurse station. Horrible!"

I was stunned. "Someone deliberately did this? Murder? When? When did it happen? Did anyone see anything? Hear anything? You were right down the hall, someone must have…"

The nurse bristled. "No one on the nursing crew heard or saw anything. Following doctor's orders, I looked in our Frankie every two hours throughout the night. At five-thirty when I checked, she was fine. Two hours later, when I came again, she had expired. I called Dr. Farr immediately. He arrived, spotted the broken vial—" The nurse sighed. "She was such a sweet young thing," she whispered.

We looked at Frankie. Neither of us spoke for what seemed like a long time, but could only have been moments. I took a deep breath and glimpsed my watch. I could not be here when the authorities arrived. I would need a sabotage update from Miss C first. They'd get to me soon enough anyway, I suspected.

I squeezed the nurse's shoulder. "I'm expected at the studio. I'll check back with you soon."

Turning to leave, the sight of Frankie's flight jacket, hanging inside the closet, stopped me. The leather was badly shredded. Blood stains marred her saddle shoes. There was something so personal about the shoes and something so ominous about seeing the spilled blood on them. The times I'd been with Frankie, she'd been wearing those shoes. That's how I remembered her. Full of life. Walking around in saddle shoes. Not some cold lifeless form lying in a sterile hospital bed, the victim of some crazed fanatic.

I marched back to her and gulped down the lump forming in my throat. "Who could have done this to you Frankie?" My voice cracked. I took a deep breath. When I spoke again, my voice was resolute. "Frankie, we're going to find the person who did this. We'll get the guy. He'll pay. That's a promise."

I brushed her forehead ever so lightly with a kiss. My eyelashes skimmed the sutures of the gash. The angry red scar—now purple—the black sutures, the crusted bleeding points filled my vision. I knew the sight would remain in my mind forever. So would the spilled blood I'd seen on Frankie's shoes.

◇◇◇

If the typing pool gals were curious about my swollen eyes and scratched face, they said nothing. Several sets of peepers flicked up from whatever project they'd been concentrating on as I whisked by. My grim persona might have warned them off or it could have been my determined pace, but not a peep as I weaved through the warren of desks to get to the hall.

It was beyond me how I would make it through the day, but I'd made a promise to Frankie. And each step I took, each task I finished, each clue I uncovered, would bring me closer to unmasking the saboteur, who it now appeared had decisively finished the job.

First up, I needed to talk with Miss C. In the booth, I placed my call. The receptionist at the hotel where she was staying— the appointed place for reaching her—reported she was out for the day. "It's absolutely not possible to contact her," said an annoying child-like voice on the other end. "She did not leave word where she was going."

I slammed the receiver into its cradle, slid to the wooden seat, and sighed. "Curses."

I heaved myself up. If Miss C could stay the course no matter what else might be going on, so could I.

◇◇◇

A telephone slip with a message from Ilka sat propped on my desk. The note said that the filming of her movie, in truth only a "briefie," would take place the next morning at MGM. She hoped I could make it.

Ilka had already made the point that hers was not a speaking part. Now I thought she might be trying to set my expectations. A briefie, as the name suggested, wouldn't be much of a film production. In purpose, briefies were similar to Victory shorts—they showed citizens how to conserve, assist, and sacrifice for the war effort, or they conveyed celebrity pleas on behalf of war charities. But while Victory shorts such as the one we were making about the WASP ran about twenty minutes in length, briefies—more of an announcement than anything—were only about one or two minutes.

Still, seeing Ilka in action was a bright spot to look forward to. I checked my calendar. I could do it, but it'd be tight. The ferrying shoot was scheduled later in the day.

A second part to Ilka's message reminded me that tonight was the Hungarian Federation auction at the Grand Hotel. I would be on my own for dinner.

My thoughts skipped back to the P-51 ferrying shoot and I slumped in my seat, picking at my cuticles. I had a lot riding on the segment. If I wanted to have a hand in developing and producing other ideas I'd proposed for improving *Sky Belles*, Novara had to be impressed with how this came off. That meant my performance and the production logistics had to be flawless.

Before going to the hospital, I'd feared my life could be on the line doing the sequence. Far as I knew, the saboteur was still on the loose. But now that it looked like he'd been after Frankie all along, could I take the P-51 up without worry? No, someone had wanted to send a message that women should not be flying military planes. A message meant to frighten us off. Which circled back to would he try to eliminate other WASPs who would dare to flaunt what they did before a camera?

I recoiled in pain. I'd torn a cuticle. As if my hands didn't look bad enough! Immediately, I was ashamed. I was worried about appearance? Frankie had lost her life. Why had Miss C left the decision up to me?

Mad Max! Maybe she'd heard something further.

I dashed back to the pay phone and got through to Max directly. That was as far as my good fortune would extend. It didn't occur to me until she picked up that Max wouldn't have yet heard about Frankie. It took a little time—I started crying more than once—but I told her what had happened. Afterwards, a few empty seconds passed while neither of us felt like speaking.

Max broke the silence. "So the bastard thought she knew something. Was afraid she'd talk if she pulled through."

My heart pounded. "Wha-what are you saying? He thought she knew who did it? That's the motive?"

"Yeah, but seems strange to take the risk, given her already near-death condition."

Recalling how proud I'd been over Frankie's small break-through in muttering some incomprehensible sounds, I felt sick. Had she been trying to give me a name? Who had I bragged to? The nurse. Sam. Gus. Miss C…Had they told others? Had I? Had word that she'd "talked" reached the killer?

It was too much to even suppose I might have unintentionally triggered Frankie's demise. I forced the nightmarish proposition from my mind.

We turned to whether I should fly. Max had seen or heard nothing to suggest that an official investigation into Frankie's crash was underway. So was it still open season?

Miss C would take the P-51 up, I reminded myself. And in the hospital, I'd had the idea of honoring Frankie by dedicating my flight—and the film—to her.

I resolved to go ahead.

After telling Max my decision, we agreed on a slight compromise. Following Miss C's suggestion, Max would conduct the P-51's final inspection. She'd test the fuel. We'd also go over the plane as a team, eyes peeled for signs of tampering.

We hung up, and I began wrestling with the next problem.

Novara had given Sam and me joint responsibility for writing up all the new segments I'd recommended. Last night, after drafting the basics of the ferrying scenario, Sam had said he'd place a call to get us the necessary technical crew and film equipment. I'd volunteered to check in with March Field to be certain all flight arrangements and protocol requirements were adequately covered. As a last step in our plan, we'd agreed on reconnoitering in Sam's office later this morning to type up the ferrying scene in script format, then go as a team to see Novara for final approval.

That had been the plan before the unexpected disastrous end to our evening. Sam had been so weird when he threw me out of his house, I wasn't sure what to expect now. Would he come through with his side of the arrangements? Would he do something to make me look bad?

I stared at the cracks in the plaster ceiling, looking for an alternative course of action. Preferably one that sidestepped my having contact with Sam Lorenz.

I got to work. First, I had to tie up the loose ends of the improvement measures I'd proposed.

Back in the telephone booth, I made the necessary calls to nail down the people I wanted to cast. I enlisted the commander of the New Castle AAF Base in Wilmington, Delaware. As someone who had more planes to move than he could handle, the WASP had come through for him time and time again. A staunch supporter, he was delighted for the chance to share his experiences.

I also got in touch with a number of pilots who offered to relay their experiences of flying with a WASP copilot. Most effective, I thought, would be an interview with the pilot who'd offered to talk about a heavy bomber experience. The positive things he had to say—especially since the plane he and a WASP had jointly flown was a B-24, a flying monster known for being notoriously hard to handle—was the exact kind of acclaim Miss C wanted our movie to project.

Highly regarded ground crewmen said they'd be happy to go before a camera and discuss their encounters with WASP. Their crew chief had enormous potential. He told me openly how, early in the war, he'd thought, *and hoped*, his dealings with women pilots would be short-lived. Instead, after working with WASP on a regular basis for the past year and a half, he'd had a one-hundred-and-eighty-degree change of heart. He raved about the professionalism, competence, and dedication he'd encountered. We needed to get it on film.

After securing permission to borrow an idle typewriter, I shouldered a borrowed canvas tote filled with carbon sheets and a ream of paper, then trudged with my load to my private dressing room office. The machine fit perfectly on Carole Landis' dressing table.

Chapter Fourteen

Perched on the vanity bench in Landis' dressing room, I pounded out each of the concepts in script form. For the first time in my life, I created dialogue, narrative for voice-overs, and scene descriptions. I was no screen writer, but the format Sam and I had laid out for the ferrying segment helped. So did the original script.

At last, a rough shooting script for every one of the new or revamped scenarios had been completed. There was an original and one carbon copy each for Roland Novara, Sam Lorenz, and Miss C. I even mapped out a shooting schedule, including alternative dates, which I typed up for everyone as well.

It was late afternoon when I finished. Tempted to rest my tired bones and drained psyche across the room on the inviting blue satin couch, I resisted. Instead I gathered the discarded sheets of paper from the floor, scrunching them in my hands as I strolled to a wicker clothes hamper in the room's far corner. My plan was to stash the discards until later when, less burdened by the items I'd hauled over from administration, I could dispose of the trash properly. I opened the lid. Someone else had gotten the brainstorm before me. Only it wasn't stored rubbish I was looking at, but film cans.

Crunched paper cradled in one arm, I lifted the top reel out. My breath caught. UFA film. I peered deeper into the bin and saw five additional reels. What were German film cans doing inside a clothes hamper in Carole Landis' dressing room? A version of the question and its ominous undertones had come to me in the hidden alcove off Della's closet. Had someone moved the cans from the Dunns' to here?

I returned the reel, flipped the lid of the hamper closed, and walked in a bewildered state toward the sofa. I spilled my crunched pages onto the satin cushions, unsure what to do next. The appearance in the doorway of MP Sergeant Winwar made my decision easy.

His gaze volleyed from the mess on the sofa to the typewriter on the vanity to me.

"These walls are thin," he said, nodding to the blue-flocked wallpapered panel at my back. "Heard a tapping noise clear outside." Tugging up his pistol belt, giving me a once over so slow and intense it was obscene, he took a few steps toward me. "Then I ain't the one who should be doin' the explainin', am I?"

Be grateful for small things, I told myself. He's not the least bit interested in what's above your shoulders, including your scratched up face.

My brightest smile in place, honey-trap training engaged, I returned the lecherous gaze.

"How great you came by, Sergeant. I'm finished here"—I glimpsed my watch—"just under deadline. Gotta run." With haste, I packed my satchel, slung it on my shoulder, picked up the typewriter. "Got a meeting at administration...with Reagan." It was a strain, especially loaded down the way I was, but, channeling Mae West, I batted my eyes, sidling close to him. "Care to accompany me, Sergeant?" I drawled.

"*Molto bello*...sure."

He reached to hitch his belt. I got there with the typewriter first. Thrusting it into his hands, I savored the shock on his face before turning for the door.

◇◇◇

Back in the secretarial pool, after asking one of the gals to air mail Miss C's packet and to arrange hand delivery to Novara and Sam, I sagged back in my chair, exhausted. Hopefully, by putting everything on paper, I'd bypassed—or minimized—any future association with Sam.

I sent a little prayer to the Woman upstairs. If today's efforts paid off, the Victory short would be a giant step closer to a successful conclusion. I'd get the chance to fly a plane of my dreams and pay small tribute to my sister WASP.

A glance at the time catapulted me from my chair. Gunnar and I had agreed I'd stop by before the end of the day. He'd promised to let me preview the training film that included Frankie's crash scene.

Winwar had been target practice for what else was on my agenda with Gunnar. He had some explaining to do, ready or not.

◇◇◇

Moments later, I arrived at the two-story brick editing building. An exterior staircase led to the second floor where Gunnar said I'd find his office.

I skipped up the stairs, entering directly into a long corridor. Most of the doors were shut, but the door of one brightly lit room stood invitingly open.

I looked in and saw an airy space with tall windows and a high ceiling. "Artist's garret" immediately came to mind. But rather than smocked painters dabbing brush to canvas, a dozen or so men in uniform manned assorted film processing equipment.

Ordered chaos. Strips of film were everywhere. They adorned the necks of the soldiers, they were clipped to shelving, they dangled from large garbage bins placed strategically around the room. Men held them up to ceiling lights or over light panels built into their desks. And film cans everywhere, stacked on the desks and on the floor; filling racks along the walls.

I started back down the hall to the office I thought was Gunnar's. The door was slightly ajar. I rapped lightly, then stepped into a long, narrow room not much larger than Della's walk-in closet.

Editing equipment and film reels cluttered two desks pushed end-to-end along the wall immediately to my left. A narrow table with a radio speaker and other sound gear was flush to the wall at the room's far end. Orderly rows of film cans in a metal shelf unit ran the length of the room directly ahead.

Another table occupied the room's center. It held a machine like a projector, but bigger and with more gadgetry. Gunnar stood beside it, a long length of film draping his neck like a stole. He held an end section of film between white-gloved hands, studying it.

"Pucci, glad you could make it." He sounded genuinely pleased to see me.

The friendly welcome and change of scenery were heartening after my brutal day. Yet I was all business. "I'm here to see the training film with the clip of Frankie's accident."

"Right. The demonstration of the new fire-fighting equipment. I'll get it."

He removed the loop from around his neck, slipping it into a nearby bin, and walked over to the wall unit. He glanced casually over his shoulder. "What happened to your face?"

My hand flew to the telltale marks. "Nothing interesting." I gingerly smoothed the raw skin. "How do you keep track of all these pieces of film? They're all over the place."

"There's a method to the madness. The tins are numbered, there's a card index, and script secretaries record what goes on at every set. They give us detailed notes of each day's work. In there." He gestured to a large notebook on the nearby desk, then pulled one of the round tins from the shelf, waving it. "Every foot of film in this can is numbered and registered."

He snapped the reel from the can, and began stringing it through the machine. "This is a movieola…"

"But what exactly do you do? In layman's terms, that is."

Gunnar stopped threading film for a moment. "A film editor joins together sections of footage to make a lucid, dramatic, and emotional whole."

"Emotional? An Army training film, emotional?"

Gunnar nodded. "It's why the Pentagon enlisted Hollywood for the war effort. Washington believes soldiers are getting the kind of training in three weeks that prewar and pre-Hollywood used to take thirteen. Know-how, especially good editing, livens up the dull subject matter. A good number of our soldiers are eighteen year olds, remember. And we're dealing in technical, often difficult, subject matter. Background music, crisp narration, bits of comedy—it's what's needed to maintain attention and retention."

I regarded Gunnar's face as he spoke. It was a kind face, and his features were strong and handsome. For the first time, I noticed the sensual curve of his lips. I blinked and tuned back in to what he was saying.

"If an editor's any good he can turn a yawning subject into something powerful." He paused abruptly. "Sorry. Sounds like I'm bragging again, huh?"

He smiled. It was a smile that under different circumstances might have melted my heart. But at the moment my heart felt bruised and numb.

Gunnar slipped the celluloid strip through the final slot. "Here, take a look."

I put on a headset. Gunnar flipped a switch and the film began. After a few minutes, I understood what he was talking about.

The training segment began in the traditional manner—a classroom scene with an instructor showing and telling about the new firefighting product, but soon an A-24 towing a target was crossing the sky. It was what I'd come to see. My stomach flip-flopped. I stared into the viewer stupefied, as Frankie's plane stalled, then plummeted out of control to earth.

I couldn't pull my eyes away. I continued to stare even after the plane hit the ground. When the crash was on the screen in the rushes, I'd been so sickened by the sight that I could hardly watch. I'd missed much of the ground crew's efforts as they brought Frankie out and tried salvaging the plane, but I had a good recollection of the scene. What was rolling now was not footage of Frankie's A-24.

I watched the fire fighters emerge from the wreck leading the pilot, dazed but ambulatory, to safety. Incredible. The pilot was not Frankie. She'd been taken away by stretcher.

I didn't need to see more. The piece was professional and effective, a good teaching tool. Most important, Frankie was in no way identified with the crash.

I straightened up. "It's good. Frankie would have been proud." The predictable happened. My voice caught.

Gunnar looked at me. His dusk-sky blue eyes caught mine. He hesitated, concern written all over his face.

I pushed on fast, fighting the wave of emotion threatening to wash over me. "Frankie's dead." Tears flooded my vision.

Gunnar produced a handkerchief. I wiped my eyes.

There was no point in bringing up the likelihood that Frankie had been murdered. The details surrounding the means of death, while suspicious, had not yet been determined. In any event, his case involving Brody was separate from mine involving Frankie. And I was here to find some answers from him.

Gunnar lifted my chin. His voice was sad, sweet. "Hey, Frankie has gone on to a bigger adventure."

I couldn't resist a small smile. "Thanks. A comforting thought."

Gunnar cleared his throat. "Ah, there's something else." I looked at him. He patted the movieola. "This footage just helped convince a certain Admiral to send thousands of tons of the foam material to the Pacific."

"Really? Why?"

"The Japs have been dropping Baka bombs on our aircraft carriers. We haven't seen bombs like these before. They cause such extensive and extraordinary damage that ordinary fire-fighting equipment can't put the fires out fast enough. Casualties have been much higher…Men have suffered horrible deaths." Gunnar paused. "After seeing this film, the Admiral believes the foam will help resolve the problem.

"So you see, the camera and the right footage—the clip of Frankie's accident, in this instance—they're as important to the war effort as any high-powered weapon the military has at its disposal."

"Right," I replied softly. I nodded to the machine. "Tell me, I have to know. How did you make it appear Frankie's plane was in flames? Her plane was badly damaged, but it never caught fire. And that wasn't Frankie being led away from the wreckage."

"The downed pilot was an actor and the rescue staged. But that was her A-24—what remained of it. After the official accident inspection, all salvageable parts were removed and allotted to special use. That's us. It was really just a skeleton, but we doused it with gasoline, then—with a fire-fighting team and the new foam at the ready—we tossed a match, and 'Roll em.'

"Afterwards, it was a matter of splicing and combining clips." Gunnar motioned toward the assortment of equipment on the adjoining desks, then swept the room with a broader gesture. "We're lucky to have superior equipment. Trick photography, dubbing, sound effects, we'll use whatever it takes to drive home our message."

"Enemy footage, too?"

Gunnar gave me a long, calculating look. "Of course."

"The Germans, the Japs, they don't just hand it over. We steal it, right?"

Gunnar gave a small shrug.

"Isn't there a German film studio…er, one called UFA Studio?" I smiled guilelessly. "One of your sources?"

Gunnar seemed to be weighing something. "Pucci, you've been cleared. I'm just not sure yet how we're going to enlist your help. There was a foul-up. Things changed, I told you that."

"You'll never know 'how' until you take me into your confidence. For all you know, I might already be on to something."

Had he not looked so skeptical, I might have been more restrained. But after the day I'd had, I decided Vesuvius had it right.

"Tell me what UFA film cans are doing in your sister's closet. And the envelope. There was a photo of Brody and a woman inside. You said he was being blackmailed. Is she the reason why? And what did the blackmailer want?" It all boiled up to the surface. "Your sister is in possession of a top secret communiqué from someone in Cairo sowing seeds about using enemy film for propaganda purposes here. What do you know about that?"

Gunnar looked startled then impressed. "I'll brief you on what I can."

"What you can? How about what you know!"

"Have a seat?" Gunnar pulled out one of the desk chairs. I sat, struggling to regain my composure. Sliding out a chair for himself, he spun it around, straddled it, and faced me, quickly explaining that the UFA film was obtained from a raid at the German site. Della, who was not actually his sister but an OSS operative, recently retrieved the film from Cairo on one of her and D.B.'s regular trips there. They also escorted back to the States two of our downed flyboys who had escaped from the Nazis—the airmen who were currently advising on the *Resisting Enemy Interrogation* training picture.

"Before the war, government wasn't involved in filmmaking, and Hollywood didn't film for political indoctrination. But in fascist Germany, the motion picture industry has been under government control since '37. And they have Goebbels, the propaganda maestro, controlling all mass media."

Gunnar leaned toward me over the back of the chair. He fixed me in a steadfast stare. "Goebbels saw immediately how topnotch films could be used to soften up or even intimidate movie audiences into opening their minds to Nazi ideals. He converted the UFA studio into an assembly operation for glorifying the cause."

The stuff mentioned in the secret dispatch I'd found at the Dunns'. I leaned forward in *my* chair.

"Riefenstahl's *Triumph of the Will* set the standard for Nazi propaganda films." Gunnar frowned. "Whole thing was staged to lionize Nazi strength and discipline, create the impression of a 'super-race.' Riefenstahl did so well that German children would go anywhere, do anything for Hitler. Yes, maybe even die for him."

Gunnar pulled a UFA reel out of his leather briefcase. The cans I'd seen in Della's closet, he explained, were the actual pilfered lot that had been delivered originally to Brody. Somewhere along the route from Cairo to Orlando to here, German operatives picked up the trail. They wanted the film back—or destroyed. They found Brody's Achilles heel—his affair—gathered evidence and sent a note. "Give us the films; we'll give you the negatives."

Brody confided in Gunnar. Certain that an insider was part of the ring, they were cautious choosing a team and making copies that might or might not hold up after an initial screening. When Brody got the call, Gunnar would follow him to the drop point. They'd keep the copied film under surveillance and catch the bad guys. If it seemed too simple, it was. When Brody got the call, Gunnar had been with me, having dinner with the Dunns at their house. His counterpart, assigned in Gunnar's absence to trail Brody, lost him turning out of MGM onto Washington.

My jaw dropped. "What happened?"

"Fate—or I should say a drunk driver—intervened. The agent was keeping a safe distance, in case the blackmailers were tailing Brody. The inebriated driver was coming from the opposite direction. Crashed head-on into the car directly in front of my colleague. Blocked the street. Brody was enough ahead, kept going."

I sighed, shook my head. "The photo in Della's closet. The lady with Brody...his lover?"

"Yes, but she's been cleared."

"She looked familiar. Who is she?"

"No need for you to know."

I was about to blurt, How can you be so sure? but caught his look. *Don't push your luck.*

"Brody had a similar envelope. He was examining it–and the contents–while I was in his MGM office at a story meeting, hours before he died."

Gunnar arched an eyebrow. "The envelope in Della's closet, one and the same. We removed it from the crime scene."

They could do that?

"In his office, Brody removed a letter from the envelope. What did it say? A pink satin ribbon was tied around the photo…"

Gunnar's eyes narrowed. "We didn't find a ribbon. I'd guess it belonged to a daughter. More pressure for him to cooperate. There was no note, either. Only the photo of Brody and the woman."

Gunnar flipped the UFA film can from hand to hand adding, "Chalmers told us he met with Brody at MGM early the evening of the murder. When Chalmers started in on his beefs about the adaptation of his novel, Brody said, 'Russell you're dealing in fiction. Here's the reality I'm dealing in.' He showed Chalmers the incriminating photo, adding, 'They snapped us checking into a hotel. They've got other compromising shots too. I think I know who's behind it.'

"Brody had just figured it out. He didn't tell Chalmers what had tipped him, and he was killed before he could relay the information to me or the others on our team. But based on what Chalmers told us—that Brody had just returned from Fort Roach where he'd made a delivery—"

Gunnar raked his fingers through his thick sandy hair. "Drop site must have been somewhere here, right under our noses."

I bounced up, practically knocking over my chair. "Have the cans been moved from Della's closet?" Gunnar looked at me like I was crazy. "If they weren't, then I know where the drop site was—is—or at least where someone is storing the copies."

Gunnar's lips curled in a sly smile as I revealed what I'd uncovered in the hamper in Miss Landis' dressing room.

I frowned. Five cans in Della's closet; six cans in the dressing room. "What's that in your hand?"

"This—" Gunnar waved the reel in his hand. "Never leaves my sight."

"Why? What is it?"

Gunnar smiled coyly. "Reconnaissance film. Care to guess?"

A picture took shape as the puzzle pieces matched up. "UFA," I whispered.

Gunnar nodded. He spoke softly as well. "Brody was making an absolute top-secret simulated bombing run film. Part of a plan to throw a monkey-wrench in the Propaganda Ministry's production output." He tucked the reel back in his case, lifted it off the floor. "I was going to give you a look, but we—I—better get over to that dressing room."

"B-but *my* part?"

I followed Gunnar to the door. He flipped off the overhead light. Behind him, illumination from the fixtures in the hall created an eerie backdrop as we stood in the shadowy doorway. "Keep an eye on Ilka."

"Ilka?"

"When Brody died, my blackmail investigation became joined with the murder inquiry. The preliminary findings suggest death was due to a dose of deadly herbs."

"Ilka and her herbs…" I said in an undertone.

"She's an expert. The connection is too obvious to ignore."

I stared at him, letting the implication sink in. "But how do you kill someone with herbs?"

"In a brew." Gunnar saw my mouth open to ask a follow-on question. "I'll explain more later, but Brody's secretary, Myra, knew Brody's blood pressure was sky-high. She'd been giving him chamomile tea for weeks now to calm his nerves. Doctor's orders."

I recalled the story conference meeting in Brody's office. Myra had brought a cup of it in that day. "So, *tea* killed him?"

"Well, yes, sort of. Myra called Brody's personal physician the minute she discovered his body. They both assumed he'd had a heart attack. But while the doctor was doing his examination, he picked up a distinct scent from Brody's mouth. He investigated the tea cup on Brody's desk. Chamomile has a flowery smell. Myra had left Brody a cup of it a few hours earlier, before leaving for the day. The remnants the doctor found were grassy in odor, different in color, and leaves had accumulated in the bottom of the cup. Myra is a fanatic when it comes to a cup of tea being pure."

"He drank a different tea? A poisoned tea?"

Gunnar shrugged. "They're running toxicology tests on the herb—we'll have that result soon—and there'll be a report on what was found ingested in another week. But the autopsy shows a healthy heart."

"In other words, you're saying—going on Myra's and the doctor's observations—evidence points to the herb being some sort of deadly strain."

Gunnar had started to walk down the hall. I'd stuck with him. He paused, checked over his shoulder, and spoke in a low voice. "The evidence isn't airtight, I admit, but the Gypsy and herb connections point so clearly to Ilka, I can't shake off the possibility."

"The Gypsy and herb theory…" I summarized. Gunnar made a move to go. I grabbed his arm. "I don't buy it. Why would Ilka murder Brody?"

"Not sure. She didn't have to brew the tea, hand it to him, to be involved, Pucci. We're dealing with a ring. Brody got in their way somehow." He started walking.

I kept pace. "Ilka is a strong, independent woman who's overcome tremendous difficulties. She's rebuilding her life. She's set on an acting career. Why would she risk getting caught up in something illegal now? C'mon. Why?"

We'd reached the exit door. Gunnar halted. His eyes flashed with impatience. "Money. The game. Fascism."

Now my eyes blazed. "Ilka would never help the Germans. Not for any amount of money. She has friends and family who are being persecuted, slaughtered by the Nazis. Her grandmother is there. A grandmother involved in underground activities, aiding the Allies."

Gunnar's brow furrowed. He was unaware of the resistance connection, I gathered.

"I need to get to that dressing room, Pucci. *Now.* I'll try to get back to the house tonight and we can talk further. If I don't show—and it's highly likely given we'll be setting up surveillance—you're flying to March Field tomorrow, right?" I nodded. "Mind if I catch a lift?"

"Of course not. But…"

"Money is a powerful motivator, Pucci. Let's leave it at that for now."

Chapter Fifteen

My assignment: cover a home front on the home front. Women's work.

There was a certain irony to being banned by Gunnar from the drop site when I was the person responsible for putting him back in the saddle on his case. Exhausted, emotionally drained, I'd let it go, returning briefly to the typing pool before climbing into the Packard and starting the journey home to the Dunns'. Adding to my day's downward spiral, Miss C had called while I'd been in the editing studio with Gunnar. *Things are heating up in Washington. I'm on my way out for the evening.* That was the entirety of her message. No word on whether she'd heard the news of Frankie or whether she'd gotten wind of any developments on the March Field investigation.

Absorbed in the complexities of my situation, I had motored blocks down Washington Boulevard before realizing, almost as if by its own will, the Packard was following a course leading away from the Dunns' and toward the ocean. I did not want to be alone. My mark, Ilka, was out for the evening at the Hungarian Federation auction. And here I was heading for the Grand Hotel in Santa Monica, where the event was being held. *Ilka a blackmailer?* I shook my head and laughed. It was going to be fun proving Gunnar wrong.

Washington Boulevard ended, and I turned onto the Pacific Coast Highway. Traffic was light, but with gas rationing in effect it was not so surprising. The hotel was on a side street. At Pico, I turned left and caught a glimpse of the lights of Santa Monica Pier. Then another left, and I was rolling past the Grand Hotel's canopied entrance.

My home front assignment had just been bumped out of the kitchen and into a luxury seaside hotel. Just past the hotel, I nosed the Packard into a discreet tree- and thicket-enclosed parking lot.

I left the car and meandered along a sidewalk, observing the hotel's brick and sandstone exterior. Head tilted back, I stared up at the tall building, unable to count, in the dark, the number of floors above. There must have been seven or eight. On the opposite side of the hotel, waves broke against the beach in a continuous rolling crash.

Nearing the entrance, I eyed the uniformed doorman at the entrance and was half-tempted to call it a day. But I'd done enough wallowing in things I could do nothing about. I needed to wrap my mind around other things. Things lively and fun.

The doorman's shoulders were broad beneath his tailored maroon jacket, distinguished with brass buttons and tails. Drawing closer I could see that the tall formal hat sat above a high forehead, a strong nose, and a neat mustache.

"Ilka Maki said if I was in the neighborhood, I should drop in," I explained to the intimidating figure, hastily adding, "She's inside with a mutual friend, Bela Lugosi."

The guard paused to give my uniform a once-over. He tugged open the door, gesturing for me to enter, but stayed on my tail.

"Wait here, if you please," he sniffed in a lofty tone. "I shall let the manager know of your request."

We were in an expansive lobby. A round table with an enormous pastel floral arrangement stood directly before me. Beyond the arrangement, tall west-facing windows that by day would look out to the ocean formed an opaque black backdrop, reflecting patterns of golden light at night. The doorman retreated toward a reception counter on the far end of the room to our right.

I savored the display of Oriental rugs, richly upholstered furniture, brass fixtures and bronze statuary arranged throughout the large space off to my left. An elderly couple, formally dressed—he in dark suit and dark tie, she in powder-blue dress with matching lace jacket—ambled by. They were speaking in the emotionally charged, harsh-sounding Hungarian I'd come to know. The couple paused to smile at me and say hello. It wasn't much, but I felt encouraged. Glancing toward the reception desk, seeing that the doorman had not reappeared, I followed in the couple's wake as they crossed into the main area.

A fair distance ahead of us were three sets of doors. The center set was propped open. Party sounds spilled out: disjointed conversations, laughter, clinking glass, frenzied violins playing high discordant notes at a fevered pitch. It was the room where the auction would be held, I assumed.

A pair of lanky legs belonging to a tuxedo-clad gentleman sprawled outward from a tall, wing-back chair positioned against one of two marble pillars. An identical chair sat beside it. Blocking the man's torso and face from view was a woman in an orange cocktail dress with a full ankle-length skirt, layered with delicate netting. Below the flounced hemline, her feet were clad in orange high-heel shoes. Above the dress' beaded bodice, on either side of a glamorous blonde upsweep, glittering earrings dangled from her ears.

Beyond the pillars, the elderly couple entered the party room. My plan was to follow them inside, get Ilka's attention, say hello, and see what developed. Nearing the pillar, I heard the woman in the orange dress speaking in Hungarian to the man slumped in the chair. I couldn't understand what she was saying, but she was definitely lecturing him. Maybe I could pick up a tip on dealing with Gunnar, I thought, passing closer, smiling at the notion.

A large colorful movie poster on a stand near the bank of the doors drew my eye. *Frankenstein Meets the Wolf Man* stood out in bold yellow lettering. I'd seen the movie earlier in the year. Above the movie title, a ferocious-looking square-headed Frankenstein raised his fist menacingly before the wolf-faced man, trying to fend him off. A reclining Ilona Massey, looking seductive in a low-cut red dress, filled in the lower corner. Bela Lugosi played Frankenstein; Lon Chaney was Wolf Man. Their names were also on the poster, the lineup supporting what Ilka had said about Lugosi's career dip. Ilona Massey, Patric Knowles, Lon Chaney had top billing, while Mr. Lugosi's name, along with Lionel Atwill's, and Maria Ouspenskaya's, appeared in smaller lettering sandwiched below those of the stars.

In the open doorway near the poster, a dark-haired barrel-chested man appeared, wearing a white peasant shirt brightly embroidered with flowers at the neckline and hem of its dolman sleeves. The wild violin playing had stopped, but the din of conversation and glass clinking continued.

"Ilona," he called to the woman in orange as he gestured for her to come inside.

The glamorous woman's profile clicked. I was standing within a stone's throw of Ilona Massey! Of course. She was Hungarian. The actress-singer must have agreed to perform for the fundraiser.

The man in the doorway cast a disparaging glance at the back of the chair and urged Miss Massey to come away. She said some departing words, then, squeezing the seated man's shoulder, started to leave. She must have noticed me out of the corner of her eye. She stopped briefly to take me in, smile, and salute.

I smiled, saluted back. "Good luck in there, Miss Massey."

She eyed the wings over my breast pocket and pointed skyward. "Thank you. And good luck to you up there."

Her skirt made a soft swishing noise as she strutted toward the man in the peasant shirt.

The slouched man in the chair propped his elbows on the armrests and clutched his head between his hands. Long-fingered graceful hands, marred by ropey veins and wrinkles, masked his face. But there was no mistaking who it was.

I walked to the chair. "Mr. Lugosi?" There was no response. "Mr. Lugosi?"

The fingers on the side of his face closest to me splayed to let a glazed blue eye with a pinpoint pupil stare blankly up at me.

"Pucci Lewis. We met in the kitchen at the Dunns'. You were with Ilka. And, oh yeah, the other night we crossed paths at their house again. You were walking arm-in-arm with Ilka and a silent film actress wearing a fur coat."

The fixed vacant stare, reminiscent of Gus' unseeing glass eye, was giving me the heebie-jeebies, and I was blathering. Luckily, a lightbulb seemed to go on. Lugosi's hands slid from his face to the armrests. Pressing against them, he squirmed awkwardly, trying to straighten up in the chair. His cape was not helping matters. It was tangled around him, restricting his movement. The high collar was askew, creating a look more zany than macabre.

"Pooo-chi," Lugosi said in a booming voice. "I am most happy to see you. Sit please a moment, vill you?"

His palm left the armrest to sweep in the general direction of the companion chair. The movement unbalanced him and Lugosi lolled sideways. Again, he fought to right himself.

I glanced toward the entrance. The doorman must have slipped back outside. A stout officious-looking woman stood behind the counter, large horn-rimmed goggles fixed on me like periscopes set to follow my every intruding move. I turned back to Lugosi.

"Thank you. I really shouldn't. I dropped in, spur of the moment. Thought I might see Ilka, have a little chat. But I had no idea this auction was such an extravaganza. Looks like you have quite the crowd. Cast of thousands?"

Lugosi chortled. "Two hundred, maybe. Big spenders, ve hope."

"Miss Massey brought in a few, I'll bet." I threw an admiring glance toward the now closed doors. "And you? Are you planning to perform?" Regarding his sagging form, I hoped not, for his sake.

Lugosi's thick eyebrows knitted at the center and he looked momentarily confused. His initial response sounded rote. "I have little act taken from my stage role. Is what I came to do.

But sadly…" He shook his head, the tall collar at his neck twisting with the motion. Regret was written on his face. "Tonight Drah-cool-ahhh has been replaced by Gypsy band." His expression brightened. "Do you like Gypsy music, Pooo-chi?"

"Why yes, I think so."

"Vell, then ve shall dance, yes?"

He struggled to get up from the chair with vigor. But sheer determination was not enough. Halfway to standing, Lugosi started to collapse. I darted forward, shoring him up by the elbow.

"Sciatica," he explained.

Or alcohol. Or drugs. Our eyes met and I registered the glazed look and pinpoint pupils again. Perhaps both?

"Oh, Uncle Bela."

It was Ilka. She'd made a flourishing exit through the double doors, the melancholy high-pitched strains of violins and the pure operatic voice of Ilona Massey bursting out with her. The melodious tune of "At the Balalaika" from the movie of the same name resonated before the doors closed, cutting off the music. The silent film star in the fur coat had also trailed Ilka out into the lobby. She had on dark glasses again. Ilka was wearing a teal cocktail dress with a keyhole neckline. A graceful asymmetrical flounce overlaid the fitted skirt. Her lips pressed into a tight line when she saw me.

"Pucci—" It was all she seemed able to say.

"I-I didn't want to be alone tonight," I explained, taking a deep breath before pressing on. "My friend died. I'm sorry. I didn't realize this was such a big event. So fancy…"

Ilka's shoulders rose then fell. She shook her head. "No, I'm sorry. That is sad about your friend. Is okay you come. I am happy to see you. It's just, well, Uncle Bela, he's having some difficulty tonight."

"Sciatica?"

Ilka arched a perfectly plucked eyebrow. "That is at the root, yes."

"Roots?" Lugosi said, as if just tuning in. "You vant to do another herbal treatment? No, no. Vhy? I have cure of the good doctor. It help me so much, it put me in such a good state of feeling…I am feeling no pain vhatsoever." His mouth curled into a silly smile. He swooned.

I steadied him. To Ilka, I said, "Can I help?"

Behind her, a slight man in a dark suit exited the party room. He looked our way then turned and made for the nearby hallway with a brass-plated "restroom" sign at its entrance. I didn't get a look at his face, but he had an olive complexion and a shock of white hair. He used a cane for support as he walked in quick, Chaplinesque movements past the silent film star, swathed in fur. She faced away from him, and us, studying the movie poster. The white-haired gentleman, pausing momentarily in the hallway entrance, glanced back at her before rapidly disappearing down the corridor.

"Pucci?" It was Ilka.

"Oh, sorry." I was still supporting Lugosi. He listed toward me but caught himself. "Yes?"

"Is okay we go now. Our auction item is delivered as promised. She sits in traditional costume on the silent auction table with the rest. She is lovely, a typical Hungarian beauty." Ilka patted her waved platinum bang and laughed teasingly. "But in truth, of the dolls, she is drawing the most attractive bids."

She showed her perfect white teeth again then shot a fleeting glance at the silent film star. Her back was still to us. "Maybe you could help Uncle Bela out to our car. The doorman will direct you. I'll be right out. My gr—" The word caught. Ilka coughed. "My great admirer needs assistance." She gestured sideways with her head in the direction of the restrooms.

"Of course, I'd be delighted." I smiled at Lugosi, gripping his elbow firmly in the manner I'd learned from Sam.

Out front, I looked for the doorman without luck. Afraid to leave Lugosi alone, fearing he might topple or wander off in my absence, I steered him past the front of the building and out into the darkened lot toward the parked cars.

"Pooo-chi, ver are ve going? We did not have our dance. Ahhh—" Lugosi tilted his head, looking skyward. For a moment

I thought he would howl. Gazing at the sky he spoke in a mysterious tone, emphasizing his words. "The cloak of night." His chin dropped and he turned his gaze on me. The queer look in his eyes made me shiver. "You prefer a promenade in the cemetery perhaps?"

I was speechless. Where was the attendant? Ilka and her fan? She said they'd be right out.

Then the sound of footsteps, quick footsteps, but only a single set.

I looked behind us to see who was coming. A long silver blade on the tip of a cane dancing toward us flashed in the headlights of an approaching automobile. Wielding the cane: the man with the wild white hair.

Lugosi surprised me. As the man rushed at us, Lugosi casually reached out his foot and tripped him. The man hurtled to the ground, his arms thrashing. The automobile's headlamps were blinding and it was hard to get a fix on our attacker. I kicked in the direction of his groin, but booted air. Lugosi's weight, rebounding from to the effort he'd put forth, shifted, unbalancing us. I stumbled. Before I could kick again, our assailant scrambled to his feet, retrieved his cane, and ran.

The car braked beside us. It was the doorman with Lugosi's sleek silver 1941 Lincoln Coupe. He threw open the driver's door, revealing a rich red leather interior, and joined us. Ilka, supporting the elderly actress, toddled across the lot in our direction as rapidly as was reasonable for the aged woman.

"Pucci, Uncle Bela, are you okay?" She was somewhat breathless. "What happened?"

Bela grinned, obviously pleased with himself. "My timing, it was good?"

Inside my chest, my heart jack-hammered. But I had to smile. "It saved one or both of us from becoming shish kabab." I looked at Ilka. "We're fine. It was that man with the crazy white hair. He came out of the auction room after you and your, uh—" I glanced at the fur-clad star. "—fan. Did you see him? Do you know who he is?"

Ilka looked pale, but then it could have been the white cast of the head lamps. She shrugged. "There was man with Einstein hair bidding on items. A guest. Eccentric Hollywood type. I can find out more, but not now, please. I am sorry." She looked from the elderly woman to Lugosi. "It has been big night. I must get them home."

We'd been close to being skewered. The smart thing would have been to investigate promptly. But Ilka looked as exhausted as I felt.

"I understand. And we both have big days tomorrow. The briefie—"

Ilka managed a smile. "Yes, will you come?"

"I'm going to try. Would you like me to drive one of your charges home?"

"No. But thank you kindly. I will take them. See you at the house shortly."

The doorman had been standing by with a world-weary expression as if he'd seen it all before. He handed Ilka the keys. While Ilka helped her aged fan into the back seat, I walked Lugosi around the car, opening the passenger door and inviting him to climb in.

He chuckled, sitting and folding his long legs inside. "Ahhh, like me, my enemies are getting sloppy. He should have known it vould take a vodden stake through my heart to kill me."

I laughed. But I had an unsettled feeling the attack had not been directed at Lugosi.

Chapter Sixteen

A blast of peptic acid seared the lining of my stomach as I walked through the typing pool. Ilka's Finn coffee. Ilka had left the coffee pot, ready for brewing, on the burner this morning with a note explaining she was going to try to sleep in. Her briefie was today and she needed to look her best.

Last night I had waited up for her, but gave in to my own desperate need for some shut eye around midnight. My flight in the P-51 was on for this afternoon. This morning, first thing, I'd placed another call to Miss C. I would have preferred telling her in person, but she'd been out again. So I left a brief message for her about Frankie with the hotel receptionist, adding, "Leave word with Major Beacock if there's anything you need to tell me before the film shoot."

Gunnar had not made it back to the Dunns', but he'd agreed to continue our discussion concerning Brody and related espionage matters on the flight over to March. I couldn't escape the feeling that last night's attempted assault had been directed at me. I also suspected there might be a link to the Brody investigation. We were meeting after Ilka's performance at MGM and I would share my theory then.

It was Saturday morning. The gals in the secretarial pool were off for the weekend, and there was no one around to disturb me as I tidied up paperwork and planned to phone Novara for his reactions to the script revisions I'd sent over.

A single cup of Finn coffee should have been enough, but I'd gulped down two. Another acid surge assaulted my stomach as I waited for Novara to pick up. He had barely been willing to listen until Sam had interceded on my behalf—what made me think he'd be responsive now?

"Pucci, sweetheart. Glad you called." Novara sounded genuinely delighted to hear from me. So much so, he was practically purring.

What did that mean? I braced myself.

"Read the new scenes. Gotta hand it to ya, kid. They're swell, *heh heh*, swell."

Incredible. What Sam had said the other day about the movie business—"One day you're in, next, you're out"—was true. This morning, it seemed, I was IN.

"You like them? Great. Going to go with them, then?" I crossed my fingers.

"You betcha." Novara cleared his throat. "The playful stuff with the gals in shorts and all was a grabber, but this new stuff, well, it's got more going for it, know what I mean?"

I absolutely did. It meant that the film was going to be a true depiction of what the WASP is doing for the war effort. I nearly clapped with delight.

"You see, things turn out for the best," Novara continued. "With this bang-up job you've done, the segments are ready to start filming, almost straightaway—without much additional effort from me. A hunky-dory result, since the Clark Gable project needs all I've got to give, pronto."

I wondered what effort he thought he'd put forth for our film in the first place, but turned to a more pressing concern eating at me instead.

"Have you talked to Sam Lorenz about any of this?"

"Uh-huh. Got off the horn with him, right before you called. Which is another reason it's so nifty what you did. He couldn't have done that script revision even if someone had been wavin' an Academy Award in his face. Those writers." Novara sighed.

"Always reaching for the little white powders when things get rough. He could barely put together a lucid sentence."

"Sam Lorenz *on drugs?*"

"Get your head out of the clouds, kiddo…What is it?" There was dead air for a moment, then the muffled sounds of Novara talking with someone on the other end of the line. *Something about shoes?* An instant later, he was back on.

"Gotta hurry, now, sweetheart. Where were we? Oh, yeah, Sam Lorenz. He was supposed to ride out to March Field with me for the ferrying segment. But he won't be going. No matter. Man oh man, I'm looking forward to seeing that new fighter in action. Break a leg up there, or whatever it is you pilots say."

"Uh-hmm."

"Something else?"

Why push my luck. "Nope."

◇◇◇

I left the phone booth and walked through the deserted office space, feeling both euphoric and troubled. Novara's report on his conversation with Sam nagged at me. I hadn't questioned his assumption that Sam was on drugs—the black mark against Sam worked in my favor—but Sam a hophead? The notion surprised me, but it also explained his erratic behavior the other night. I sighed. The bizarre attempt at dancing. His shock at seeing someone at the window. Perhaps there'd been no one there at all. He'd been hallucinating.

I stopped at my desk briefly, then proceeded outdoors to a gorgeous morning.

Thoughts of the wacky evening with Sam persisted on the walk from the administration building to the parking space where I'd left the Packard. An image of Sam at May Lee's flashed to mind. The flushed coloring of his face that I'd attributed to alcohol, a symptom of drugs? The nervous scratching, also related? At another vision, this one of a sickly-looking Sam visiting the hospital, my toe caught on an uneven portion of pavement and I tripped, luckily recovering before I tumbled.

Well, so what if he was an addict? I'd washed my hands of him. He wasn't my problem any longer. At least not on a personal level. There was still what he knew about Frankie's crash to deal with. But maybe Max would have some answers. Or Miss C.

My spirits picked up as I caught sight of the Packard's dark green and chrome exterior, the cut-down doors, the tan leather interior. The runabout was a sporty dream machine, especially the way it looked now, top down. I loved the car and would miss it terribly when my mission was over.

"Oh, What a Beautiful Morning" was playing on the radio as I motored out of Fort Roach, then down Washington toward MGM. I put my soul into singing along with "everything's going my way…"

◇◇◇

Gus wasn't at his newsstand when I rolled past. Apparently, he had taken the day off as well. A dark-haired fellow with a walrus mustache was standing in for him. I didn't stop. If Gus had been there, I definitely would have, but the sooner I got to MGM the better. I wanted to see as much of Ilka's picture as possible before flying out to March Field.

◇◇◇

I parked the Packard in a lot behind the executive office building. I got my bearings and began the short journey to Sound Stage 5. There were few people about, but the tall, thin woman wearing a smart black suit, long red gloves, and fashionable pumps walking toward me would have stood out, even in a crowd. Her face was familiar, but I didn't place her right away. She was nearly abreast of me when it hit. Wilma Wallace, the OWI representative. But with an entirely new look. When we'd met three days ago in Brody's office, her hair had been secured in a severe bun. She'd worn thick, horn-rimmed glasses. Now her longish ash-blonde hair hung in tight defined waves. Her pencil-lined blue eyes popped between lashes lush with mascara; her lips, painted an alluring bright red, picked up the shade in her gloves. What was equally if not more arresting was that I'd seen Wilma in this glammed-up persona before. The woman in the incriminating photo with Brody.

"Hello, Miss Wallace." She paused and squinted, trying to place me. "We met the other day at the story meeting. *Adrift with the Enemy.* I was just observing."

"Oh, right."

"Mr. Brody invited me." At the mention of the director's name, she turned away. "Sorry, you must miss him." She nodded, sniffled, dabbed a gloved finger to her nose.

"You look nice."

When she turned back, she smiled, but there was a glum edge to her expression. "Why, thank you. I have a friend in the make-up department." She finger-combed a side of her hair. "Ordinarily, I wouldn't dream of showing my nonbusiness side in the daytime. But the other evening I ventured out to a fundraiser. A palm reader there was incredibly gifted. If you think my outside has been transformed, well, there've been inner changes too."

Had Ilka read Wilma Wallace's palm? It appeared that way. The serendipity was uncanny. My astonishment must have shown.

This time her smile was genuine. "It's true. Through studying the pattern on my hand, she revealed things about myself I'd forgotten or ignored or hadn't recognized. She asked questions and we talked. She helped me to uncover my calling. She encouraged me not to hide who I am. To know that I can be feminine in my appearance and still get things done."

"Bravo." I echoed what I knew Miss C would say. "That's wonderful."

The pearl bracelet Wallace had worn in Brody's office adorned her gloved arm. The contrast of the smooth creamy gems against the red fabric seemed to reflect her new mindset: power and grace combined.

She polished a pearl with her finger, and from the look on her face I guessed the bracelet had been a gift from Brody. "I believe we are all on this earth to touch others' lives in positive ways. I've quit OWI and applied to join the WAC. I want to drive an ambulance on the front, devote myself to a meaningful cause. Step away from my Movieland fantasy existence. Find peace. Maybe learn to forgive myself."

Wallace had been so absorbed in the bracelet and conveying her thoughts, it was as if she'd forgotten I was there. She looked up. "Oh, sorry." She blinked. "Of course, if the WAC assigns me to ambulance driving, I'll be back to wearing a uniform and my glasses." She smiled.

Wallace was trying to find a silver lining. But leave town? Did Gunnar know about this?

Ilka might be psychic, but I was getting a strange foreboding sensation myself. Could the enemy operatives involved in espionage and Brody's death also be saboteurs? Was their mission somehow tied to what happened to Frankie?

"Miss Wallace, this is very delicate and I'm sorry to have to ask. But a friend of mine died yesterday, also under suspicious circumstances." She looked at me wide-eyed. "Yes, I know signs point to Mr. Brody having been murdered. I'm part of a team investigating. I also know, uh, sorry, that you and he were, well…in love." My face felt hot and I knew my coloring was closing in on the shade of her gloves. "Was anyone else wise to what was going on?"

Wilma's lips had gone dry and her lipstick was caked. She circled her mouth with her tongue. "No one."

"Please think. It's critical to our inquiry. You want us to find the killer, don't you?" If she didn't, *that* would be telling.

Her eyes shifted. "Well, possibly Myra," she conceded. "Secretaries seem to know everything."

◇◇◇

I hoofed it down a side street toward Sound Stage 5.

Things were much quieter than when I'd first visited the MGM lot. Probably fewer people worked on the weekend. I thought of the secret memo's description of the UFA Studio's round-the-clock schedule and hoped that there was more going on inside the surrounding buildings than was visible to the naked eye outside.

Three men in tee-shirts and jeans rounded the corner just ahead and came toward me carrying rolled up cords, cables, and a camera. From their equipment, I guessed they were grips or electricians. We all reached the door at once. Their arms were full. I held the door for them. They were part of the film crew. The trio couldn't tell me the briefie's subject matter, but their faces broke into devilish grins when they reported that nine starlets were participating in the shoot.

Nine starlets? A two-minute production? Not exactly a "star maker" opportunity for Ilka.

I trailed them to a lighted set about halfway down the cavernous sound stage. They threaded their way through the clutter of people and equipment already surrounding the set, while I halted at a spot ideal for observing the goings on.

The set was a replica of an office interior. A sterile office interior. Eight gorgeous young ladies, starlets, I presumed from what the grips had told me, were seated on a long bench. The bench was the centerpiece of the set's furnishings. On the wall behind the starlets, Uncle Sam in tall hat and stars and stripes pointed accusingly from a large poster that read: SILK & NYLON STOCKINGS FOR UNCLE SAM. A waist-high round trash canister overflowing with stockings stood next to the benched ladies.

I looked at the lineup more closely. They all wore dresses and high-heeled shoes. Ilka was not among them. Then I saw her, a large straw basket hooked on her arm, off to one side of the set. She was the only blonde of the bunch and her platinum hair was pulled into the compulsory upsweep.

A man in a white dress shirt and dark pleated trousers was giving the women instruction. I gave a discreet wave, trying to catch Ilka's attention, but she was glomming on to his every word, like the other gals, and didn't notice.

After a few moments, the man walked to the camera facing the set. The camera sat atop a crane-like arm attached to a movable dolly. A seat for the cameraman was mounted on the adjustable arm, and the man who'd been giving direction to the girls slid onto it. After peering through the camera lens and studying the set, he made a few adjustments. He dismounted and turned so I had a full view of him. Mid-fifties, he had the droopy expression of an aging beagle. His dark hair had thinned to a few strands on top and there were prominent bags under his eyes.

Settling into a tall chair slung with a canvas seat emblazoned with DIRECTOR, he lifted a megaphone to his mouth. "All right, let's have a rehearsal."

The set grew quiet. He shouted into the megaphone again. "Ruthie, where are you?"

"Here," a female voice chimed from across the set.

A middle-aged woman with thick glasses perched atop dark straight hair was picking her way through the sprawl of technicians, grips, and equipment. Toting a clipboard in the crook of her elbow and wearing a stopwatch around her neck, she might have been a gym teacher or swim coach.

"Got the script?" the director asked.

Ruthie nodded, sidling in close to his chair.

The director pointed the megaphone at the line of starlets and spoke loudly. "All right. This briefie we're doing here this morning has only four scenes. The three involving you gals run back to back. We're going to do all three, boom, boom, boom. Got it?"

A gal on the end opposite Ilka said something in an undertone. There was some murmuring from the other starlets.

The director, ignoring the disruption added, "Fourth scene will be spliced in later."

"How about splicing in some furnishings for the set?" One of the ladies wisecracked. The others giggled.

"I got news for you, Charlene. This isn't supposed to be the parlor of some Southern plantation. And you're not Vivien Leigh."

The director's retort unleashed some teasing comments and more laughter. Even Ilka, who'd remained silent and unsmiling at her post to the side, could not contain a broad grin.

Aware his control was ebbing at a dangerous rate, the director bellowed, "That goes double for the rest of you. Stop acting like a bunch of dizzy belles waiting for your beaux to come and escort you out for a spin around the ballroom."

Naturally, the admonishment only egged the girls on more. The director's face turned borscht red. It astounded me that when he took another stab at quieting his unruly cast, he stuck with the same tack.

"We're not doing a remake of *Gone with the Wind* here," he screeched through the megaphone, invoking yet another twist on the laughable analogy. "We're doing *Uncle Sam Wants Your Old Stockings to Sock the Axis.*"

I knew a director worked with cast members to help them understand his sense of vision for the film, but what was he going for here? Mass hysteria? I grinned. Listen to me! My concept gets approved for a film and what happens? Poof! I think I'm Master Director.

Pandemonium threatening, the director at last changed his approach. "Ladies," he said in a strained whisper that required absolute quiet to hear. "We're going for austerity here, because this piece is about sacrificing for the war effort. What we're about to do may help save lives and win the war. It may help bring our men home sooner." Then, as an aside, in a more forceful voice he added, "Perhaps you should practice some austerity with your mouths."

The entire set became somber.

"No, no, no," the director bawled. "I want an austere setting! Not grim faces. I want pert! Perky! Not murrrky!"

The director's emotional rantings—particularly the way his jowls shook with his exaggeration of the word "murky"—were so overblown, they made me smile. I once had a flight instructor who was a pussycat underneath his gruff exterior. The director reminded me of him.

Fortunately, the ladies under the lights were taking the situation with a grain of salt as well. Posed quietly now, they awaited further direction.

"Okay. Let's get started. Everyone, right leg over left."

The ladies sat up straight, crossed their legs, and stared into the camera lens.

"Nice," the director said after a moment. "I think we're ready. Ruthie will read the narration for the rehearsal. Bette Davis will be the voice in the final cut."

Another stir rippled through the starlets at the mention of the famous actress.

Impatiently, the director shouted, "Knock it off! I'll see to it you gals never get a big-time role if you can't give me what I want here!" The starlets responded with instant silence. "Now, let's see what you can do. Ruthie, go!"

Ruthie cleared her throat. "Off with the stockings girls," she read. "They're due for the discard and the war effort needs them."

I stared. Her voice was high-pitched, quavering, a dead ringer for our First Lady's.

While she spoke, the ladies stood and formed a line in front of the bench. They posed as though a chorus line, right foot in front, toes pointed, each foot angled "just so." Next, they bent down, pretending to roll their stockings from the knee down over the calf.

Ruthie continued, "In a silk and nylon campaign, the government is asking us to turn in our stockings…" The ladies recrossed their legs, so now the left foot was forward. "Not new ones or good ones, but worn-out stockings. Here, motion picture starlets contribute theirs."

The trilling speech? Was it real, or was she acting? But if she was playing a part, why not take on the voice of the film's narrator, Bette Davis?

Again, the starlets on the set acted out rolling down their stockings.

"That's it, that's it," the director said quietly in the background.

Ruthie continued in her high, quivering voice "Rising film star Ilka Maki collects the stockings at the MGM Studio in Hollywood…"

In my mind's eye, Brody's secretary appeared, entering his office during the story meeting. Like Ruthie's voice, Myra's overbite and receding chin had reminded me of Eleanor Roosevelt. At intelligence school, we'd received instruction in the use of facial disguises. Detachable gum pads puff sunken cheeks or transform the profile by filling out the upper and lower lips. If such a pad could be inserted into Myra's chin, it would change her looks dramatically. For the better, I suspected. An adjustment to her chin might also improve her lisp. Now what about Ruthie? Was that the way she normally spoke?

Like a row of upended dominoes suddenly toppled, the ideas rippled into one another until I noticed Ilka had taken center stage.

Carrying the basket, she walked behind the ladies who had returned to the bench and were seated again. As Ilka passed, the starlets turned and placed their stockings in the basket. When she'd finished, Ilka stopped at the front of the set, placing the basket on a small stand that had been slipped in front of her. While she slid a fist into a sheer stocking pulled from the collection, the others gathered behind her. They smiled over Ilka's shoulder as she held her stocking-covered hand and forearm aloft examining it. After a second, Ilka looked into the lens with an approving grin.

In the background Ruthie said, "There's an explosive reason for the silk and nylon drive…"

The director took up his megaphone. "Cut."

He gave a quick synopsis of the scene that would follow. Bette Davis would explain that the stockings were intended to be used in making powder bags for heavy guns. A finished bag looked like a huge long nylon tube and was filled with gun powder. Actual footage of one of the bags being hoisted by crane onto one of the big artillery guns would accompany the narration.

Miss Riefenstahl, Dr. Goebbels…eat your hearts out. The script was corny, but it was sure to grab the public's attention. The message was compellingly clear. I was certain that women all across the country would respond by pitching in their stockings.

I felt a pang of unease. Miss C would probably think that Ilka and the other gals were allowing themselves to be exploited. Ah, well. This little flick wasn't her responsibility, nor mine. And it was for the cause.

"After the gun gets loaded," the director finished up, "the audience will hear Miss Davis say: 'Girls, here's how your worn-out stockings will go to war and give the Nazis and Japs a great big sock!' The finale is the resounding boom of the gun firing."

The starlets smiled and nodded agreeably.

The director took a look through the camera again. "Okay, let's get a picture."

The actresses returned to their places on the bench. Ilka went back to her spot on the sideline. The director called for quiet. The buzzer sounded and the set doors locked. "Roll sound," he commanded. Then, "Roll camera."

The clapper boy held up his slate reading "Uncle Sam Wants Your Old Stockings—Scene 1, Take 1." Giving it a curt snap in front of the camera, he stepped out of the frame.

"Ac-tion," the director barked into the megaphone.

Camera rolling, the ladies stood and took up their chorus-line position.

Right away, the director called, "Cut."

Impatiently, he shouted, "Second from left, your stocking has a giant snag in front."

The starlet looked up, wide-eyed. "I thought that was the point. We're giving up our worn out stockings!"

The director released an excruciating sigh. "This is a movie, Barbara Jane. Not the real thing. Your leg is what's gonna sell. And it's not gonna sell anything looking like ninety-eight-year-old Great Aunt Martha's beat-up gam." Another heavy sigh. "Stocking, Ruthie!"

Ruthie dispatched a bystander to fetch a fresh stocking. As the aide left, a portly man in a fine suit with a handkerchief protruding from the breast pocket arrived on the set. Ruthie spotted the newcomer first and immediately began making a fuss over him. The director joined in. They had a three-way conversation for a few minutes, then the director addressed the cast and crew.

"ATTENTION, EVERYONE! We're gonna take a short break." The director checked his watch. "Take fifteen, but don't leave the set. I want to shoot this before lunch."

I inched my way across the set. "Psst. Ilka."

Ilka's face lit up when she saw me. "Pucci. Thank you for coming."

A caterer had brought in coffee and sweet rolls. I followed Ilka over to the laden table, where we each grabbed a cup of coffee. Canvas folding chairs were spaced around the set. Many of the cast and crew were already sitting in them, reading trade papers or conversing in small groups. We found two vacant seats and drew them together far enough from the others so that we could talk in private.

Settling into her chair, Ilka asked, "Well, what do you think?"

We discussed the picture, both of us agreeing that, though it was a small film, she had a big part.

"I thought Mr. Lugosi might be here."

"No, as you have seen last night he is in bad way."

Sam was also "in bad way." I buried the errant thought. "The first time we met, I saw the leather case. The vial. Needle. Is he on narcotics?"

"Morphine. Doctor prescribed." Ilka shook her head. "The drug, it relieves the pain, it is sure. But it is potent. Makes him a little loco." She spun her finger in a circle near her temple. "Naturally, I worry."

Recalling I'd been outside the kitchen and had overheard her tell Lugosi, "It can kill," for an instant *I* was worried.

"The roles he is getting now are beneath him," she continued. "Typecast as monster, bah! Frankenstein his big comeback, fie!" Ilka shuddered. "Imagine. Great actor who at the most famous National Theater in Budapest was cast as Romeo. Jesus Christ.

Now plays the devil's disciple. It is sad. I fear the escape to opiates will increase in keeping with declining offers."

"But it's a living. He's paying the bills, right?"

Ilka shrugged.

I felt the tug of the heartstring connected to my soft spot for immigrants. Lugosi had been through a great deal and clearly was up against tough times now. Ilka's journey here couldn't have been easy either. She, like Lugosi, struggled to get ahead in the dog-eat-dog world of movie-making. I studied her, trying to imagine what she'd been through, though I didn't have a prayer of truly understanding the hardships of leaving everything familiar and starting over from scratch somewhere new. What I did know was that it'd taken incredible courage and great strength. Yet the person sitting next to me projected no hint of having ever suffered anything more than a broken fingernail. Even her speech hardly gave her away. And, with her Jean Harlow platinum hair, terrific looks and glamorous figure, Ilka fit in perfectly with the Hollywood starlets scattered nearby. No, she stood out. Hadn't the director said she was "up and coming"? Still…

"Acting is a brutal profession. Even Lugosi with all his experience and talent is getting tromped on. Why are you so determined to follow him? It's gotta be tougher for women. And movie people, the movie business…it can be so much phony-baloney. You've been through such harrowing experiences. And you survived. With the kind of inner core that's gotten you this far, you could do anything. You have other gifts…"

Ilka's eyes widened. She cut me off. "Think, lady. I already told you. I come from phony."

It was my turn to be pop-eyed.

Ilka's laugh was tinkly, nervous. She looked around. Two grips, part of the threesome who'd entered the sound stage with me, were seated nearby absorbed in magazines. Her expression softened.

"Sorry," she said softly. "You cannot imagine the number of times I was caught—or nearly caught—stealing chickens. So many times, it is a wonder I am here." She rolled her eyes and smiled. "Hoo! The lies I have told to farmers in order to save my skin. So you see, acting it is at the heart of who I am. This is my chance, Pucci." Her eyes pleaded for understanding. "I am without education, pedigree, or financial security. I have looks, that is it. I must use them to my advantage.

"When I am actress, I will make money and help friends left behind in the old country. I will help Uncle Bela as he has helped me."

I'd really stuck my nose in where it didn't belong. What did I really know about what was right for her? Or, for that matter, about what she'd been through.

"Good plan," I said, meaning it with all my heart. "Didn't mean to get on a soap box like that. I was thinking of your palm reading. I bumped into Wilma Wallace outside. She was over the moon raving about the guidance she'd gotten. I assumed from you?" Ilka thought a moment, smiled, and nodded. "The silent film actress you brought home the other evening for a special session. She's another fan..." Ilka frowned. She looked confused, or was it troubled? "You said so last night."

Ilka shook her head "Last night, it was very strange night."

"Did you get a chance to follow up with any club members? Learn more about the eccentric Hollywood type with the Einstein hair? You said he was a guest. That he was bidding on auction items."

The coffee had been hot and I'd been letting mine cool, holding the cup in my lap. Ilka raised her cup to her lips, blew on the dark black liquid. "The man, an I-tal-ian—" Ilka narrowed her eyes seductively and winked, "he is collector. The auction organizer, she got word beforehand. She put notice in paper, a call for Hungarian dolls. He was bidding on our doll in the silent auction before we left. The price it was going higher and higher..."

"*Our* doll?"

Ilka's eyes shifted. She sipped her coffee. "Yes, my fan who was there once give it to me as gift. The doll, she was in costume. A delicate porcelain face, little leather boots, hand-embroidered apron and vest, beaded headpiece. She was beautiful. A reminder of home. It was not easy to part with her." Ilka smiled stoically. "But to fill the war coffers for fight against Hitler. To give him a big sock…" She nodded toward the set. "I would do it yet again."

"But did you find out his name? Where he lives?"

Ilka looked crushed. "No, I did not. I was too shocked to ask. Our doll, it disappeared."

"You mean it was snatched? Before the money was collected? How could that be?"

"A waste basket on the stage in front it caught fire. Naturally, people, they were looking there. While they look, the doll it vanish."

Arson on the *Resisting Enemy Interrogation* set. Now fire at a fundraiser. A wild-haired eccentric…

The news vendor was an eccentric. But he wasn't Italian, he was Hungarian. Or was he? I'd just assumed from his accent he was Eastern Bloc.

Ilka's face filled with concern. "Pucci, you all right?"

I cleared my throat. "Ilka, the collector. Did he have different colored eyes? One false?"

"I cannot say. The lights in the room, they were dim."

The director's voice boomed through the bullhorn. "Back to your places everyone!"

"Ilka, I'm sorry." I scrambled out of my seat. "I need to get to March Field for my film shoot. Gotta run."

Chapter Seventeen

The Santa Monica residential area gave way to the camouflaged perimeters of Clover Field. I swung the Packard up a side street, following it to the south end of the field where Miss C's Staggerwing was being stored. At the small hangar, I climbed out, immediately noticing the canary yellow plane perched near the flight line.

On the field, cadets in dark coveralls were sopping up their lessons on the tarmac-campus. I wove through the small student groups stationed at models of airplane sections while keeping an eye out for Gunnar. He'd asked to hitch a ride out to March Field; now where was he? The flight to March would take only about a half hour, but I had an 0930 appointment to keep with the P-51 test pilot. He needed to brief me on the plane's special features before I could take the new fighter up. And I wanted to leave enough time for practicing a few maneuvers before the actual shoot. *After* Max and I went over the plane with a fine-toothed comb.

I checked my watch, hoping he still planned to show up. Some critical new and unfinished business needed our attention.

At last I spotted him walking out of one of the half-hangars at the Douglas facility. Bulk, the AAF mechanic-instructor keeping an eye on Miss C's Staggerwing, was with him. They skirted a Havoc, a side section of its fuselage pulled apart for repair, saw me, and waved.

Locked in amiable discussion, walking more briskly now, the two men skirted the end of the runway. Gunnar wore a leather flight jacket, dungarees, and the beat-up cowboy boots he favored. Tall and fit, his bearing casual, he strode as if at ease with himself and the world. Bulk, who was medium height and barrel-chested, wore grease-stained coveralls stretched taut over his stout physique. He swaggered with the effort of moving his full frame, especially at the stepped-up pace, but he appeared perfectly satisfied with the man he was, as well.

They drew near. Bulk removed his billed cap. "Great day for blasting off into the wild blue," he said, brushing a hand over a bristly crew cut. "Gunnar tells me you'll be flying the P-51 later today. That's some hot plane. Impressive they've agreed to let you fly it."

His admiring look and the reminder of the impending flight sent blood rushing to my face.

"Taking the P-51 up is an honor, all right. Kind of bowled me over, too, getting the nod." I checked the cloudless azure sky. "Yup, perfect day. But this is the hot machine I'm going up in first, right?" I nodded to the Staggerwing.

Bulk sensed my impatience to get underway. He flashed an okay sign and lumbered over to the plane. With a grunt, he mounted the wing and climbed into the cockpit to inspect the interior. Gunnar and I remained on the ground.

"You're too modest," Gunnar said. "Getting approved on the P-51 is a huge privilege only an ace pilot would have been allotted."

I shrugged and began my walk-around check. Gunnar stayed with me. "You're an ace saleswoman to boot. The Pentagon isn't usually looking for publicity for a prototype plane. In fact, the strategy is generally the opposite. Keep the enemy in the dark whenever possible." Gunnar's mouth spread into a slow grin that dimpled a tiny spot on his cheek.

"Miss Cochran called the base commander. She secured the P-51."

Gunnar shook his head. "Miss Cochran's support carries weight. Not in this instance, though. Decision to extend you permission for the P-51 had already been made by the time her call came through."

I started to ask where he had gotten his information then realized: Gunnar had an inside track to the brass. I continued checking the landing gear and other inspection points. Gunnar followed along, observing. At last, walking to the front, patting the plane affectionately on the nose, I turned to face him.

"Why are we talking about the P-51? What's going on with drop site? Any developments? Did the minnow take the bait?"

Gunnar's shoulders fell. "No. No activity. It's almost as if he's been tipped off."

I took a big breath. "Gunnar, I think I had a brush with the minnow. Possibly *one* of the big fishes."

Gunnar's sandy eyebrows peaked in the center. He stared as I told him about the attack at the club.

"We nearly had him, but he bolted before I could even get a good look at his face."

"How do you know he was trying to skewer you, not Lugosi?"

"I can't say for sure, but I don't trust the coincidence…"

There was a slight thump as Bulk dropped from the wing. A Hershey's wrapper escaped his pocket. While he bent to pick it up, Gunnar leaned close to my ear. "To be continued," he murmured.

"Everything checks out inside," Bulk called out. "You two ready?"

I pulled the speed prop a few times to clear it. "Yup. Ready."

◇◇◇

Gunnar and I strapped in, then taxied away from the hangar. I spun the radio's dial to the proper frequency and called the tower. A reply crackled from the plane's receiver.

"Beech one-three one-three able. You're cleared to runway One-Niner. Wind's from the southeast at fifteen knots. Altimeter setting, two-niner-eight-six."

I rolled to the end of the strip, turned into the wind, and paused to do my pre-takeoff run-up. Instruments, controls, engine magnetos "checked." Fuel mixture, nose trim, carburetor heat, throttle "adjusted."

Cleared for takeoff, I advanced the throttle. My feet dropped from the brakes, the Staggerwing lunged forward, and we sped down the runway. A quick climb to cruising altitude and I banked sharply, taking up a course to the east. Easing the power back, I leveled off, scanning the instrument panel and rotating the wheels to adjust the trim tabs with the engine speed. The Pratt & Whitney hummed low and even. A few more alignments and I turned to Gunnar. He was staring over the side.

"That camouflage netting. Incredible."

I looked out my window. "Yeah. The Ocean Park Boulevard painted across the top of the Douglas plant blends so perfectly with the pavement at each end, it's impossible to tell where the fake street stops and the real one begins. Look, oil streaks and tire marks even."

I banked the plane giving Gunnar a clear view of the cloth and framework reproduction of the Santa Monica Douglas aircraft plant nearby. "And there's the dummy Douglas plant— fake field and all."

Once the U.S. Army Engineers had successfully obscured the real factory with the camouflage netting, making it look like an extension of the surrounding residential neighborhood, they realized the unmistakable bulk of the big hangar was impossible to completely disguise. So, a dummy plant was built as a more obvious diversion. Only a short distance away from the real thing, the fake facility was dominated by an imitation of the big hangar and flanked by a perfect—but bogus—airfield.

"Brilliant," Gunnar said. "Shrouding the fake facility with shoddy camouflaging to catch the eye of an alert bombardier."

I nodded, maneuvering the plane back on course. "The effort and skill that it took to disguise the real plant is one thing. But think of the thousands and thousands of dollars that went into making the reproduction."

"In the bookkeeping of war, it's a small price to pay. Throwing an invader into momentary confusion and jumbling his plan of attack gives defending planes and gunners their chance."

At a sputtering in the engine's sound, my grip on the throttle tightened. I held my breath, listening. A pilot's ear, like that of a symphony conductor's, is constantly tuned to perfect pitch. The slightest deviation is jarring.

Gunnar looked over. He'd heard it, too.

A scan of the instruments read normal and the engine's hum was smooth again, yet neither of us spoke. We remained all ears, concentrating on the powerful vibration of the Pratt & Whitney and the normal hiss of airflow seeping into the cabin through vents and joints in the fuselage.

I made a few adjustments to keep us on course.

Finally, Gunnar let out a long breath. "What do you think it was?"

I looked over with a blasé smile. "That little hiccup?" My voice sounded calmer than I felt. "Probably nothing. A random, normal sputter." Of course, sputters weren't the norm. But we were 9,300 feet up, and that's what I was willing it to be.

I entertained thoughts of heading back to Clover Field. But so much was riding on our getting to March Field on schedule, I quickly ditched the idea. Bulk had gone over the plane and I'd personally conducted the preflight inspection. There was nothing to be jittery about.

Except that a saboteur may be lurking about.

Shoving the thought aside, I said, "We were discussing camouflage. This morning I bumped into Wilma Wallace. She looked different. A stop in the make-up department, she said." I looked over. "She was Brody's lover." Gunnar nodded. "You said she was questioned and cleared. Did you know she's planning to leave town? Possibly the country?"

Gunnar gathered his thoughts for a moment. "It's a complex matter, but yes. She's enlisted in the WACs, a good place for her to be."

"Chalmers is off the hook, so's Wallace. Brody's secretary, Myra? What about her?"

The possibility that she might somehow be mixed up in Brody's death had occurred to me immediately, and I was somewhat shocked to learn Gunnar did not consider her a suspect. I told him what Wallace had said about the likelihood of Myra knowing about the affair.

"So Myra could have been blackmailing him." I looked over. Gunnar nodded, but he was holding something back. "You don't still suspect Ilka, do you?"

He didn't answer. We hit a few bumps. My stomach knotted as we rode out the turbulence, then uncoiled as the air settled again almost immediately. I adjusted the trim tabs. The bar on the artificial horizon gauge leveled out.

Gunnar sent me a wan smile. "This is getting to be an interesting flight."

My eyebrow lifted. "I was asking about Ilka."

"Yes, she's still a suspect. The herb found in Brody's cup, remember? Got a message as I was leaving that the toxicology tests are in. Haven't followed up, but I'll know more soon."

"You said money was her motive. Ilka's got a job. Three jobs, if you count palm reading and acting. Why would she need more money?"

Gunnar shifted in his seat. "Family back home."

I bit my lip, recalling Ilka proclaiming she would use the money she made as an actress to help friends in the old country. Help Lugosi. Could Ilka have gotten involved in a crime ring as part of a desperate attempt to raise funds to help secure the release of her Grandmother Roza and other relatives in Hungary? Was that what Gunnar suspected?

"But you don't have any evidence."

Gunnar shrugged. "I'll let you know what toxicology says."

"Identifying the herb won't be proof."

"Pucci, Ilka has access to film studios and sets. She was there last night when you were attacked. Ilka's a Gypsy…"

I interrupted. "Hold it. Enough with the stereotype…"

Even as I was saying the words, I was remembering what Ilka had said about her Gypsy heritage this morning on the set. *I come from phony.* She'd admitted criminal activities were part of the Gypsy culture. Hadn't she even acknowledged that she'd personally lied and stolen many times? What if she'd been tantalized by something irresistible? Something like getting family out of harm's way?

I concentrated on the instruments and checked our course. Gunnar was completely silent. "Have you talked to your *sister* about this? Della has complete faith in Ilka."

"I would if I knew where she was." He smiled, but I was not in the least bit charmed. The smile faded. "Pucci, don't look so distressed. She's only a suspect. One suspect. And now you've served up other leads. We'll look into the news vendor. And Winwar. I'm also going to delve deeper into the secretary's background." He scratched his neck near his Adam's apple. "You know, there's something else it might make sense to reopen."

Gunnar at last came clean about his reasons for wanting the film segment of Frankie crying. In the clip, he'd picked out a woman's image in the background. On a wild hunch, he thought he might turn up a connection to Brody's blackmailers. A cameraman from the P-51 film crew had caught the scenario. It was taken just before Frankie went up. The image was fuzzy, and it was not possible to make out who else was in the shot. With nothing else relevant to go on, he'd dropped the thread. Now, building on my suspicions about Myra and keeping in mind she would have had access to the hangar, he would check back with the cameraman to see what he remembered.

Goosebumps rose up and down my arms as Gunnar talked. Could the woman in the background be the culprit who'd put sugar in the A-24's tank?

Argh! There it was again. A momentary roughness in the engine hum. Barely perceptible. Gunnar's "son of a bitch" was drowned out by yet another sputter.

A hot rush of adrenaline charged through my veins. "Dammit," I muttered before I could catch myself, "they've gone and sabotaged this plane, too."

I scanned the instruments.

"What's going on?" Gunnar asked, clearly alarmed.

Preoccupied with weighing what to do about the situation, I didn't answer right away. I looked out my window. The rugged peaks of the San Bernardino Mountains cut a jagged line against the horizon to the north. We were maybe ten minutes from March Field. Would we be better off putting down in the sage brush country below and taking our chances on the terrain, or pushing on to where an emergency crew would be on hand if we needed them?

Gunnar picked up on my thoughts. "Think we should get this machine out of the air?"

March Field seemed the right choice. Now all I had to do was to keep Gunnar—and myself—calm until we got there.

"No. No need to panic," I replied, firmly. "Miss C's been experimenting with some fancy schmancy high-octane fuel. My guess is that's what's going on."

"You mentioned sabotage," Gunnar said, evenly, rubbing at a kink in his neck.

Where was that hearing problem when I needed it? I'd hoped he'd missed my slip-up.

The stress of carrying around the secret truth of what happened to Frankie seemed overwhelming all at once. Miss C was not available, but it was definitely time to confide in someone higher up and get some answers. And if anyone could learn why the findings of Frankie's accident were being kept hush-hush, it'd be Gunnar. He knew Beacock at March; he was G-2; he obviously had an in with the brass hats. But what about my promise to Max? She'd been given orders to remain silent and had gone out on a limb telling first Miss C, then me. Her future was riding on my keeping the secret.

Ah, but Max hadn't asked me not to tell anyone about finding sugar in the tank of the wreckage. She'd only said I couldn't tell anyone where I'd heard it.

"Miss C told you I'm on a case…" I began, quickly bringing Gunnar up to speed.

Gunnar was astounded by the news. If he was to be believed—and I'd decided to trust him, hadn't I?—he had no knowledge that sabotage was behind the incident. If he, with his connections to the intelligence community, wasn't aware of the sabotage, did that mean the enemy could be ruled out? Could it be, as we'd been speculating all along, that the deed had been "friendly fire," meant as a warning to WASP pilots? That someone in our own Army Air Force wanted us to throw down our wings and leave the flying to the men?

Gunnar didn't have any ready answers to what was going on. Not even any guesses.

"But, Pucci, if the objective was to frighten off the WASP, why has the discovery been kept under wraps? Wouldn't the idea be to publicize the incident?"

"And launch a full scale investigation?" I shook my head. "No way. The incident is being kept hush-hush because the saboteur is 'one of their own.'" I glanced over at him. "Word about the crash will get out soon enough via the grapevine. They'll make sure of that. Then the news will leap like wildfire from one ready room to the next."

Gunnar looked at me long and hard. "I'll make some contacts soon as we're on the ground. See what I can learn."

"One more thing," I said. "You brought up the P-51 cameraman. Sam Lorenz was on that crew, and he was a friend of Frankie's. He's got a drug problem, did you know?"

"We know…"

According to Gunnar, Sam had been assigned to Fort Roach in spite of the known addiction, the shortage of writers having worked to his advantage. That, and the certificate indicating he'd completed a three-month treatment program at the state hospital. Gunnar hadn't known he was back on drugs.

"But I'm not shocked…"

The engine lurched; my stomach heaved. The engine sputtered, and the gyro and every needle on the panel hiccupped wildly.

Tiny beads of perspiration had formed along Gunnar's hairline.

"You all right?" I asked when everything was steady again.

"Fine." He swiped the line of sweat with his finger. "You might have told me about the sabotage before I buckled up."

I sighed. "That's funny coming from you. You know what it's like to be sworn to secrecy."

Gunnar cleared his throat.

"Sorry. That was unfair. Our little tight-lipped conspiracy put you in a dodgy plane."

"At least I'm with you," he said with goofy grin meant to cut some of the tension.

I smiled then grew serious. "The fact that the problem is intermittent suggests it's something in the fuel feed. We're almost at March. I think we can make it."

There was no hesitation. "You're the pilot. March Field it is, then."

I smiled at the vote of confidence.

March Field came into view in the distance.

"We're there." I reached to flip on the radio transmitter. Without warning, the engine shuddered, then quit. Heat surged through my body. Instinctively, I dropped the nose in an effort to hold a glide pattern. I looked below. We were over chaparral country. There were clumps of dwarf trees and dense thickets of mesquite brush. There was plenty of flat open space as well. Could be worse.

I tightened my seat belt. Gunnar followed suit. An uncanny calm came over me as I began running emergency procedures, rapidly checking lines, gauges and controls.

"Can I do something?" Gunnar's voice sounded loud in the eerie silence.

With a swift motion, I flipped a switch to put us on another tank. My tongue pressed against the parched roof of my mouth, making a sticky sound. I swallowed to get some moisture going.

"Not yet," I managed finally, the voice sounding nothing at all like mine.

I pumped the throttle with vigor. The engine failed to react. I put the Staggerwing into a gentle turn, heading for the clearest flat area around. We continued to lose altitude. The propeller caught a shaft of sunlight. I watched it slowly windmill in the slipstream. I glanced at the altimeter, then over to Gunnar. He didn't say anything, but signaled thumbs up.

I went back to manipulating the pump lever, mixture controls and throttle. Suddenly, the engine backfired—once, then twice. I held my breath. A sputter. Then, with a roar, the Pratt & Whitney sprang back to life.

I shoved the throttle to stop the descent and gain airspeed. Gently, I pulled up, banking to the left to get us back on course.

Chapter Eighteen

My stomach settled slowly.

"Nice work," Gunnar said calmly, looking a little pale.

I grinned. "Thanks. Nothing to it."

Gunnar studied the instruments. "Still think the problem's in the fuel feed?"

"More than ever. The tanks are on separate systems. We were on a wing tank. I switched us to the reserve. Seems to have licked the problem."

Gunnar smiled thinly. "How about setting us down before the reserve goes bonzo?"

I called the tower for clearance, entered the pattern, and began a slow descent.

As we were approaching our runway, Gunnar said softly, "You cannot go up in the P-51 until we know what's going on."

"But all the arrangements are made. Novara, the film crew, they're driving out to March, hauling out all the equipment. They may already be here. Besides," I added, already knowing he was right but reluctant to give in, "it's possible the fuel system wasn't tampered with at all. Could be mechanical failure."

"Your pal's plane was sabotaged. That's enough for me. Should be for you, too." Gunnar checked his watch. "You can try to catch Novara and the film crew. They may not have left Fort Roach yet. Afterwards, we'll fix things with Beacock together."

A chance to fly the P-51 was hard to walk away from. I sighed. "Righto."

Set up for the landing, I cranked the handle for the landing gear and cocked the nose into the crosswinds. Dropping us gently onto the runway, I worked the brakes and flaps to slow us down. A turn near the end of the runway, and we were taxiing toward our designated spot. At Hangar Ten, I flipped off all switches and cut the engine. Gunnar and I breathed loud sighs of relief.

Down on the tarmac, we went our separate ways. I searched out Novara and the film crew, discovering to my relief that only a team of gaffers and grips had arrived so far. My luck held when I called Fort Roach. Novara was still there. Without providing any detail, I explained that a crisis had arisen at March Field and that filming would have to be postponed. He was irritated, but grateful they hadn't wasted time making the trip. An urgent new film project had been thrown his way. He'd be working late into the night as it was.

Gunnar and I joined up again to meet with Major Beacock. We provided a different spin, indicating that a snag had developed back at Fort Roach necessitating a delay in the film shoot. Beacock agreed to reschedule whenever we could pin down a date in the future.

Gunnar stayed on to talk with Beacock and I went to see Max. She had taken on the post-flight inspection of the Staggerwing. She thought she could get back to me this afternoon.

I hitched a ride back to Clover Field with the film crew.

◇◇◇

It was time to put Gunnar's Gypsy and herb theory to rest. I navigated the Packard in the general direction of the Dunns', taking a slight detour through the streets of Culver City first.

The dark-haired man with the walrus mustache who'd been filling in for Gus earlier in the day was still at the kiosk. I parked and scooted up the walk.

15 JAP WARSHIPS HIT; THREE SUNK. I saw the bold headline before I reached the kiosk. Closer in, I read the subhead: U.S. NAVY FLYERS DESTROY 88 NIP PLANES. Good work. Way to go boys, I cheered inside.

The man had his back to me, straightening a pile of papers below the counter. I felt a twinge of regret at noting the absence of the can of flowers, but my greater remorse was the growing certainty that I'd been deceived by the immigrant news vendor Gus…or whoever he was.

Gus' sub straightened and turned to face me. "Top o'the day, darlin'." He had a pug-nosed Irish face and spidery, oversized eyebrows to match the expansive bristly patch above his lip.

"Help yourself." With a sweep of his arm, he backed away from the news racks so I could browse.

"Where's Gus?"

The man's eyes narrowed. "That scalawag? Skipped without word. The wife's sick. I'm needed at home. Signed him on to fill in for a month. Now he's gone." A worried look seized his face.

"You're the owner, then?"

The man nodded.

"And you don't know where to find him? No address?"

"Darlin', this here's no military operation. I take what I get. Say—" He pinched an end of his mustache. "Fella was just here askin' about Gus. Smelled like a copper. Now you're nosin' around too…"

My cheeks felt hot, but I looked him straight on. "I'm not *nosin'*," I huffed. "I've been stopping here every morning for a week. Curious, is all."

Turning on my heel, I marched back to the Packard, my hunch about Gus' involvement in blackmail, espionage, and possibly murder coming into sharper focus.

◇◇◇

A ringing telephone greeted me as I entered the side door at the Dunns'.

"Ilka…" I called, racing down the corridor.

She didn't appear and the phone was still ringing when I arrived at the settee near the staircase. "Hello," I answered breathlessly.

"Hi, Pucci. Gunnar Rask. Everything okay?"

"I'm fine. Just got in. What'd you find?"

"I need you to keep the particulars confidential for a day or two. Agreed?"

My pulse, which had begun to return to normal after my double-time dash down the hall, speeded up again. I twisted the cord in my hand, pivoting in a circle to glance up the staircase, then into the living room. Coming around full circle, I peered through the open doorway of the library. No one was around. Still, I lowered my voice. "Agreed."

"You need to be on alert. We're zeroing in on the saboteur, but we don't have him in custody yet."

"What's that supposed to mean?"

"We've talked to the officer who oversaw the accident investigation team. He confirmed what you told me about the mechanic's findings. The officer decided, on his own, to keep the sabotage conclusion under wraps." 'Officer' came out as more of a snarl than a word.

"Why'd he bury the findings?"

"What you suspected. He saw it as a get-back. A chance to rattle some nerves. *Ladies'* nerves."

Anger was thudding heavily in my chest. All along we'd speculated that an embittered airman at March might be the saboteur. Still, I never really thought we'd be right. In my heart, I didn't want to believe that a fellow American would be capable of committing such an act. Now I had to believe it. *How could someone be so twisted?*

Gunnar continued, "The major claims he doesn't know who did it. That he merely decided to falsify the cause of the accident by deeming it a 'mechanical failure' for the record." Gunnar cleared his throat. "Said he assumed he was covering up for one of his men. But, supposedly, he doesn't know which one.

"His crew, along with anyone else who might have had access to Frankie's A-24 that day, is being sought for questioning. We're doing our best to keep the investigation quiet, hoping we'll catch the rat off guard."

I sank to the bench nearby. "I'm not sure Miss Cochran heard about Frankie's passing. Do you know? Was she informed?"

"Uh-huh. Within the past hour."

I sighed with relief. Gunnar continued. "She asked me to tell you to expect a call from her in the morning. After she's had a chance to sort things out."

I forced myself to remain calm, speak reasonably. "Did you talk to the cameraman who took the footage in the hangar?"

"Uh-huh. He remembered Frankie had been arguing with Sam Lorenz. A lover's spat. He turned his camera on her to get a laugh. Got the opposite. Once he stopped filming her, she went back over to Sam. They made up and everything seemed hunky-dory. He also said there might have been a mechanic there, they're always in and out of the hangars, but he couldn't be sure.

"There's some good news," Gunnar added. "The insider involved in the blackmail scheme finally showed for the film cans in Landis' dressing room."

It had to be…"Winwar?"

"Yup. I've done some digging. Winwar in Italian is *Vinciguerra*—"

Gunnar knew some Italian and pronounced the name "veen chee gwer ah." He explained the verb *vincere* was "to win," and *la guerra* "the war." His working theory was that Winwar had Americanized his name.

Since Pearl Harbor, Italian immigrants living in coastal communities were subject to travel restrictions and a curfew; some had even been forced to move from their homes and relocate inland. Those considered "possibly dangerous" were interned in a camp in Missoula, Montana. Fear of accusation was very real for many innocent Italians; for Winwar, changing his name would have been critical.

My mind leapfrogged. Had I proven myself? Was Gunnar at last ready to pull me from behind the lines, place me at the front? "So Winwar is our man. What do you want me to do next?"

"Er, nothing. We've got him under surveillance."

"And?"

It wasn't an assignment as I'd hoped, but Gunnar had another bit of good news. While probing Winwar's affairs, he had unearthed a black market scheme. Novara had indeed purchased Italian leather shoes through him. But, he cautioned, it was unlikely that charges would be brought. Too difficult to prove Novara knew he was buying contraband.

"I've been doing all the talking," Gunnar said. "How about you? Any more discoveries?"

"The vendor I told you about at the kiosk has vamoosed," I said. "But you already know that. Say…what about Myra? You were going to check into her background."

Sounding contrite, Gunnar admitted there'd been another oversight. Myra, whose full name was Myra Blade, had taken a two-day leave for a family emergency. She'd left an address where she could be reached. It was bogus.

"Er, MGM personnel also told us she'd been with them for only three weeks. Don't worry, we'll track her down."

Myra *Blade*? My hand slipped into my pocket. I fingered the swastika earring I'd found in my tea cup. Perhaps he shouldn't be so sure.

"Pucci, there's more."

From the tone in his voice, I was glad to be already seated. "Yes."

"The leaves in Brody's teacup have been identified. It's *ma huang*."

"*Ma huang*?" I asked, stumbling over the pronunciation.

"Pharmaceutical name's *herba ephedrae*. It's a Chinese herb."

"So it's true. An herb that kills. How's it work?"

"There are plenty of herbs that can kill, Pucci. People have allergic reactions, some are poisonous by nature. Especially in large doses. *Ma huang* causes constriction of the blood vessels. That brings up blood pressure, which, in turn—in someone susceptible like Brody whose blood pressure was already in the danger zone—can bring down the curtain."

"Can anyone get ahold of *ma huang*? Where do you get it?"

"Not in a store. The killer most likely obtained it in China-town or from some private herb source."

"Why are you telling me this?" I asked, already sure of his answer.

"Just a reminder about Ilka…"

"Not that again…"

Footsteps echoed in the corridor that I'd raced down minutes ago. A woman in high heels. I could tell from the click-clacking on the stone.

"Pucci, I thought I heard you." Ilka rounded the corner. "I am making tea. Will you join me?"

Chapter Nineteen

Ilka clapped a hand to her cheek when she saw I was on the phone.

"Sorry," she mouthed, tiptoeing away.

"It's okay Ilka. I was just hanging up." She waited while I spoke into the mouthpiece again. "Gunnar, I've gotta go."

"Ilka's there?" He sounded concerned.

"Yup. She's just invited me to join her for tea." I flashed Ilka a warm smile. "Hopefully chamomile. I could use a relaxant."

I pictured Gunnar on the other end of the line, scowling over my being so glib after having just moments ago confirmed that Brody had been killed with a deadly brew. Well, Gunnar might be worried, but I wasn't. Yes, Ilka had admitted to the misdeed in her past life, but supply a deadly herb knowing it was intended to kill someone? Ilka was a healer. And she despised fascism. No, while I could understand Gunnar's reasons for suspecting Ilka, I couldn't go along. In fact, after hearing what he'd learned about Brody's secretary, Myra, my suspicions ran in a different direction. But to prove to Gunnar that he was wrong about Ilka meant digging up some convincing evidence. Sooner rather than later.

Speaking into the phone, I queried, "Will you be joining us for dinner?"

"No, I'll be here late, with luck following our rat to the nest." He paused. "You know I'm not wild about your being alone with Ilka. Be careful, would you? Keep your eyes and ears open."

"Don't worry," I said firmly. "I'll wait up for you. We can compare notes. Besides, I'll be on pins and needles until I get word from Max."

"Yeah, it's a long shot, but if someone tampered with the Staggerwing there might be a lead in it to Frankie's killer. Meantime, call if you need me. Leave a message with the duty sergeant if I'm not here."

I wrote down the numbers he gave me. "Got it. See you later then."

In the kitchen, a steaming copper kettle simmered at a low whistle on the stove. I sat at the table watching Ilka pour the hot water into a delicate yellow teapot painted with a scrolly green and pink pattern. She placed the lovely china pot on a trivet before me. Fine Oriental lettering, not apparent at a distance, was also part of the design. Next, she set out matching china cups and saucers, sugar, cream, and tiny lemon wedges. After retrieving a plate of orange marmalade and wafer-like biscuits from the counter, she took the chair opposite me.

Ilka was wearing the simple black dress she'd worn the day we met. The dress' bodice boasted an asymmetrical sweep of large buttons continuing down the full skirt. The skirt's side seams were set with deep pockets. A paper that had been partially stuffed inside one of the pockets slipped out, dropping to the floor between us as she sat.

My hand shot out. It was a typed memo like the one that had been stuffed under the bread box the other morning. Ilka had maintained the earlier memo was a "project list" from Della, not the OSS-MO document I'd initially believed it to be. She'd be hard-pressed to insist that what I was holding in my hand now was anything other than OSS agency correspondence. My grasp was loose and she easily slipped the paper from my fingers, but I'd already noted the words OFFICE OF STRATEGIC SERVICES—CAIRO—SECRET before I gave it up.

"Ilka, what are you doing with an OSS intelligence memo?"

She flipped the long platinum swoop off her face. "What? What is it you want to accuse me of?"

The flowery scent of a garden in bloom drifted up from the teapot's spout. I stared at the Asian lettering. Ilka was innocent of Brody's murder, I felt sure. But she was up to something. What?

She had folded the paper and stuffed it back into her skirt. I looked directly into her tawny eyes. "Ilka, please let me look at the memo."

She lifted a manicured eyebrow. A moment of tense silence followed. "It is secret."

"Does it have anything to do with a sudden windfall of cash? Or with getting someone out of the old country?"

Ilka's eyes widened and she pressed her lips into a tight line.

Her guilty look surprised me. I'd expected her to answer both questions in the negative.

"Ilka, it's best you tell me. The investigation into Brody's death has revealed he died after drinking tea laced with an Asian herb, *ma huang.* You're an expert with herbs. You're suspected of somehow being involved. I don't believe you are, but you've got to help steer me to the real culprit."

"*Ma huang*? How would a European know about Asian herbs?"

I clenched my teeth. "Ilka, this is serious. Show me the paper."

Reluctantly, Ilka pulled the memo from her pocket. "This will prove I am innocent, but in showing you I am betraying trust of the Mrs. It is secret project to aid the cause. The resistance network in Hungary, it is involved. She has asked for me and Uncle Bela to help. Code name, *Magyar Amerika.* This is all I will say, no more."

Her hand covering the vital information at the top—the "Date"; the "To and From"—she placed the document on the table, turning it so I could read.

#29174

KINDLY PLACE ADVERTISEMENTS IN HUNGARIAN
NEWSPAPERS.

START TO OBTAIN MESSAGES RECORDED ON PLATTERS
OF 33 1/3 REVOLUTIONS PER MINUTE.

ASSEMBLE A COLLECTION OF HUNGARIAN MUSIC
DISCS. BEGIN TO SEND US THE ABOVE MATERIAL BY AIR-
POUCH AS SOON AS IT IS AVAILABLE, AND LET US KNOW
HOW YOU ARE PROGRESSING.

Ilka saw my puzzled expression. "Any questions, you must
pose them to the Mrs. But now you know I am not killer. I am
helping the U.S. government."

*This proves nothing other than she got hold of one of those docu-
ments stashed in the Dunns' loft office.*

Really. Had that ratty little voice in my brain been secretly
indoctrinated by Gunnar?

"I'll check with Della when I see her. She'll be able to tell me
about the note I saw the other day, peeking out from the bread
box as well. They seem to go together."

A cryptic smile flickered across Ilka's lips. "I already tell you
fibbing it is in my blood. But killer, I am not."

Call me crazy, but I believed her.

Unfortunately, it complicated my speculation about who
was behind the blackmail plot, Brody's death, and also Frankie's
murder. If I was right about the mastermind, the assailant at
the club the night of the auction had been after me. But had I
been mistaken? Did the attack have to do with the secret MO
project? Had Lugosi been his intended victim?

"Ilka, why would someone steal your doll at the auction?"

She shrugged. "This I do not know."

"Think, Ilka. I may believe you, but they suspect your motive
for getting in bed with the enemy is helping family in the old
country."

"They?"

Gunnar's true profession was a sensitive matter. I chose my words carefully. "The investigators. They have the impression that immigrants who have family overseas might be tempted to aid certain enemy operatives stealing movies from our studios in exchange for money—or, for a loved one's safe passage. Once involved in the operation, they might be asked or forced to do other things."

Ilka's eyes blazed with anger. "What do you say? I would aid the Axis in trade for Roza's passage out from Hungary? Why? I have no reason. Grandmamma moves with the underground. No trading was necessary. Once in Cairo—" Having unwittingly let the cat out of the bag, Ilka's sudden rage evaporated.

I felt my heart thumping wildly in my chest. "Roza's here?"

Ilka sighed. "A month ago, it becomes clear Grandmamma must leave Hungary before is too late. Gypsies, Jews, they are being singled out more and more. Grandmamma, she is seventy-three. Her health it is failing." Ilka pointed to her forehead. "Her mental health, that is."

Moved by her sorrowful expression, I reached across the table and patted her arm.

Ilka cleared her throat. "As you can imagine, it was difficult journey."

I nodded. Nearly impossible, considering the Germans now occupied Yugoslavia, the escape route Ilka had used. In fact, every country bordering Hungary was under Axis rule. How had she managed? The Gypsy underground must be powerful indeed.

Ilka's lips crept into a wan smile. "She made it. Is so wonderful to see her again."

"Where is she staying?"

Ilka's smile broadened. "Here. In this house. Actually, she is with Uncle Bela at this moment. But she will be back soon. Lia, she is off tonight. I am making chicken *paprikás*." She was suddenly serious. Her eyes held a pleading look. "Please, you must go along. No one can know she is here until the proper paperwork it can be arranged. And hiding her, this sometimes is not so easy."

Ilka explained that although she understood the necessity of staying undercover until her immigration status could be resolved, being forced to lay low indoors went against Roza's Gypsy nature. But then she had discovered the labyrinth of secret passages that ran throughout the Dunns' home, and her declining mental power became a menace. I learned that though the fuses outside had indeed been faulty, the lamp in my room had not had a wiring problem at all. Roza had been the culprit behind the strange business of its turning on "by itself." She'd sneaked in and pulled the chain-switch while I slept. The disappearance of my jade green satin pajamas—and their subsequent reappearance—had been part of Roza's adventures also.

I'd seen "Cairo" on the memo in Ilka's pocket before she grabbed it away. The Dunns traveled there on OSS business regularly. "Do Della and D.B. know that Roza is here?"

Ilka hesitated but an instant. "Yes, the Mrs. she know. Grandmamma, she help to inspire the secret project." Ilka flashed a proud smile.

"When your grandmother traveled to Cairo, did she have with her a couple of escaped prisoners of war? Heisted German film, perhaps? Reconnaissance film?"

Ilka's tawny eyes widened. "This you must ask the Mrs."

"But if you're hiding her, what's she doing out with Lugosi? And what was she doing at the auction last night?"

"Like I already tell you, at the briefie, there was call for dolls. Grandmamma she bring doll with her from Hungary. We donated…"

The swastika earring in my pocket felt like it was on fire. "Ilka, this is important. Why did she bring the doll with her?"

Ilka stood and walked to the sink, leaning over it to peer outdoors. Dusk had fallen and the outside lights were on, but it must have been difficult to see. She shaded her eyes, straining to catch sight of someone or something, probably Roza and Bela.

Finally, she turned from the window and leaned back against the sink for support. "Morality, it is prewar luxury. Being in underground requires wheeling and dealing. Stealing, lying, cheating, all are part of the game. But those involved they have different motives. Some they are anti-German, some they are profiteers. Others, they are both. So, it would not surprise you, then, that some hard crooks exist in the Gypsy network?" Ilka raised her eyebrows inquiringly.

I shook my head. "No surprise at all."

Ilka began to pace in front of the sink. "This Zolton Laszlo, he is in with many bad characters. To make money, always to make money."

"With Roza?" I inquired.

Ilka stopped pacing. "No. No." She shook her head adamantly. "Laszlo, like Grandmamma, has his own Gypsy tribe. Similarly, he transport goods and people. There the similarities they stop. Grandmamma, she take risk because she want to help save lives. Of dissidents and other Magyar who suffer under Hitler. Zolton, though, he involved only in those smugglings which will put money in his pocket."

"What are you trying to tell me, Ilka?" I asked, impatience creeping into my tone. "Who is this Zolton Laszlo? Why is he important?"

After a significant pause, she gave me an even glance. "One incident will tell you all that you need to know about Zolton Laszlo.

"In September, 1940, Laszlo accept money from underground contact to transport Austrian refugee from Sopron in the north of Hungary down through back country to southern border. There, they are to meet another transport for exit out through Yugoslavia."

Ilka's shoulders slumped a little. She returned to the table, taking the chair opposite me again. "Along the way, Laszlo, he turn refugee over to Germans. Do it to double his money. Can you imagine such treachery?"

I stared at my empty teacup, fingering its delicate handle, picturing Frankie lying in the hospital bed. "Yes, Ilka, I can."

Ilka went on, "This same villain, when he learn Grandmamma was soon to leave with goods to aid Allies, he gives to her—under threat—the doll. Somehow he has put together she will not be coming back. That she will come to Hollywood to join me. Zolton tell her, 'Take doll with you or I hunt down precious little Ilka, adjust her looks so that *never* she will be actress. Expect word about what to do next with doll, after you arrive.'"

A chill moved through me and I shuddered visibly. "What are you saying?" I glanced across the table expectantly. "You weren't surprised that the doll was snatched?"

Ilka shrugged. "When we see notice in paper calling all dolls for auction, we know this it. And Grandmamma, she insist she must go to see who is there to take it."

"The man with the Einstein hair?"

Ilka nodded. "Or his associate, the woman playing his wife."

I raised my eyebrows. I was back on track.

I had blamed the secretaries for the swastika earring left in my tea cup. Then Gunnar told me about Myra's short stint with MGM, and I instinctively knew Cardillac was responsible. She had recognized me that day in Brody's office. *Cardillac, mistress of disguise.* The prematurely grey hair could have been a wig or a masterful coloring job. I didn't get a good look at her eyes, but contact lenses could make them any color she chose. And that overbite? I'd been speculating how to fix her receding chin. Now I'd bet she was using a mouth insert. But it was the name that had really tipped me. The double-entendre was a Cardillac weakness. Or forte? Myra *Blade*. The scar on my forearm was testament to Cardillac's pride in her expertise with a stiletto.

Nazi operatives in Hollywood would need money. The doll likely contained something of value. Jewels, money, drugs. Cardillac had pulled off a similar scheme in Detroit. Cardillac. The archenemy I'd sworn to bring to justice.

We heard the distant ringing of the telephone.

"I have to answer it," I said, leaping to my feet.

Chapter Twenty

It was Max.

When I'd seen her at March Field, there hadn't been an opportunity to let her know I'd shared her sabotage findings with Gunnar. Initially, Gunnar had been with me when we'd asked Max to go over the Staggerwing, and when I saw her again later, other mechanics had been nearby. The secret slipped out, I hastily explained now, during our close call coming in.

"Don't worry, Pucci. Everyone's gonna know soon enough." She lowered her voice. "They're trying to keep a low profile about it, but an inquiry's finally in the works."

"Excellent," I said, feeling greatly relieved that Max wasn't upset. Also, that she was already in the know about the investigation. "But how'd you find out?"

"I was called in for questioning."

I gasped. "Really? Why?"

"Nothing to worry about," Max assured me. "Everything I did was in line with procedure. Turned out the officer in charge had decided, on his own, to keep a lid on my findings. Some perverted idea about scaring women and covering up for one of the guys. Like sabotage was a fraternity prank or something. Can you believe it?"

My stomach knotted with indignation though I'd already heard the news from Gunnar. "Yeah. Har-har. Real funny."

"I've finished checking out the Staggerwing," she said. "Gotta tell ya, someone was watchin' out for you. Problem was in the fuel-feed, just like you suspected. Switching to a different tank was what saved you and the lieutenant. Switching to the right one that is."

"Huh?"

"You were on a wing tank first, then you switched to the reserve, right?"

"Yup."

"Both wing lines weren't feeding correctly. If you had tried the other wing, you wouldn't have recovered. Like I said, luckily, you picked the right tank."

I let out a low whistle. "So, why weren't the lines feeding properly?"

"Paper wads plugging the suction lines."

"What?"

"I was dropping fuel from one of the wing tanks when I noticed the outlet clogging intermittently. I started experimenting. By jiggling the wing, I got the fuel flow to change from heavy to light to nearly nonexistent. I took a closer look-see. Saw a little clump moving in and out of the flow valve. Same thing on the other wing tank."

"And…"

"After fishing around through the filler caps, I pulled several wads of paper—same size, same color—from each of the tanks. They were the culprits interfering with the fuel drainage. When you were in flight, they would have been plugging the suction line."

I clutched the receiver tighter. "So, it was sabotage." A brain-wave struck. "Did you keep the wads?"

"Hold on a minute. They're nearby. I'll get one." The receiver clunked as she set it down. She was back in a minute. "You know something? That was a great question. Wait a sec. I'm trying something."

The receiver clunked again. An instant later, Max came back on. "The wads I pulled out were fuel-soaked, but the one I'm looking at has had a chance to dry out. Maybe it's the texture or coating…it didn't shred when I unwadded it and smoothed it into its original shape."

"Yeah..."

"Looks like someone had a few cupcakes." She chuckled wryly. "Hey. Maybe 'the someone' had to hide the wrappers in a hurry."

"What?"

"A joke." Max chuckled again. "I was picturing a mechanic eating a secret stash of cupcakes. Someone comes along—maybe his boss...Wait! Maybe it's an official from the ration board checking for sugar hoarding!" Another chuckle.

Max was obviously enjoying her silly fantasy, but I didn't laugh. I'd been having my own vision involving the Hershey wrapper escaping Bulk's pocket. Bulk, a saboteur?

"Max, cut it. It isn't funny."

Max apologized immediately. "You're absolutely right. Sorry."

"You said you were dropping fuel. A mechanic responsible for routine maintenance wouldn't have gone through that sort of testing, right?"

"Not unless he had reason to suspect a problem."

But what if he had deliberately created a problem? "Tell me more about the wrapper."

My suspicions about Bulk fell away and a lump formed in my stomach while I listened to Max describing a pink pleated cup like those that held the custard tarts Sam had ordered "to go" from May Lee's the night of our disastrous "date." I remembered the crazed look I'd seen on Sam's face just before he chucked me out the door of his bungalow. My God! Had Sam tampered with the Staggerwing?

My hand shook as I hung up. I hadn't shared my suspicion with Max. I had to think first. *What possible reason could Sam have for wanting to sabotage my plane?*

A scare tactic to frighten off the WASP? Why would Sam give a hoot whether or not women flew for the military?

"...s-s-...s-s-...ah-ah-aaahh...p-p-p...s-s-mmm...m-e-e..." Frankie's utterances pierced my thoughts. I tumbled the sounds on my tongue. S-s-...ahh...p-p...s-s-...*mmm...me...*Had she been saying "Sammy?" What had the cameraman told Gunnar? They'd had a lover's spat.

But sabotage? And why me?

The photos on his dining table that he'd claimed had to do with an upcoming shoot all at once seemed worth another look.

My mind raced forward with a plan. When I'd called Novara from March Field, he'd mentioned an urgent new film project. Desperate, he was planning to bring Sam on as a writer. Novara had also said they'd be working late into the night. Likely Sam wouldn't be home. If he was, I'd confront him. Why not? He didn't frighten me. He was just a druggie. If he wasn't there, evidence of his guilt might still be lying around.

At the sound of approaching footsteps, I reeled around. It was Ilka, her forehead furrowed with concern. Before I could second-guess my decision, I started toward the staircase, calling back over my shoulder. "Ilka, can't explain right now. I have to go."

◇◇◇

Upstairs in my room, I dug the B-4 bag out from under the bed and grabbed Gran Skjold's pocket revolver.

The blue steel finish of the snub barrel shone dull and menacing in the lamp light as I held the small revolver in my hand, checking it over carefully. I'd fired the gun just once, in Detroit. The memory sent a chill up my spine. Any hesitation passed quickly. Frankie had died; Gunnar and I could have died as well.

A metal nail file in my cosmetic's kit caught my eye. I slipped it into a pants pocket then rummaged in the flight bag again, this time for my ankle holster. The strap fitted tight to my left leg, I slid in the break-top. At rest just above the ankle bone, the gun in its case felt awkward. But it always did when I first put it on.

◇◇◇

Downstairs, I gave the operator Sam's number. Butterflies flitted in my stomach while I waited. Ten rings later, we gave up. The coast seemed clear.

I tried Gunnar next. No answer. A call to the duty sergeant's line was greeted with a busy signal. I headed for the side door exit.

◇◇◇

Ilka looked up as I entered the kitchen. She was standing at the counter next to the stove, chopping onions. The white pock-skinned breast of a whole uncooked chicken was visible, protruding from a roasting pan resting nearby. The onion's pungent odor enveloped me when I stopped, a few feet away.

I was torn. What if Gus or Cardillac or one of their goons showed up here?

"Ilka, you have to trust me. Promise me that you'll try to reach Gunnar." I wrote down two numbers, explaining which was which. "Tell him Della enlisted you for a secret project. Tell him about Cairo and Roza. It'll explain a lot. He'll…we'll all work on a way to turn the investigation away from you." I didn't think I had to spell out Gunnar's ties to intelligence. "Another thing. Let him know I've gone to Sam's house. Something to do with what Max found, tell him. Can you remember all that?"

Ilka chin shot out. "I am actress. Memorizing lines it is what I do."

"One more thing, until Lugosi arrives…even after he arrives… keep the doors locked, stay alert, will you? The thug who came at us the other night in the parking lot might try it again."

While I was talking, Ilka's tawny eyes had skimmed the length of my body, stopping at my ankle. I looked down. My pant leg was bunched at the bottom. My holster was visible.

Engaging my opposite foot, I quickly worked the fabric back over the holster.

"Not to worry about us," Ilka said, looking up. "You had best take good care of yourself."

We both heard the rumble of an approaching automobile. Moving quickly, we followed the flagstones to the front of the house and watched, hidden under the archway, as headlight beams crossed through the open gate. I strained to identify the car as it circled the courtyard, its tires rolling along the stone floor in a steady muffled crunch.

Ilka recognized it first. "It is Uncle Bela's car. He has returned with Grandmamma."

We crossed the courtyard as Lugosi, looking handsome in a dark suit, circled the front of the sleek Lincoln Coupe and opened the door on our side.

Roza wore the fur coat of the incognito actress, only tonight she wasn't wearing sunglasses. The muted outdoor lighting cast a feeble glow. Enough to observe her dark complexion, dark eyes, and wizened face as Lugosi helped her out of the car.

"Grandmamma, meet Pucci Lewis."

The woman's deeply lined face was kindly, especially when she smiled. But unlike her granddaughter's teeth, hers were not perfect. They were dark and some were broken, others missing. But she wasn't shy. Ilka repeated my introduction in Hungarian and the smile broadened.

Lugosi's one hand supported Roza; his other held a smoldering cigar. The acrid smell traveled through the night air, blanketing us in its heavy aroma. My nose twitched in revulsion.

"Mr. Lugosi," I said looking at him. "I need to go, now. I have some urgent business to take care of. I'm a little concerned, though." I hurriedly explained my fears.

Lugosi straightened his spine and drew himself up to his full height. Head slightly canted, he said, "Pooo-chi, I once vas cap-i-tan in Hungarian Army. I serve at Russian Front remember? This—" He threw out his arm and waved his cigar in a theatrical sweep. "This is Holly-vood. Kitten's play in comparison."

I smiled. His eyes looked normal and indeed with his proud bearing in place he looked prepared for battle.

Chapter Twenty-one

I doused the Packard's headlights, coasting to a stop a block from Sam's. Unsure of my next move, I sat quietly in the dark, challenging my reasons for breaking and entering. *Personal threat, connection to Frankie's death, evidence.* Before my insecurities could regroup, I fished a flashlight from the glove box and exited the car.

I leaned against the driver's door, surveying the street. The temperature was mild, yet I shivered. It was darker and quieter than I'd expected. No street lamps, no traffic, no dog walkers. No use fooling myself, either. What I was about to do was dangerous. Knees a little weak, I zipped my leather jacket with a jerk and headed down the street.

Most of the homes I passed had a light or two on. Sam's bungalow looked completely dark. No car in the driveway and no garage. My hope that he would not yet be home was playing out.

My heart beating wildly, I knocked at the front door, ready with some mumbo-jumbo regarding script consultation. There was no answer. Still, I wanted to be certain he wasn't around. Concealed in the shadows, I rounded the front of the house, keenly aware of the enemy rosebushes and our recent encounter. The scent and related thoughts were so offensive, I began breathing only through my mouth.

At the driveway, I swept a final look up and down the deserted street. Then, spotting a gap in the shrubs bordering the left side of the house, I ducked through.

Deep in the foliage, I sidestepped along the stucco wall to the back door. I flicked on the flashlight, running the beam up and down the door jamb. The door opened outward, and there was gap between its edges and the frame. I removed the metal file from my pocket. Flashlight clenched in my teeth, the beam positioned on the crack at the latch, I slipped the file in, sliding it at a downward angle until it met resistance. Then jimmying it, I worked the file deep in behind the latch until there was enough leverage to press it back. Keeping the file tight against the depressed latch, I turned the knob and opened the door.

Ear cocked, I listened for sounds of life beyond the thumping of my heart. I slipped into kitchen.

Moonlight washing through the windows over the corner sink permitted a surface view of the room. A wall phone, an orderly lineup of small appliances, a bowl of fruit, a chopping board leaning against the wall, the tea service Sam had hauled out the other night.

The dining room table was next. The photos I wanted to look at again had been on the table. But as I parted the veil of beads, I headed instead for the velvet floor-to-ceiling drapes along the interior dining area wall to see what was behind them.

I tugged a drawstring on the side. A hushed "my God!" escaped my lips.

On an altar table set into a narrow alcove, a large golden Buddha sat upon an elaborate gold and red lacquer throne. Legs crossed, eyelids shut, the pensive figure was flanked by candles, flat brass discs—one containing a pile of straw-colored twigs and the other a white powdery substance—and a framed photograph of a stiff-looking Asian man and an unsmiling, traditionally dressed Spanish woman. I blinked several times. A small hill of sugar cubes and a pink pleated cup were also part of the shrine arrangement.

Excitement flooded over me. The incriminating evidence I was after. It would be easy enough to compare the dessert cup before me with one Max had taken from the fuel line of the Staggerwing. And the stack of sugar cubes. We'd thought sugar had been *poured* into the fuel tank of Frankie's A-24. Tossing a few cubes in might have been easier, more discreet.

I took a closer look at the straw-colored twigs. Herbs? *Ma huang?* And the white substance? I was no drug expert, but heroin perhaps?

A low moan came from across the room behind me. Every muscle in my body tensed. Twirling around, my arms squared protectively before me, I assumed a semisquatting defensive pose.

Sam Lorenz, a gag of white tape across his mouth, was bound, his arms behind him, to one of the metal and leather dining chairs.

I panned the shadowy living room, then relaxed my stance and went over to Sam and yanked the tape from his mouth. His head lolled to the side, but otherwise he did not react. Beside him, the silvery gooseneck lamp had been left on. The flexible neck was bent downward, its shaded bulb creating a globe of light reflected in the glass table-top. Next to the lamp, I could see Sam's typewriter and a neat stack of papers, but there was no manila envelope. Afraid Sam had slipped into unconsciousness, or worse, I twisted the lamp's arm, adjusting the shaft of light so it was directed at his face.

He looked awful. His face was haggard, dark circles rimmed his eyes, and I was reminded of his brief appearance at the hospital when he'd claimed he was suffering from some sort of bug. This time without his telling me I thought I knew what had bit him.

Sam was not wearing his glasses. He stirred, squinting against the light's glare. I turned the shade slightly. His lids slowly opened.

"Sam?" I repeated. He looked at me with a dull stare.

The other evening at the auction, Lugosi had been under the influence of drugs and his pupils had been pinpoints. But unlike Lugosi, whose blue eyes had made the telltale characteristic obvious, Sam's eyes were dark brown, his pupils barely distinguishable. But the vacant look in them was unmistakable.

"A f-f-fix. Need a f-fix."

For an instant, my thoughts turned to what it would be like to give him his drugs. An *overdose* of his drugs. I could almost see his eyes rolling backward in their sockets, see his chin falling limply to his chest. I shook my head. Angry as I was, that would get me nowhere.

"Sure, I'll give you a fix," I said agreeably. "Soon as I get some answers. The sugar cubes, the pink dessert cup"—I nodded sideways in the direction of the shrine—"You sabotaged Frankie's plane and mine. Why?" There was venom in my tone, but gritting my teeth helped keep my voice even. "She's dead, did you know? Who killed her? You?"

Even in his rough condition, the shock on his face was obvious. "N-no. I didn't do it. *They* did. Nazi agents."

"*They're* the saboteurs? *They* murdered Frankie?"

His gaze shifted and he fought to focus. "Y-yes…I took pictures."

"*Took pictures?* To aid the Nazis. The saboteurs. Murderers. That makes you an accomplice." I took a breath, fought for control. Strange as it may seem, I wanted to know how it could have happened. When we first met, he'd been supportive of me, of women generally, and I sensed—*he'd even said*—he loved Frankie. "How could you do it? Why?"

"Gave me drugs…"

"But you were clean. You went through rehabilitation."

He concentrated, then as if remembering the shrine, looked in its direction. "My parents…Spanish…Japanese."

He shifted slightly in the chair, struggling weakly against his bindings. I checked them. Behind the back of the chair, rough rope encircled his wrists. On the floor, his feet were trussed at the ankles. The ropes did not look tight, in fact I thought they might be too loose, but he grimaced with his effort.

His body grew still again. He looked up. His expression was imploring and he looked so helpless and broken I almost felt sorry for him. *Almost.*

"W-when met you, thought you could help me. That night, here, tried to confide—"

What had he said when we were dancing? *Don't worry, I'll tell you want you want to know.* "Why didn't you then?"

"In too deep. Need drugs. F-f-fix."

I looked at the photo. His father was Japanese. Not his mother. "Uh-huh, in a minute. Lorenz … you kept your mother's name?"

Something odd crept into Sam's expression. There was a strong but almost out-of-body timbre to his voice and it suddenly strengthened considerably. "These are dangerous times for the American Japanese. Remember I told you my mother…" He frowned. "My father worked as a costumer at a movie studio? That he brought me along to work and that I amused myself by reading and writing while he sewed?"

I nodded.

"Ha!" Sam sneered. "That was the Pollyanna side of the American tragedy. My father gave twenty-five years of his life to that studio. Twenty-five years! And when he needed someone to stand by him, stand up for him, IT gave him nothing in return. They call *us* yellow…"

His face went slack. Then in an angry outburst he told me that the day after Pearl Harbor soldiers had come onto the studio lot and taken his father, forcefully, with them. His father, interned at a camp, committed suicide a year ago.

"I'm sorry." I sighed. I really was. I gestured to the shrine. "Is that to honor your parents? Him?"

"*She* made it." Sam's lips were raw from the adhesive. He'd ejected the words with such force, a wound opened, and a droplet of blood ran down his lip. He ran his tongue around his mouth. "To focus blame for Frankie's crash and Brody's death on me."

"That's why you're tied up? They've got the goods and while they make their escape you'll be left to take the fall?"

"Dead. A suicide note-confession. *Ha ha.*"

There was no joy in Sam's laugh.

Beads of perspiration wetted my temples. A Nazi operative would be coming back here. I had to get every scrap of information I could before he did. "You took photos for them—*her*. Of what?" I scanned the table for the envelope of photos. It wasn't there. "Brody and Wallace?"

"No, *she* took that. I took reconnaissance photos. Douglas Manufacturing plant, Fort Roach. For the sub commander…"

I swiped a finger across my moist forehead as the very high stakes involved in what had been going on began at last to sink in. Taking out a plant like Douglas Aircraft would mean not only the loss of a critical manufacturing facility and a large inventory of planes, it would also be a huge blow to the citizenry's sense of security. Destroying Fort Roach and its vital contribution to the war effort would be a huge coup for the Nazis.

I recalled Frankie had taken a civilian for a joy ride the day before her crash. "And *Frankie* helped you?"

"No, Frankie tried to stop me. *She* was there. Heard Frankie say she'd tell the authorities if I didn't." His eyes welled up making his glazed look all the more eerie. I pressed on.

Stop Sammy. Frankie's garbled message was at last clear. "Who do you mean, *she?*" My breath caught as I made the connection. "*She* put sugar in the A-24's fuel to silence Frankie, tampered with my plane…Who is *she?*"

"Goes by a code name. Can't remember." His brow furrowed, then his head lolled sideways again. "Need a fix…"

Code name. The scar on my arm throbbed.

"Okay, I'll help you. Really, I mean it. But where are the photos now? With *her?*"

Sam briefly rallied. "No, I outsmarted her." He smiled then looking down, seemed surprised to see that he was tied up. "Maybe *she* outsmarted me."

There was a barely audible rustling of beads.

In one fluid motion, I doubled over and pulled out my gun. The toes of a pair of military boots were visible below the curtain. Springing upright, the revolver secure in my right hand, my left stabilizing the wrist from below, I pointed the barrel, chest level, at the figure behind the beaded veil.

The nose of a Walther P48 emerged, parting the beads. "Ciao, Pucci," an accented voice said nonchalantly from the other side.

It was Gus. My hands shook, but somehow I mustered a calm demand. "Step through to this side. No funny business. My gun's aimed straight at your heart."

If you have one, my mind echoed.

The voice belonged to Gus, but the man who strode through the curtain was younger. Much younger. His hair was not white or fly-away, but jet black and neatly slicked back. The tanned, deep olive hue of his skin was Gus', except not so deeply lined. Ah, but the eyes were the same. One brown, one blue. It was Gus. The incarnation of Gus who'd also been on the *Resisting Enemy Interrogation* set and released the canister-missile from the catwalk, narrowly missing Sam's head. I'd only caught a glimpse of him from the back while trying to chase him down, but there was no doubt in my mind.

"You are not wearing our gift, the earring," he said, his Walther continuing to hold me in its sights.

"Earring?" I shrugged and smiled. "Oh, you mean that Cracker Jack prize left in my tea cup?

"Let me guess: courtesy of your associate, Myra? Or should I say, *Cardillac*? Why isn't she here? Afraid to show her face? And what about yours? Why have you been hiding behind Gus, *Tazio*?" Tazio was *Cardillac*'s Italian boyfriend. We'd never met, but this had to be him. My finger tightened on the trigger. "Did you sneak into a Hollywood hospital and inject a vial of potassium into a patient's I.V. line? Is that why you were in disguise, *Tazio*?"

He remained silent, staring at me with a cocky grin. Behind that quiet, dark handsome exterior, I knew, his mind must be racing. It was gunfight at O.K. Corral. We were in a standoff that was sure to end badly for one of us.

What about Sam? Might he rally? Provide a diversion? Dream on. Beside me, Sam was so quiet I feared he'd passed out. No, I had to keep Tazio engaged until I could pull a trick from up my sleeve or until Gunnar or a member of his posse rode in to the rescue.

It's your chance to learn more about what we're up against, my pragmatic side chimed in.

"Why'd you…er, Myra kill Brody? Wasn't he cooperating?"

Tazio's gaze shifted to the living room area and he slowly sidestepped away from the curtain. "Brody figured out that Myra was running the blackmail scheme. From the shot of him with Wallace when she was posing as a cigarette girl. Director's eye. He remembered the evening and restaurant from what Wallace was wearing. He also recalled the cigarette girl's earrings. They were identical to the pair his secretary, *Myra*, always wore."

His movement and the taunting tone he used in saying her name, unnerved me a little, but my gun remained steady, fixed on its target. "He told Cardillac this?"

"She'd returned to the office for her house keys. He'd just figured it out." Tazio smiled. "She offered him a cup of tea."

"He drank it?"

"She'd brought her stiletto along."

I struggled to keep my voice even. "So why'd you come here? What you're really after is at Fort Roach."

Tazio laughed. "Vinciguerra told me you were in the dressing room. Didn't want to believe you'd seen the film cans. *We* suspected differently." Facing me, he took a couple more cautious sidesteps in the direction of the living room. "*Questa è la guerra.* This is the war. Why did I come here?" He waved the Walther. "You mean besides to give our friend his fix? His final fix? And now I have a bonus—I can take care of you…"

Moving ever so slowly, keeping his gun level with my heart, Tazio crept closer to the L-shaped sofa. My finger itched against the break-top's trigger as I watched, helpless to do anything. I could fire, but a reflexive return volley might also mean my end. He shook his head. "Too bad the paper balls did not do their trick."

I felt a hot flush as anger seized me. "Stop where you are."

The force in my voice seemed to rouse Sam. He moaned. At the sound, Tazio, gracefully bending at the knees, reached his free hand under the sofa cushion and pulled up a large manila envelope.

"What is that?"

"A piece of the bigger plot to help our side." His mouth stretched into a smarmy smile. "We'd been counting on the photographs Sam took. He'd also agreed to be our liaison with the sub commander. Our drug fan speaks Japanese, did you know?" For the first time since intruding on the scene, Tazio acknowledged Sam's presence with a flicked glance. "Shame he changed stripes after learning the truth behind his girl's crash. Tried to trick us with stock film. Of the Rhine…" Tazio waved the envelope. "Not these."

So Sam had been playing with fire. Now it was my turn. Where was my break? Where was Gunnar? Had Ilka called him? Would he know to come to Sam's house?

Tazio's brash manner, his superior smile, were wearing thin. But I needed to keep stalling.

"So you've outmaneuvered Sam. But who'll be your go-between with the Japanese now?"

"Sam has been under guard. But tonight I—*we*—discovered a new attraction at the Santa Monica Pier." Tazio stared at me with a sly smile. "It is why I wasn't here to greet you when you arrived."

Then Sam lunged for Tazio, a human-chair projectile.

I heard a whistle of air and then the crack of gunfire as the Walther fired wildly. Sam hit the floor near Tazio's feet, striking his ankles, crashing him to the floor and separating him from his gun.

Sam was out cold, his head at an odd angle, his cheek flat against the area rug. Nearby, Tazio was sprawled in a semi-seated position, his chin against his chest, his back against the sofa.

Gun straight out in front of me, I moved toward him. He rolled sideways. I wasn't expecting his punch to my stomach. I reeled toward the coffee table, dropping my gun. Doubled over, I held the table's edge, gasping for air. A hand grabbed my neck firmly from behind. The fingers dug in hard as another hand came around from my left.

My combat training kicked in. Fired by pain and adrenaline, I let loose a scream that rose from my depths and echoed off the walls. "AHHHHH…You killed my friend, you bastard!"

My hand closed over the marble Samurai warrior, swinging it upwards with a force I hadn't known was in me. One moment, I saw the point of the Samurai's sword and Tazio's icy blue glass eye. The next, heavy marble met flesh and bone. The dull crunching sound of the impact paralyzed me.

With a cry, Tazio fell to his knees.

Shattered glass glittered around Tazio's collapsed socket, spurting blood. Shards pierced his torn skin. A red stream poured from a thin slit between the collapsed lids. Pulses of crimson carried tiny slivers down his cheek. One jagged piece poked grotesquely through his upper lid.

Tazio was screeching, curled like a baby, writhing in anguish on the floor. His bloody hands clutched at his face. No longer sleek and handsome, he had the twisted visage of a horror creature straight out of a Lugosi picture.

My stomach roiling, I forced myself to search out the guns. When I heard rapid footsteps coming through the kitchen, I grabbed the Walther. A muted male voice called, "*Pucci!*"

It was Gunnar.

"Pucci, are you all right?" His gorgeous gray-blue eyes were filled with concern; above them, his eyebrows were scrunched into a V at the center.

"I'm fine. But they're not so hot." I nodded to the two figures on the floor. "One of them's the big fish you're after."

Gunnar glanced at Tazio, then where the bloodied Samurai rested. He lifted an eyebrow and there was something admiring in his glance.

He knelt down. Turning Tazio slightly and carefully pulling a hand from his ruined face, he felt for a pulse. He shook his head. "Gone."

My knees gave way. I slid to the floor and sat, leaning against Gunnar. My body trembled uncontrollably. "I-I killed h-him."

Gunnar put his arm around my shoulder, waiting until the trembling subsided. "That's one for Frankie."

I'd never killed anyone before. I glanced at Tazio and immediately looked away. "He's a Fascist…conspiring with Cardillac to take out Douglas…FMPU." My words, hesitant at first grew stronger. "They murdered Brody, Frankie. Tried to kill us!"

"Good. Get it out, Pucci. This is war. War on the home front. You've just helped even out the scales of justice." He squeezed my shoulder.

Sam, his eyes closed, his cheek plastered against the rug, remained secured to the chair. Gunnar went over to him, gently lifting an eyelid. "He won't be going anywhere for awhile."

I still had unfinished business to attend to. I scrambled to me feet.

"Cardillac—she must have the doll, who knows what else. She's going to meet the Japanese." In a rush, I told Gunnar about the reconnaissance photos and what Tazio had said about having made contact with their Axis counterparts.

Gunnar stayed calm. "Pucci, I've got to call my office. Get help here, incognito, on the double. We're gonna keep things quiet until we can sort it all out, but you've got my assurance. Forget about that sub. The coastline is secure. Also, Winwar's in custody. He picked up the film and our team nabbed him. Winwar or your pal there"—he gestured in Tazio's direction—"will lead us to Myra… or Cardillac, if that's who Myra really is."

"But the doll. She must have the Hungarian doll."

"I know about the doll."

"It's got something in it. Probably jewels. Diamonds. If Cardillac has the doll, she needs to captured before she meets up with the Japs. I promised Frankie I would get her and I'm not about to let Frankie down!"

"You won't, Pucci. Listen…"

Chapter Twenty-two

Gunnar convinced me that there was nothing more I could do for Frankie at the moment. Ilka and Lugosi should be outside Sam's house waiting in a separate car, at his request.

"They'll take you to Lugosi's house." Worry clouded Gunnar's dusk-blue eyes. "I'll feel better knowing you're together, out of harm's way."

My .38 at the ready, I stood guard in the living room while he phoned for help in the kitchen. Returning almost immediately, he glanced at the motionless figures on the floor before walking me to the front door. Lugosi's sleek silver Lincoln Coupe was parked at the curb. Gunnar signaled with a wave, then lifted my chin till I met his gaze.

He smiled. "Frankie would be proud. I am." He ran his fingers down the side of my face. The light caress, the tenderness in his eyes, made my heart pound. "How will I ever be able to thank you?"

I gingerly rubbed my bruised stomach and smiled at his suggestive tone. "Once they're all behind bars and we've caught up with Cardillac, how about I let you take me to dinner?"

"You got it."

"Oh, and maybe you'd like to volunteer for our Victory short? Work with Novara?"

He wasn't looking so flirty now. But he laughed and shook his head. "I'll consider it."

Lugosi locked the back of the driver's seat into position again after helping me inside. "Comfortable?"

Ilka was in front, riding shotgun. Roza was in back. Her broken-toothed smile greeted me as I squeezed in. She radiated mischief, dark eyes twinkling.

"Grandmamma sees in you a comrade in danger."

Roza had been impressed to learn that I was a U.S. secret agent. She understood that I helped bring down those strong-arming her into aiding the Nazis. She had specifically asked Ilka to convey her gratitude to me.

"But you are all right?" Ilka was alarmed that I sank back in my seat.

Cardillac was at large. I had killed a man in there; I had nearly been killed myself. I was wrung out, depressed, and unable to hide it. "I'll be fine."

"Poo-chi, vee are completely with puff-chests to have you in the car. You have slain the evil beasts—" He paused for dramatic effect. "They vil ne-ver rise again."

Anticipating his audience's reaction, his gaze flicked to the rearview mirror. I stared back. The dashboard lights gave his handsome, slightly bloated features a sinister appearance. Perfect for the comical delivery of the menacing lines. I should have laughed. But it was no good. Melancholy held me in a firm grip. I sighed. Looking out into the traffic snarl along Santa Monica Boulevard, I knew I would never regain my peace of mind if I failed to avenge Frankie.

We passed a street sign that triggered something Tazio had said. In a blinding flash, I knew where Cardillac was going to meet the sub.

"Mr. Lugosi, the Santa Monica Pier, please. And step on it. I'm after a Nazi agent."

He needed no further urging. At the next corner, he spun onto a deserted street and hit the gas. "Do not vorry." Lugosi hunched over the wheel, his hands tight. "A getaway route I know vell."

He drove with precision and a faultless sense of timing, hurtling through the night, careening along a twisty westerly backstreet route, away from the Hollywood Hills and toward the ocean. I explained who we were trying to chase down and why. Next to me, Roza didn't understand a word, yet she loved the chase after Cardillac. It was written all over her dark, wizened face.

Lugosi attacked the Pacific Coast Highway at high speed. We passengers hung on with frozen smiles and a collective silence.

"There it is!" Ilka sounded as relieved as she was excited, pointing to the illuminated archway at the pier's entrance.

I scooted to the center of the seat for a panoramic view as Lugosi, tapping lightly on the brake, swung the Lincoln onto the entry ramp and drove beneath the grand signage:

SANTA MONICAYACHT HARBOR
SPORT FISHING * BOATING
CAFÉS

◇◇◇

We motored alone along the paved path leading to the pier's end. The lampposts were lit at wide intervals, but the arcade entrance was strung with lights. The pavement ended abruptly, the Lincoln's tires bit into wooden planks, and our ride got a little rougher. But it was not the time or place to speed. We crawled along, passing gift shops, food stands, and cafés, looking for signs of our mark among the pedestrians, couples smooching, and individuals looking over the pier's railing.

We were coming up on a vast white structure.

"The La Monica Ballroom," Ilka whispered, interrupting our silence. I was mesmerized by the grandeur of the freshly painted building.

Rolling the two side windows down, we surveilled the passing scene to the rhythm of tires softly thumping against uneven wood.

The pier was not just a recreational mecca. It also serviced Santa Monica's mackerel fleet, sustaining the nation's war effort.

Our headlamps picked up a fisherman enjoying a cigarette leaning with his back against the railing, his pole at attention by his side. He turned away, adjusting the floppy brim of his hat and flicking his smoke to the ground as we slowly cruised past.

I felt a quick spasm of recognition. *That's no fisherman.* His face was too smooth, and an earring—a swastika earring?

"Stop!"

Lugosi stood on the brake.

Leaping out, he shoved forward the driver's seat, extended a graceful hand. I eagerly grasped it.

I panned the shadowy area where I'd seen the fisher*woman*. The pole was there, but she had vanished. A dim street lamp showed an opening in the railing near where she had been standing. I squinted into the dark, sick with panic. That had been Cardillac. I wasn't losing her this time.

I pounded down the wooden planks. Behind me, the harsh sounds of heated Hungarian grew fainter as I tore away from my friends.

At the edge, I surveyed an expansive railed deck below. A boom and rigging for moving cargo and small boats jutted from the far end of the pier. Just short of the tall boom, I found an opening that gave me access to the water. "You won't get away," I vowed clambering down a short metal stairway. "Not this time."

I leapt off the bottom step. The deck was not lit—moonlight was not enough. A thick iron ring caught my toe. I belly-flopped to the deck. Pain smashed through my knee.

"Pooo-chi," Lugosi called, his feet clunking heavily as he started carefully down the stairs. Behind him, Ilka's voice carried loudly. "We are coming."

Either my body was adapting to physical abuse or I had less air left to expel. In the hush that followed, my ears picked up the starting sound of a small outboard motor. Seized with adrenaline, I stumbled upright and charged from the platform, bolting down a gangplank to a small floating dock. A line of thick rope was thrown carelessly along the dock's edge, but the puttering motor was gone. I stared into the shadowy moonlit expanse straining to see the boat, appalled and helpless as a dinghy, manned by a passenger in a floppy hat and oversized life vest, churned out to sea.

It was like watching the final scene of a gripping movie and knowing the director had chosen the wrong ending. I wanted to rewind the scene playing out before me, return the boat here, to the dock, apply the skills I'd absorbed from Sam, rewrite the scene, put in the proper ending. Cameras rolling, I'd make it to the pier on time.

The dock rocked with the motion of the water. I *could* change the ending. I drew my gun.

"Cardillac!" I shouted with all the force in me.

She faced out to sea, gripping the outboard motor's handle. At my shout, the boat veered leeward. She turned and looked toward shore.

"Pucci!" Her voice was recognizable even at a distance. "Come to see me off?"

A lilting laugh I'd once considered charming tinkled through the cool night air. Like chalk on a blackboard, it raked my spine, raising goose bumps along my shoulders.

I shot, shot again, and again.

No luck. The boat continued its course.

Outside the breakwater, a powerful beam flicked on, illuminating Cardillac. A mighty engine roared. The ominous black outline of a large cruiser powered in on the path of the dinghy. The deep rumbling increased.

The spotlight remained on my mark. Cutting the dinghy's motor, she stood. A breeze stole the hat away. The hair, the smirk, made me grind my teeth.

She waved a festively dressed doll at me before stuffing it in her life vest then she pulled a Walther. "You'll never catch me!"

Now or never. Steadying my .38, as best I could on Cardillac, I pulled the trigger. She reeled and fell overboard with a splash.

Chapter Twenty-three

Miss C's call came through early the next morning.

"It's truly sad," Miss C said, her voice catching. "We'd just located Frankie's uncle, were cutting the red tape to bring him home when I got word. He's put us onto another relative stateside, and she's been contacted as well. Funeral arrangements are underway. Her uncle will get to Hollywood in a day or two to accompany the body back home. I gave him your name as a contact."

"So you're suggesting I stay on here?"

"You're *expected* to remain there. There's an investigation—investigations—to wrap up. You'll be summoned to the inquest at March. Can't believe that goon of an officer tried to cover up the incident. He'll be facing a court martial for what he did...*didn't* do. What was he thinking? You could have been killed, too!"

The officer hadn't been involved in the sabotage of my flight, but I didn't bother correcting her, since his lack of action had contributed to all the events that followed. She'd spoken of investigations in the plural, and it was likely she'd already been briefed. But Gunnar was running the other case involving the blackmail and murder of Brody, and she was sensitive about my nonflying duties. Last night Gunnar had been consumed with activity, dealing with the enemy triumvirate Winwar, Abbado (deceased), and Lorenz. I didn't know how much she'd been told about them or even about my face-off with Cardillac, and I wasn't sure how much I should say.

I began a different tack. "Your Staggerwing…"

"Oh, don't worry. Bulk's taken a look. She'll be fine." She cleared her throat. "Rask called. You didn't stop at putting us on the right track with Frankie's incident; you helped take down another enemy cabal like you did in Detroit." Clear across the country, I could feel the warmth of her approval pulsing through the telephone line as she added, "You know, Lewis, these are just the sort of direct—and indirect—contributions that will have a positive impact on my…*our* program."

Before I could get in a "thank you," she let me know she'd also spoken with Della.

Admitting she had no business talking to me about such things over the telephone, she lowered her voice to a confidential tone and told me what she'd learned. Did I know that Della's friend Bela Lugosi was orchestrating Hollywood types to record messages for Allied patriots in Hungary? It was hush-hush and that was all she could say *except* it was rumored that besides Lugosi, Bela Bartok, Charles Vidor, Ilona Massey, and Zoltan Korda were all planning to broadcast personal appeals to native Hungarians in the underground to resist the Germans. Della's housekeeper's seventy-something grandmother was in on it. Who would have thought? "Our kind of gal, right Lewis? Did you meet her?"

I was speechless. I'd never bumped up against this side of Miss C. Besides, as an intelligence operative I was sworn to secrecy. Was this some sort of test?

Ignoring the barrage concerning *Magyar Amerika*, I thanked her for the earlier compliments relating to my work. Then I got down to the disheartening business preying on my mind since last night.

"Miss C, Cardillac's body has not been recovered. The Coast Guard searched the waters all night. The beaches in the area are still being combed. The doll washed up with the diamonds still in it, but as of this morning, there's been no sign of her. I can't figure it out."

There was a moment of silence. My heart thumped loudly. Had I spoken out of turn?

"Lewis, all that can be done is being done. It's highly possible Cardillac has been carried out to sea or that sharks or such have taken care of the matter. The situation is out of your hands. We can't control everything."

Her search for Earhart, mine for Cardillac.

"I read your script revisions," she continued, "they arrived by courier pouch last night. I also had a long chat with Novara. You've done an excellent job in turning the film—and him—around. Thank you. I'd like to rely on you to complete the ferrying and towing scenes, oversee the rough cut of the film. And…show off the P-51. Will you agree?"

I wasn't looking forward to an extended tutelage in filmmaking under Novara, in spite of the long way he'd come. I'd rather fly, or do more undercover work. But on the bright side, there was the promised ride in the P-51.

"Fine," I said, evenly. "And can I get your go-ahead to convince Novara to dedicate the Victory film to Frankie, and to the memory of the other nine WASPs who've gone before her?"

"Of course. Now why didn't I think of that?" She paused. "Lewis, it's clear you have talents beyond being a pilot. Talents needed by our country. Delicate matters, with many layers of complexities and subtleties…" She cleared her throat. "Be assured, if while working on the WASP film something comes up where your skills are absolutely needed, I'll be in touch." Then, as if she'd been holding back a laugh, like we were in on a private joke together, she chuckled. "Oh, and I suspect you'll find it easier to walk in Novara's shoes now…" Another chortle. "Now that he's wearing made-in-America."

I laughed out loud.

Factual Postscript

The WASP program met its objective in showing that women could serve as military pilots. Their statistics compared favorably with those of their male counterparts: the women had as much endurance, were no more subject to fatigue, flew as regularly and for as many hours as the men.

More than 25,000 women applied to become WASPs, 1,830 were accepted for training, and 1,074 won their wings. In all, thirty-eight WASPs died in service of their country.

The WASP program existed from November 1942 to December 1944. The women exceeded expectations and made a huge contribution to the war effort, yet were not militarized during the time they served. Indeed, until 1979, the nation refused to recognize WASP as veterans for purpose of disability and other benefits. March 8, 1979, Congress at last passed the GI Improvement Act which authorized the Secretary of Defense to determine that WASP duty was active military service.

◇◇◇

Jackie Cochran went on to become The First Lady of Flight.

According to the National Air and Space Museum exhibit, Smithsonian Institution, 1981:

At the time of her death on August 9, 1980, Jacqueline Cochran held more speed, altitude and distance records than any other pilot, male or female, in aviation history. Her career spanned 40 years, from the Golden Age of the 1930s as a racing pilot, through the turbulent years of World War II as founder and head of the Women's Air Force Service Pilot WASP program, into the jet age, when she became the first female pilot to fly faster than the speed of sound. She was a 14-time winner of the Harmon trophy for the outstanding female pilot of the year and was accorded numerous other awards and honors in addition to the trophies she won with her flying skills."

To receive a free catalog of Poisoned Pen Press titles, please contact us in one of the following ways:

Phone: 1-800-421-3976
Facsimile: 1-480-949-1707
Email: info@poisonedpenpress.com
Website: www.poisonedpenpress.com

Poisoned Pen Press
6962 E. First Ave. Ste. 103
Scottsdale, AZ 85251